THE VAMPIRE KING

N. MALONE

ALSO BY N. MALONE

ETANI SERIES

Etani

Trapped Princess

Always A Fae

Goddess of Death

The Vampire King

Queen of Nothing (Forthcoming)

The Slave Queen (Forthcoming)

Lost Soul (Forthcoming)

Creator (Forthcoming)

The Great Mother (Forthcoming)

Unnamed Book 11 (Forthcoming)

Unnamed Book 12 (Forthcoming)

STANDALONE BOOKS

The King's Daughter (Forthcoming)

Last Men Standing (Forthcoming)

Aquaphobia (Forthcoming)

For my Family and all who have come to support me and my dreams.

THE VAMPIRE KING

CHAPTER 1
HER

His entire world ended on the day Anubis took the sun from him. The day he had ripped her from all of their lives and hidden her away somewhere they couldn't find.

It had been a perfect day, the sun warm on them, and the grass soft under their bodies as they enjoyed the last bit of peace they would experience for quite some time.

They had been talking, the men around him congregating like sheep to a shepherd. She was their shepherd, and they were eager to be near her.

She had been standing by the lake, watching her twin and the hybrid in the water, a slight frown tugging at full lips as she contemplated the male that was courting the one sibling she had left.

He knew she was ready to kill Hunter the instant he did something wrong, and they regularly taunted him about the matter. He hadn't quite believed them until he found her observing him, ever watchful of his actions.

He stopped ignoring their taunts after that, knowing that she would end his existence in an instant if she thought for even a second that he would betray Letari.

1

She watched them, both happy and afraid for her twin, wanting her to be happy and safe in equal measure.

Did she know how utterly perfect she looked standing there? Her skin almost shimmering in the sun, her long, black hair trailing past the perfection of her arse and taunting them all as it got to touch something none of them likely ever would.

Did she know how all of their eyes lingered on her, studying the minute movements of her face as thoughts passed through her mind?

She had turned to look at them all, alert and wary of threats, but then her tension left, and her frown faded.

She was beautiful, painfully so. Small compared to the rest of her kind, with slender, toned limbs, and rounded hips, a perfect hourglass figure, and a full chest that had all of them salivating to taste. Alabaster white skin, smooth like silk, with just the faintest hint of a grey-blue tint to it. Delicate hands and feet, long fingers, and silver nails that could slice through metal if she put her mind to it.

An oval face with sculpted, arched brows, a delicate nose, full lips, and the most amazing cheekbones he had ever seen. Long, tapered ears, and the best of all, those eyes. Eyes that put the vibrant blue of a Ulysses butterfly to shame, vibrant and deep at the iris and darkened at the outer edges with irises that were slightly oblong. They said her eyes were the colour of blue lightning, but even that couldn't give their shade a proper identifying name. There was nothing in this world, or any, that could properly describe that colour, and they were framed by thick lashes that kissed her cheeks when she looked down.

No, she had no idea just how agonisingly perfect she was to look upon. They all knew that. But she did not see herself in that way. She saw herself as a freak, thanks to the bastards who had taken 'care' of her when she was but a child. They had taught her to hate herself.

She watched them, and they watched her, ever alert to her movements and even more so now that she had been returned to them, broken and abused, with a swollen belly that had been filled with life that had then been stolen from her by that monster.

They watched her because they all loved her, each in their own way.

They watched her because they all wanted her.

Dirdos was one of the few men who was brave enough to approach her like she was not the killing machine she was, and Versalis smiled in amusement as the giant man offered his hand to her.

She had smiled, a smile that could end a thousand lives in an instant with the devastation that was her lips moving upward. It was like seeing the sun rising when the sun had never been seen before, and they would all be blinded by it, though none of them could look away.

The demon had a flute and played an upbeat, steady tune that the dragon stepped into with ease.

WHEN SHE DANCED, he could see light inside her that was a slow and steady glow. She never had that light except when she danced, and none of them knew what it was. But he suspected it was joy, her pure joy that had been a gift from the cat Goddess Bast. It was not the happiness she felt when she was around them, but undiluted joy, and it sang out from her and made their bodies ache with the need to rise with her. There had been a myth that the humans invented a creature who would lure away the children of the humans who betrayed him, and it was like that then, with her.

She lured them with her dance, and none of them ever dared tell her of the way their bodies burned to move with her. They loved her, but they were not stupid enough to let her know. They worshipped the very ground she walked on, but they would not give her ammunition. She might be a rational creature, but she was still a creature, and she was dangerous. They would have gladly killed for her, but no matter how long they kept a lioness leashed, she would always be ready to turn and rip out their throats.

Etani might be civilised, but she was a wild creature who would never be tamed.

It was part of what drew them all to her, that danger and constant threat that she could turn on you, but such was the allure that was Etani. She was a monster, but one who would steal one's soul in exchange for her love. And every man in both worlds wanted her love.

She moved with a grace that rivalled the wind, feline and carnal in a way that should never be allowed. No being should be able to move like that, especially not a woman as beautiful as her, and he felt all eyes turning in her direction, watching that body moving.

It was not a sexual dance, but she could make eating dirt sexual just by moving.

They were captivated by her, the way her hair shimmered in the sun, the way her head tilted, the way her eyes lowered, and her cheeks flushed with a delicate pink.

They watched, and that was how they missed the God moving until it was too late.

Malik saw it, the one they all hated for his relationship with her. Her scion who could touch her and love her when none of them could.

He sensed the threat, and he moved with vampiric speed to block the jackal-headed God, but it had been a foolish gesture, his arms spread in a defensive posture.

She felt his fear and turned, her smile fading into confusion as she took in the sight, and then there was a sickening thud as the axe came down on the vampire's head.

It was the most terrible thing he had seen happen to a man.

The God discarded the vampire and moved forward, determined, with dark eyes set on Etani, and they realised what had happened.

Her scream of his name broke the frozen spell of their shock, and they all moved, but then they were stopped by the Gods around them: Hades and Loki, Sobek and Bast, Amun and Eile.

"No, you will die if you step in," the cat Goddess had whispered, and he hadn't cared. That scream, that primal scream of terrible grief, was calling him to her.

But she did not need them. He could feel her reaching down into her with her rage, and Sobek jerked as she ripped the binding to shreds. Her wrists flared scarlet, and then the bindings fell from her, burnt gold chain on the grass.

Her magic exploded out of her in a physical wave that turned the grass to frost, and they were all shivering, their bodies refusing to move as the ice crept up their legs and caged them in place. The dragon had been sent flying, and when he landed, he was frozen to the ground. Versalis knew she had not meant to do it, but her magic was uncontrolled in her rage to destroy the God.

Drawing those knives sent a chill through them all, and the blades glowed with a blinding white light, extending until they nearly reached the ground, and her skin glowed with them, marked and beautiful.

Her lips had turned dark purple, her eyes bleeding into blackness as she tapped viciously into the magic of Winter, and it screamed with her.

"Anubis!" she raged, and the God looked for an instant like he was afraid, but then he had no time to be afraid.

SHE MOVED LIKE LIGHTNING, flashing in a violent blur of fury that left gouges in the ground, and her explosion left a crater in the ground.

They could do nothing to help her, nothing to protect her as they had all sworn secretly to do. They were helpless, and they hated it.

A terrified scream came from Letari, fear and desperation to help her sister, and it was the distraction Anubis needed.

Her need to protect her sister drew her attention away from the threat, and he moved for her, blocking her view, and her body jerked.

Her magic snapped off like a cut string and she stood frozen, her lips parted, and brows drawn down in a look of child-like confusion. She didn't understand what had happened, but they had all seen.

They saw when he thrust his fist into her, her blood splattering his chest and arm. They saw it all with a terrible, agonising clarity.

He felt it inside himself then, as Anubis closed his fingers around her heart. He felt her weakening, the same weakening he felt when she was starving or injured. She was dying, and they couldn't stop it.

She looked down as the God had done, and the flash of surprise, and then understanding, crossed her face. She knew in that instant what he had done to her.

He said something they could not hear, and her face registered her terror.

Kai and Letari started screaming the moment the God pulled her heart from her chest, and a part of Versalis vanished, the part that was a sense of her existence. A light inside him that snuffed out, her fire doused in water.

She stood there, her body too confused by the finality of it to move, and they realised her magic had broken, the ice had melted, and Versalis was moving.

Skidding on the grass, her body fell, and he caught her before she could touch the grass, eyes closed and face relaxed, her head limp over his arm.

His fingers felt dirty and ugly against the perfection of her skin, and they trembled as he touched her, knowing she was already gone where he couldn't reach her.

"You bastard!" Daemon raged, but Anubis had already slid sideways through reality and was gone, taking her with him.

"Come back ..." he whispered, stroking her cheek, but she couldn't come back to him. She was gone, and he knew the God had taken her heart with him for a reason.

He couldn't feel her in The Nameless Place. She was not there, nor was she in the spirit world. She had not died; she had simply been ripped from her body.

"Please ..." he begged her, little drops of liquid patting down onto her throat and trailing down along her jaw. His fingers stroked back her hair, smooth as silk and soft as a feather. She would have come back to him if she had been able. But she was not able to. She was gone and this time he didn't think she would be coming back. It felt different, and that scared him.

Someone was standing nearby. The two linked to her were screaming bloody murder, and there was a terrible kitten crying coming from the cat Goddess.

"Etani!" Versalis screamed, his head bowing over her as he lifted the empty shell of the woman he loved against his chest.

She was gone, and he couldn't reach her. She was gone and none of them would be able to find her again.

She was the love of his life, the love of all their lives, and the dog God had stolen her away and left them all alive in a sick joke. It would have been better if he had killed them all, merciful even.

"Bring her back!" Daemon screamed. "Bring her back right now!"

He couldn't bring her back. She wasn't in The Nameless Place, and even if she was, he could only guide her back when she wanted it. But she wasn't there, and he couldn't access The Nameless Place without her.

"Bring her back!"

"I can't!" Versalis roared, drinking in the perfection of her pale face. "She's not in The Nameless Place! She's not anywhere! I can't reach her!"

"Fuck!" Daemon howled, a wounded dog who had been kicked one too many times and was begging for mercy.

"Don't leave us ..." he begged as he pressed a kiss to her forehead. It was a kiss she wouldn't feel. That was not her. She had left. "Don't leave me..." He breathed, but he knew she had already left.

THEY DID NOT MOVE until her body had disappeared into that same black dust that it always vanished into, leaving nothing but her clothes and the earrings she insisted on wearing, and that ring.

He scooped them up, considering throwing the ring into the lake, but then he clenched it hard in his fist, determined to shove the thing down the Hunter's throat.

Folding her clothes neatly with shaking hands, he slid the small, silver hoops onto the top of his pinkie finger and stood, clutching the fabric to himself as though that would be enough to bring her back.

"Where is she?" Daemon demanded, getting in his face.

"I don't know. Anubis took her."

"What do you mean Anubis took her?"

"She isn't fully dead. She is still somewhere."

"He trapped her?"

"He stole her heart," Dirdos said softly, and they all turned on the giant dragon, his shoulder slumped in a terrible grief they all understood.

"What?" the demon snapped.

"Do you remember the story of the Winter Queen who stole the heart of the Summer King to spite the Summer Queen?"

Evidently no one did, and the dragon sighed.

"There once was a Queen of Winter who fell in love with the Summer King. When he did not return her love, to spite him, she stole his heart and kept it in a box. It continued to beat, and he was trapped inside it, unable to be with his love until the heart was destroyed. It ends with him killing the Summer Queen when he learns she replaced him, but you get the idea. Anubis is the weigher of hearts. He took hers. She is trapped inside her heart, and he is probably sticking it in a box."

"She hates those wooden boxes ..." Bast whimpered.

She did, ever since she saw the box of hair that Neah had kept. She had thrown out all the wooden boxes and replaced them with little glass bowls instead.

"Let's hope it's not wooden, then," Dirdos said. It was not a joke;

she would be terrified.

"Can you feel where it is?" Daemon demanded.

Versalis thought for a moment, his mind lingering on her image and her name. He got an odd sense of wrongness, and he frowned, trying to figure out what it meant.

"I don't know how to explain it. But I feel like ... it's wrong. Like that feeling you get when you're being watched by Cat when he's about to try to chew off your foot. Something is wrong, but you can't tell what it is."

"Fix it," the demon snarled, enraged at his own impotence as much as Versalis' lack of power.

"How? How the fuck am I supposed to fix it, Daemon? Don't you think I would bring her back if I could? Don't you think I would call to her? You're not the only one who loves her!" Versalis snapped, infuriated with the man who would have others do his job for him. "You're the one who is supposed to protect her!"

The demon was incensed, yellow-gold eyes snapping to a gold glow in an instant.

"We all were," Dirdos said to calm the demon down. "We were all supposed to keep her safe."

He turned to see Kai and Letari; Hunter was dragging the screeching woman from the water, and Jaia was trying to contain his violently writhing twin.

It had been like this before, that agonised screaming that hadn't eased until she had opened her eyes in The Nameless Place. They were so completely connected to her, so tightly linked that their connection was shredded with the loss of her, and all they could do was scream.

They stopped being functioning creatures at that point and they just screamed. Nayishma would be screaming, too, and he could imagine the beautiful Adella trying to calm her wife, who couldn't hear her. All the others she had returned to life would be the same, and like Kai and Letari, they would be tucked away to wait for her return.

CHAPTER 2
MEMORIES

"Get the vampire's clothes," Dirdos said, and Jagum moved away to obey, his posture limp and broken.

No one ever paid much attention to the werecat. He was always so quiet and watchful. But he was always there, watching them instead of watching her as they all did. He had accepted that she would never be his early on, and had made it his mission to keep her safe from them instead. It worked for the most part, their flirting always cutting off when those gold feline eyes turned on them as if to say, 'you dare to try that with such a perfect creature?' It always worked to get them to back off, knowing they would never be good enough to touch her.

But now Jagum was not glaring at them. He was slumped, and his fur glittered with his tears. He too had failed to keep her safe, though he had not thought to keep her safe from the God who had been so quiet for so long. Everyone forgot about him, and he had used that to get to her.

He turned to Uzo, and the Fae was frozen in place, eyes on the spot where she had fallen, as though he could still see her there, bloody and still in death.

Uzo and he had become close since she had come back from the Hunter compound. The only ones who were allowed close to her. Why she had chosen him was a mystery, but he knew why she had attached herself to the Fae. He was her kin, and he was violently protective of her, even if she had never seen him do it.

Jaia had seen the full brunt of the Fae's wrath when they had learnt what he had done.

Uzo had been careful not to kill the vampire, but *Mother* it had been close.

The incident might have been funny had it not been so utterly, unexpectedly horrifying. The Fae had seemed perfectly calm about the whole thing when she left, leaving them all to wait for her return with her blood still on the floor. He had poured the vampire a cup of tea, the pot still fresh from before the fight. Daemon had been indignant at the sight of the Fae offering the rapist tea. But Jaia had refused, his eyes furious at the attempt to kill him.

No one saw the Fae move; it was so fast, and the vampire screamed. Those pale fingers curled around the back of the vampire's head and he smashed the delicate porcelain into the dark eye that had so captivated her. Blood splattered as the Fae ripped the cup out again and smashed it back in, and then a third time. When the cup shattered, he used the saucer and, with a terrible calmness, smashed the shards of porcelain into the vampire's eye. Over and over and over they watched in horrified fascination as the Fae beat a teacup into a vampire's eyeball, and then the saucer broke.

Without missing a beat, the Fae picked up one of the knives Etani had left behind and drove it again and again into the vampire's gut, his face entirely devoid of emotion, except for that same smile he always wore, small and polite.

The vampire doubled over and Uzo held him by the back of the head, stabbing and stabbing until the knife no longer met resistance. Only then did the Fae stop, blood covering his clothes and face.

Turning, he tucked his hands into his pockets and walked away, whistling a soft tune that had always drawn Etani's eyes to the man, though no one knew why.

The vampire slumped to the floor, barely moving, and his twin went to him, desperate for the life of his rapist twin.

None of them helped him, none of them wanted to sully their hands by touching him, and none of them ever drank another cup of tea again.

They had never seen the Fae the same way since, and they all came to the same conclusion: one does not fuck with Uzo.

None of them told her what her uncle had done. She had no idea of what the man would do to any one of them if they hurt her in any way. All while smiling and whistling to see if he could get her to smile.

THE SOBBING COMING from the Goddess tore at his heart and he turned to the woman, so elegant and beautiful with her black fur, tall ears, white eyes, and feline face. She looked back at him, silently begging for something he couldn't give her, and when she saw his face, she turned away bitterly.

He wanted to comfort her, but what could be done? He was just a man, and she was a Goddess who had lost someone so precious to her.

Hunter had managed to get the writhing woman from the lake and wrapped his arms and legs around her to keep her from hurting herself, screeching like a banshee even as she sang for the loss of her twin.

Vincent moved to help his friend and not for the first time, he wondered when the two had become close. Perhaps while they were hunting Etani down? Perhaps it was as Daemon suspected, and they hadn't been hunting her at all but hiding her.

With what they knew about Neah, it was seeming more and more like that was the case. She had never mentioned the man before, and then he had been watching her when she returned from her attempt to run from them.

Even he hadn't been able to sense where she was for much of her journey. The ocean was one barrier, all that saltwater causing a barrier they all experienced. Then the mages in Istralis had kept her hidden. They got a few glimpses of her, but then she vanished again. He had not felt she was in danger, only sad and lost. She appeared again in his mind a few months later and Daemon ordered them to go get her.

She had looked clean, tidy, and fed, somewhat confirming their suspicion that she was hiding out in the compound with the Hunters.

She had escaped from them again and he felt her loss so keenly. But her scent was that of caves.

The demon demanded to go to the caves after that, certain he would find her there, and he hadn't been wrong. She appeared in his mind just as fast as the demon vanished, and they had their orders.

None of them liked the plan, knowing it would mean a loss of her trust in them, but the demon would not be refused, and they planted themselves in the forest.

She appeared with the vampire male who made them all wary, maybe even jealous, but the plan was in place, and they knew her.

Letari was the perfect bait and she fell for it, the man standing back to watch the two. He watched her in the same way they all watched her and none of them liked it.

Daemon arrived with the other two, and they all watched as the creature inched forward, her need to be with her sister clear on her face.

They were perched in the trees and she looked for them. She knew they were there, and yet she couldn't not go to her beloved twin. Letari was too much of a lure.

Daemon was panting in his excitement. She was so close, and they waited, eager to have her back.

She cried for the vampire to run, and they ran for her, knowing they had only seconds to get to her before she was gone again.

She threw her twin off her and she was gone, vanishing into a blur of movement, but Kai was after her. Kai would catch her; they all knew he would.

It was only minutes later that they heard the scream as they crashed through the trees and then the whistle, all heads turning. He had caught her. She was contained.

Turning in that direction, they found her on her side on the ground, beautiful and perfect even with blood running down her arm, blood that screamed for Versalis, demanding he take it. Jaia moved for the vampire whose face was covered in her blood, trembling with the need to take what didn't belong to him. He wanted to hold her down and drink from her, to bury himself and move inside her while he revelled in the blood. He didn't resist his twin, and Versalis stood watching that wounded animal who had been betrayed by them all.

HE FELT terrible in that moment, like they had caged a lion and it could do nothing but pine for freedom. But then, she was back with them, and he was happy about that. They couldn't live without her in their lives. It was impossible, unthinkable.

Daemon had her by the jaw and they all saw the resentment, the betrayal. They all saw her hurt, and yet they were all too selfish to care that she was betrayed. It meant they got her back, and that was all that mattered.

The dragon pulled her up and she yanked her arm free of him, Versalis feeling a savage glee at her rejection of him, and he found himself unable to focus on the conversation as she stood there, captivating him always and forever.

The scum vampire had returned, and he was dragging along the vampire man. Her cry told them all his name, and a vicious jealousy ripped through Versalis as he saw the way she looked at him. She must have created him. Epharis recognised the man and when she reached him, they all tensed.

There was too much tenderness in that touch, the way her body moved around him, drawn to him.

The vampire looked incensed at the name of the one holding him, but he went to her and clung to her like a child at his mother's skirt.

He had been horrified and fascinated by the fact that she was even capable of turning a human. It shouldn't have been possible for her; she was less than a halfling, but so much about her defied the rules of magic. So little about her made any actual sense.

The thought that she was capable of turning a vampire was terrible, and he knew that she would be in even greater danger with this new development. She had the capacity to become a Vampire Queen with enough effort, and what would the vampires do if they knew she could turn humans? More than that, she had created a vampire who could walk in the sun.

Versalis felt a thrill of fear for her as the demon reached for the stake. He couldn't just kill the vampire, it was sadistic. It was exactly something the demon would do if he felt threatened by her creation.

Her cries for mercy were terrible and her magic exploded out of her at the demon, ripping its way through her bindings and her flesh. How powerful was she that she could rip through the gold chain like that? He didn't think it was a good thing, and he turned his head to meet the concerned eyes of her uncle, exchanging a worried glance.

She begged for his life as he knew she would. He understood her fear. She was his creator, and they had an incredible bond. Deeper than that of a mother and her child, it was boundless, and to lose him would devastate her. Odds were she would not recover from that loss, just like so many first-time creators didn't survive the loss of their scions.

THE MEMORIES MADE him sad as he moved into the aura of the dragon and the world vanished into fire, dumping them out in the room that smelt of her; lavender, and her skin.

"Get them down into the basement," Daemon ordered, and Versalis turned to watch Jaia and Hunter moving away with Kai and Letari, leaving the rest of them to endure the scent of her in that place.

Lifting her clothes to his face, he inhaled the heavenly scent of her and headed into the bedroom, pausing as he found a dress laid out for her. That was odd, given almost everyone had been at the lake, and he took a moment to sniff the room, wary of who it might be.

There was no scent except for those known to him, and finally deciding not to worry about it too much, he set her clothes down on the chair and hung the dress back up in the closet.

How many times had he come in there to clean up after her? She was so careless with her clothes and cared so little about possessions that she would often throw them around when searching for something, or else she would leave them in a pile in the corner, not caring what happened and not noticing when someone picked them up.

She was by no means lazy; she just didn't have the mind to care about clothing as most women would. Clothes were useful to her only to guard her modesty or allow for objects to be placed on her person. Outside of that, they were a nuisance that she didn't care for.

He smiled sadly, his hands running down over the soft fabrics, and forced himself to close the wardrobe door, still open from where she had left it when getting dressed that morning.

There was nothing in that room that indicated a woman lived there if the wardrobe was shut. It was exactly the way she had found it when she was first moved into those rooms, the only additions being the cases of weaponry under the bed, and her clothes and boots in the wardrobe.

She had left so little personalisation that it did little more than enhance the alienness of her. She was so far removed from the rest of them that she might be from another world entirely.

He knew it was only a matter of time before she returned to them, but Mother it hurt to know she was gone even if it was only for a few days.

He didn't think it would only be a few days this time, however. He felt that there was something different this time. She was not where she was supposed to be.

The Nameless Place was the place Uzo had once described to them after he returned to life. An empty void that, at the time, had been dubbed 'the place with no name.' They tried to ask her what she called it, but she refused to give it a name. It was not her place to name it. And after a while it had become 'The Nameless Place,' and they used it often enough that she called it that herself and that was it. She had given the place a name, even if it wasn't a name.

It amused him to see her frustration when they told her that she had named it, and she told them off, but none of them listened to her scolding. It was too fun to see her flustered to stop and then they simply got used to it, and forgot about the origin of the name.

He didn't know why she wasn't there, or how the God had managed to take her as Dirdos had suggested.

HEADING BACK out into the sitting room, he found the rest of them sitting around awkwardly, confused. It was always odd to be in that room when she wasn't there, almost like it was a violation of her privacy, even if they knew she wouldn't care if they were in there or would call them stupid for thinking she would be so possessive of a room.

The vampire's clothes had been set out on the chair in the corner and Versalis noticed a small chain he had never seen before. Making his way over to it, he picked it up and examined it carefully, curious and wondering.

"She gave it to him a few weeks back," Uzo said from the couch, his head bowed but hearing the sound of the chain.

"How do you know?" Dirdos asked.

"I helped her pick it out. She wanted him to have something that would remind him of her when she wasn't with him."

On the end of the chain hung a simple carved wooden form and as he lifted it higher, he realised it was a small dolphin. It was both intricate and basic, and he had a sudden pang of jealousy as he realised that odds were she had made it herself.

"Did you know she could carve?" Versalis asked the room, seeing the tiny imperfections.

The global response was a resounding no. None of them had known, and he wondered what other talents the woman had that she hadn't told them about.

"Do you think she will be able to bring him back?" Daemon asked as Versalis set the chain back down, resenting that she had only ever made one thing and that was for her scion.

"I don't know if it's possible to resurrect a vampire," Dirdos said slowly, weary of it all.

Versalis didn't think it was. They were only modified humans, and without that modification, they were simply human. It was likely Malik had gone to the underworld and wouldn't be coming back.

"I would be surprised if she could," Versalis said softly, and Daemon groaned.

Turning, he found the man sitting with his head in his hands, agony written over every inch of him.

The demon had changed since the witches took them, almost as though he was indignant that she hadn't stayed with him after. None of them liked to think that he had been with her, but the fact that he had spelled her to make it easier on her was soothing. She had not gone willingly, but he had not assaulted her.

The witches had suffered for abusing them both, and yet not all the witches had been taken. Only those aligned to Hecate had been taken. It left the witch Elizabet to step in close to Alaric, and Etani had been indignant that she missed any of the witches at all.

Etani did not like Elizabet. Elizabet loathed Etani with a burning passion, and so they avoided each other, though no one knew why they hated each other.

Any time they asked her, she muttered something about the colour green and changed the subject.

"You can't feel her?" Daemon asked the floor.

"No, it's not like it was before where I could feel her asleep. This time there is nothing except that feeling of wrongness."

"What are we going to do? What if Dirdos is right?" Vincent asked, and everyone looked around at the man, surprised that he was still there. He was much like Sebastian in that they both crept around like spiders and often hours went by without them making a sound and scaring the others when they were finally noticed.

"Then we go find her heart," Daemon said.

"How do we find it?" Versalis asked, grinding his teeth as he thought about the underworld and having to go there. He knew Etani had been there to meet with Hades, but Anubis wouldn't be in the same place as Hades, and Hades wouldn't help them.

"We go to Anubis," Dirdos said.

Well, it looked like they were going to Anubis.

CHAPTER 3
HATE

The plans to go to Anubis were being made, and the room felt wrong without Etani in it, especially now that there were only men in the room and he found himself studying each of them, his rivals.

The dragon was his biggest threat. Dirdos knew what it took to make her laugh and could take her away and hide her for an eternity if he wanted to. He was also the most physically intimidating. He knew that Dirdos appealed to her, the danger and domination of the man. They had almost been together more than once, but so far it had not happened, and Versalis hoped it never would.

Daemon came next, though he thought she likely didn't care for him anymore. He had chained her like a cat on a leash, and that had been the ultimate betrayal. Worse than Kai, worse than anything except Jaia, but nothing was as bad as what Jaia had done and the man himself, the rapist, was sitting quietly, his head bowed and attention focused on the drawings of what Daemon said was where the God lived.

There he was, the vampire who had so completely destroyed her. The one she had trusted and loved beyond all others. Jaia.

20

How the vampire had not been executed was beyond him. Versalis didn't know how. It was a disgusting miscarriage of justice. His head should have been stuck on a pike outside the city walls for his daring to touch her when she did not desire it.

But then, he wondered, did Epharis and Alaric actually know what he had done? Did they know how he had brutalised her? The words of the crazy twin echoed in his mind, the words that had devastated him as much as any of the others. 'The only reason you weren't the first to create a world is because you damaged her too much.'

He wanted to rip the vampire apart, to destroy him and not stop as Uzo had done.

Jaia felt the hostility and those dark, empty eyes turned in his direction. He didn't know what it was she saw in him, the cold, empty shell of a man who had never seen her as anything but a toy to be played with and then discarded. She was nothing but a conquest to him, bragging rights, and taunts that he had gotten to touch the most perfect creature to ever exist.

He would not allow the scum to hurt her again, would not allow any of them to hurt her again.

Closing his eyes, he saw her again as she stood before him, her eyes blank with that bite marring the smooth skin of her throat. He knew something was wrong, that something had happened. He simply couldn't see what it was. His jealousy at the scent of Jaia on her made him blind to the truth for far too long.

She had changed, and he still didn't see it; still didn't want to see it in her, but he had suspected, to watch the way the vampire stared at her, the way she avoided him and kept her eyes down. He knew; deep down, he knew.

They had kept it a secret from everyone. The dragon knew, the brother knew, but none of them said a word. Versalis suspected that everyone had at least an inkling of what had happened, but they couldn't say for sure and then it came out and the mood shifted. Everyone turned on Jaia. He wanted to cheer on Daemon when he produced that stake, wanted to scream his satisfaction as the life drained out of that bastard's eyes, but it wasn't his blood that was spilled, it was hers.

Their world came crashing down as she fell, and he moved to her side, terrified and lost on what to do. He wanted to save her, but he couldn't. There was nothing any of them could do but be with her as her life drained away and the stake meant for the vampire ended her life instead.

"What?" the scum demanded, but Versalis only shook his head, trying not to think about the thought of her under him, pleading for him to stop as he held her down. The thought of that monster forcing himself inside her and her tears as she tried to comprehend why. She understood the Gods, they wanted her magic; she understood her husbands, they owned her body; but Jaia was something she couldn't understand, and he knew she would have cried as he destroyed her. He could smell that he had spilled himself in her and had been so jealous that he hadn't seen the traces of black on her cheeks, the scent of blood or the swelling at her lips. He hadn't been able to see that he forced her into his bed. He had been so enraged with jealousy that he ignored the fact that she had been raped by someone she once wanted to be with.

None of the men around them looked at the vampire the same way. None of them wanted him around, but he was a tactical master and a skilled swordsman. Daemon deemed him to be too valuable to kill or expel from their lives, and Versalis hated the demon for that.

Why would he force her to be near him? But then it clicked. The demon wanted her to kill the vampire, to exact her revenge on him and obliterate him. It was her right, and so he forced the vampire before her, and even though he understood, he didn't think she had ever realised or thought it to be her right.

He didn't even know if she would have been able to kill him.

"Thinking," Versalis said to cover his anger and furious glare on the vampire. He couldn't let jealousy get the best of him. He couldn't focus on the thought of that man moaning her name while she cried for him to stop and then left his visible claim of ownership on her flesh.

His thoughts returned to the little dolphin carving and Malik. He had been the Prince of Istralis and had saved her life. In return, she did the same for him, turning him into a vampire when he was on the verge of death. None of them had ever known her to care for a human. She saw them like the humans saw cattle. But then there was Malik, the human who didn't fear her. Who saw nothing more than a wounded Fae and moved to help her, not because she would have owed him, but because he was a decent man.

She saw that in him and acted on impulse, returning the favour, and she loved him as only a vampire could love their Scion.

She adored him and he saw how her face lit up at the sight of him, and how she moped when he wasn't around. Their desire faded just as it always did and after the lust was gone, things settled down. Malik was no longer a threat to their claims on her and it turned out he was an enjoyable man to be around. A wicked sense of humour and a dirty mind that made them all laugh and made even Letari blush. Etani only listened, watching him with a slight curiosity.

He knew she would have gone on to question him on his experiences in love, and it had then been his turn to blush as he tried to explain sex to the inquisitive Goddess. Malik might find it funny to brag about sexual exploits that could rival even Daemon's, but when she asked him to describe what it felt like, he went red.

None of them except Dirdos and Hunter had been able to give her much of an answer on that. It was like trying to explain it to your mother. It felt wrong in the weirdest way.

She was more curious than a kitten, wanting to know everything.

The one and only time she gave her body to a man ended badly, with Neah kidnapping her and holding her for months. She said that while it felt good, she didn't feel any connection to the man like they described.

Versalis was glad for that, and his mind went to showing her what a real man could do for her, not the emotionally stunted sociopath.

None of them liked the idea of her exploring sexual pleasure with Neah and they all tended to pretend it hadn't happened, but Versalis made himself remember, very aware of how the man had stalked her, and it was a sharp reminder that not all beings wanted her for her magic. He wanted her because he had fixated on her. She was beautiful and exotic, wild and feral. He wanted to tame her and make her his, simply because he thought he could.

In part, he had been successful. That ring was still on her finger even though she had thrown it into the lake twice and once off a canyon, but it always appeared back on her finger as though it was magnetic.

Vincent and Dainin hadn't known how the magic worked, but they also had little to do with the special Hunters. Most of the Hunters avoided them unless they had to be around them. They were creepy and cruel, more likely to end up as Neah had.

Vincent had also suffered for the lack of action of his species, ousted by the rest of them as Jaia had been. They knew he hadn't done anything wrong, but it was hard to forgive him when they all could easily imagine the sounds of her trying to escape, and that he had ignored. He could have brought her torment to an end half a year earlier. But they had ignored her as they ignored countless others before her, leaving them to be abused, killed, and then eaten by the creature. They couldn't forgive him for his negligence, not yet anyway.

Versalis supposed it was normal for them to find someone to punish when the responsible party was out of their reach.

That meant the blame fell on the unfortunate man and his cousin. Vincent seemed to understand and hadn't taken any of it to heart. Dainin, however, seemed to consider it a personal insult and took it upon himself to give her flowers weekly ever since.

She was deeply confused by the gesture and when she asked Uzo, the Fae smiled at her and explained.

Uzo was far more eloquent than the rest of them and he seemed to understand her better. He helped her to understand, and it was an odd moment for the woman.

She wanted to tell him to stop, but also didn't want to make him feel guilty and so she kept quiet and accepted them. In time, he thought she actually appreciated the gesture. His trying to make up for the sins of Neah. Versalis thought only death could do that, but the gifts were a start.

It was one of the confusing things about her. She loved flowers of all kinds and he found her leaning over them more than once, eyes closed, lips pulled up in a smile as she inhaled the soft scent. He always meant to ask why she liked flowers and what they reminded her of, but he hadn't gotten the chance.

The thoughts cut off with a sharp stab of pain at her loss, and he forced himself to focus on the situation. It was hard not to think about her, especially when they had so recently lost her.

"Are we all going?" Versalis asked, and Daemon nodded, still focused on the map and the vague, scattered information they had.

"Yes, if given the chance, we will try to find the box and retrieve it, though the odds of that working will be low. It's still worth considering as an option, just in case."

"You know he won't just leave it lying around," Dirdos whispered.

"I know, but it's worth the attempt, just in case he hasn't got his defences up yet."

"Do you think he planned it?" Uzo asked, standing to light candles as the room grew dark.

"Not for today. He seemed surprised and happy about her using her magic. It was opportunistic, but I suspect he had the plan ready for some time and was just looking for an excuse," Daemon replied, scowling as he turned the pages to better see the map of the entrance into Anubis' domain.

The news was met with silence, and Versalis found himself

staring at the demon with everyone else, confused as to what he meant.

"What do you mean 'using her magic'?" Versalis asked when no one else spoke.

Daemon looked up at them, frowning in thought, but then his head turned to look at Dirdos, who shrugged.

"None of you felt it?" Daemon demanded.

Versalis hadn't felt anything at all except the need to get up and move with her. His thoughts shared by the others as they shook their heads.

"She was creating another world," Daemon said, unsure of if they were messing with him or not.

"What?" Jaia snapped, and as much as Versalis hated it, he had to agree with the sentiment.

"When she was dancing, she started drawing her magic in and it took form. I don't think she intended to do it, but it happened."

Dirdos looked distraught at the idea that he had contributed to Anubis taking her.

"How?" Uzo asked, his voice low in his concern.

"I have felt it happen a few times, only when she is dancing or had ... been taken," the demon said, skirting around the subject of her forced impregnation. "If it is her on her own, it only happens when she is dancing. I suspect it has something to do with how happy she is when she dances."

Bast made a tiny sound, and they looked around at her, her mouth ajar as she looked at them all in horror.

"You don't think ..." she whispered, looking at Daemon, but the man only shrugged.

"It's possible, Bastet," the demon said with a sigh.

"What?" Uzo demanded, looking between the two.

"Bast blessed Etani so that she would always find love and joy in dance. Creation comes from joy."

"Why didn't you tell me? I could have removed it ..."

"Could you have taken that from her? Could you have removed that pleasure she gains from it?" Daemon asked.

Bast looked at him, her face torn. Could she have taken that from Etani?

"You should have told me, at least!" Dirdos snarled, his eyes glowing a faint red. "I wouldn't have ..."

"It doesn't matter now; I didn't know for sure, and I couldn't just ... she loves it when you ask her to dance. I couldn't take that from her when so little in her life makes her that happy," Daemon said to the floor.

The room was silent once more, all eyes lowering to the floor in shared grief for the woman they loved.

"We have to get her out of there ..." Jaia murmured, and everyone nodded, though no one looked overly happy to be agreeing with the vampire.

At least Versalis had one thing to look forward to. The bastard might get killed. At least he would if there was any justice in the world.

"How are we getting her out of there?" Uzo demanded.

"I don't know ..." Daemon growled, frustrated and angry at his own inability.

"But we have to have a plan."

"I know, Uzo, I'm trying to figure one out."

"We can't leave her there."

"I know, Uzo! I don't know, okay!? I'm trying!" the demon exploded, and everyone went still, tense and nervous with so much stress and fear. "Sorry ..."

"We will get her back," Uzo soothed, and Daemon nodded, running his hands through his hair for the hundredth time that evening.

"Yeah, we will ..."

"Has anyone stopped to think that ... maybe she won't want to come back?" Versalis asked, knowing they weren't going to like it.

"Why wouldn't she?" Daemon asked the floor.

"The question is ... why would she? She's been beaten and broken so many times. She's been betrayed time and time again. Why would she want to come back to that?"

They all looked at him and he saw their fear, that terrified realisation that she might simply not wish to return to them.

"She would want to come back ..." Uzo whispered, his head turning to look at the others. "Right?"

"Would you?" Vincent asked.

"No." Uzo sighed, his head bowing.

"How do you think she managed to stay sane?" Vincent asked.

"She's not like a normal woman," Daemon said, and Versalis nodded his agreement. "She doesn't see things like we do. I think it's something she can mostly understand, given the type of being she is. She believes Epharis and Drizdan have a right to her." He refused to think of Neah having that same right to her body. "The Gods ... They are power hungry, and they see her as nothing more than a vessel to get their own desires. In a way that makes sense to her, at least somewhat."

He saw their glance towards Jaia, but Versalis chose to pretend he didn't see it, not wanting to bring up that subject.

No one believed what Jaia did was in any way understandable or forgivable. He caught the glances and clenched his jaw, forcing his eyes back down.

Not for the first time, he tried to understand what it was she could have possibly seen in him as a mate, but he couldn't. Jaia was like Neah, he manipulated her to get what he wanted.

"Stop looking at me like that," Jaia growled.

"Did you stop?" Daemon said in that same flat, lethal voice he always used when speaking to the vampire.

"You don't know what you're talking about."

"I know exactly what I'm talking about."

The tension in the room rose as Jaia looked up at Daemon, both trying to stare the other down.

"Now is not the time," Dirdos said, trying to calm the tension.

Daemon, like Uzo and all of them, wanted to destroy the vampire for his actions. Daemon was actively looking for a fight with the vampire, so he had that excuse to kill him.

"The only reason you aren't in the same place as Malik is because she loves Kai," Daemon said, ignoring Dirdos.

"She loves me, too," Jaia snapped.

"You're a delusional little leech. She hates you."

Jaia's face twisted and Versalis stood, moving to place a hand on Daemon's shoulder to keep him sitting.

"Wait and see, demon. I'll have her in the end."

You could have heard a pin drop, his eyes meeting Uzo's for an instant as they tried to figure out what to do.

"I'll be burning in the underworld before you touch her again," Daemon snarled.

"And yet if I asked her, what do you think her response would be?" Jaia was smug.

"Rip your throat out with her teeth, I suspect," Uzo muttered, Versalis nodding.

"Arrogant little shit, considering it took you *raping* her to get her under you," Daemon said.

"And it took a coven of witches and your magic to get you there," Jaia barked.

"That's enough. This is my niece you're discussing," Uzo growled.

"At least she agreed to my magic," Daemon muttered, but dropped his eyes when Uzo glared at him.

"Daemon did it under threat of torture and death, it's not comparable to what you did," Uzo said. "She is the only reason you still exist, and you had best hope she chooses to come back, because the first thing I'm going to do if she doesn't is finish what I started." Uzo's eyes were on his cup and he clicked it down into the saucer, everyone in the room flinching at the sound as though he had shouted.

"I'm going to bed - we'll head out at first light," Daemon said and stood, his eyes lingering on the bedroom before he growled and stalked into the room, grabbed a pillow, and flopped down onto the mattress, face buried in the downy softness.

There was a brief pause and then Dirdos was up, Uzo grabbing him by the shirt and dragging him backward to keep him from claiming the second pillow. Vincent was moving but Dirdos snatched him by the hair. Versalis ducked under Vincent's attempt to grab him and snatched up the second pillow, dodging Dirdos and settling himself into the windowsill, clinging to the pillow for dear life.

It smelled so strong and wonderfully of her hair, and he knew they would be trying to get to it. Curling himself around it, he nuzzled his face into it, and he fell asleep to the sweet smell of the woman he loved.

CHAPTER 4
THE UNDERWORLD

He woke first the next morning, still curled protectively around the pillow he had claimed, though Daemon no longer had the other one, Uzo did, and he was face down in it.

Versalis didn't think it was possible for him to suffocate like that, but it didn't seem comfortable when one needed air to breathe.

Looking around at the lightening dawn through the window, he frowned as he realised his feet were about three feet above his head on the window frame and he was almost on his back on the bottom sill, neck bent awkwardly, but oh Mother did it feel good. It might look weird, but it felt wonderful to sleep like that and the pillow was clenched to his chest with his nose just touching the softness of the case.

Twisting to place his feet on the ground, he yawned and stretched, clutching the pillow in one hand, and then plopped it down in his lap. Bending over, he buried his face in it, inhaling deeply.

As much as he wanted to stay there, he knew it was time to get up and get ready. He was the first one up so he got to shower first, meaning he would get privacy for at least some of it.

Taking advantage, he slunk out of the room and headed for the bathroom.

They all had spare clothes in there, given how often they refused to leave her rooms unless she forced them out, and it had gotten to the point where they had pitched in to get a standing dresser installed in the bathroom, each of them getting a shelf with spare clothes. It was less likely to get her trying to kick them out if their stuff wasn't piled up on every available surface.

Smiling slightly at the memory of her trying to kick them all out, he stripped and headed into the water fountain to bathe.

She had been so enraged by having to dig through their clothes to get to her own, that she stalked out, stark naked, with their belongings in her arms and threw them in a heap on the floor.

"All of you out. I've had enough. Get your stuff and go back to your own rooms!" she snarled, and they looked up at her, various faces of appreciation, wariness and stubborn refusals.

"Darling girl ..." Uzo started, but then fell silent when her blazing eyes turned on him.

"We practically live here already," Daemon said, his attention back on his book.

"This is *my* room, not a dormitory," she snapped.

"We should get bunk beds," Dirdos said, watching her with amusement, and then ducking as she picked up a shoe and threw it at him.

Versalis thought it was likely one of Kai's shoes, but it was hard to tell.

"Get out!"

"You don't really want us out," Versalis wheedled, and when her glare turned on him, he refused to back down.

"Out," she demanded.

She was so gloriously radiant when she was angry, and he simply shook his head in refusal. He wasn't leaving.

32

"Don't make me kill you ..."

It was a threat she made fairly often, but as yet, she hadn't killed any of them except Kai and Daemon.

"Come on, Etani, you love us being here," Kai said, and he was next to duck a projectile shoe.

"I want you all gone before I get back," she yelled and turned, stalking back into the bathroom and slamming the door.

They were still there when she got back, clothes neatly folded and waiting to go back into the bathroom, a dresser already purchased and ready to go.

She hadn't said a word, simply glared at them before stalking into her bedroom to get dressed.

How many times had she tried to kick them out, and they simply refused? More times than he could count, and he sighed at the loss of her as he stood under the streaming water, his hair plastered against his body.

Resting his forehead against the wall, he clenched his eyes shut and brought the image of her face up in his mind. It wasn't hard to do, she was always in his thoughts, and it was even truer when she was gone.

Things had been quiet for a long time, peaceful almost, and then Anubis had to go and ruin it for them all. He simply had to take her away from them.

First Neah had almost destroyed her, and now this.

Reaching blindly, he found the lavender oil without needing to see and pulled the cork out just enough to fill the air with the scent and he could more readily imagine her there with him, watching with that same confused expression or otherwise trying to punch him. He had learnt to read her reactions and knew when she was about to turn on him.

HE SMILED FAINTLY as he thought back on the time they watched her, bent over and doing up those boots that they were all certain Epharis had deigned.

Delightfully tight cotton and boots that required her to spend several minutes bent over to lace up; he caught the eye of Daemon, who was smirking.

Making the most stupid choice of his life, he crept closer while she was occupied and, with both hands, grabbed her backside. It was the most glorious three seconds of his life, his hands on her rear, but then she turned on him and her fist clipped his jaw.

They all laughed while he ducked and dodged her fists and then her legs. She might look little, but she could hit like a raging bull and she finally got him, sending him crashing through the bathroom wall, and he lay there wheezing. It had been worth it to have his hands on that perfect, heart shaped arse for just a few seconds.

He wasn't the only one to do things like that; it was fun for them to see her react, and they knew she in part liked the challenge. It was a win-win for them all when it was an ambush like that.

He could still feel the coolness of her skin on his hands and then the pain of her kicking him through the wall.

Sighing, he made an effort to keep from breaking down and grabbed the soap, scrubbing himself down and heading for clothes just as Uzo shoved the door open, black hair in his face and looking like he'd been punched in the face a few times.

Pretending not to notice, Versalis dried off while Uzo headed for the shower and there was a thump as the man's head hit the wall, his breathing slow and deep as he almost dozed back off against the wall. Picking up a cork, he threw it at the man. Uzo looked down at it, then lifted his hand with the middle finger extended.

"Love you, too, Uzo," Versalis said as he pulled on his pants.

"Die in a fire, vampire boy," the Fae grumbled, stealing a line from his niece.

Heading out, he paused as he spotted the odd object on the table, the papers pushed aside, and a single white rose set in a tall glass of water. It hadn't been there the night before and he glanced around the room.

Nothing else was out of place and, shaking his head, he decided not to worry. Odds were it belonged to Dainin, and he had left it there as a gift to her memory while she was gone. But it was still hard to see it there and so he turned away, not needing more memories of his loss.

The others were stirring and there was a general grumbling of annoyance as the queue went toward the water shower.

Heading for the bedroom once more, he shoved the mattress and Daemon growled, irritable as always in the morning.

"You said first light, demon. Let's go."

Daemon didn't move and Versalis sighed, reaching down and grabbing the mattress. Heaving it up, the demon rolled off onto the floor with a grunt, but Versalis glanced down, and he frowned as he saw something on the boards.

Reaching down, he picked up a small figure made of wood, only about the size of his thumb, but as he looked at it, he realised what it was. It was a little figure of Kai.

His eyes turned to the others on the board, and he saw them in a neat row of tallest to shortest, all meticulously carved out of a deep red wood, but it was the second smallest that drew his attention. Placing the figure back, he noted that the smallest was a little feline, but the one beside that was female, at least mostly ... It didn't really have a shape like the others, hair and limbs that were too long for the body. A visage that was twisted and anguished with tear marks running down the terrible face.

Was this how she saw herself? Anguished and hideous? He knew she didn't see herself as the creature she was, but this?

Daemon appeared over the top of the mattress and looked down at what he was holding, the anger vanishing in a puff.

"What's that?" he asked.

"I think Etani made these ... It's all of us."

Picking up the small carving of the demon, he held it out to the man himself. Daemon took it and studied it carefully.

"She even got the horns ..." he said, sounding more than a little impressed.

Holding up the female figure, Daemon's brows pulled into a scowl.

"Who is that?"

"It's the only female," Versalis said slowly.

Daemon stepped around the bed and crouched down to look at the figures, picking up the small cat and setting it back down again, his hand out for the figure in Versalis' hand.

Handing it to him, the demon studied it, twisting it in his fingers before he set it down carefully in the position it came from and pulled the mattress back down to hide them.

"We're not saying a thing about this," he said.

"But ... that's her, right?" Versalis demanded.

"I think so. Not a word. No one else needs to see them."

"Why would she make herself look like that?"

"Not a word, Versalis. Nothing. To anyone," the demon demanded, standing to glare at him.

"Daemon ..." Versalis whispered, trying to put all his fears and concerns in that one word.

"I know. We can worry about it when she's back. But not before," he said. "No one is to know."

Versalis exhaled but then nodded, smoothing the sheets out, and with one last glance towards the bed, he followed the demon from the room.

THE SITTING room was full of men and Versalis stopped to consider them all as they stood around and prepared for the assault on the underworld.

Jaia was a cold, empty man with black eyes that seemed to suck away at your soul. Shorter than Versalis by only a few inches, with an arrogant face, and he always seemed to have an aura of coolness around him.

Kai was his polar opposite, all brightness and warmth with black eyes that almost seemed to glow from within. A smile that could last for years and a determination and loyalty rarely seen in anyone, let alone a vampire.

Daemon stood taller than Versalis by an inch, his starkly handsome face almost permanently set with a scowl when Etani wasn't around. Angry and resentful, he prowled around like a lion after his missing lioness. He was proud once, similar to Jaia, but that had gone when the witches had taken them. After that he seemed to realise the error he made in Etani's creation and the life he had hoisted onto her, and regretted it. One could always see it in those yellow-gold eyes, the self-hatred that hunched his shoulders and made him snap.

Dirdos was the tallest by over two feet, long limbed and cruel, but he had a deep love for Etani that trumped his cruelty. He seemed to see her more as a kitten than a tiger and he doted on her. Crimson eyes that now blazed with anger had once blazed with lust for her, but that had cooled somewhat since she was leashed, and Versalis could only assume it was Daemon's doing. They knew Dirdos was the one she asked to be her first attempt at pleasure, but he hadn't gotten the chance, and then Daemon's time with her probably put a stop to it altogether.

Dirdos was quiet now, watchful and alert. He liked it when she would play with his hair or touch him, especially with how the heat that radiated off him counteracted the coldness of Winter inside her.

Uzo was the most openly relaxed of them all, just under seven feet tall with wild black hair and incredible blue eyes that watched them all day and night. He was openly hostile to anyone trying to get near to Etani, though he never showed it when she was nearby. All smiles and sophistication, usually with a teacup in hand that had everyone moving away from him.

Jagum was enormous, muscled but sleek in that way only the werecats could be. He was like granite, hard and immovable until Etani gave him her affection, and then he was putty in her hands.

Vincent was all glares and eerie silences, his mask never leaving his face when around them. Since Neah, he had changed to be more introverted and watchful.

Versalis knew he was hiding things, but didn't know what they might be. So long as Neah stayed away, Versalis didn't care.

Always reeking of blood and magic, his crimson eye was unfocused unless Etani was nearby, then he watched her. He was always watching her with that same scowl as though he were trying to figure her out. They were almost on a level with each other, though Vincent never looked down from his two or three-inch height he had on Versalis.

Sebastian was always nearby, reserved and just as watchful as the others. He didn't speak unless he had to and was always willing to help with anything they needed. Aside from being creepy, he was generally just a nice guy and as reliable as any. Quick to volunteer for babysitting duty or to supply information. Daemon, Dirdos, and Jaia hated him for the power he had over Etani, but Versalis liked him well enough.

Hunter wouldn't be joining them; he had wanted to stay and watch over his love and Kai, though Kai was likely only incidental. It was good, as they would both need to be fed while they were gone.

Hunter was an anomaly. A crossbreed that was so incredibly rare that it was believed to be impossible, but to hear him say it, he was not the only one. Rugged and almost feral. He had a wicked grin and laughing eyes. He enjoyed teasing Etani only to a very careful extent. He was absolutely terrified of her even as he was drawn to her like the rest of them. She might care for him, but she wouldn't blink an eye at killing him if she felt it was necessary and she could do it.

She was faster, stronger, and more callous than him. And the fact that she was violently protective of Letari only made him more afraid. But she did care for him, quite deeply. Versalis asked her why once, and she said it was because he took care of her after Jaia abused her.

Hunter refused to explain why she was in the cell and unable to be woken and no one wanted to ask her about that day.

She looked at him, her face blank and eyes unfocused as she recalled the man.

"He promised to help relieve..." She trailed off, her lips parted, and he smiled faintly at the sight of the tips of those tiny fangs. "He helped me after Jaia. He did everything he could to look after me," she said, and he saw her distress at the memory, the way her lips turned down at the corners and her brows drew together even when she was being so careful to hide her thoughts.

He saw then just how badly the experience had affected her. Jaia was not the first to abuse her, but he was the only one who truly hurt her.

Kissing her cheek to distract her, he smiled and offered her a flower picked from the garden. She looked confused for a moment as he drew her back from her thoughts and she took the flower, fingers cold and gentle as she placed it behind his ear instead, and he shivered in delight as she brushed his hair back from his face and scolded him for being silly.

He hadn't meant to make her unhappy; he had been curious and after that he didn't bring it up again.

DAININ WASN'T in the room, but he would be joining them, and it wasn't long before the creepy guy rocked up, his mask that of a wide, grinning face with sharp teeth that matched his crimson eyes. He was the same height as his cousin, longer black hair and those creepy eyes making him look like a ghoul, but he made Etani laugh and that was all that mattered to Versalis.

The supplies of weaponry were gathered and checked over before being applied to their bodies.

"First one to shove Jaia into the river gets to keep her pillow until she gets back," Daemon said, eyeing the vampire with hostility.

"I'm not going if you're just going to try and kill me," Jaia snarled, his sword in his hand.

"Oh, you're going, little vampire. You owe us."

"I don't owe you shit."

"You owe her," Uzo added, and all eyes turned on the Fae, a long knife in his hand as he was looking down the blade and polishing away any lingering prints. "You owe her your life and you will give it to her if she calls for it."

Jaia was silent, staring at the Fae for a long moment before he nodded.

AFTER ANOTHER HALF hour they were ready and the tension in the room rose as they prepared for the likely chance that someone wasn't going to get out of there alive.

How they would die seemed obvious, but they had to try to get to her. They couldn't leave her trapped there.

He took Daemon by the arm, felt another hand come down on his shoulder, and the group headed through the tear in reality and stepped out into a barren wasteland with nothing in it for miles in any direction.

"You sure we got the right place?" Dirdos asked, a few hands back in the chain.

"Positive. Can you feel her?" Daemon said, turning on Versalis.

Versalis didn't even need to check to know she was nearby. Her aura was everywhere, and he shivered as he looked around himself as though he could see her.

She was everywhere and nowhere, the air and nothing, and she was deeply asleep.

"She's asleep," Versalis said slowly, trying to get a sense of it. It wasn't like the sleep she had been in within The Nameless Place. This was the sleep of the dead, endless and unfathomable.

"Can you call to her? Wake her up?"

Closing his eyes, he exhaled as he drew up that exquisite face in his mind, the scent of her almost immediately filling his senses, but still it felt wrong somehow.

"Etani?" he asked, frowning when he didn't get so much as a stir from her. "Etani, love, wake up." Still nothing. "Come on, sweetheart, just open your eyes. We're right here."

He shook his head slowly; he was getting nothing from her. "It's like an echo, I don't think she can hear me," he said, frowning at the sensation.

"Let's go," Daemon said bitterly, and they all followed after him.

It was weird, they were in the middle of nothingness with nothing behind them, nothing in front of them, and nothing in any other direction, but Daemon had stalked off like he knew exactly what he was doing and none of them questioned him.

No one was game enough to question him, though. And so, they followed like ducklings after their mother.

The opening appeared out of nowhere and they all froze, looking down at a giant split in the land that seemed to vanish down into nothing.

"Where are we?" Vincent asked from the end of the row.

"The wastelands of Summer. It's why the lot of you didn't get a power hit. There's no magic here," Daemon said quietly.

"Why not?"

"The courts destroyed it during the war."

There was silence as they took in the information, but then Daemon was heading down into the crack, and they followed into the bowels of the world.

THE STAIRS SEEMED to go on forever, and the further down they headed, the more he could feel her, and he was soon pushing at Daemon to hurry up.

"She's here," he snarled when Daemon growled, but still hurried his descent, almost running down the remaining steps, and they burst out onto the most disturbing and fascinating world they had ever seen.

The world had turned red and brown, seemingly endless with giant pillar-like mountains that seemed to have been placed on the ground to hold the surface of the sky up.

There was an enormous river that ran through it, snaking all over the place, and in the distance, they saw the largest temple any of them had ever seen.

It was almost entirely white, though there was no white stone in that place for the builders to have used. There was no way that place belonged only to one God.

"Who lives here?" Versalis asked, his eyes locked on the temple, and he found he was twitching in time to her beating heart coming from that place.

"Many people, most of them don't hang around much. But there is ..." Daemon squinted, following Versalis' eyes to the temple. "Osiris, Isis, Amun, and Anubis here most often. Hopefully if Amun is here, we can get him to force Anubis' hand. But many of the Gods live here."

"Where do you live?" Vincent asked curiously.

"With you idiots."

"Where did you live before that?"

"None of your business."

There was an awkward silence for several minutes and then the group set off after Daemon, following along behind him.

IT WAS a matter of hours before they reached the river, and oddly, there was a barque floating there with enough space for them all to sit on.

"Everyone get on, keep your eyes on the temple and don't look away. Except you, Jaia; you look around all you fancy. Look everywhere," Daemon said eagerly.

Jaia growled, but they all climbed into the little boat and, with a start, the thing moved up the river and against the current.

There was a low whisper around them, calling his name, and he wanted very badly to look around to see who it was calling for him, but he kept his eyes locked on the temple in the distance, even when he saw a flash of light out of the corner of his eye.

When his eyes weren't on the temple, he kept them shut and blocked out the sounds of the whispering around him, his mind on the steady thumping of her heart that he could feel vibrating through him.

He wanted to get to her, to pull himself into her arms and stay there for eternity. He wanted her, more than anything he had ever wanted. He simply wanted her.

CHAPTER 5
THE GOD OF DEATH

I t felt as though they had spent years on that boat being pulled upriver, and by the end of it, Versalis was visibly vibrating with the sound of her heart thundering in his ears. He was staring around wildly once they were off the boat and on hard ground again, knowing she was there but unable to see her.

He was desperate to reach her, but he couldn't do anything when Daemon was still trying to get himself organised. Ignoring the demon, Versalis started for the temple, twisting free of the restraining grip of someone he didn't know, and running for the steps.

She was so close, so incredibly close, and he was almost with her again. She needed him; he could feel it.

The temple itself was spectacular, the walls made of a rich, white stone and covered in ancient symbols he didn't know, large statues standing guard on either side of the small door. The doorway itself was likely sixteen feet high, and the statues were at least twice that height, some of the women in their magnificent headdresses were even bigger than that.

He didn't pay them much attention, his footsteps echoing as he ran inside and turned, eyes wide as his head ached with the sound of her.

He was in a large chamber filled with carved pillars and flowing, gauzy fabrics in blues and whites, fluttering in a breeze that hadn't existed in the world outside.

Warm yellow light flowed in through the large openings in the walls, and he could see blue sky when the sky outside had been red.

It was as though he had stepped into another part of the world, and it was fascinating. But still he was struggling to focus, and he could feel her nearby.

Footsteps announced the others following him, but he ignored them, running into the next room and stopping dead in his tracks as four people looked around at the noise, curious and wondering who it could be.

The first two Versalis knew: Amun and Anubis, looking as splendid and terrifying as ever.

Amun was around seven and a half feet tall with an enormous plume headdress that rose another two feet above his head. Wearing golden armour from head to toe with bronze and silver detail, a skirt and pants underneath it. He held a golden ibis bird staff in one hand, and a golden khopesh sword in the other, as though he was prepared for an attack, a second blade still at his hip.

"Versalis?" the giant man asked, stumped by the appearance of the vampire.

Anubis was as huge and terrifying as ever with his fierce dog head and tall ears, muscled body, and wearing nothing but his usual skirt and belts.

In his right hand he held a long staff with a set of scales hanging from the tip, an odd sight to behold.

He wasn't armed that Versalis could see, but it didn't mean he couldn't be armed in a second.

The last two were unknown to him, but the man had green skin and a long, bound beard that reached his collarbones. Dressed in layers of robes, he stood around seven feet tall, and his headdress made up another one, tall and white with a green plume on either side of it.

His white and green robes were decorated with bird wings, and a heavy crimson belt held a flail and a dark green khopesh.

"Who's this?" the man asked Amun.

The woman was beautiful with golden skin that matched the others and kind dark eyes, long black hair, and elaborately feathered headdress.

She had kohl around her eyes and delightfully plump lips, a small nose and thick eyebrows. Her headdress was a golden disk between two golden horns, and with her white dress that left her midriff bare he realised with a start that he was looking at the Goddess Isis.

That meant the green-skinned man was likely Osiris.

He was in the presence of some of the oldest and most powerful beings in existence, and he was staring at them like an idiot.

"One of *her* boys," Anubis growled, and all eyes lifted.

Looking up with them, his head spun as he saw it above them all. A large, wooden box that was suspended by at least one hundred ropes that shot out in all directions, the box itself wrapped around with the ropes, and then chained by another few dozen lengths of heavy, dark grey metal, and elaborate padlocks.

"Give her back," Versalis snarled, making them all look back at him.

"Versalis, you need to go ..." Amun said, his eyes lifting as the others arrived.

"Eros?" Osiris asked.

Daemon waved slightly, amused and worried. "Where?" the demon asked, and Versalis pointed up.

The eyes of all the intruders went up, and they studied the thing that was easily twenty feet above their heads.

"Leave. She is safe and secure here," Anubis growled, angry at the lot of them for intruding.

"Give her back to us," Jaia snapped, drawing the eyes of all four Gods to him.

"No. She is staying here with us so she can't cause any more problems."

"What is this?" Isis asked, confused by the whole conversation.

"They are looking to get their girl back," Osiris said.

Isis nodded, looking down at them all. "She is safe here with us, we can protect her," the woman said kindly.

"That is not protecting her!" Versalis yelled, pointing up once more. "That is dead!"

"She's not dead," Isis said gently.

"I can feel her, I am connected to her, and she's as close to dead as can be!"

"What are you to her?" Osiris asked.

Daemon growled in warning, but he ignored it.

"I'm her bearer, give her back."

There was a moment of silence as Daemon slapped his face down into his hand and the Gods glanced at each other.

"She does not have all of her magic right now?" Isis asked, suddenly wary.

"I ..." Versalis was stumped on what to say, realising his mistake.

"How powerful is she?" Osiris demanded.

"Idiot ..." Daemon growled.

"We can control her ..." Versalis said.

"No, you can't, you're too busy ogling her to notice she was creating. She's going to stay here, in her current state," Anubis snarled.

"You can't keep her trapped like that," Dirdos shot back.

"I can, and I will," Anubis said stiffly.

"We can convince her to give her magic entirely to Versalis," Daemon suggested.

"Entrust that much power to the control of a man who is so blindly in love with her that he can't see how dangerous she is?" Amun asked.

Versalis blushed, angry at the lot of them.

"Then to the others. We can split it up between them. Dirdos can take creation, Versalis has death, and she can keep Winter."

Both Dirdos and Versalis nodded, not caring what it took to get her back.

"What about the rest?" Amun asked.

"What rest?" Daemon said.

Anubis snorted. "He doesn't even know what he has created ... How about you go in the box with her, demon? You can enjoy the visitation with your precious creation."

Daemon's eyes lit up. "Yes!" he gasped.

"Daemon, no ..." Dirdos said gently. "We need you here to help us."

"But ... I could be with her..." he said, and they all saw a flash of that desperate need he had been hiding from them all. He wanted to be with her just as badly as they wanted her back.

"We need you more than she does," Versalis reasoned.

"We should put the bearer in with her," Osiris said.

Versalis jerked back a step in alarm.

"Yes, it would ensure she can't be called back ..." Amun said.

"Run," Daemon whispered, and the group scattered as Anubis swept down on them.

Versalis sprinted for the door and there was a snarl as the God came for him, knowing he was going to be in trouble if he got caught by the man.

Leaping off the steps, he staggered, but managed to stay on his feet, running full speed. He knew he was not going to be fast enough, Anubis was as fast as Etani and he was never able to keep up with her.

Dirdos was there, reaching out from behind a pillar, and the world erupted into flames as he was dragged to a stop and the canine roar of fury followed. Anubis had been alarmingly close to catching him.

DUMPED OUT IN AYATHIAN, the dragon was gone again to collect the others and he looked around for one fleeting moment, hoping to find her there but she wasn't, and his head bowed.

"You idiot vampire," Daemon snapped, and Versalis looked up just in time to have a fist rammed into his jaw. "If I knew you were going to tell them exactly how strong she really was, I would have left you here with Sebastian as a babysitter!"

Dirdos had returned with Jaia and Jagum, dropping them off while the others made their own way back, the Hunters appearing in that same swirling red, while Sebastian seemed to just sidestep through reality. Uzo came last, his eyes narrowed as he searched the room, but they seemed to be alone.

"They are going to be coming for him," the Fae said.

"We can deal with that if they decide to come for the idiot," Daemon growled. "You're a stupid child."

"I didn't think they would jump to that conclusion!" Versalis snarled back, already angry at himself; he didn't need to be reminded of his mistake by the angry incubus.

"It was an easy mistake to make," Uzo said, but Daemon only snorted and turned away.

"If you think it was going to be hard to get her back before, they've probably buried her heart by now," Daemon ran his hands through his hair, eyes clenched shut. "Mother ... she was right there ... right above us."

"We couldn't have gotten to her even if we had the chance. Those locks were enchanted. We would need one of the curse breakers or the magic breakers to get her out," Dirdos said gently.

"But we could have brought her back with us. She could have been safe here, protected here ..." Uzo reasoned.

"Where would we have been able to keep her?" Sebastian said.

"What?" Daemon snarled.

"Think about it, Daemon. This is the heart of the single most powerful and dangerous being to ever exist. And in that state, she is entirely vulnerable to having her magic abused. Until we can get her free, she is safer being in the underworld where the Gods can protect her. Anubis isn't going to abuse her magic, Amun wouldn't let any of the other Gods abuse her. In all honesty, where she is right now is the best place she could be in order to be safe until we can get her back to her rightful state."

Daemon's face twisted as though he had bitten into a rotten piece of meat.

"None of us could have protected her heart if we brought it back with us. We would have been responsible for her protection and so far, none of us have done particularly well on the grounds of keeping her safe," the cambion explained. Daemon was glaring, about ready to explode. "We need to figure out how to get her free. Only then do we go bursting in there and get her out. When we can free her, not just move her to a higher risk hiding place."

They were silent, not wanting to agree with him, but he was right.

"Seb's right," Versalis said softly, making the man jerk. "We have to find a way to free her first. We need to get in contact with the curse breakers or the magic breakers."

All eyes turned on Vincent and Dainin, the two men exchanging a wary glance.

"Will the Hunters help?" Daemon asked.

"I think so ..." Dainin replied, unsure of the actual answer. "But it will be a risk. They will want to know why. Would saying she's a trapped Goddess be enough?"

"We can try," Vincent said with a slow exhale. "What about Neah?"

"What about Neah?" Daemon snapped, infuriated as always by the name of that man.

"We need to make sure he doesn't find out about any of this, or he will want to become involved ..."

"The issue is, those like Neah tend to talk, so we will need incentive to try and give them a reason not to tell Neah his wife is in need of magical help."

"She's not his wife," Daemon snapped.

"She is."

"No, she's not," Dirdos growled, but Vincent only shrugged, looking away from them.

"Are there any who aren't like Neah?" Versalis asked and the two Hunters exchanged another look.

"We can go to Jason," Dainin said.

"Who's Jason?" Daemon demanded.

"The mask maker," the two Hunters said together, their faces grim but determined.

It was another couple of days before they managed to get hold of the man, and Versalis was on edge the entire time, just waiting for the Gods to show up, but they never did, and when he asked Daemon, he shrugged.

"Likely waiting until you're alone," he said simply and then left, leaving Versalis to himself.

Versalis scrambled to get up and followed the laughing Demon.

But they had all settled in for a quiet night of waiting for the Hunters to get back, and when they did, they brought a tall figure with them. He had jaw-length black hair and a mask that was white and featureless except for a red-brown smile that had been painted on the front of it. How he saw, Versalis had no idea, but he was looking around at them all curiously with his hands linked behind his back.

He was thin, standing a good six inches above Vincent's head. He was wearing a dark blue button-up shirt that was a size too big for him, and black slacks, he had no shoes on, and Versalis saw that his feet were bruised and bloody, though none of the dirt or blood rubbed off onto the white carpet.

"Everyone, this is Jason," Vincent said.

Jason was breathing in slowly, deeply, as he looked around the room.

"This room belongs to a woman," the man said. His voice was muffled by the mask, but it was low, more of a murmur than anything else.

"What does he know?" Dirdos asked.

"Nothing as yet. He only knows he is to keep this all a secret from Neah," Vincent explained.

"Though I would like to know why I need to keep it a secret from our psychotic little friend," Jason said in a perfectly cheerful voice.

Lifting his mask up to better see them all, Versalis was surprised to see just how normal the man looked.

Pale skin, large, blue eyes that oddly had no pupil or iris at all, just a solid deep blue. His mouth was wide, but not unusually so, and thick brows were lifted in curiosity.

Versalis noted that his hands were also covered in dirt, bruises, and blood.

"Where is the woman who lives here?" he asked, making everyone tense. "I recognise the scent, is this the woman you and the hybrid kept in the compound?"

There was a moment of stunned silence as all eyes turned on Vincent, who looked defiant.

"Yes. This is Etani's room," the Hunter said.

"I knew it ... you lying little shit!" Daemon exploded. "You weren't looking for her at all!"

"Kill him later. We have work to do," Dainin said, but Daemon was still glaring.

"I'm not going to apologise for doing what she asked. She didn't want to come back, we kept her safe in the compound."

"Yes, so safe that Neah started stalking her," Dirdos growled.

"Is that where he's been? Stalking after this woman?"

"Etani is dead," Dainin said.

"That's a shame," Jason said with a slight frown. "She was a unique creature."

"Did you ever see her?" Versalis asked.

"Not directly; she was always hooded any time she was in the dining hall when I was there. But I could feel her aura, quite a chaotic being," Jason said, turning to look at him. "You have her magic inside you."

"I'm her bearer," Versalis said slowly.

"Isn't that a God thing?"

Versalis nodded and Jason made a soft sound of surprise. He had the same sharp teeth as the rest of the Hunters, but he looked normal when his mouth was closed.

"So, why am I here?" he asked. "I assume none of you want masks."

"We need your abilities," Daemon said, drawing the odd blue eyes of the Hunter toward him.

"Please elaborate," Jason said politely, pushing his mask up to the top of his head and linking his hands against the small of his back.

"Etani has been trapped by Anubis, her heart stolen and placed inside a chest," Uzo said.

"You have a similar aura to hers ..." Jason said as his eyes turned on Uzo.

"I am a member of the Fae," Uzo said in a dark tone that had Jason's brows twitching up.

"Is that so?" Jason said, dropping the subject. "Anubis took your girl's heart and put it in a chest. Why?"

"You have to swear to secrecy," Daemon said.

"I already swore not to tell Neah any of this."

"You have to swear not to tell anyone."

"I'm not going to do that."

"Why not?" Versalis asked, the man looking around at him with a faint hint of a smile.

"It's not as much fun if there is no risk involved. I would like to meet your girl when she has returned to life. That is my offer."

There was silence as they all took that in, wary and uncertain.

"Meet her how?" Jaia asked.

"As we are now. I will sit, she will sit, and we may talk. She is interesting and I am curious."

"And that is the payment you seek?" Daemon asked.

"I do not know what I am exchanging payment for."

"Freeing her," Vincent said.

"Freeing her from the chest?"

"She is trapped behind enchanted locks. We need your powers to get her free."

"I see. Then yes, I will exchange my abilities for a chance to talk with her. For a few hours."

"You are not to touch her," Daemon said.

"I will not touch her unless she asks me to."

"Why would she ask you to?" Versalis asked.

"Jason can read the truth of a person with a touch. It's how he makes the masks. He can read a person's true being and moulds the mask based on that," Vincent explained.

"What does that say about you two?" Dirdos asked.

"Vincent is hiding everything behind his mask. He is secretive and prefers no one to know him unless he chooses them to. Dainin is a happy soul, but he is also vicious and will smile as he rips your throat out," Jason said, and the two men flinched.

"And Neah?" Versalis asked.

Jason turned to look at him, his face neutral. "Neah is empty. He is a psychopath from conception and while he might love your girl in his own way, he is incapable of being *in love*. He is exceptionally good at manipulation, particularly of women. He also has sociopathic tendencies, prone to rages and some impulsive behaviours."

"Like kidnapping," Daemon said.

"Yes, like kidnapping, rape, murder, torture ..." Jason frowned slightly, his eyes meeting those of the Hunters.

"Are you like him?" Uzo asked.

"No, I am not a psychopath or a sociopath as some of the others are. I am the anomaly in this situation. I might be cold or violent, but I am capable of empathy, guilt, and remorse just as many of you are."

His eyes landed on Jaia before turning away again, the vampire frowning.

"So, tell me everything," the man said as he moved around the room, examining the few trinkets Etani owned. "She's not much for keepsakes, this girl of yours."

"No, she's not," Daemon said and exhaled. "Etani is the culmination of fifty generations of careful breeding. Each generation was new and never repeated."

"Why?" Jason interrupted as he picked up a small pot of lavender perfume, sniffing it carefully before setting it back down.

"A prophecy foretold that death would be a Creator. It was a challenge and a race amongst the Gods to see who could be the one to create that being. Everyone thought it would be male like the rest of the Creators."

"But she turned out to be a female."

"They were all female except for her father. I was so certain that he was the one we were waiting for ..."

"You are the one who bred her?" Jason asked, looking around at Daemon.

"Yes, it was my doing."

"I see, go on."

"Lutheral was born, and I was so sure he was going to be the Creator, and given he was the only one born I was really confused."

"Lutheral, as in Captain Lutheral of the Winter Court?" Vincent asked, sounding strangled.

"Yes, Lutheral is Etani's father."

"Lutheral had a brother," Jason said.

"What?" Uzo demanded, looking around.

Jason held up two fingers. "From what I understand, there were two born to Tatialia. Twin boys. Is your Etani one of a set?"

"Yes, Letari is in the basement," Versalis said.

"Twins tend to reproduce twins. Surely you would have figured that out."

Daemon looked like he was trying to swallow glue, his mouth opening and closing repeatedly.

"Who is the brother?" he managed to say.

"No idea," Jason said, his eyes falling on Uzo, who was making choking sounds. "You look like you're going to have a stroke, my friend."

"Lutheral didn't have a brother," Uzo snapped. "He would have told me."

"Unless he didn't know," Jason said, amused by them all.

"Regardless of the existence or status of this brother who may not exist, please continue with your story."

"I ..." Daemon spluttered, shaking his head as he tried to focus. "I lost track of Lutheral during the war, he had become interested in something in the human world and hid from me. Several decades later I hear rumour about a painting that had been found depicting Lutheral, a woman, and two infants. I managed to get a glimpse of Etani right as they were escaping Faerie, but I couldn't get to her in time. That was nine hundred years ago and then it was several years ago that I found her again. She had no idea who or what I was. But I could feel it in her, all that magic that hadn't yet been tapped into. It was all turned on, but she had never had cause to use it until I showed up."

"What does she look like?" Jason asked, lifting up a long silver chain with a cat ornament hanging from it.

"Imagine Aphrodite but better," Daemon said.

"Like nothing you have ever seen," Dirdos added.

"Her skin is like milk, smooth like silk. Her lips are rose petals touched by frost, eyes that could put the most vibrant Ulysses butterfly to shame, with a wicked intelligence and primal hunger that could turn on a ghoul. Midnight hair that is softer than a feather, and a face one couldn't come up with in their wildest imagination. She doesn't compare to the word perfect; she is more than perfect. Small, delicate, and stronger than most vampires. She could shred your skin to ribbons or comfort you better than any mother with those hands and she smells of ... magic and honey, lavender and sex," Versalis said, his eyes lowered to the carpet.

There was a silence so complete that it seemed no one was breathing, their minds all on the woman they loved.

"And that laugh ..." Dirdos said. "That laugh that was somehow both entirely innocent, and a million times more wicked than any succubus all at once. A voice that is so sinful it should be illegal."

"A smile that could bring even the most powerful man in existence to his knees," Jagum said, his voice pained. "It could topple Kingdoms, leave Gods begging for more ..."

"And when she loved you, there was nothing in this world that could be more perfect, for if you earnt her love, it made you special," Daemon said, voice shaking. "It made you worthy of something, it made you good."

"And on top of all that ..." Dainin said, "she is absolutely and completely oblivious to just how utterly, blindingly, soul-shatteringly beautiful she really is."

CHAPTER 6
JASON

They were all silent, pain pulsing through them all as they tried to keep strong for her, so they could bring her back to them.

"She sounds magical," Jason said, setting the necklace back down. "I will help you bring her back."

"Thank you," Versalis sighed, dropping his head into his hands and rubbing his eyes hard. He wasn't the only one whose eyes stung with tears; almost all of them struggled with the thought of her being gone.

"Tell me what she is, the full truth of what she is," Jason said after a short break to give them all time to recover.

"That is hard to give an answer to, but from what we can understand she has aspects from the last twenty species. Those are the thunderbird, Genii Loci, three Gods, an iron witch, a pixie, and siren, the witches associated with Hecate, Strigoi, abarimon, were-cats, asrai, aswang, banshee, nephilim, the Fae, and the Celestrials. Many of those are personality or physical changes, others are physiological or magical. On top of that, her husband Epharis tried to turn her into a Lich and then that *thing* and his brother tried to turn her into a vampire," Versalis said, jerking his thumb toward Jaia.

"She is the personification of death, the only female Creator to exist, and she is a Goddess."

"What else could she be?" Versalis asked. "They suggested there was more."

"I don't know," Daemon sighed, shaking his head.

"Is that not enough?" Versalis demanded.

"Who are the Gods?" Jason asked.

"Apophis, Sobek, and Theseus. But further back is Loki, Hades, and Mara," Daemon supplied.

"Would explain why she is so powerful, especially after she became a Goddess herself. What did Dominick offer her?"

"How...?"

"Dominick is the only Nephilim."

"The magical addiction," Daemon said, squinting at the man. "Those who lay eyes on her become addicted to her presence."

"Seems easy enough to keep track of. What is she the Goddess of?"

"Death, beauty, lust, creation, and destruction."

"And rebirth," Versalis pitched in.

"Rebirth?" Jason asked sharply.

"Etani can give immortality to others," Daemon said.

"I'm sorry, what?" Jason said, turning fully around to look at them all.

"She can create vampires for one; she created Malik."

"Which one of you is Malik?" Jason asked.

"Malik died trying to protect Etani. She ripped right through the chain bindings in her rage."

"Coming back to that ... how else can she give immortality?"

"Etani can remove your soul with a kiss."

"Yes, the Hunters were all talking about that. Vincent," he answered the questioning look Daemon gave him. "He talks about her incessantly, quite the crush on her."

Vincent was glaring, his face as red as his eye.

"But it was believed that she simply consumed it."

"No, she can then take that soul and put it in a new body. It makes the being immortal."

"My brother is one of her creations," Jaia said moodily.

"Same with her sister and the Queen of a neighbouring Kingdom, and a handful of others," Daemon said.

"Might I see these two?" Jason asked.

"Not right now," Jaia said warily.

"Very well. So, she can grant immortality. That in and of itself is miraculous as it would seem that she is not changing them. She is taking a vampire and simply making him a more immortal vampire. What would happen if she did that to a human?"

"I don't know that she would be able to resist the urge to consume a human," Dirdos said. "Humans are her primary food source; it would be difficult to keep from simply eating them."

"But if she could?"

"They would ... I suppose simply to be an immortal human ..." Daemon said.

"A being who can grant pure, unperverted immortality," Jason said. "What about her creation magic?"

"She created another world, under duress by the witches. She then took the witches and stuffed them into that world and severed the connection to Faerie."

Jason looked at Daemon, his face blank and mind working hard.

"Let me be perfectly clear here. Your girl, Etani, created an entire other world ... and then took all the witches from this world and put them there. Then she broke that world's connection to this one. You are saying that she created another world, entirely capable of surviving without a connection to Faerie. A standalone world."

"Yes," Daemon said.

Jason sat down beside Jaia, his eyes unfocused and trying to come to terms with what he was learning.

"Your Etani ..." He broke off, trying to wrap his head around it.

"Your Etani is ... she's a magic Creator. She's not a Creator, she is The Creator."

Dainin exchanged a glance with Vincent and Vincent only shook his head.

"What does that mean?" Jaia asked.

"A magic Creator is what is supposed to have created Faerie and the human world. A being capable of creating Faerie. But she never created another one, because it is believed she did not have the capacity to create it perfectly. So, she waited ... is waiting, for the one who is capable. Your Etani is that being. She can create another Faerie, complete and perfect. She could create a million Faeries, a million human worlds if she chose to. All interconnected. She could create a universe of them. Not only that, but she could tear this one apart if she wanted to."

He exhaled, rubbing his eyes, and then looked up at them all.

"Do you find you feel stronger when around her?" he asked.

"I don't know," Daemon said.

"Yes," Dirdos said.

"That scent of magic you get from her ... It's not just her, it's the magic she is creating that is leaking out of her. She is *creating* magic out of herself, and it is being fed into each of you. It's why her aura is so chaotic, her magic has no outlet, so it just builds up and up until, like a cup, it simply overflows and is pushed into whatever being is nearby. That would be all of you. That would be why you are addicted to her; she is giving you the same high you feel going into Faerie. You are addicted to the magic she is putting out into the world. It's like a drug and being around her means you will never stop being addicted to her. It will lessen if she can use her magic more, but it will never go away."

Versalis sat back in the chair and studied the man who had so easily explained so much that they had all been unable to under-stand for so long. It made sense, and how she could control them all was given voice.

She had never done it on purpose, they knew that, but it didn't make her any less alarming. She was both terrifying and amazing at the same time, more so now.

"Okay, so where are they keeping her?" Jason asked, lifting his head.

"Last time we saw, suspended about twenty feet off the ground inside a chest," Daemon replied.

"Do you think she's inside a box?" Versalis asked, his voice pained.

"Why does that matter?" Jason asked.

"She doesn't like wooden boxes."

"Why not?"

"Neah keeps a box full of hair from his victims. He put hers in there when he took her, and she hates them now."

"Seems reasonable," Jason said, frowning. "Have either of you seen it?" he asked Vincent and Dainin.

"No," Vincent said, his face still red.

"Did you hear her?" Dirdos asked.

"Hear her?" Jason lifted a brow, looking up at the dragon.

"When Neah had her. Vincent did but didn't realise it was her."

"No, my rooms are a floor below and on the other side of the compound. I didn't know she was there," Jason made a face, his eyes pained.

"What?" Versalis snarled.

"There were jokes going around about Neah having a good time with someone," Jason said, his eyes lowering. "It's how they all cope with the thought of his victims. We can't stop him, so they try to mask it with humour. Wouldn't be as funny had they known she was there, she's quite a popular source of discussion."

"Do you think they would have stopped him if they knew?" Jaia asked.

"Probably not. They would have feared her being executed if they spoke up, but they would have gotten word back to Vincent and you all. We don't interfere with the activities of the other magic breakers."

"Monsters ..." Jaia growled.

"Yes, but not all of us. Those two are decent men."

The two in question shifted and looked away, embarrassed by the attention.

"So, what can you do?" Versalis asked.

"I can break through the magical locks, you just have to tell me how to get there, and what to do with her once I've got her."

"Bring her back here."

"And then what? Do you know what to do with her heart?"

They were all silent, looking around at each other as though someone would be able to give them an answer.

"That's what I thought. You will need to destroy it, crush it, or stab it. It must be completely destroyed, and you must prepare for the rebound of when she wakes up. How does she normally come back?"

"There are two ways, the Celestrial method, which is her resurrecting in the soul pool in Ceress. Then there is the way she is reborn with Versalis," Daemon said.

"I don't know how that's going to work since the crystal shattered." Versalis sighed.

"We will experiment when she's back."

"So you are the bearer of death?" Jason asked.

"I am," Versalis said warily, uncertain of that man.

"And what happened when this crystal shattered?"

"Shards pierced my skin and changed me."

"Might I see them? I've never met a bearer before."

Glancing at Daemon, the demon shrugged and Versalis sighed, standing and pulling his shirt up over his head.

Their looking at him like that was making him uncomfortable, but he stood still as the tall man approached, a good near half foot taller than Versalis, and he smelt of blood like all the Hunters.

"Interesting. They look like wings," Jason said, reaching out to press his cool finger against Versalis' chest, tracing along the smooth lines that spread across his chest and up to his shoulders.

"Etani has wings when she appears as death," he said, trying to ignore the cool breath that washed over his skin as the man bent forward to look closer.

"Does she? Black?"

"Yes, with a span of what? Thirteen feet?" he asked Daemon.

"Each wing is taller than she is, she's five ten, isn't she?"

Versalis nodded and Jason snorted.

"Tiny little thing for a Fae."

"Don't ever say that in front of her if you want to keep your lower legs," Versalis muttered.

"Oh Mother, I forgot about that ..." Daemon laughed.

"What?" Jaia asked, sounding confused.

"About three months ago there was an Elf who came through to speak with Alaric," Daemon started. "He called her little, and so she chopped his legs off at the knee, and just goes 'Now you're little, too.'" He mimicked her voice and burst out laughing.

"She's a feisty woman," Jason said, amused. "Did the Elf recover?"

"No, he died, and Alaric was so angry. But he knows better than to try and punish her. He's all talk, but he's absolutely terrified of her. Most people either want to fuck her or want to kill her. Often both, probably at the same time."

"Both," Dirdos said, amused.

"I was like that at first, too," Vincent said. "Absolutely terrified, but I couldn't *not* try and get into bed with her."

"Former for me," Versalis said and Jaia nodded.

"That's my niece you're talking about," Uzo said, and the clink of a teacup made them all flinch.

Jason caught the reaction and lifted a brow, but Versalis only shook his head.

"You're an odd bunch," Jason said, stepping back from Versalis. "Can you feel her right now?"

"No, I could feel her in Faerie, but not as much here. In Faerie she was just asleep."

"You were almost flinching when we got to the temple," Jagum said from the corner.

"Her heart was almost screaming in my head."

"Interesting. So, the enchantments are likely keeping her asleep or is it simply to keep you all out?"

"We don't know," Daemon said. "There were possibly ten or fifteen locks on that thing."

"Likely both, then," Jason said, moving away, and Versalis was able to put his shirt back on. "You realise that they will simply try again if you get her back. You will need to come up with another method to keep her safe."

"What do you mean?" Dirdos asked.

"You might need to have another bearer, or otherwise find a way to bind her so that she is contained. They want her because she's dangerous, so you need to make her less so if you want to keep her."

"You're not binding her again," Versalis growled, glaring at the demon.

"No, but we might ask her to surrender her magic to me," Dirdos said.

"Why you?" Jason asked.

"Least likely to give in to her whims," Daemon said and Dirdos nodded.

"She can be a dangerous creature when she wants something, and you are refusing to give it to her. I can neutralise her magic if in contact with her, which means she cannot force her magic back from me."

"You're a dragon?" Jason asked.

"Yes. I love her dearly, but I won't let her destroy herself because she is angry."

"That is a wise idea. The rest she is likely capable of controlling on her own."

"We hope so," Dirdos said, glancing at Daemon, who was frowning.

"First things first; we have to get to her. Then we get her out of the chest and whatever else she might be inside that chest. After that, we get the heart destroyed, and she's back."

"After the heart is destroyed, she will wake up, but then Versalis will need to draw her back and she may not want to come back," Daemon said.

"Why wouldn't she want to come back?"

"Neah is not the first man to take her."

"Oh," was all Jason could say in response. "Is this why Neah is so obsessed with her?"

"Etani is also a universal breeder," Dainin said, and that made all of them look around with an angry growl.

"She's not a broodmare," Uzo snarled.

"Peace, friends, it is a term we use in the compound and not intended to disrespect your girl," Jason said, his eyes turning back to Dainin. "And by universal, you mean?"

"Any being who isn't entirely sterile."

"Neah was asking questions about procreation not that long ago. I assumed it was a generic question, not one relating to Etani. He likely had her?"

"Yes, she was pregnant," Versalis said, his face tight.

"Interesting creature you have," Jason said. "I would suggest you not mention this around the others. The rules of mating in the compound will not matter if they believe she can provide them all with offspring."

Dainin and Vincent nodded, and Jason let out a slow breath.

"He has mentioned a new bride. I take it that is your Etani?" he asked, sounding exhausted by the whole thing.

"Yes. However, he had taken her under false pretences. It is entirely possible the marriage is invalid," Vincent said.

"Speak with the elders, they'll be able to give you an answer. In the meantime, I will see what I can find out about these locks. Give me a week and I'll get back to you on how things are. We will monitor the Gods and see if they take her anywhere. For the time being, just try to be patient."

"Easier said than done," Daemon growled.

"Try," Jason said darkly, eyeing the demon.

"How do you see through that mask?" Versalis asked as the white thing was pulled back down.

"I do not see as you do. I see in auras," he said, and his tone suggested the end of the conversation.

"What do you think the creepy smile means for him?" Jaia asked after the man had vanished.

"Drawn on smile," Dirdos said and Daemon nodded. "I think it means we will need to be wary of him. He might seem like a reliable figure, but he is dangerous."

"Don't underestimate any of them," Dainin said as Vincent vanished. "They are powerful, and they all have their own agenda. They will bring this entire world crashing down if we give them a reason."

CHAPTER 7
THE VAMPIRE QUEEN

They were still waiting, impatient and trying to figure out what to do, but they couldn't just check out of their lives while they waited for Etani to come back.

Jaia had returned to working for Alaric and taken Dainin with him in order to cover for the missing Kai.

Daemon was a freeloader who did pretty much nothing, same as Dirdos.

Uzo, Sebastian, and Jagum acted as advisors for Alaric and Epharis to their respective people, but no one had told them that Etani was gone, at least not yet. They were hoping neither of the royals would really be paying attention, and with the war upcoming, it had been nine days since her death, and they still hadn't noticed.

It was a bit sad really, but Epharis was respecting Etani's wishes not to be touched and that had lasted months; it was unlikely to change soon. Versalis himself was meant to be an emissary to the vampires, given his rank, but he didn't do much. It was a title in name only.

Sitting in the garden, he was drawing idly on the frosted surface of the table and scowling as Cat thumped his way around in delight.

The cat didn't get to be out often while everyone was still pouting, and the poor beast was getting pretty chubby from the lack of exercise. Etani was going to be furious at them if she came back ... when she came back.

Closing his eyes at his mental slip up, he didn't immediately feel her approach until her shadow fell over him and he jumped, looking up when the scent of her hit his nose.

"Hello, little King," the woman said, and Versalis swallowed.

She was exquisite, not Etani's level of impossible beauty, but she was ravishing with long, wavy black hair and ivory skin. Her eyes were a deep, almost liquid silver colour, and she had dark crimson lips and a slender but full frame. She was around four inches shorter than him, and she seemed to rather like the height difference.

"Who are you?" he asked, but he already knew what she was.

She was a Vampire Queen; he could smell it on her. Raw sexual hunger, blood, and magic. Sharp fangs when she smiled, and a slight discolouration on her forehead in the shape of a crescent moon with the points facing upward. She had two small red circles just under her lower lashes and looked good enough to eat in a black dress that hung off her shoulders, her hair unbound and wild to the middle of her back.

"Helena of the Lamia Clan," she murmured, and he jerked back, alarmed. Lamia was the largest clan to ever exist, consisting of some hundred thousand vampires, all under a single woman. It was an unprecedented number of vampires to one Queen, and she had created every single one of them.

He swept the garden and found them all, the members of her clan who were there to keep him from laying a finger on such a precious commodity.

The Queens might be numerous, but when compared to the sheer number of vampires to exist, a Queen was incredibly rare. One in a million, or so they assumed.

"Why are you here?" he asked warily.

She smiled, looking him over for a second.

He hadn't taken any effort to look presentable in black slacks and a dark grey, button shirt that hung open to show off some of the markings on his chest. His hair was bound loosely at the back of his neck but much of it had come loose and was everywhere.

Mother she was so beautiful, and that smell, that smell was turning him on more than he could have thought from a being who wasn't Etani.

"I'm looking for a husband," Helena said gently.

"Pardon?" Versalis said, hearing her just fine, but he wasn't entirely sure she had meant what she said.

"I am looking for you to become my husband, Versalis ... the only Vampire King in existence. I rule the largest clan in existence, it is fate," she said happily, as though he would be delighted to hear that.

Sure, he would love to fuck her a few times, but marry her?

"I'm not interested," he said, and her eyes widened in surprise, her chin lifting as he stood and made a clicking noise that brought Cat spinning around to look at him, bounding over and almost knocking him over with a shoulder-barge of affection.

"Why not?" she demanded, looking down at the feline, and when Cat hissed at her, she hissed right back at him, the cat darting behind Versalis' legs.

"I already belong to someone."

"You are not married," she said, motioning to his empty ring finger.

"Not yet, but when she is back ..."

"Where is she?"

"Dead."

Helena blinked at him once, her expression one of disbelief. "You are waiting for a dead woman?" she demanded, irritated by his apparent stupidity.

"She is immortal, trapped by the God Anubis, and she will be back."

"Are you insane?" Helena asked with genuine concern.

"No, Etani cannot stay dead," he said gently.

"Why do I know that name ...? Etani ... Isn't that the name of the Goddess?"

"Yes, she's a Goddess," Versalis agreed, fascinated that she would know of her.

"Some of my scions worshipped her. Goddess of Beauty and Death or something like that."

"She's also the Goddess of Rebirth. She will be back, very soon." He hoped ... he deeply, madly hoped.

She made a sound, but he pretended not to hear it, bending down to pick up Cat.

"What is that?" she asked.

"This is Cat, Etani's companion," Versalis said, and her brows lifted slightly.

"You do a lot for this dead woman," she said.

Versalis shrugged, not really wanting to go into detail of what he would and wouldn't do for that creature.

Trying to step past her with Cat in his arms, he frowned when she blocked him, her body moving with a feral grace he found oddly hypnotic.

He knew getting involved with her was a bad idea; she was powerful, physically strong, and there were a very large number of vampires under her control who would gladly die for her. He wasn't one of them.

"Do you have a clan?" she asked, Versalis frowning as he looked down at her.

"I do not," he said, wary of how vulnerable that made him.

"Why not?"

Versalis paused, looking down the few inches into her lovely liquid metal eyes as he tried to think about why he hadn't.

"I have been searching for something for a very long time, Helena," he said, and he frowned, thinking about that. He had been searching for something for at least twenty years, and then it was no longer searching, but staying near to that thing. He hadn't ever stopped to think why he had stopped searching, but he realised then that it was because he had found it.

With a dawning horror, he recalled the corpses he had always seen and thought nothing of. He had just seen them as belonging to some creature that lived in the area. He hadn't been wrong; they had lived in the area.

He had been following along after a siren call for at least twenty, possibly even thirty years without ever really paying attention, and that siren call had pulled him right along behind the woman who was now dead, and whom he was awaiting to return.

He had been hunting her for decades, always a few days or even a week behind her as she danced her way around with Cain on her heels. He had been following along behind.

Why had he been stalking her?

He was frozen in thought long enough that Helena cleared her throat, and he looked at her, confused and uncertain of himself.

Why would he have been hunting her? How had he been able to hunt her? Was it her magic calling to him?

"You went somewhere just now," she said and Versalis shook his head to clear it.

"Apologies, something came up in my head," he said politely. "I am grateful for the offer, but I will not be available to marry you."

Helena looked annoyed by that, chewing on her nail in a way that sent a pang of pain through him.

Etani chewed on her nail like that when she was thinking.

"Perhaps you need time to think about it. It must be quite a shock to have me show up."

"Yes, how is it you found me?" he asked warily.

"You are technically in my territory. I've been aware of your presence since you set foot here. Did you really think I wouldn't know when someone of your rank set foot in my land?" She laughed. "It could be *our* land though. Or I could have you evicted."

His eyes narrowed as her smile turned cruel, and he took in that information. She could easily have him kicked out, it wouldn't be hard, and then he wouldn't be present to help return Etani. He had to be there for that; he couldn't be apart from her like that.

"I am needed here," he said.

"This is my territory," she countered, and he felt himself growing more alarmed by the idea of being evicted by the woman. Yes, she was entirely within her right to throw him out, but then she would have to deal with Alaric as well, and no one wanted a war with the maniacal King.

"And if I consider your offer ... you will let me stay?" he asked.

"I will consider letting you stay," she countered, and he couldn't hide the frown as he looked at her.

"I will consider your generous offer of marriage," he said, her lovely face lighting up as she offered him her hand.

He took it, and it was small, warm, and delicate in his fingers. Lifting it to his lips, he kissed it gently, and she seemed delighted by his manners.

"You will make for a good husband," Helena said, and he had to wonder if this was what it was like to be Etani, men chasing her and demanding she be with them. It was bad enough it was happening once in his opinion.

He would have to figure something out, but he would put her off as long as was possible in the meantime. How long she was willing to wait for him was a mystery, but hopefully it was long enough for him to get out of it.

HEADING BACK UP to the castle with Cat in his arms, he clutched the beast to him, and Cat mewled, rubbing his face against Versalis' and making soft chittering noises as he looked around from the new, much taller vantage point of his arms.

"What do I do, Cat?" he asked the beast, but Cat didn't give him a response. "Oh yeah, you talk to her but when I have a question? Ignore. Pretend Versalis doesn't exist. I'm Cat and I'll only talk to

Etani because she's nicer to me and gives me treats. Who cares if I get fat?"

He was muttering to himself as he carried the heavy beast back up to the castle and Cat leapt free of his arms and prowled across the room toward Bast, who was sitting on the couch.

"I hear you boys had an interesting time in the underworld a few days ago," she said, and the soft purring voice of the cat Goddess soothed him as it always did.

"You could say that," he said, heading straight for her and dropping down onto the floor by her feet. She dug her nails into his scalp, and he very nearly melted right there into a puddle of goop on the carpet.

"What were you thinking?" she asked, those long fingers working.

"We wanted her back ... I think we were all a bit crazy, but it did tell us where she is."

"Yes, I suppose so. But did that help you? Are you able to get to her with that knowledge?"

"Yes, we are working on it."

"I miss her ..." Bast said and Versalis looked up at her, taking her hand from atop his head and kissing the palm gently.

"We will get her back. I promise we will find a way to get her back."

"Please ..." she whispered and Versalis rolled up onto his knees, hugging the shivering Goddess.

She clung to him, her face burying into his neck, and he sighed as he stroked her, his fingers tracing down over the back of her soft head.

"I will not rest until we have her back. She is going to be back here with us, I swear."

He was still holding her tightly to him when the door opened and Daemon strolled in, his face going still, and then pain crossed his handsome features.

He approached and wrapped his arms around the Goddess from behind, his forehead resting between her shoulder blades.

She clung to his arms, crying quietly as they did what they could do to comfort her, though he was feeling inadequate.

"Hey, it's going to be okay," Daemon said, turning his head to nuzzle his cheek into her back. "She's going to be back, making us all frustrated in no time."

"It's been almost two weeks, Eros ..." She wailed and Versalis kissed her cheek hard, looking at the demon over the Goddess' shoulder.

"And this time next week you'll be wondering why we don't just kill her ourselves when she's trying to do something stupid," he said, making the woman laugh.

"No, you're right ... I just ..."

"I thought we agreed never to tell Daemon when he was right, it might get to his head and make it bigger than it already is," Versalis chipped in.

Daemon glared, but Bast laughed fully, always pleased when someone got away with picking on the demon.

"This is why homicide needs to be legal," Daemon grumbled.

"You're not killing my Versalis," Bast said, and Versalis smirked at Daemon.

"Yeah, Daemon. I'm *her* Versalis," he teased.

"Oh good, if you belong to Bast then you no longer must want Etani. Better odds for me." The door opened, and Daemon looked up. "Hey Dirdos, Versalis is bowing out of the race."

"Good, saves me having to kill him later," the dragon said, his eyes on a giant plate of cooked meat he had managed to get from the kitchens.

"Are you going to share that?" Daemon asked, popping up from behind Bast.

"Hadn't intended to."

"But you will because you love me."

"At no point have I even indicated I liked you, let alone loved you."

"Your mouth on my cock suggests you liked me," Daemon said dryly.

"Don't be crude," Bast scolded, but Dirdos was looking at Daemon, his lips pursed, and then he sighed, rolling his eyes, and held the plate out to him.

Daemon grinned, moving forward and taking several hunks of meat. Bast stole some, too, and Versalis snatched two pieces before the dragon managed to get teh remainder away and he was left with a single piece.

"I hate you all ..." the dragon said

"You love me at least," Bast said, amused as she chewed on the meat.

"Only because you're cute."

"I can work with that," the Goddess said.

Versalis stuffed the meat into his mouth as Dirdos looked at the two pieces and then growled, stalking back out of the room to get more while popping a piece in his mouth.

"You'd think he would have learnt by now. We will always take food," Bast said, amused.

"You'd think ..." Daemon agreed, chewing.

"Old dog, new tricks, and all that," Versalis said, swallowing, and eyeing Daemon's pile but the demon glared at him, moving away to protect his food.

"You love me too, don't you?" Versalis asked.

"Blow me and I'll consider it," Daemon said.

"You're not really my type," Versalis said, and Daemon looked around curiously.

"Which part?" Daemon asked.

"Not that into demons," Versalis said, amused by the demon's curiosity. He didn't fancy men, but it was funny to lead the demon on.

"And here I thought you were a boring straight man," Daemon said.

"Excuse me? Being straight is not boring," Bast said.

"You don't count. I'll give you this if you kiss me then, Versalis," Daemon offered, holding out a large chunk of the cooked meat.

It was a very tempting offer, and he considered the meat, then the demon, and back again.

"Tempting, but Etani is the only one I want to kiss."

"Two?"

"All of it," Versalis countered.

Daemon's eyes narrowed, and he shook his head. "No way; I got this fair and square."

"No kiss for you," Versalis said.

Dirdos sidled back into the room, and the smell of fresh food made them all turn around.

"Get away, you greedy bastards, this is mine."

Daemon pouted and Versalis frowned, considering.

"Did you know Versalis was into guys?" Daemon asked.

Dirdos laughed, amused by the whole concept.

"Versalis is as straight as Etani's hair," the dragon said, biting half of the giant cube of meat and then looking around. "Why? Is he changing his mind? Because dibs on that first experience."

"He agreed to exchange all of my dinner for a kiss."

"Doesn't mean he likes men, just means he's hungry ... But then again. Half of this for a kiss."

Versalis looked at the plate, then at Daemon and then at Dirdos.

Daemon looked annoyed.

"One kiss, on the mouth," Versalis clarified.

It didn't matter to him; a kiss didn't mean much. Vampires kissed each other a lot and the sex of the one being kissed never mattered.

"Deal," Dirdos said, pouring half of the meat into a bowl and offering it to Versalis.

Versalis took it and smirked at Daemon, the demon looking agitated.

Dirdos bent down and Versalis considered the man for a moment but then shrugged. Picturing the beautiful face of Etani, he grabbed the Dragon by the back of the head and kissed him hard.

Bast laughed, Daemon swore, and Dirdos was frozen, not expecting the kiss to be so much.

The dragon's mouth was hot and dry, smelling very faintly of cooked meat, fire, and mint. It didn't really taste like anything with the flavour of the meat still in his lips, and so while it wasn't doing much for him, it wasn't unpleasant.

Letting go of the dragon, Versalis padded away with more than enough food, offering some to Bast who gladly accepted.

"That was unexpected," Uzo said from the doorway.

"Food," Versalis explained, and the Fae looked down at the enormous pile and nodded.

Like most mythicals, they couldn't gain energy from food, but it did help slow down the consumption of energy; not as much as sleeping, but it worked, and so they tended to eat and sleep constantly. Plus, spiced meat tasted so delicious.

Uzo slunk into the room and Versalis offered him some of the meat, the Fae taking it happily and stuffing it into his mouth while Dirdos got himself back in order.

CHAPTER 8

THE MASK MAKER

It was another five days before Jason returned, skidding into reality with a wicked grin and an enormous burn covering a good half of his body.

Another form popped into reality behind him, bent over and panting, while a third appeared in the corner, a thump announcing his face hitting the wall while he groaned.

They were all smoking a little, smelling of sulphur and burnt meat.

"Evening," Jason said as though he wasn't half cooked with half of his mask missing, cleanly sliced across where the nose should be. Judging by the blood on his face, his nose had been hit in the process.

"What happened?" Dainin jumped up, looking around at the three of them.

"You two get back to the compound, report back to Vincent and then get more of the normies. See if we can bury them," Jason said, and the two others grunted their agreement and vanished, leaving Jason alone.

"Your Gods tried to shove us into a lake ... except that the lake was on fire," Jason said, seemingly delighted. "I've never seen a lake on fire before, but I want one."

"How many have you involved?" Daemon asked.

"Six at the moment, but we're going to get more. We can bury them in a mass of people. Would be easier if we could just kill the Gods, but that's out of the question. Vincent said no murder."

Pulling off his shirt, he looked down at the tattered shreds that remained and Versalis saw that the man was a lot more muscular than originally thought, painfully thin with almost no fat on his form.

The bruises seemed to stop just above his wrist on one arm, and all the way up to the elbow on the other where the cage contraption was wrapped around his forearm.

"They're fun to play with at least," he said, frowning at his clothes. "We don't get to play with the Gods."

"Have you had any luck?" Versalis asked, anxious.

"No, they moved it somewhere else. I can't get a read on her, and Vincent is otherwise occupied. Do you have anything with her blood on it?"

"Her clothes from that day haven't been cleaned," Versalis said.

Uzo nodded, heading for the bedroom and returning with the dress she had been wearing.

He pushed down the stab of jealousy as the gaunt man took the clothes and put the bloody, tattered edges of the rip into his mouth.

Sucking on it and mixing the blood with his saliva, he frowned as his eyes unfocused, trying to get a feel for her.

"Either they have her intentionally hidden or this is too old," he said after several seconds.

"Can we sacrifice the blood packs?" Versalis asked.

Jaia growled. "You're not giving away the blood," the furious vampire snapped.

"Blood packs?" Jason asked.

"Etani keeps a store of blood for this situation, so Kai doesn't starve."

Jason nodded, frowning as he licked the fabric once more.

"The other option is I take the vampire with me and use his magic to find her," he said.

It took Versalis a moment to realise that meant him, and he looked at Uzo, who was frowning back at him.

"If we lose Versalis, then we lose that connection," Daemon said, his eyes on Versalis as well.

"You have my promise that he will not be harmed while under my protection," Jason said, accepting a shirt from Uzo that was a little short, but worked for him.

"Those are your choices, the blood or the vampire."

"You're not getting the blood," Jaia snarled.

Jason only shrugged and turned to look at Versalis, offering his burnt hand.

"If he is injured, I will find a way to kill you," Daemon said.

"He'll be fine. We'll go to the compound first and then get our next strategy," Jason said.

Versalis accepted the hand and threw one last glance at the worried-looking Uzo, before the world disappeared.

STEPPING OUT INTO COOL DARKNESS, he turned to find the room in turmoil as robed figures moved around.

Vincent was standing on a small landing and Versalis was on the opposite side. Looking up, Vincent gave a slight nod to the two of them before turning back to a man with a solid gold male face mask, complete with a moustache and large smile.

Versalis watched the men moving, one in particular stopping to look up at him before turning away. Versalis only got a glimpse of grey before they were gone again, and he followed Jason down the stairs to the floor, and then across to Vincent.

"The vampire agreed to help, hopefully we can get a sense of where she is now," Jason said, Vincent turning to shake Versalis' hand.

"Good, it's impossible to get an idea of what's going on in there. So far, we have gotten into the temple, but the place is so big it's hard to figure out where we should be aiming."

"I can get an idea of where she is. But they will want to come for me if they spot me," Versalis said. "They want me in the box with her," he explained when Jason looked at him.

"Makes sense, we'll make sure that doesn't happen," Jason turned on the crowd of men who were finishing their organising and vanishing one or two at a time, heading off for the assault on the temple.

"How many live here?" Versalis asked.

"A few hundred; we're sending in volunteers right now. We will recruit the rest if needed. On top of that, we have an extra ten magic breakers."

"You're not sending Neah in," Versalis snapped.

"Neah doesn't know why we're going in. He only knows he needs to get to the box and if he finds it, not to touch it until Jason gets there," Vincent said. "He has no idea that she's in it."

"I don't like this," Versalis growled.

"We don't have much of a choice. We need all the men we can get," Jason said.

Versalis looked at Vincent, but the Hunter could only shake his head.

"We need all the magic breakers in there, I wouldn't let him near her if there was any other choice," Vincent said gently.

"All right," Versalis said, not liking it, but trusting Vincent, at least somewhat.

"Come on, we'll disguise you to make it harder to tell who you are," Jason said.

Heading down the corridor, he looked around with fascination and blinked as he saw again that flash of grey that was gone before he got a real look at it, and he was getting the weird sense that he was being watched.

The man pulled him down another corridor and then down a flight of stairs that would have been impossible to find had he not been guided to it.

It was hidden in what looked like a solid wall, but there was a tiny crack that they could squeeze through, the stairs well cut and smooth from use.

Heading down, there was very little difference in the two caves, one simply having a flat roof instead of disappearing above them into nothingness, and Jason rather pulled him into another little slit in the walls.

The room they stepped into was full of masks of all shapes and sizes. Some of them simple, some of them enormous with feathers and inlaid gems.

Jason looked at him and then crossed the room, pulling down one of the masks and returning to him.

It was simple, black, with a trail of crimson dripping down from the right eye and from the corners of the mouth.

"Lovelorn vampire," Jason said. "It's not fully accurate, but it is close."

Looking around the room, he stared at all the tools of the man's trade, fascinated by all the masks and other things he needed to make them. Some were leather and others clay. One even looked to be made of solid gold.

"Put it on, vampire, we're wasting time."

Versalis pulled the mask on and Jason moved behind him to adjust the straps so that the mask was tight against his face, one strap going around the back of his head, and the other closer to the nape of his neck, holding it securely and allowing him to see through the eye holes without the mask getting in his way.

Jason stepped back around, pulling his hair out around it to hide the straps, and then nodded.

Throwing aside the scraps of his own mask, the man pulled on a new one that was an almost exact duplicate, though the smile was slightly different. It seemed that the man drew them all by hand and no two would be exactly alike.

"All right, vampire, are you ready to go to battle?"

"Versalis," he corrected the man. "Let's go."

JASON TOOK him by the arm, and they stepped through to the red world once more and Versalis was surprised to see that they were right outside the temple. He got only a second to appreciate how close they got before the first thump of her heart beat hit him.

"She's below," Versalis said, his muscles clenching in time with the slow thumps of her calm heart.

"Excellent," Jason said, looking at him curiously. "Below," he called, and the word was spread between the men who were streaming into the temple. It seemed to Versalis that most of the Hunters were present, and he had to wonder how, or what, they had agreed to, in order to come.

Jason grabbed his arm and pulled him up the stairs and again Versalis was unable to appreciate the beauty of the place as his mind went to her, her silent thoughts.

"Etani, love …" he murmured, trying desperately to reach for her. "You just need to open your eyes."

Jason could only shake his head when she didn't respond, and so Jason pulled him forward.

"Down here," a voice growled, and they headed down a flight of stairs that had been hidden by slabs of marble. Versalis had no idea how the Hunters had even found it.

The sound of fighting faded and there was a peaceful coolness to the area under the temple, but it wasn't really able to register in his brain, and before he knew it, it was he who was pulling Jason along, the man clutching tightly to his arm.

He sprinted between the pillars and past wary-looking figures, ignoring all possibility of traps in his eagerness. They came across a wall where he stopped, looking over it as he considered it.

"We have searched the room from top to bottom, there's nothing down here," a man reported, but Jason was watching Versalis as he stared greedily at the wall.

Shaking off the Hunter, he felt along the wall, and he knew she was there, right on the other side of it, waiting for him.

"Behind here," Versalis said.

"There's nothing behind there, it's the foundation. There's nothing but rock."

"Here," Versalis insisted.

"Jason, we've tried. It's solid stone all the way around the base. The rocks just slide right out."

"This is the Gods we are talking about; odds are there is an enchantment to hide the truth," Jason said slowly, inching closer and running his hand over the wall.

Versalis was feeling it as well, searching for an opening, but the man appeared to be right. Had he not felt her on the other side, he would have believed it was nothing more than solid stone.

Jason made a noise after a good ten minutes and Versalis turned to see the man on his hands and knees, peering under a small gap where the wall met the floor, face flattened to the floor and mask askew.

"Hello there ..." he crooned, smiling slightly, but when he reached for the gap, he yelped and pulled back. His fingers were gone, and the gap was gone with them.

"Motherfucker!" Jason yelled, nothing left of his fingers but half of the lower part below the first knuckles. "Tricky little Gods."

"Trapped?" Versalis asked, and Jason was about to snarl at him when he saw Versalis twitching with the quickening beat of her heart. Had she heard the yell, or did she sense him nearby? He didn't know, but it was making him visibly twitch with her closeness.

"Yes, trapped. But I saw red glowing inside there and a large golden chest with padlocks. You're right, she's in there."

His fingers had stopped bleeding in the time it took him to finish his sentence and it would only be a matter of time before they regrew, but he was certainly more wary of the wall after that.

"We need to get into that wall," Versalis said, considering it.

"Yes, but how?" Jason asked, licking the blood from his hand, and contemplating the problem before them.

Using his bleeding hand, he stood and smeared his blood along the wall at elbow height, considering it, and then bent down to repeat the process at knee height. When that didn't work, he tried again just above his head and then frowned, looking around.

"This is not the right wall," he said.

"This is where she is," Versalis growled.

"Yes, but there must be a passage. This is not where we get in. Get someone to find the others and bring them down here. We need every wall checked, including all the pillars."

It was half an hour before nine men were standing before them, all looking around but alert to the words of Jason.

"We need every wall covered for signs of magic. Watch out for traps."

Versalis tuned them out as he studied each mask in turn in search of the one that was Neah. None of them had dared ask Etani what his mask looked like, so he had no way of knowing which one was the man, but he searched them all anyway, hoping to find the one who had abused the woman he loved.

He couldn't decide who it was, and he didn't want to ask for fear of drawing attention to himself.

If Neah suspected she was inside, it might cause issues for the plan to get her out.

"Go," Jason said, and Vincent blinked when the men scattered, moving around the large room and setting to work on checking the walls.

It turned out that it was the wall on the opposite side of the place where she was hidden, and a man wearing a black demon mask had found it, stepping back as Jason and Versalis approached.

"Send in the normies," Jason said, and an order was given.

A handful of men approached, peering inside the hallway, and it was a good thing they were first in, because six spikes shot out of the wall and impaled the first man.

"Figures ... it can't possibly be easy." Jason sighed, and the man was dragged off the spikes and left in a heap on the ground to recover.

"Is it actually possible to kill a Hunter?" Versalis asked as the man twitched, even though he had a very large hole in his head.

"Yes, but it's not easy, and I'm not telling you how to do it," Jason replied, watching as the men filed in and one by one, and were brought down by traps.

More were called for and the pile of limp forms was growing, but they had made it partway around the corner and down the adjoining wall.

"We need to move faster, the dog is coming," a man said, and Versalis looked up. His mask was almost round and dark grey with large, black eyes that seemed to be leaking black down the front to the jaw of the mask, his wild black hair falling down over the top.

"Right, let's go!" Jason called out, and there was a general sense of urgency as Versalis turned back to the task at hand and others were moving the limp forms out of the room.

The growling was getting closer and Versalis looked in the direction of the stairs, then back at Jason, the man looking toward the stairs as well.

"Go!" the grey-masked man yelled, shoving them through, and a yell came from across the room. "Let's go!"

Jason grabbed Versalis' arm and dragged him down through the hallway, leaping over limp forms and groaning men as they sprinted down the hall and around the corner, then down the long end of the wall. Skidding around the second corner, they came into the room that was glowing a rich golden red.

THE SIGHT WAS both terrifying and amazing at once. The chest was suspended from a giant, gaping hole in the ground, and a hundred feet or more below was the river of the dead.

What might become of her if she fell into that river in her current state was a mystery, he didn't want to guess, but she was right there.

"We have to get it down without it falling ..." Jason said, looking from the chest to the water far below, and a canine roar came from only a few metres away.

"Sounds like dogman is here," the grey-masked man said.

"We are out of time, what do we do?" Jason called, but Versalis didn't know; they needed more time.

"Cut one side and drag it up the other?"

"Yeah, good idea," Versalis said, and he reached for his knife, crouching down, and starting to hack at the closest rope. He screamed a curse. "It's metal!"

"Shit!" Jason yelled and shook his head. "Retreat. We have to retreat!"

"No! I'm not leaving her!" Versalis cried, grabbing onto the rope and trying to rip it free, but it wasn't moving.

"Versalis, stop! We have to go or he'll be on us!"

Versalis struggled against the man and then the grey-masked man was grabbing him as well, both dragging them back as he reached for the chest.

"Etani!" he screamed, and the heart seemed to skip a beat. He felt her moving, her head turning just slightly as she heard his voice. "Etani! Wake up!"

He could hear her sleepy thoughts, see the faintest hint of blue in her eyes before a wash of exhaustion overcame her, and she nuzzled into the blackness, warm and content within the safety of the noth-ingness that held her.

"No! Wake up! Wake up!" he screamed, but she couldn't hear him, she was too deep now. He had lost his chance to get to her, and tears stung his eyes as the men dragged him back and the world vanished from around him.

They tumbled out into Ayathian and Versalis dropped to his knees, his face on the carpet as he screamed his grief and pain.

"She was so close, you bastards!" he raged. She had almost opened her eyes; she had almost realised he was there and then she was gone. He knew he could have gotten to her if they had just waited a few more seconds, but they hadn't let him.

Then a voice made his mind freeze over as the name sank in.

"Neah?"

CHAPTER 9

NEAH

There was silence in the room and Versalis lifted his head, tears dripping out of the bottom of the mask as he turned to look up at the grey-masked man. He was two inches shy of seven feet, or so Versalis guessed, willowy with hidden muscle and neat clothing. The mask was creepy in normal light whereas it had suited the dark, underground room very well.

"Neah?" Dainin asked, stumped on why he was there, and why he had Versalis.

"You're Neah?" Versalis asked, rage building inside him.

"Where's Etani?" he asked, his voice a calm, low murmur.

A growl enveloped the room from where Daemon had stood frozen, but now Versalis saw he was tensing, ready to attack in an instant.

"Neah, what are you doing here?" Dainin asked.

"I helped bring back your vampire. He was flipping out over a chest and yelling at it."

"You found the chest?" Uzo asked, sitting up straight in his chair where he had been almost crushing the teacup and staring at Neah with that same deadly calm that had left Jaia blind and wheezing for a week.

"Where's my wife?" Neah demanded, his head turning to take in the group of men and the Goddess Bast.

"She's dead," Versalis said, pushing himself to his feet and taking a step back, his hand sliding behind his back. A blade was slipped into his hand by Dirdos, who had been sitting in the chair.

"She's immortal," Neah countered, lifting his hand to shove the mask up out of his way.

Everyone recoiled from the sight of his face, those huge, empty black eyes that seemed to be leaking down his face, a mouth that was too big and filled with razor-sharp teeth.

Versalis saw what she would have found so appealing in the man. He looked like a predator and had the aura to match it. He knew what he wanted and would take it. That kind of person appealed to her on a primal level, and that was why she had allowed him to be close to her. He was also a master manipulator and had played on her anger and uncertainty to get close to her, and it had worked perfectly.

"She's dead," Versalis repeated, and those terrible shark eyes turned on him, making him shiver slightly. Oh yes, he knew exactly why she had gone to him. He would have hit all of her buttons in a potential mate. Had he not been a psychotic killer, he would have been perfect for her.

"She can't be dead, she's immortal ..." Neah snapped, irritated with him.

"It's a long story."

"Tell me where she is."

"Etani was taken by Anubis," Dainin said warily, his face blank, but Versalis could see he was thinking.

"Why?"

"Because she is dangerous."

There was an odd expression on Neah's face, a mingled pride and malicious desire that made them all uneasy. "I want her back," Neah growled.

"You can't have her back, she belongs here with us," Uzo said in a terrible calm that had everyone near to him glancing down at the teacup in his hand.

"She's my wife!" Neah snarled.

"I think you'll find she's actually my wife," a cool voice said from the side of the room.

Epharis had come to see what the commotion was, and was leaning in the doorframe, his arms crossed and a dangerous smile on his lips.

"You think so, do you?" Neah asked with a feral grin.

"I know so. She's been my wife for several years now," he said, lifting up one long fingered hand to show the shadow band on his finger.

Neah focused on it, and his grin faded, eyes narrowing. "She's my wife now," Neah snapped.

"Is she legally bound to Neah?" Jagum asked.

"Yes," Dainin said in a tone that made it sound like the word was sour.

"How can she be married to both of them? And Drizdan?"

Neah looked around at Jagum warily. "Drizdan?"

"You're not even her second husband. You're the third," Epharis taunted.

Neah growled again, glaring with malicious intent at the Lich.

"What, didn't she tell you that while you were *raping* her?" Epharis said.

"She gave herself to me first, Lich," Neah snarled.

There was absolute silence while Versalis exchanged a wary glance with Uzo, both having been careful to avoid the subject. They didn't want anyone to know until she was ready to tell them.

"What do you mean?" Daemon growled.

"I never raped her. She gave herself to me the first time and then she was my wife."

"She ... went to you willingly?" Jaia asked, his face snow white in his horror.

Neah was utterly delighted by their fury. "I seem to recall her moaning my name as I fucked her," Neah taunted, grinning maliciously. "And while she was riding me, and begging me to hurt her."

The mood in the room went from anger to homicidal rage in an instant, and then the man turned around and lifted the back of his shirt, showing two sets of scars that interjected a million others, small and long, in a pattern they all recognised.

"She's a feisty little slut when she's horny," Neah said, their eyes on the marks that could only have come from their beloved Etani, in a position that suggested she had been actively participating.

"How is it legal?" Jagum interjected to try to bring down the rage, but barely anyone was focusing on the question, Neah turning back to them, grinning suggestively at them.

"She's the Queen of Winter, firstly. She can have as many lovers and husbands as she desires to have. The more the better, so long as they are fertile," Uzo said and Neah looked at him.

"Excuse me?"

"Not much time for pillow talk?" Daemon snarled.

"Not really. She found my storage room shortly after and I had to ..." he mimicked, whacking something over the head with a bat or similar object. He was so calm about the fact that he had beaten a woman over the head that it threw Versalis off his nerve and he was utterly disgusted by the man. "She's the Winter Queen?" Neah asked after the awkward silence. "She said she was valuable to some people; how many people is 'some?'"

"You'd be hard pressed to find anyone, mythical or otherwise, who wouldn't find her valuable," Dainin said angrily, glaring at the man, and Neah made a thoughtful sound. "Aside from her position, the women who come to the compound are permitted as many lovers and husbands as they desire as well. We do not follow the rules of monogamy as is common amongst the other species. It is not uncommon for a woman to have two or three husbands and several children amongst them. They are not required to stay, but can only take the girls with them if they choose to leave."

"I'm not sharing," Neah said, looking Dainin up and down. "She's mine and you, or any of the Hunters, aren't allowed to touch her."

"You know that's not up to you," Dainin said.

"I don't care. I'll kill you if you try to touch her."

"What does that mean?" Versalis asked warily.

"A woman can choose however many husbands she wants, and the men have no say in if she stays with him or goes," Dainin explained. "If he isn't to her liking, she simply tells him she no longer wishes to be married and finds another husband, or leaves. They are under no obligation to stay and continue to breed with the Hunters. Some choose to stay, others like the dryads only come in during their fertility seasons and then leave again with their daughters. It's why everyone likes the dryads the most, they only want the girls, we only want the boys, and they like to leave after. Everyone gets what they want."

"You have a weird culture ..." Jagum said.

"Coming from the man whose clan doesn't have marriage and shares custody of children," Dirdos said in dark amusement.

Jagum shrugged. "You get a lot of gifts for your birth date when you have fifty parents."

"What else makes her valuable?" Neah demanded. "What is she?"

"Fae," Uzo said.

"Who are you?"

"I'm her uncle."

Neah simply looked at the man, his brow lifted slightly.

"She's not pure Fae. I've tasted Fae before and she's not it," Neah said finally.

"You'll have to ask her when she's back," Dainin said, and when they all looked at him, he grinned. "Assuming she's not trying to rip your face off."

"She wouldn't be able to do that," Neah said, smirking.

"You haven't seen Etani at full strength. She's a raging comet of homicidal intent and strong enough to kick Epharis through three stone walls," Dainin said, nodding toward Epharis.

Neah looked at the Lich and then back at Dainin, his face thoughtful.

"She's like nothing you have ever faced, and she will be angry," Dirdos said, his eyes on the map he'd picked up at some point during the conversation.

"I can handle her," Neah said.

Daemon burst out laughing.

Dirdos grinned.

Uzo snorted.

"We wish you luck. She's going to decimate you," Daemon said.

"We shall see," Neah growled.

"Can she divorce him?" Dirdos asked.

"Vincent is off trying to find out if it's legally binding. She was coerced into marriage and that's forbidden. We are never to trick a woman into being with us, it's consensual only."

"She was the one who suggested it," Neah said.

"Only after you had been stalking her for a few weeks and manipulated her into thinking you cared about her," Dainin snapped.

"I do care about her."

"You're not capable of caring about anyone, Neah. She's just a prize for you."

"She's going to be the mother of my children, Dainin," Neah snapped.

"You're never going to see her again."

"None of us may ever get to see her again if we can't get her freed from Anubis," Uzo growled.

The door opened and Hunter walked in, followed by Sebastian, their voices low but cutting off as they saw the strange scene before them.

"What's going on?" Hunter demanded.

"How's Kai and Letari?" Jaia asked.

"Who is Kai and Letari?" Neah asked.

"Kai is my twin, Letari is Etani's twin."

"Etani has a twin ...? Is she like Etani?"

The tension ratcheted up and Hunter's eyes glowed white.

"Who the fuck is he?" the hybrid demanded.

"Neah," Dainin said.

"Neah ... Neah as in the man who kidnapped Etani?" Hunter's feral eyes turned on the man and they all saw the shimmering as he fought to control his need to rip the man apart.

"I didn't kidnap her. She came willingly, I just didn't let her leave."

"That's the definition of kidnapping ..." Uzo sighed.

"Semantics," Neah said dismissively. "I didn't take her, I just kept her."

"Why is he here?" Sebastian asked warily.

"I want my wife."

"We already told you she's dead," Dainin snapped.

"You said she was taken by Anubis."

"She's dead, and taken by Anubis," Versalis clarified.

"What are you?" Neah demanded.

"Vampire King."

"There's no such thing as a Vampire King, only the Queens."

"I'd say it's a pleasure to meet you, but fuck you."

Neah laughed, delighted by the lot of them.

"Where's Vincent?" Sebastian asked.

"Talking to the others about the legality of Etani's marriage to Neah," Dainin replied in a quiet voice, looking tired.

"She's my wife," Neah snapped.

"She's mine, actually," Epharis grumbled.

Versalis was getting a headache from all the arguing, and he rubbed his eyes. "Etani was killed and taken by Anubis. She's in the chest that was hanging over the river."

"Which river?" Daemon asked, his eyes still on Neah.

"The river with all the dead inside it. Not the river Jason was thrown in."

"What would happen if she fell into that river?" Uzo asked.

"She would be gone. Forever."

The finality of that hit them all, and they swallowed down their fear.

"She was really in the chest?" Neah asked, his eyes turning to Epharis and glaring at him.

"Yes, she was really in the chest," Jason said, eyeing the lot of them warily.

"How was she in that chest? I know she's small, but that small?"

"Anubis only took her heart."

The two Hunters looked at each other.

Taking advantage of the distraction, Versalis stepped forward and shoved the knife into the underside of the shark eyed man's jaw.

He jerked back but by then it was too late, and blood showered on them all.

The room cheered, but Jason only dropped his head into his palm as Neah dropped into a heap on the carpet.

"Immortal, idiot ..." Jason sighed.

"I don't care, he deserved it," Versalis snarled as he stepped forward and kicked the man in the gut.

"Who's got some gold chain?" Daemon asked.

Epharis dug around in his pockets, pulling out a length of the gold chain that bound magic.

"I'll need him in a few weeks for the next assault. Have Vincent come get me when you're done," Jason said in a bored voice as Neah's hands were bound behind his back.

"Will do, let us know if you figure something out," Daemon said, coming over to slam his boot into the man's back, and the snapping of his spine was incredibly satisfying.

Jason left, and they all took turns kicking or punching the dead man, none of them deeming it necessary to remove the blade from his head. It would take a few hours for his body to reject the metal, and until then, they hung the man from a picture hook on the wall and either beat him or shot him with Etani's crossbow.

It was incredibly cathartic to beat on the man who had abused her and destroyed their child, and they were more than happy to keep him there as long as needed.

A SECOND KNIFE seemed to materialise in the man's head by the next morning, and while no one owned up to it, no one cared who did it so long as the knife was kept there.

It gave them something to do aside from moping and it helped them deal with the loss of their loved one.

Even Bast took a turn shooting the man, her face lighting up when the *thunk* of the bolt hitting his chest reverberated around the room.

"You know he's going to try and kill you, right?" Daemon asked Epharis as the Lich took a turn with the crossbow.

"Oh yeah, I know. But I'm not overly concerned," the Lich said as he took aim with the bow.

"I'm sure it will be amusing to watch," Dirdos said, and the two men nodded in agreement.

"It will be fun to see what he tries," Epharis agreed, and the bolt hit the man's gut.

"You need more target practice. If you want, I can give him a push," Daemon offered.

"Tie a rope around his ankle and pull on it," Uzo suggested.

"She's going to be so angry when she sees the damage you did to that wall," Bast said, her eyes on her book and accepting a cup of tea from Uzo.

"Worth it," Versalis said.

They all knew that if she was mad then she would be alive, and that was all that mattered.

"How is it you knew she was dead?" Versalis asked Epharis.

"These walls are thin. I heard you all talking the moment you got back," Epharis said.

There was an awkward silence at that, but Versalis' mind had wandered away.

"I almost had her ... I was so close, but Anubis was almost on us."

"Did you talk to her?" Daemon asked, turning on him.

"She heard my voice, and she almost opened her eyes, but there is something keeping her asleep. She wanted to wake up when she heard me but couldn't."

"The magic breakers will lift that if it doesn't break automatically," Dainin supplied, waiting his turn with the crossbow.

"I could feel her, warm like she was wrapped up in Dirdos' arms. It made her feel safe."

"Do you think they are making her think she's with us, so she doesn't try and fight?" Daemon asked warily.

"I don't know. She sounded so tired."

"We'll get another chance, Versalis," Uzo said quietly.

Versalis nodded, knowing it was true, but still, he wanted to argue.

"We will get to her next time and bring her back here," Dainin said.

"Then we will destroy her heart and she can come back fully," Dirdos said.

"Yeah, it's only a matter of time," Versalis agreed, hope filling him as another bolt thudded into the limp Hunter's body.

CHAPTER 10
ASSAULT ON THE TEMPLE

It was at least another two weeks before they saw Jason again, and he only popped in to tell them they needed to stop playing with the dead Hunter and give him back. He would be back in another four days and Neah needed to be alive and healthy for that.

They kept the man dead by the simple act of removing the knife when it had worked out to around halfway, and stabbing him in a new spot. It was working remarkably well and keeping them all quite happy. He was also entirely riddled with bolts, so much so that they had been forced to replace Etani's quiver of twenty, and that one had arrived the day before. They had planned to see just how many bolts they could put in the man, but they didn't get the chance.

"Not it," Versalis said, and the room echoed, all eyes going to Dirdos, who had been eating at the time and unable to get enough room to mutter the phrase.

That left him as the one forced to remove the bolts and knives from the man, and he looked irritated as he set to work.

It had taken several hours for the Hunter to recover and he was prowling around in a surly mood, lashing out at anyone who looked at him and then disappearing at the end of the third day to annoy the

Hunters with his presence. None of them were nice to him, all wishing they could stick more knives in him, but they were all looking forward to seeing just what Etani did to him once she was back. They didn't think Neah was just going to go away after they got her back, and they still hadn't heard back from Vincent about the legality of her marriage.

"She could just say she doesn't want to be married, right?" Daemon asked after they had watched the Hunter disappear.

"She married him under your religious customs, wouldn't Matthew be able to tell us?" Uzo asked.

"Where is that blood bag, anyway?"

No one had seen the man in what... months?

"Etani's not going to forgive us if he turns up dead," Versalis said.

"If he turns up dead, we'll just stick him under a rock and pretend he didn't turn up in any state," Dirdos said, flipping the page of a large book in his lap.

"Let no man say dragons aren't pragmatic," Daemon said with a note of amusement.

"We should find him," Versalis said.

"Not it," the room immediately burst out and Versalis swore, the last this time. He sighed, knowing it was going to be painful to try to track down a human.

"Good man," Uzo said, slapping him on the back and grinning.

"Shove it," Versalis grumbled, making the Fae laugh.

THE INITIAL ENQUIRIES into the presence of the man turned up nothing, and he didn't make it to the next, distracted when it was only one day later when Jason was back, and they were all being ordered to prepare for the next assault on the temple.

It seemed that the Gods had left her where she was, but the layout had changed and now they needed to find the opening to the room she was hidden in.

They hadn't figured out what would be best to cut the metal ropes, but a local blacksmith had been happy to make them several pairs of large bolt cutters. It may have also been the fact that it was Dirdos who had gone to ask for them, and the dragon was terrifying when he wanted to be.

He had paid the blacksmith very well, but he still scared the man into working.

"Where did you get the money?" Uzo asked as he took a pair that had the handles wrapped to keep the iron from burning him.

"Same place you lot get your supplies from," Dirdos said.

"Steal it from Etani?" Versalis asked.

"Steal it from Etani," Dirdos agreed.

"She's going to be broke by the time you lot are done," Uzo said, opening the cutters to examine the blades and then looking at Jaia with a thoughtful expression.

"Please, the crown throws money at her and she's terrible at hiding it from us." Dirdos scoffed.

"Could be that you just have no respect for her privacy."

"That's beside the point, Uzo," Dirdos said, grinning as the cutters snapped together.

"She has more in the vaults. What's up here is just an emergency," Versalis said, picking up his own pair.

"Is that right?" Dirdos asked, a greedy gleam coming over his face.

"Leave her something, would you? I love her, but I don't want to have to bail her out of financial troubles because of you lot," Uzo said.

"I'll leave her a bit," Dirdos said, and Versalis nodded his agreement.

IT DIDN'T TAKE them long to prepare, and by the time Jason got back, they were ready to go, loitering around the room reading or otherwise stuffing their faces or cleaning weapons one last time.

Jason stepped through to the room and looked around at them all, nodding and motioning them forward. "Neah will be there. Please refrain from killing him, I need his abilities," Jason said, eyeing them.

"No promises," Dirdos said. "Bring your teacup," he added to Uzo, who grinned savagely.

Jaia looked uncomfortable, but let no man say he was a coward, his chin lifting and eyes focused on the Hunter as he arranged them to make it easier to move them all at once.

"All right, children. This is an active war zone, our job is to get in, get the chest, and get back out again. We have... *convinced*... some mages to come along and help keep the chest from ending up in the river should it fall. It shouldn't, but we are taking that precaution. They are on a boat under the hole. We can't get up that way, unfortunately," he said, seeing their suggestion. "It's in and out as fast as possible, the Gods are being drowned in bodies so we should have enough time. We need to get those ropes cut and the chains off as quickly as possible. If you die, you're shit out of luck because I'm not going to try and get you back. Questions? No? Good. Don't get killed."

"Good pep talk," Dirdos said, grinning as he wrapped an arm around Daemon and Versalis' shoulders and the world vanished.

WHEN THEY STEPPED out into the red glare, the place was in chaos as men and Gods battled it out. There were way more than the 'few thousand' Jason had mentioned; likely closer to several thousand or even more, and they were easy to distinguish from the Gods. They either wore robes or dress pants and shirts, but they all wore masks.

The Gods in comparison were wild and beautiful, and it wasn't only those who lived in that part of the underworld who were present. The blue-skinned, six-armed Goddess was certainly not from that area.

Hades was there as well, and an enormous, three-headed dog was at his back, a massive paw holding down a robed form while the bloody mouth bit into the corpse.

The Hunters had managed to get a couple of the Gods down in gold chains, but that would only hold them for so long, and the Hunters were being careful not to injure the Gods in any way.

Her heart thudded in his head, and he turned to the temple, seeing that the Hunters had made an attempt to dig down through the stone to try to get through the ceiling of the room, but it had failed and they had abandoned the attempt.

"She's in the same place?" Jason yelled over the fighting.

Versalis nodded, unable to take his eyes off the spot where he could feel that steady thump.

"Don't worry, sweetheart, we're right here..." he muttered, knowing she couldn't hear him. To his surprise, he felt her shifting and he could feel a sense of anxiety from her, but it was gone so fast he wasn't sure he had felt it at all.

Jason led the way up the stairs, and they followed along behind him, Dirdos keeping their backs safe and grinning when Hades looked in their direction, scowling but making no attempt to try to get up to them. Was he on their side? Versalis didn't know, and he could only barely think with the volume of her heart in his head that was making his face ache.

Running up the steps and then into the room where the four had been standing the first time, he saw that nearly every available surface was smeared with blood in an attempt to break the magic that was hiding the door.

"We're running out of places to look," the demon-masked man called, Neah standing not far behind him, his head tilted back up, looking up into the space above them where she had been suspended.

"What about up there?" Neah asked, deep in thought.

The demon-masked man turned and moved to stand at Neah's side, looking up as well. "You think?"

"Good place... not like we can just walk up to it."

"True. But how do we get up there?"

Neah lifted his hand and pointed to a narrow bar that ran along the wall, turning as he followed the bar with his finger and down to where it joined the ground, hidden amongst the carvings and symbols painted on the walls. It was just wide enough for them to stand on if they were careful.

The demon-masked man nodded and headed for the wall, beginning a quick pace up, one arm outstretched at his side and the other gripping the carvings for support.

Sidling his way up, he looked down at them and shrugged before he twisted his wrist and smeared his blood over the walls.

There was nothing, and Versalis turned, his body shuddering with each throbbing beat of the heart that was both so close, and yet so far away. Frowning, he looked up at a spot that seemed somehow out of place, and he tilted his head at it. Her heart slammed, and he flinched, seeing a weird ripple of the stone that his brain struggled to understand.

"There," he said, pointing up to it. "She knows we're trying to get to her." He could feel that anxiety again, her vague thought for freedom that only lasted a fraction of a second before it was gone again.

"What?" Daemon demanded.

"She's worried about something. Maybe it's the noise," he said, only half paying attention as he stared up at the spot that was shimmering.

The man was making his way around slowly, seemingly unable to see what Versalis could see. But he was going anyway, trusting Jason and his judgment.

Reaching the spot, he twisted his wrist in order to renew the blood and after a moment, smeared his blood over the spot. The wall seemed to hum for a moment and then it changed, the door darkening until the enchantment broke and the wall was suddenly gone.

"Get the normies to bring in something to climb up here and start flooding it," Neah said, and the men around him dispersed to call for more men.

They went with rubble from their attempts to dig down to the room, piling heaps of stone and dirt into a mound and then stamping on it to ensure it was stable.

It took a surprisingly short amount of time to get the rubble piled up high enough for them to be able to climb it and the men from Ayathian stood back to watch.

"What's a Normie?" Dirdos asked, watching the mass of bodies moving supplies.

"Non-magic breakers," the demon-masked man said.

"Oh, okay," the dragon replied.

Versalis looked up at the giant man and he shrugged. What else could be said?

ONCE THEY WERE able to reach the doorway above, the men started to pile in and it was a good thing so many had come, because the traps that had been set up were numerous and aggressive.

One man ended up with his head and body being dragged out in two pieces, another was still smouldering, and a third had been doused in some form of acid.

They looked more annoyed than anything by what was going on, and that meant they were more determined to get through, their irritation growing into an obsession.

Even if they didn't know what they were trying to get to, they wanted to get to it solely because the Gods were trying so hard to keep them out. It was an interesting tactic, and it was working; the Hunters threw themselves into the traps with a suicidal glee only the immortal could pull off.

"Stairs," one man said, holding his right leg in his hand which was flung over the arm of another man who had a rather large hole in his chest, and while he was wheezing, he seemed to be fine.

Jason nodded, and the men shuffled off, seemingly in fairly good spirits considering one had to regrow a leg and the other one could be seen through.

"I wish I could have that level of indifference to injury," Daemon said, watching the men go.

"When it's almost impossible to kill you, injury is meaningless aside from a fun story to tell your buddies," Jason said dryly.

A roar came from outside and Jason turned, swearing in irritation.

"We've got the dog!" a bellow came, and there was a general cheer, and then screaming. "Never mind!"

"Inconvenient ..." Jason sighed, turning back toward the opening above "Why is this so difficult? What do they hope to accomplish?"

"They want to ensure she can only be used when needed," Dirdos said, leaning against the wall with his hands in his pockets.

"Like a sword? Surely there are better ways to contain her."

"Before, they bound her, and it made the Gods come for her ... The only way to tap into her magic was to impregnate her," Versalis said. Jason's head turned slowly in his direction. "Etani was taken a few times, but thankfully she has measures to stop it from going anywhere."

"Measures?" Jason asked, his voice flat.

"She has nails like a razor and an extensive knowledge of anatomy. She knew how to stop it," Daemon said.

Jason shuddered, all of them able to imagine how she had done it. "Who was the father of the world she created?"

"Me ..."

"You raped her?" Jason asked, sounding shocked.

Daemon turned to look at Jaia, the vampire's face darkening. "I would never rape her," Daemon said, and Jaia growled while Jason looked between the two men with interest. "The witches took us; I used my magic to make it easier for her. We created the world and then Etani took the witches and changed the world so that the witches and Hecate couldn't use magic."

"Divine punishment from a divine being," Jason said, and Versalis exchanged a wary glance with Uzo. The man sounded far too interested in Etani. "I look forward to meeting with her."

"Everyone does," Daemon said darkly.

It was another hour before they reached the room and the shout came up the chain, Jason leading the way up the rubble and into the passage.

They ran down the passage and then the stairs, Versalis very aware of how deep they were going into the ground, and then he saw the warm, orange glow, racing until he was on Jason's heels and they burst into the room.

The chest was suspended still, secure and locked.

They set to work cutting the metal ropes they could get to, but then realised their issue. Many of the ropes below were out of reach, and even with Dirdos dangling them down, they wouldn't be able to reach them all.

"I have an idea," Jason said, looking up at the rocks, and then down at the chest.

"We don't know what will happen if you end up in that river," Neah warned.

Versalis, Uzo and Daemon looked around in sudden interest at the man and the prospect of throwing him headfirst into the river below.

Neah growled and moved away, following after Jason as the man paced around to the heavily bound side of the chest.

"Rope," Jason said, and Neah sighed, motioning for one of the normies to come forward.

They used rope to bind around Jason's middle, and Versalis

watched as the man backed up and then ran forward, leaping off the edge of the opening and hitting the side of the chest, clutching onto it and panting as the wind was knocked out of him.

The ropes groaned but managed to stay anchored, and the man grinned, sidling around to the side of the chest that opened. He stood between two of the ropes, one foot on each one and holding onto the chest to stay upright.

Leaning to the side, he examined the first lock and tapped at it.

Versalis screamed, clutching his head as Etani's mind raged against him, furious and aware of her restraints.

"Get me out!" he screamed, her words filling the cavern and making the walls tremble. "Let me out or I will rip these worlds in two and watch you die!"

She was utterly furious, blindingly angry at the Gods, and he could feel her need for revenge.

Dirdos clapped his hand over Versalis' mouth, but she was screaming profanity and so he screamed profanity.

"I like her," the demon-masked man said, amused, and even more so when her rage turned on him, but she was silent, aware of what was going on.

"Versalis, what are you doing?" Her change of mood alarmed him, and he shook his head, unable to reply with her controlling his vocal cords. "Look around, I want to see."

He obeyed, looking around the room and then landing on Neah, a low growl in his chest. His eyes turned to Jason, and his head tilted to the side just as hers did in his mind.

"Nice butt ..." he muttered, the words coming out of his mouth. Jason was too busy trying to work the lock to notice, and his eyes lifted at the growl coming from Daemon.

"Oh, shut up. Where am I?"

"In the underworld with the Gods," Dirdos supplied.

"I take it I'm in the chest."

"Yes, you are."

"Fucking Gods ..." he sighed, his tone perfectly mimicking her irritation. "Why is Neah here? You clearly didn't try hard enough to kill him."

"He can't die. We haven't tried the lake, though," Daemon said.

Versalis crawled to the edge of the opening and looked down.

"Oh, it's like the Styx... First one to push him in gets a kiss," she called out, and Neah immediately looked around in alarm. "So, who's the honey playing tightrope?" she asked.

"Jason. He's one of the Hunters," Dirdos said.

"Jason?"

Jason looked around and jerked as he saw them. "Sweet Mother," he yelled, clutching onto the chest to keep from falling off.

"Careful, you don't want to go swimming. It would be a shame to waste that arse to the river."

"Etani …" Uzo warned, even as Jason tilted his head and she tilted Versalis' head to mimic him.

"You try having your heart ripped out and stuffed in a box, uncle." She was still watching Jason through his eyes, though talking to Uzo. "Then tell me how *in the mood* you are for chit chat. I am going to make a nice pair of boots out of the dog's hide."

"He'd make very nice boots," Dirdos agreed, and there was an enormous *boom*.

"Speak of the devil," Etani murmured. "Let's get a move on, shall we?"

Jason shook his head to clear his thoughts, and turned back to the lock, smearing blood on it.

Neah approached and Versalis' fist shot out, driving the man's nose up into his brain, and he dropped.

"I like vampire strength," Etani purred through him. "Daemon, I want vampire strength for my birthday."

"You … when even is your birthday?"

"No idea."

"August twenty-fifth," Uzo supplied.

"Apparently August twenty-fifth. Thank you, Uncle."

The power of her mind inside him wobbled violently, and his stomach heaved, suddenly in control of himself again.

"Sweet Mother I'm going to puke ..." Versalis groaned.

"Versalis?" Dirdos asked, and he nodded.

"She's chained down inside there, and she is so, so very angry."

"Wouldn't you be?"

"I am talking about destroying the world levels of angry."

Daemon frowned at him as he stood, their eyes turning to Jason as the first lock fell free and he threw it aside.

"I think she'd prefer Jason for her birthday," Uzo teased, and there was a general angry growl from the men.

The second lock followed the first, and they turned at a ferocious bellow coming from somewhere behind them, but it seemed Anubis was still outside.

"Hurry up, Jason!" Versalis yelled.

"Yes ma'am ..." Jason grumbled, irritated.

"Etani's back asleep, move it!"

Third, fourth, and fifth fell into the abyss and Jason considered the mass of locks and then nodded, lifting his arm up above the chest.

His arm twisted and blood poured down, the chains sizzling, and then fell away, just as the wall behind them boomed.

THE MEN SCATTERED and Jason lifted the chest, looking inside and bending down to pick up a small metal box, the thing seeming to vibrate with the heart beating inside.

Jason lifted his mask and looked down at the thing, ignoring the rampaging, bloody form of Anubis behind him.

Opening the box, he grinned wide as he found the red, still-pumping heart inside the box, and he picked it up.

Etani's eyes opened and Versalis shuddered as he saw them, enormous and blazing blue as her head lifted and she blinked in confusion, not understanding or remembering the situation for several long seconds.

"Hello sweetheart," Jason crooned to the thing, and Versalis felt her head turning, listening to the voice.

She was bigger than he imagined her to be, her face turning, and he could see Faerie and the human world reflecting in those luminous eyes, her lips pulling up into a savage grin as she reached and the world shuddered as her fingers dug into the world. Their reality seemed to warp, the world squashing slightly as it was pressed down by her hand and then rebounded back up again.

"Throw it in the river!" Anubis roared.

Jason was hanging onto the chest for dear life.

"Jason, give it here!" Dirdos yelled, reaching for Jason. "She'll kill us all if you don't throw it in the river and destroy her!"

The world was shuddering around them, their teeth rattling as she curled her fingers around the human world.

"Etani, stop," Versalis said, and she lifted her eyes, seeming to see right into his.

If they weren't mythical creatures, none of them would have heard his gentle words over the screaming terror of the men and Gods around them.

She couldn't speak to him now, only look at him, her eyes flicking down to the two worlds and then back up again, her eyelids lowering and her expression turning sly.

"No. You need to stop this right now."

The screaming had stopped, and the world was silent inside the room, his eyes focused on the her he could see over the top of the world around him. "You can't do this. I know they hurt you, but you have to be better than them." She looked annoyed, turning away from him, and he got the oddest sense of self hatred. "You are better than them. You are amazing, perfect. I know how you see yourself, but that's not you."

She looked back at him and her fingers slid free of the two

worlds, her body liquid as she slid around between him and the two joined worlds, her head turning, and he saw the other world she had created with Daemon.

"Yes, see? You can create beautiful things, but you mustn't destroy this one. You must create a better one first. You can't just rip these two apart. You would kill us all."

She shook her head, distressed and wanting him to understand, but unable to communicate.

"Etani, please, we need you to stop trying to tear the worlds apart. We need you to come back to us."

She shook her head again, her eyes dropping, and he was horrified to see tears in her eyes.

"We want you back. We won't let them hurt you anymore. No one can force you to create again. We will make sure none of them can hurt you ever again."

Looking up, she stared hard at him, turning to look at the worlds and then back at him, torn.

"Please, love, come back to us. I swear on my life that I will keep you safe."

She wanted to believe him; he could see it.

"Please come back," he begged her.

She watched him for several long seconds and then nodded, her eyes lifting to the bug far above that made a high-pitched zipping sound as it flew for her like an arrow, her hand lifting for it, but before she could reach for it, the connection between them snapped off and Versalis dropped, his brain switching off with an explosion of blood.

CHAPTER 11
TRUTH

When he woke, he had the oddest feeling that something important had happened, but he couldn't quite remember what it was. Lifting his head, he took a silent note of the number of bodies on top of him, and the sheer amount of blood all over the bed. Etani was not going to be happy, but then again, they were likely going to have to replace her mattress and he knew she preferred his, so he'd get her one like his.

He might even pay for it with his own money. Maybe.

"What happened?" he asked, his mouth tasting like sandpaper, a steady throbbing pain starting up in his throat.

"Your brain was a bit like the shower thing in the bathroom. Was quite interesting to see actually," Dirdos said from somewhere nearby.

"Where's Etani?"

"Anubis took her..." someone said. Was that Jason?

He twisted to find the long form of the mask maker sprawled under Dainin and Uzo. "You appear to be missing an arm..."

Indeed, he was. Ripped off at the shoulder and only half regrown.

"Shove it, vampire," the man growled irritably.

"What happened? Last I remember we were in the room and Etani said she would come back, and then nothing."

"She agreed?" Daemon asked, sitting up so fast someone thumped to the floor with a grunt of pain.

"Yes. Where is she?" Versalis demanded.

"You were talking to her, and then Anubis ripped off Jason's arm, shoved her heart back in the box, and you were screaming bloody murder and bleeding everywhere. Out of your eyes, ears, mouth, everything," Daemon said. "What was happening to reality?"

"She wanted to rip the two worlds apart. Mother, she's so beautiful in that state."

"I know, right?" Uzo asked from the floor where it seemed he was quite content to stay.

"So, any time she grabbed one of the worlds, everything sort of moved ... but what happened after Anubis got her?" Versalis asked.

"After you started spouting blood like a hose, Anubis sort of... expelled us. We all ended up outside of the underworld and the entrance was gone. He seemed to have moved it," Daemon said.

"You can move it?"

"You can if you're a God of the Underworld."

"The Hunters are still trying to get in. But it's going to be a while before they can locate the entrance again."

"We'll find it," Jason mumbled, yawning.

"What do we do? Do we go help look?"

"We can't have you lot running around Faerie. We stay here, let the Hunters do their thing, and go in when we're ready." Daemon was watching him, his lips set in a sulky pout.

"What are you pouting about?" Versalis asked.

"I want to see her like that."

"Die and you probably will," Uzo said.

"I don't want to die," Daemon grumbled.

"Then stop bitching."

"How long have I been out?" Versalis asked.

"Two days. Go shower, you stink," Uzo quipped.

Versalis sighed and crawled out of the bed, much to the annoy-ance of the others, and headed for the shower to wash off the blood, and then headed out to eat.

RETURNING A FEW HOURS LATER, flushed and satisfied from his feeding, he returned to the rooms to find the mattress had been stripped off the bed and, with a moment of panic, he recalled the wooden figures.

"Where?" he whispered to Daemon as the demon came out of the room.

"Hidden," the demon replied, throwing the sheets and pillows down onto a pile on the floor. "Know what she likes?"

"She tried to steal mine."

"Seriously?"

"Completely. It was just after we got her back, and I had gone to my rooms to get more clothes... bed stripped, blankets everywhere. You could see the drag marks where the dust had been cleared away, so I followed. Three corridors away there she is, this tiny little monster dragging this giant mattress along as happy as you please. Then when she saw me, she put on that innocent face and just says 'Hi, Versalis' like nothing was wrong. Just meeting in the hallway, not her stealing my bed."

Daemon laughed and Dirdos grinned.

Uzo had his face in his hand, shaking his head. "When I told her to put it back, she just sort of looks at me and then goes 'No' in that defiant way she does. Like she thinks I'm not going to retaliate."

"Or is daring you to try," Dirdos said, trying hard to keep from laughing.

"So, I grabbed her, threw her over my shoulder and dragged the mattress back to my room, and threw her down on it, bound her up with the sheets, got my clothes, and left. She wasn't very happy, but she didn't try to steal it again. Has she tried to steal yours?"

"Not my bed, but I don't think she's ever seen my room," Uzo said

"She's been in mine back in the cave, but she didn't try to steal it. Stole other stuff, though," Dirdos said.

"Like what?" Versalis asked, taking one of the pillows and stripping the case off it.

"Clothes, mostly. Some jewellery. Did you know she likes shiny objects? Like a bird, though she doesn't seem to be entirely aware of it."

"It's a Fae thing. We all attach to something. Shiny, furry, feathered, wooden."

"She likes shiny. I'm betting she had a collection of shiny things she's stolen."

"I would never have picked that," Daemon said, and his eyes swept the room. "I didn't think she had quirks like that. If I were Etani, where would I hide it...?"

Versalis looked up while the others peered around them. "Up there," Versalis said, and they all looked up. Above them he saw that while the walls appeared complete, one of the boards was slightly off as though she had replaced it in a hurry.

"How would someone that small get up there?" Dirdos asked.

Versalis pointed to a chair that was almost never used, and he could imagine her standing on the arms, reaching up for the spot. Versalis pulled the chair over and stood on it, climbing up and pressing the board out of the way.

Inside the little space behind the board, he found a small cloth bag, and a little metal box, eyeing them. These were something she had worked hard to hide from them; looking at them was a true invasion of her privacy. Should he really be going through them?

"Come on, get them," Dirdos said.

"Should we?" Versalis asked, looking around at them all with their eager, impatient, hungry faces.

"We all want to see," Daemon said.

"That doesn't mean we should," Versalis said.

"Do it," Uzo ordered, and Versalis sighed, grabbing the bag and the metal box, stepping down from the chair, and heading for the table between the couches.

Setting the box down first, he opened it and they all leant forward to see what was in it. It wasn't what he expected; a huge pile of precious stones or something similar. It was a button, a small rock, a ribbon, a chain with an inverted cross, a clay tooth, a chunk of jagged stone, a large leaf that had been dried and carefully pressed, a bolt from a crossbow that had flecks of blood on it, a white glove, a piece of cloth with a bloody kiss on it, a chunk of wood, an elaborate silver hair pin, a blown glass cat wrapped in crimson velvet, a page from a book, a crude little wooden figure, a silver cross on a leather thong, a wolf carving, a real snake fang, a little silver bead, and a finger guard.

"That's... that's the rock she gave me in the cavern," Dirdos said.

"And the button off Kai's jacket. The ones he had to get fully replaced." Versalis pointed to the button. "Avadari's hair pin."

"Do you think ...? There's no way these represent us, right?" Daemon asked.

Versalis had been staring at the ribbon for several minutes, trying to figure out when he might have lost it, and when she might have gotten it.

"That's mine," he said, lifting the ribbon out of the box and looking at it. It was stained with dry blood. "I had that when ... I can't think of the last time I had it."

"What does this mean?" Dirdos asked, picking out the rock and looking at it, the pebble an odd, quite pretty mixture of colours.

"Maybe she actually likes us after all," Daemon said.

"What do you mean?" Jagum asked, the dried and pressed leaf cupped in his paws that he lifted to his nose and sniffed.

"I always assumed she simply tolerated us. I didn't think she actually liked us."

"Me too," Dirdos said.

"Yeah," Versalis added.

"Of course she likes you ..." Jagum sounded annoyed by their suggestion.

"How would you know?" Dirdos snapped.

"She's more like a cat than you idiots think. She wouldn't let you near her or touch her if she didn't like you. She wouldn't be in the same room, even. She would either be snarling, or would simply leave if she didn't like you. You live with Bast, me, and Cat, and you didn't see the similarities there? Aren't you lot supposed to be intelligent? We all sleep on the same bed ..."

They were stunned for a long time as they took that in.

"Well ... she does tend to just sit there and watch you like Cat ..." Dirdos said, considering.

"And she does have a tendency to hiss when in a bad mood," Daemon added.

"And nuzzle when she's happy," Jagum supplied.

"I never realised how much like a cat she really was," Versalis said.

"They'll rarely be outwardly affectionate, but you can see it in the little things they do. Touching, nuzzling, sleeping at your side, giving you things, staring at you, getting angry when you're being overbearing or too clingy, simply being near you ... She might seem aloof, but she is absolutely crazy about all of you. I thought it was obvious."

"It is, now that you mention it ..." Uzo said.

Looking up, he found Jaia was staring down at the button on his palm, but ignored him, having nothing to say to the man.

"Whose is that?" Dirdos asked, touching a white glove.

"Kai's," Jaia said, looking at it.

"Kai is the button."

"The button is mine. It was my jacket Kai was wearing that day, it's why he was so upset about the button. He was worried I might get upset."

Versalis didn't like that she had kept something from Jaia, even after what he had done to her, and judging by the expressions of the others, they didn't like it much, either.

Uzo was still and silent, the piece of rock in his hands. It was obvious what it was, a small piece of the stone that he had become when he died, and yet it was worn down slightly; something she handled frequently enough that her fingers had smoothed the jagged edges.

"Can we guess who everything belongs to?" Dirdos asked.

"The ribbon is mine; the stone is you ..." He picked out the long length of silver with the inverted cross, and Daemon snatched it.

"Sneaky brat, I wondered where that went ..." the demon growled.

"Daemon then, the tooth? That's made of clay, isn't it?"

"One of the Hunters' maybe? Dainin has teeth like that," Jaia said slowly, looking at it curiously.

"Possibly ... So, the button is Jaia, the stone is Uzo, the leaf is Jagum, and the bolt?"

"Definitely Vincent. That's her blood, and he's the only one who's shot her."

"Malik's man shot her, didn't he?" Jagum asked.

"I think the wood is likely to be Malik. It looks like the same wood they use to make ships," Versalis said. "Vincent might be the bolt; the glove is Kai. The hair pin is Avadari, the glass cat is very likely Letari. The page?"

Daemon unfolded it and snorted, turning it to show them. "It's about how to kill a Lich."

"Epharis. The cross is likely Matthew, the two carvings. One is a wolf so maybe Hunter."

"The figure is of Alaric, they sold them in the markets not long ago," Daemon said. "I didn't think she liked Alaric."

"I think he amuses her," Dirdos said. "That's a snake fang, isn't it? Nayishma, possibly."

"That leaves the kiss, the bead, and the guard, assuming the rest are correct," Versalis said slowly, considering the three items. "The blood smells weird, I don't know who that belongs to. The bead could be anyone, and the guard looks familiar, but I can't place it," Daemon said, frowning at it.

"There are too many people for those to belong to, for all we know the guard could be Hunter's, or even Malik's," Dirdos said, and they all fell still, considering the items before them and what they represented.

"What's in the bag?" Daemon said, shaking his head to clear it.

Versalis set the bag down as the men reluctantly returned their items to the box and closed the lid, locking away the possessions that none of them could bring themselves to take back from her now that they knew at least a trickle of what she felt for them all.

The bag was heavy, and moved easily, so it was no surprise when Versalis undid the knot and the fabric fell open to reveal a large pile of very shiny objects.

Bells, coins, jewellery, precious and semi-precious gems, pieces of glass in a variety of colours, little metal scraps, and beads.

"She's a baby hoarder," Dirdos said, sounding proud about that. "Hang on ..." he added, eyes narrowing at a ruby the size of a duck egg.

"Isn't that ...?" Daemon said, looking at the same ruby.

"Sneaky little bitch ... when did she steal that?" Dirdos was indignant while Daemon was laughing.

"No wonder she didn't want to give it back to Alaric, she already had it." Versalis laughed.

"How did I not know that was missing?" the dragon demanded.

"That's what you get for underestimating her," Uzo said with a wide smile.

"You can't have it back," Versalis said as the dragon reached for it. "It belongs to her now, fair and square."

"And I can take it back fair and square," Dirdos growled.

"You know full well she will castrate you," Uzo warned.

"She can try. Might be nice having her hands that close to ... certain parts of my anatomy," Dirdos muttered.

"That's a little too kinky, even for me," Daemon said.

"Whatever gets you off, man," Versalis said, tossing the ruby to him.

"Whatever gets him off had better not be my niece," Uzo growled.

"No, sir, wouldn't dream of it," the dragon lied, catching the ruby and tucking it safely into his pocket.

CHAPTER 12
ALLEGIANCE

Everything had gone quiet on the side of the Hunters, and they were all impatient, unsure of what to do in the meantime. As always, everyone fell back into their roles around the castle, and they barely contained their burning rage to get moving.

Talks with the local communities were underway and that meant Uzo, Jagum, and Jaia were all occupied with negotiations with the prospective species as Alaric tried to pull more and more mythicals to his side to help in the war.

It didn't seem to be going all that well, and the King was in a foul temper most of the time, so it was a surprise when the man in question grinned at him and Versalis went on guard, but the King didn't approach, nor did he speak. The lack of communication only made the grin all the more unnerving.

It had been three weeks since they found the hoard of items Etani had stolen from them, and that in and of itself made things a little awkward between them.

Now that they were aware of her tendency to hide things, they had found a number of other objects she had hidden.

The books she had used to press the leaf for one; another book on how to carve stone, and they speculated that she planned to shape the rock that had once been Uzo but never had the chance.

Behind the wardrobe they found a small collection of language books and Versalis was left in tears when he found them, easily able to imagine her stealing hours while they slept, her face intent as she tried to learn another language, all while not making a noise or allowing anyone else to know.

When Daemon found him, the demon saw the books in his lap and stalked from the room, screaming his rage at the world from across the castle, and there were renovations to repair whatever he destroyed.

There were so many little things they had never noticed before: her ability to repair clothes that none of them had known about, a small bag of mint lollies in a drawer, a silver bangle stuffed in the back of the wardrobe.

A set of earrings showed up, and the jeweller was alarmed to see so many angry, intimidating men glaring, but he handed over the earrings and left. None of them knew what to do with them, so they left them on a shelf in the little cloth bag.

The bowl of rotting strawberries she had hoarded in her room that no one knew about and she was unable to eat.

Even a small toy she had been in the process of making: a sock stolen from Kai and stuffed with fluff and feathers.

It all amounted to a lot of pain for the men in her life, all waiting for months for her to return.

The Hunters hadn't been present for a while, Dainin avoiding the place due to Alaric attempting to recruit the Hunters in the war, or else involving himself in the attempts to find the underworld.

It was hard to obey orders when they wanted to be out in the field searching for it as it meant they would be looking for Etani as well, and that meant they would be doing something.

The thoughts taunted him, and he rubbed his face, pacing along the corridor for the millionth time that day.

He knew he was wearing a track in the marble, but he didn't care;

he needed to move or he might go insane from the loss of the brightest spark in his life.

He kept coming back to the thought of the amount of time he had spent stalking her in what he had thought at the time was aimless wandering.

He stopped only to eat and sleep, something inside him pulling him along and ignoring all the signs that he was actively tracking something. Now that he thought back on it, he realised just how far he had wandered without realising it; the sheer number of corpses should have been a warning, but he had been so intent on moving that he hadn't been paying attention to the fact that it was thousands of miles, and he was still coming across the same villages and the same corpses.

It should have been a red flag, but he had been too drawn up in whatever it was that was leading him along. As it turned out, it was she who had been leading him, and he had been following along in her footsteps without ever realising it.

How she could have been drawing him like that was a mystery and he was hesitant to ask Daemon or Uzo for fear of coming off as a creepy weirdo, but perhaps Dirdos would be able to give him an answer?

He considered going to find the dragon when a voice called out and he turned, frowning as he spotted the dark-haired Fae hurrying in his direction.

"Uzo, what's the matter?" Versalis asked.

"I've been looking everywhere for you. You need to get out of the city, fast," Uzo called and Versalis tensed, unsure of how to respond.

"Why?" he asked, chewing on the inside of his cheek as Uzo came to a stop before him, eyes sweeping the corridor for signs of eavesdroppers.

"Man, you need to run ... there's this crazy vampire woman with

Alaric, trying to buy your hand in exchange for the vampires helping in the war," Uzo said.

Helena jumped to mind, but it wasn't unlike Uzo to mess with him like that.

"Ha, ha. Very funny," Versalis muttered, hoping it was a joke.

"I'm serious. She's mental, and he's seriously considering it."

"He can't do that ... I don't belong to him," Versalis said, worried.

"You're a King, Versalis ... on foreign soil and in territory not owned by your clan. It would take him about three beats to declare you a diplomatic prisoner and hand you over to her. He wants the vampires."

"What about Etani?"

"What about her?"

"She won't be happy if she finds out."

"He doesn't care, once you're married it's no longer his problem. She can bitch and moan all she wants but it'll be too late, and I don't think you're ever going to be allowed out of that woman's sight."

"This is bad ..." Versalis growled, trying to decide what to do.

"Go talk to Alaric and get out of it. Tell him she's a mental case or something. If you can't convince him, prepare to bolt."

"Where are they?" Versalis asked, aware of how Etani must feel any time a royal leader came stalking in demanding her hand.

"War room. I'm going to find Daemon to see what he thinks."

Versalis nodded and Uzo hurried off, his mind going to what he was going to do.

Heading for the war room, he considered the arguments but couldn't think of anything, really, aside from the fact that he didn't want to marry the damned woman.

Bursting in on the two of them, Helena looked up and smiled, Alaric glancing over with a frown of irritation.

"What are you doing here, Versalis?" the man asked, his expression making it clear he wasn't welcome in the meeting.

"Word reached me about this," he said, motioning between the two of them.

Helena laughed, and it did interesting things to his libido, but he ignored it. She was a succubus who could trigger all of his sexual hungers and she knew it.

"Is that right? Who told you?" the big man asked.

"That's not important. What is important is I have no interest in getting involved in clan politics. More so, I'm not interested in a wife."

"Unless it was Etani," Alaric said.

"Who is this Etani woman?" Helena growled. "She's all anyone ever talks about in this city."

"She's the Winter Queen, Epharis' wife, a Goddess, and a few other things," Alaric supplied.

"She's already married?" Helena asked, looking around at him in irritation.

"The Queens of Faerie can have multiple husbands, but only men who are fertile, or something like that."

"Vampires can't procreate, Versalis." She sounded only half sympathetic.

"Etani can procreate with any species so long as that being isn't sterile," Alaric said.

Helena frowned at Alaric; her eyes narrowed in consideration.

"That's interesting. She might be capable of producing vampires … from birth?"

Versalis growled at where her thoughts were leading.

"I'm not going to allow you or any of your clan near her," he snapped.

"I wouldn't dream of it," the woman lied, smiling as though they were best friends.

"Regardless of the possibilities of this woman, you are still eligible and a valuable asset in and of yourself. The only Vampire King ever known to exist, without a clan to protect him and in another clan's territory," Helena said.

"You said you would allow me to consider it."

"I did, you've had weeks and have not come back with an answer."

"Where is Etani, incidentally?" Alaric asked, looking around at him.

"The underworld, with Anubis."

Alaric shook his head, rubbing his eyes, annoyed. "She and I need to have discussions before this war. Have her come see me when she is back."

"She's dead, isn't she?" Helena asked.

"Technically, she is sleeping," Versalis said when Alaric looked around.

"Who is the heir?"

"Aurora. But you're not going to have much luck discussing it with her, I get the feeling she doesn't care much for the affairs of this world." Versalis sighed.

"I want a husband, Alaric," Helena said. "You want the vampires. It's a win-win."

"I'm not for sale," Versalis snapped.

"You are if I say you are," Alaric growled.

"You can't sell me," Versalis demanded.

"Yes, I can."

"No, you can't," Uzo said from the doorway, stalking in with Daemon and Dirdos. "Versalis is under the protection of the Winter Court."

"Says who?" Alaric snapped.

"Says me, the emissary of the Court. If you threaten my courtier, you will be declaring war on the Court."

"Versalis isn't a member of the Court," Alaric snapped, Helena looking distinctly unhappy.

"He is once he declares fealty to the Queen," Dirdos said, his eyes lingering on the woman who glared at him.

"I declare fealty to the Queen of Winter, and the Winter Court," Versalis said, making the King scowl and Daemon grin.

"There, now you can't touch him," Uzo declared.

Alaric fumed and Helena looked like she was going to scream, but the rest of them smiled happily, eyeing the two.

"I can declare you all prisoners. What is the Court going to do? Come here?"

"No, probably not. But Etani will have something to say about it."

"I'll face your little Queen. You're all political prisoners. Including Etani when she gets back," the King snarled.

"That was a very unwise move, Alaric," Daemon muttered, reaching out and taking Versalis by the arm.

THE WORLD BURST into crimson flames around them, and they stepped out into the middle of a crowded room that shrieked in surprise.

The four of them had stepped out into the middle of the Winter Court in the throes of some sort of mourning celebration.

"Uzo?" a soft, sweetly feminine voice called out from the throne, and they turned to find the pretty, pale form of Aurora sitting on the throne. The sight made Versalis' eyes widen.

The lights had gone dim, the tree seeming somehow sad and wilting.

"I'll get the rest of them," Dirdos growled, and stepped backwards into the flames.

"We are evacuating Ayathian for the time being, Your Majesty. I'm afraid there was an attempt to take us all prisoner," Uzo said smoothly.

"By the King?" Aurora asked, her lovely face turning down into a frown. "On what grounds?"

"He hoped to trade Versalis for assistance in the war."

Aurora looked at Versalis and frowned, considering him, before she shook her head. "We will be glad to welcome you all here."

"Versalis has sworn allegiance to the Winter Court," Daemon

said, throwing an arm over Versalis' shoulder. "Aren't you lucky, you get to spend time with the world's first Vampire King."

The words hit the Court like a slap, and they started whispering, making Versalis squirm as so many lovely and intimidating people craned to see his face.

"We are exceptionally lucky," Aurora said, her smile warm.

"I suppose there has been no news on Queen Etania?" a tall, elegant woman called. Her dark violet skin faded down to a warm pink-orange at her bare feet. Two large horns stuck up out of the top of her head and long ears stuck out on either side of her head. Red-pink hair trailed down to her knees even when bound up in a twist that fed down into a long braid.

In one hand she held a cherry blossom branch staff, and she wore a pink, frothy dress with a red bow at the front. She also had a long, slender tail that ended at a tuft that matched her hair. Large, yellow-white eyes and a small, bow-shaped mouth added to her exotic, almost alien beauty, and to accent it all, she wore little blossoms in her hair.

"The Court recognises the lady Karnia," Aurora said, the lady stepping forward with the gentle tolling of a bell.

Fire burst up around them and the others were dumped off, Jaia and Sebastian deeply confused, Hunter snarling, Jagum hissing, and Vincent a little amused as he bowed to the Queen.

"I need a place to store Letari and Kai," Dirdos said to Aurora without preamble.

"Take them to the Queen's suite. The guard will assist," Aurora said.

The dragon vanished again and Versalis turned to the others, counting heads to ensure they were all present.

"What are we doing here?" Hunter growled; evidently, the magic of Faerie was having an effect on his magic, and he was trembling as he tried to both shake out of his skin and stay within it.

"What news do we have of the Queen?" the dark beauty asked.

"Nothing as yet, my Lady," Vincent said. "We are still searching for the entrance to the temple."

Karnia turned to look up at Aurora, who only sat back on the throne, her pretty mouth turned down into a disappointed frown.

There was a shimmering and Jason popped into existence, his hands in his pockets as he looked around with the creepy mask smiling at them all. "What's happening, folks?"

"Evacuation of Ayathian. Alaric was making threats," Daemon said, Jaia looking up with a frown, but before he could open his mouth, a terrible conjoined screaming came from somewhere and then was muffled by a slamming door.

"Kai and Letari," Versalis explained to the terrified crowd that had grown larger as the curious beings of Winter came to see what was happening.

"We will have rooms for you prepared, might I suggest you go out into the garden for now?" Aurora suggested, and they all nodded, filing out like the obedient little boys they were.

THE GARDEN WAS the one he had seen Etani dancing in, radiant and exquisite with her silver hair and the markings that glowed on her skin, her body moving with the incredible grace of a natural-born predator.

She had never looked so happy as she had in that moment as Dirdos swept her along and Winter vibrated with the beat of her joy, the world and her body changing between the steps of the dance.

He had never seen magic like that before, minor changes that, when combined, made huge differences to the world around it until the world was no longer recognisable.

The garden hadn't changed since that night, the dance floor still swept clean, and the men were subdued as they looked out over it, very aware of what had happened that night.

"She looked so pretty with my blood on her face ..." Vincent sighed, staring out towards the tree where they had found the would-be lovers. "Lying in the snow and so angry she could turn the world to ice. She never even thought to use her magic to defend herself, she was so unused to it."

"You should have seen her before she was running for her life," Daemon said.

"Oh, I did, with her dress up around her waist," the Hunter growled, grinning. "Didn't get to see much though, the dragon was in the way."

"What a shame." Versalis snorted even as Daemon fumed and Jaia choked on his rage.

"It was, but she was still lovely. She looks good with silver hair, but I prefer brunettes."

"We all do," Versalis said.

"I don't know, her as a redhead was pretty delicious," Daemon muttered, jumping down the steps to the dining area, the tables still set up and dusted with snow.

Jagum growled his agreement, prowling down the steps to the dance floor.

"I'm going to stay with Letari. Don't call me if you need me," Hunter growled and stalked back inside, his face dark with their attitudes.

"Such a buzzkill," Daemon said.

"Wouldn't you be if your love was screaming bloody murder all day every day?" Jagum asked.

"My love is dead, Jagum," Daemon snapped, and the werecat flinched.

"Right, sorry."

"First one to make a snow angel wins the first hug," Uzo said, already running, and the rest of them sprinted after him only a second later.

CHAPTER 13
THE HEIR TO WINTER

It was another eleven days before anything further was heard about the entrance to the underworld, and they moped around, bored and irritable, though they were all getting a lot of attention from the various members of the Court.

The Court was fascinated with the newcomers and the newcomers were more than a little starved for attention; it made for an interesting mix.

Versalis and Dirdos in particular, but Jagum had slunk off more than once with an eager female of his species, his eyes sly and amused, always returning with a satisfied growl to his voice.

"At least someone is getting laid ..." Daemon muttered, ignoring the attention of a young woman with small horns and a wicked smile.

Versalis was getting nervous about the whole thing, far too many women interested in him for what he was, and it only made Daemon laugh when he appeared to be anxious around yet another exquisite creature who was trying to catch his eye.

"Come on, Versalis, you know you want to. All of these women would kill to get into bed with you."

Versalis knew that the demon was hoping he would get attached to someone else, much like Hunter had. It would take him out of the race for Etani, but he wasn't giving in. Etani was the woman he wanted, and she would be back soon.

It had been over three months, though, and it was getting harder by the day.

Jaia was also drawing a lot of attention with his dark brooding nature and empty shark eyes. He was attractive, but there was something about him that set Versalis off. It might simply be the knowledge of what he had done to Etani, as he had liked the man before that. But now he could only see the vampire as a predator of the worst kind.

He seemed oblivious of the women around him, focused on trying to plan things out with Vincent, and debating on where the entrance to the underworld might be.

He was a tactical genius, and his suggestions appeared to be playing out. Vincent was growing angrier by the day as Anubis or Osiris kept moving the entrance every time they got close to finding it.

"Can't we just go in through one of the other entrances?" Versalis asked, looking down at the map that was utterly riddled with little red pins that showed the past locations of the entrance and a handful of black that showed possible locations.

"Yes, but there are creatures down there you don't want to mess around with," Daemon said, his head tilted as he tried to understand the pattern, though no one else could find one. It seemed the entrance was random, but couldn't be in the same place twice.

"Can we simply flood the unused space with Hunters, so they are forced to put it where we want it?" he asked.

"No, I don't think they would care if they allowed a few Hunters to fall in ..." Uzo trailed off, looking up at Daemon from his spot crouched down beside the table to consider it from the bottom. "You don't think we could get in that way?"

"It's better than facing the monsters," Daemon growled.

"Will the Hunters go for that?" Uzo asked Vincent and Jason. Both men shrugged.

"At this point it's a game, they no longer care what they're looking for, they simply want the chest," Jason said, amused.

"What about after we get her free?" Daemon asked, voicing something that had been bothering Versalis as well.

"I simply want my conversation with her. The rest of them will bargain for a universal deal with her. A favour, most like," he said dismissively.

"I would also like a favour," Vincent said. "But I will discuss that with her personally."

"Good luck with that," Daemon grumbled, but Versalis thought it was likely she would agree for the effort they put in. He felt he knew her well enough for that, at least. She valued those who put value in work.

"We will try this plan, but there is still a lot of land to cover, we will need to keep pushing them back until we have less land to work with," Vincent agreed.

"You have my suggestions, but we are running out of time before they start going against instinct. Eventually they will go entirely random," Jaia said, his low voice grating on Versalis' nerves.

He could imagine what that voice would sound like, growling her name as he violated her.

Pushing the dark thoughts away, he stood and stretched.

"I'm heading out, I'll be back later."

"Where are you going? Got yourself a lover you're keeping secret?" Daemon asked.

"Running," Versalis growled.

"Sure you are. Tell her we said hi."

Rolling his eyes, he left the room they had stolen to work as a council room, and headed back to his room, stripping out of his shirt, jacket, and shoes in order to go running.

RUNNING HAD BECOME a form of stress relief for him while cramped up in the palace with the rest of them, constantly being taunted and ridiculed about having a secret lover somewhere in the palace. He wasn't interested in any women who weren't Etani, and nothing he said was changing their minds, so he simply stopped trying.

Heading back out of the room, he came to a slow stop as he saw a group of men standing around the base of the dais, and a harassed Aurora.

"Good …" What time of day was it? Was it day? "Hello, Your Majesty, how are you?" he called out, and Aurora looked up, seemingly relieved by his appearance.

"Versalis, what a pleasure. What are you up to?" she asked, smiling at him as she always did when he appeared.

"Just about to go out for a run, is there anything I can do for you?"

"Your Majesty, please, this is important," one of the men, a satyr by the look of him, called to her.

"What seems to be the problem?" Versalis growled, his chin lowering to glare at the men intimidatingly. He was taller and wider than all of them, his bare chest making him look bulkier than he was, more so when his shoulders pushed forward, his spine straightening and his chest puffing out.

"Nothing," the man squeaked, eyes going huge.

"We were discussing the regrowth of the deadlands," a second said in a small voice, with large deer antlers strung with silver and diamonds. Otherwise he looked entirely human.

"Regrowth?" Versalis asked.

"It appears to have stopped," the antlered man said.

"It would appear that the deadlands have been repairing." Aurora looked annoyed at the suggestion.

"Isn't the deadlands a result of magic being killed there?" Versalis asked, a dawning thought breaking in his head. "When did it start?"

"We noticed it a year ago or so. But it fluctuates, speeding up and then slowing down for several months. Then it sped up again and now it has entirely stopped."

Aurora was watching him, her eyes narrowed. "What are you thinking, Versalis?"

"It's Etani. The repair is a result of her," he said, frowning at the men and holding out his hand. "I'll bet my life that this started right around the time she came into her magic, slowed when she was bound, increased when she broke the bindings and stopped when she died."

"How is Etani doing this?" Aurora demanded.

"Etani creates magic. She seems to generate it somehow, and it lifts off her like steam. The less she actively uses, the more it simply flows out of her."

"So, why didn't this happen when she was born?" Aurora asked, looking for a loophole.

"She wasn't tapped into Winter," the satyr said, staring at Versalis. "She had no connection, and Winter would be feeding off her in an attempt to reclaim lost land ..."

"Exactly," Versalis said, looking down at the map. "Without her, it will simply stop, but it will restart again when she's alive again. I wonder if it would speed up if she was in Winter ..."

"Possibly ... But how is this possible? She's just fixing the damage?"

"No, Winter is fixing the magic, she is simply supplying the power needed. She's the fuel needed to make Winter work."

"How can we know for sure?" the antlered man asked.

"Monitor it constantly. If it doesn't change and then starts again when she's back, there's your answer."

"This seems too easy," Aurora said. "That land has been destroyed for eons and now she's just ..." she snapped her fingers. "Fixed."

"I doubt it's that easy, Aurora. It is a lot of land to fix, it could take another several eons for her to recover it."

They looked at him oddly and he blinked.

"You shouldn't speak to the Queen so informally, even a stranger like you should know that," the satyr hissed.

"Apologies, I meant no disrespect, Your Majesty, it's a habit I will endeavour to break," he said, bowing to her.

She was watching him; her cheeks flushed a delicate pink and lips parted.

"It is no issue; thank you for clarifying this for us."

"You're most welcome. Please do not hesitate to call on me if you need anything else," he said, wanting very much to run away, and possibly even die if he could pull it off.

He just knew it was going to come back and bite him on the arse.

HE WAS RIGHT; the huge grin on the demon's face told him how fast rumours spread in the Court.

"So, Aurora, huh?" Daemon grinned. "All sweaty and dishevelled. Is she fun in bed? She looks like she'd be fun in bed."

"That's my Queen you are talking about," Versalis snapped, feeling the lovely woman deserved better than that.

"Etani is your Queen," Uzo said from the corner, his eyes lowered to a cranky Cat, who had been rescued after being forgotten for a day. He didn't much appreciate their forgetting about him.

"Aurora is acting Queen," Versalis said back.

"*Aurora is my Queen*," Daemon taunted, grinning widely. "Etani is going to be thrilled when she finds out you and Aurora have been getting it on. She might be so happy she'll just set you on fire. I have matches if you'd like to practice."

"Be nice," Uzo scolded.

"I'm not having an affair with Aurora. It was a slip of the tongue."

"A slip right up her—"

"Daemon!" Uzo snapped. "That is the Princess you are speaking about. You will show some respect."

Daemon glared at the Fae, and then looked back at Versalis, eyes narrowed before hissing and turning away, grumpy that he didn't get to taunt Versalis any further.

Versalis growled and headed for the shower.

"If you need to jerk off to your lover, make sure you clean up the shower!" Daemon called out, and Versalis slammed the door to the bathroom, anger flooding through him.

That was entirely unfair; he loved Etani more than life itself. But still that lovely Aurora kept creeping up in his mind. He rested his head against the shower wall as he tried to understand what was going on in his mind.

Etani was almost too perfect to touch; she was a literal Goddess, and so far out of his league that it was laughable. Aurora was a beautiful, gentle, and sweet creature who also deserved better than him, but still he knew she fancied him; he could see it in her eyes.

As far as he knew, she had no suitors. Would Etani be so unhappy if he didn't wait for her?

It dawned on him that his thoughts were likely the exact same ones that Jaia had considered all that time ago when he chose to stop waiting.

Growling, he grabbed the soap and washed himself, irritated with his thoughts.

No, he felt she would be sad, but ultimately, she would be happy for him. She was not a cruel creature in that sense.

She could be a monster when she needed to be, but if she felt he would be happy, she would release her claws from him.

Especially if that other being was the lovely and kind Aurora. Biting his lip, he thought of the pale beauty whispering his name as he kissed her neck, the first time he had ever thought of her as such.

With her it wouldn't require effort, it would come naturally, and he wouldn't have to fight his instincts.

It would be gentle and slow, not the raging inferno of lust and passion that Etani would provide him. Their love was volatile, a Molotov that only needed to be lit.

Aurora was a slow flame, a candle that he could love without being burnt.

He could have a gentle, sweet, and kind woman at his side if she would have him, or he could have the Goddess who made his heart skip a beat when she looked at him, the woman he had been hunting for years.

Would he end up like Hunter? Falling madly for another woman and turning away from her fire without being able to fully let go?

There was no denying the hybrid was insanely in love with Letari and they would spend an eon chasing each other across the worlds, loving and being happy, and bringing more of them into the world. But Hunter would always have half an eye on Etani, wary and at least somewhat wanting.

Closing his eyes, he thought of the two women, and for the first time, it was not Etani who came forward to claim his attention, and he sighed as he found the pale beauty taunting him with her perfection.

His hand fell to his side and then moved around, his cheeks flaming as he imagined her under him, her quiet cries of pleasure as he moved inside her, that long, blonde hair splayed out around her like a halo.

Grasping himself, he clenched his eyes shut as he pictured her naked, small, perfect breasts in his hands, nuzzling them and biting them, her blood pulsing through his veins. The feel of her wrapped around him, the coolness of her flesh as he clutched her to him.

He clenched his jaw to keep from making a sound as he stroked himself, his breathing ragged as he heard her whispering his name, a soft husky sigh of pleasure as he claimed his new bride.

She would have his ring on her small, delicate finger and he would feel it against his fingers as he clutched her hand, her back arching as he took her for the first time, and her body accepted him.

She would be ripe with his child, belly swollen, and cheeks flushed as she scolded him for something silly he had done, but then she would move into his arms and they would make love on the rug before the fire, ever careful of the growing life inside her.

She would know exactly what to do to turn him on, and he would know how to drive her wild with need, satisfying each other time and time again while his past faded behind him.

They would have beautiful children, and he would love her like he had never loved before.

His body clenched, and he shuddered at the thought of her before him, her hand on him, stroking him.

His release left him tingling, and he rested his forehead against the tiles of the shower wall, keeping his breathing slow and steady as he felt relief, and then a terrible shame flooded through him.

Etani's eyes opened before him, her fear and need for escape in his mind.

He had let her down in fantasising of another woman, and he finished his shower, wrapping the towel around his waist and dropping onto the bench.

Mother, how could he be thinking about another woman when his woman was trapped and crying for help?

What kind of man would simply abandon her like that?

Even if the soft smile of Aurora lingered in his mind, he couldn't not think about *her*, his Etani. She was life for him; she was everything to him.

But then there was that little spark of fire that started up in his chest and he clenched his eyes shut, realising with dread that he had allowed himself to fall for Aurora.

He was a disloyal man; even if Etani wasn't his, she owned him.

Would she be able to sense it in him, the betrayal? He thought she would, and for a moment he thought only to throw himself headfirst into the damage he had already caused.

She would forgive him in time, wouldn't she?

He didn't know, and he could only hope she didn't hate him for his feelings.

CHAPTER 14
SHARING

"Remember when she threatened to kill you and bring you back as a goat?" Dirdos was saying, grinning at an amused Jagum. "And then you were taunting her about not being able to do it, so she went out and actually got the goat?"

Jagum burst out laughing, followed by the others sitting around in the room.

"Whatever happened to that goat?" Uzo asked, trying to remember.

"Fairly sure Hunter ate it ..." Dirdos said.

"Poor Goatee ..." Bast sighed and Versalis jumped, not realising the woman was in the room.

She laughed and hugged him, nuzzling his jaw before pulling away, and he felt a stab of shame as he realised Etani did something very, very similar to that when she hugged him.

"Noticed it, too, huh?" Daemon said, amused by his expression and the realisation.

"What about when she threatened to rip out your spleen?" Jagum said, missing the last comment by Daemon.

"What do you mean, threatened? She was *holding* it! She was holding it ... in her hand! Outside of my body!" Daemon cried, drawn back to the conversation. "How someone can remove a spleen without breaking a rib is beyond me, but she did it."

"Well, you shouldn't have been staring at her arse ..." Uzo said, stirring a cup of steaming tea.

"Is ... is it possible to not stare at it?" Daemon asked, his eyes wide.

"No," Dirdos said. "Especially not in those cotton pants ... when she's tying up those big boots ..."

There was an appreciative silence for several long seconds.

"How about when you caught her trying to smuggle strawberries into her room ... and instead of giving them up, she stuffed them all in her mouth and flipped you off," Sebastian said, his eyes dancing as he looked at Daemon.

"She is a menace for food smuggling ... I swear if we didn't catch her there would be standing room only." Uzo sighed, shaking his head.

Daemon was too busy laughing to respond.

"Or the time she almost stabbed that werewolf in the eye when he grabbed her," Versalis added, recalling the incident. He was fairly sure it had involved those cotton pants, and the man sitting up to her standing right in front of him. It was hard to not want to grab her when that happened.

"And when she punted Epharis through three walls?" Versalis said.

"Best day of my life." Daemon sighed.

"That was the greatest thing I've ever seen," Jaia said, hesitant to join in on the fun.

"How about when she said she was going to feed you your own stomach and then had to stop to think how that would work," Jaia added.

"She was so sure you would choke on it before you managed to get your stomach back into itself." Dirdos laughed. "And then she just gets that evil look, and you know it's time to run away before she starts experimenting."

"And there was the time she tried to drown Sebastian before realising that he was part siren and could breathe underwater," Daemon said, grinning.

"And then we tag teamed and went after Hunter and Letari," Sebastian said, his smile hidden under the mask.

"And Hunter was so sure he was going to drown. I swear that man has never been that scared in his life," Dirdos added.

"He's absolutely convinced that Etani is going to kill him and then refuse to bring him back," Versalis said.

"If I was dating Letari, I'd be convinced of that, too," Dainin said, enjoying the memories, though he hadn't been there for any of them.

"Oh, what about when she poisoned Uzo's tea?" Daemon said, turning to look at the Fae who was looking down at his tea suspiciously.

"I didn't know that was her," he said.

"She wanted to know what would happen if you ingested a new concoction and didn't want to test it on herself."

Uzo rubbed his eyes. "That girl is going to be the death of me ... again." There was a moment of awkward silence as Uzo realised what he said and shook his head. "You know I didn't mean it like that."

"She was responsible for your death?" Jason asked, leaning against the wall beside the bookcase and hidden from Versalis' view.

"Not directly," Uzo said, setting down the cup and saucer. "This was when the Creators were still alive."

"Did Erlking die?" Jason asked, looking at the other two Hunters.

"Who's Erlking?"

"The Creator."

"What do you mean? A Creator survived?" Damon asked, alarmed.

"Yes, the only one to survive. I thought that was common knowledge. He came to the compound to hide out for a while. But that's incidental. What happened?"

"I ..." Uzo looked stumped for a second but then shook his head. "We thought everything went fine, she was back, and then the Creators came. But they shouldn't have been able to if she had her magic. They should have been neutralised, but they came and ... when you get killed by the Creators, you turn to stone and if anything touches it, it crumbles. She was too late and touched my face..."

"She just stood there for a few seconds, staring down at you. And then she exploded, screaming, and people just started dropping like flies. She killed them all. She was devastated for months," Daemon said in a soft voice. "Barely functioning and blaming herself. She wanted to kill herself and go be with Uzo wherever it was he went. But then Hades taunted her into going and finding him."

"She looked so terrified," Uzo breathed, his eyes wide.

"So ... what does that mean for your body?" Jason asked. "Are you like Kai and Letari?"

"No, it seems that my body was regenerated from her flesh. Sort of like how she is reborn through Versalis'. She created me of her flesh, not of clay."

"I would like to see her making one of these bodies one day."

"It takes ... I don't know, about twelve hours to fully make a body," Jaia said slowly, uncertain. "I wasn't fully in my right mind when she started."

"About that, maybe a bit more. No one was really watching the time," Daemon said.

"Considering all of this, it's fascinating that you haven't all run away screaming," Jason said.

"I think about it. But I'm fairly sure she would drag us back out of spite," Jagum said.

"Yeah, revenge for bringing her back." Daemon agreed.

"Why did you have to bring her back?" Jason asked.

"There was an incident, Etani was injured, and Sebastian offered to help. It didn't go as expected and she sort of..." Uzo said, looking at the others for help.

"She went bat shit crazy, wanted to fuck everyone and then eat them," Dirdos supplied. "Hottest thing I've ever seen, and Daemon almost fell for it. She went for Kai, something she would never have gone for before."

Jason looked towards Jaia, who shrugged, eyes on the ground.

"Later, I found the two of them in the basement, she was kissing him and... I called her a whore, so she left," Jaia said.

"She's not a whore, not even easy. She has given herself to exactly one man in her entire existence," Uzo growled, looking at the vampire.

"I was jealous and angry. She said she was only curious, but that it wasn't to her liking, and she would try one of the others."

"Idiot boy, you can't seriously think she meant it?" Dirdos snapped, looking indignant.

"Why would she say it, then?" Jaia snapped back.

"Because Kai kissed *her,* and she didn't want to make you resent your brother. So, she pulled your hatred on herself," Dirdos sighed, sounding like he was dealing with an angry toddler.

"What?" Jaia demanded, looking at the dragon in disbelief.

"Do you really think she would just kiss Kai to experiment? When has she shown any inclination towards either experimenta-tion, or Kai? She sees sex as procreation only, not for pleasure, at least not until she met Neah." Dirdos looked annoyed.

"She... she made me hate her to protect Kai?"

"Of course she did. She might have liked kissing him, but I would be extremely shocked if she instigated that kiss."

"She wouldn't have," Daemon added, shaking his head. "Etani endures, she doesn't instigate."

Jason had a weird look on his face.

"Jaia raped her, didn't he...?" Jason asked in a quiet voice.

There was a sudden silence, all eyes turning on the vampire who had gone pale.

"What makes you think that?" Dirdos asked.

"You're all hostile, Daemon's comment about him never abusing her, this conversation."

"Yes," Jaia said, his expression carefully blank.

"Why is he still alive?"

"Etani," Daemon said. "She made us promise."

"She did?" Jaia asked.

"Why would she do that?" Dainin asked. He knew of the story but not the reasoning.

"Because of Kai," Dirdos said, sounding unsure.

"No," Daemon growled, his expression one of someone eating a sour grape. "Because part of her still loves him. Is still in love with him. How can I put this in a way you will understand...? Etani is incapable of seeing things the way we see things, the way the average woman sees things. She sees sexual abuse at the hands of her husbands as their natural right to her. She believes she belongs to them, and as soon as she's back, we will have to deal with Neah. She has not married any man because she wanted to, but she will submit to them if they want her. She would let him do what he wanted to her because she is his wife. Zeus... she can at least understand what he did, because he wanted her magic."

"Zeus?" Jason asked, horrified.

"Zeus had her for a couple of days. She had a chance to give us a clue," Vincent said.

"At the time one could... force her to create a world for you... if you were a man," Daemon said, the men in the room flinching at the implication even if they already knew.

"He took her, and she was pregnant. Kai killed her. She was... she learnt how to disassociate from that. She goes somewhere else so they can do what they want without her feeling it," Vincent supplied.

"Whether she is capable of remaining present in that situation remains to be seen," Daemon growled. "It may be that she will simply never want to be touched again. Or she may bounce back."

"We hope she will recover, but she's different now. She tries to hide it, but she doesn't sleep with us anymore. Only Versalis or Uzo," Dirdos said.

"She's ashamed," Versalis said, Uzo watching him. "She doesn't want you all to look at her differently."

"Why would you look at her differently?" Jason asked, frowning.

"We wouldn't," Dirdos growled. "Why would she think that? What did she say?"

They were all looking at him, greedy and hungry for information that he was hesitant to give.

"She's ashamed because she gave herself to him. She didn't see what he was, because she didn't want to see what he was," Uzo said.

"She has been talking to you two?" Daemon growled, indignant.

"She doesn't want you to think less of her because she fell for a manipulative man. She thinks you will look at her like a stupid child who should have seen it coming. Like she should have expected it ... Because why would anyone *actually* care about her without there being an ulterior motive? She no longer thinks anyone would ever want her simply for being her. She thinks everyone is trying to get something out of her. It is going to take a very strong man a very long time to change that thought," Uzo said, eyes lowered to his knees.

They were all silent again, trying to wrap their minds around the damage that had been caused to her self-esteem and self-worth.

"She stopped seeing herself as a woman, and now thinks she is nothing more than a tool to be used and discarded by the next man who decides to take her off the shelf," Versalis said, trying to drive it bitterly home to them all.

Daemon's eyes clenched shut, his face screwed up in pain, and Uzo stared blankly at the wall, refusing to listen to it all again. Versalis saw her face as she sat huddled in the space.

CHAPTER 15
SORROW

Those huge, blue eyes stared at nothing as she whispered her private thoughts to them, trying to make them understand.

"I don't want them to touch me."

"Why not?" Uzo murmured, stroking her hair from his spot wedged between her legs and the wall.

"Because I don't think I could handle their rejecting me. I saw the way you all looked at me before I ran away, and that was before you all thought I was a silly little girl."

"No one thinks you're a silly little girl," Uzo scolded her. "There's nothing wrong with what you did."

"You only say that because you're my uncle and you have to love me," she said, turning away from him. "I can't be near them again. Not yet, maybe not ever. I can't ..." Tears welled in her eyes and Uzo hissed at her, pulling her closer until she was in his lap. "Not again... I can't do it again ... I don't want to be touched again ..."

"It's okay, love," Versalis whispered, taking her hand, and pressing his lips to it.

They were silent for a while, her eyes shifting as whatever it was went through her mind.

"Do you think they love me?" she whispered, eyes unfocused and broken.

"Who?" Uzo asked, turning his head to see her face from above.

"Everyone. All of them. Daemon, Dirdos ... all of them. Do you think they love me, or is it like Zeus?"

"Of course they love you ... How could you think that?" Uzo asked, devastated by the question.

"I don't know if they can. I was just wondering, what if they only want to get something from me, too? What if they only want to use me, too?"

She looked up at Versalis, but there was no fear in her, and with a terrible realisation, he knew she saw the abuse as normal. It was what she knew; it was what she would expect from a partner.

"Etani, not everyone is like that. They love you, truly and deeply," Versalis said, clutching that delicate hand between his.

She met his eyes, searching his face for something he could only fathom. "Okay," she whispered, dismissing the conversation and closing her eyes.

Versalis looked up at Uzo, the Fae's eyes burning with rage as he clutched her to him, and Versalis thought the Fae was thinking along the same lines as he was.

She was long asleep before Uzo was able to bring himself down enough to speak, his voice a clipped snarl.

"She thinks everyone is going to abuse her, doesn't she ... and that it's entirely okay for them to do it."

"I think so," Versalis whispered, watching her sleeping face. "It's like ... she doesn't care anymore. She hasn't given up, has she?"

"No, she just can't get her head around the idea that someone would actually want her without wanting her magic, at least that's what I'm getting from this."

Uzo shifted her in his arms and she mumbled, nuzzling her cheek against his chest and curling herself up against him.

"You think so? What do we do?"

"Keep the rest of those idiots away from her until she can figure it out. Try to convince her that not everyone wants to abuse her ... keep her safe," Uzo murmured, resting his cheek against the top of her head.

"How can she think that ...?" Versalis whispered, her brows drawing in as she dreamt.

"If abuse is the only experience you've had in a relationship, isn't that what you see as normal?"

"I suppose it would be ..." Versalis sighed, kissing her limp hand that he had refused to let go of.

"None of them are to touch her. Not any time soon; she needs to recover."

"Yes, I agree completely."

"I knew I could rely on you, Versalis," Uzo sighed, eyes closing.

They fell into silence, listening to the steady pace of her breathing.

THE MEMORY MADE tears swell in his eyes as he thought of how distant she had been with the others for so long, wary and only allowing them close to her when she had to. It was agony for them, but they hadn't demanded she let them near. They sensed that she needed space and gave it to her.

"If a single one of you touches her when she is back ... I'll kill you," Uzo said. "She needs time to recover. If you ever loved her, you would respect that. None of you are capable of repairing that damage."

"Is any man capable?" Dirdos asked, his eyes on the floor. "Is any man alive or dead worthy of trying to repair that?"

"I don't know," Uzo sighed. "I hope so, but I don't know."

The men within the room exchanged glances, judging each other for their respective abilities and the likelihood of their being anyone good enough to try to help her, let alone be worthy of loving her.

But no one stood up and demanded to be given the chance. No one opened their mouths. No one wanted to be denied.

Versalis headed into the bedroom to get dressed, returning to Bast and taking her hand. She tried to put on a brave smile, but it was forced.

"Did you really name the goat Goatee?" Dainin asked after a while, and Daemon snorted.

"Yes, Etani thought it would be funny, and it was entirely accidental."

"She's a strange and twisted woman. I like her," Jason said, his words lightening the mood.

They fell back into talking about the random conversations and events of the last years with her.

"Who is it that taught her such foul language?" Sebastian asked after a while.

"She spoke like that as soon as she arrived," Jaia said. "She just didn't use it as much before you lot started showing up."

"How did she even get stuck in Ayathian, she seems way too bright to be in a place like that," Jason asked, sitting down on the floor against the couch beside Bast's feet.

"Epharis caught her," Daemon said.

"Caught her?" Jason asked, curious.

"To hear him tell it," the demon started. "She was feeding. She had cornered an Elf or something similar and he had put up a fight, ripped off her arm, and so she was eating to regrow it. He felt her presence and went to investigate. There she was, chowing down. She pretty much told him to fuck off, and that she wasn't sharing. He was immediately hooked on her and decided he needed to know what she was, so he got out that gold chain and she didn't know what it was, so she didn't try to defend herself. She just looked up at the chain and that was it. She figured it out once the chain was around her, but by then he had her. He said he pulled her apart trying to learn what she was, but never managed it. He eventually got her to tell him."

"She didn't have a clue that she was about to spend the next ten years being abused and tortured," Uzo said darkly.

"Before that she was simply keeping Cain busy so Letari and Avadari could have a normal life," Daemon finished.

"What does that mean?" Jason asked.

"Cain is one of her people ... well... he was one of her people. He was assigned with tracking her and Letari down, killing them, and retrieving Avadari. Letari is 'mentally delicate,' or so Etani calls it. Avadari is the younger sister to the twins, but she passed at Cain's hands. For nine hundred or so years she kept him on the run, chasing after her so the other two could have a normal life and relationships. Several years back Cain caught up with her, and when he couldn't get to her, he went after the sisters. Both Letari and Avadari were killed. Avadari wouldn't come back, Etani accidentally dragged Letari back."

"Mother, no wonder she's so ... distant," Vincent said, staring at Daemon. "Being on her own for all that time? With nothing but an assassin trying to kill you for company?"

"It's assumed that's part of how she ended up as she is. More creature than anything, and as cold as a block of ice," Daemon replied. "Surviving on instincts."

"How could you live like that and stay even vaguely normal?" Jason asked. "Fae are the ultimate social creatures; they need others around them to function."

"You can ask her when she's back," Uzo said. "But I'm betting she will simply say 'I did what I had to do for my family' or something similar."

"Was Letari always like that?"

"No, her mind was damaged when Etani first died, around twenty-two or twenty-three years old."

"What do you think Letari would make of Jason?" Versalis asked thoughtfully, and all eyes turned on the Hunter, his eyes wide in alarm with his mask atop his head.

"I'm betting she would like him," Daemon said bitterly. "Probably wouldn't even warn him off."

"Warn me off what?"

"Etani. Letari warned almost all of us off, except Versalis and Dirdos."

"And almost ripped out Jaia's throat," Uzo added.

"Why you two?"

"The rest of us she doesn't see as worthy of Etani. She can read surface thoughts and emotions at times. Did she warn Kai off? I never asked."

"Don't think so," Jaia said in a whisper.

"So you three ... that's not fair," Daemon complained.

"Why Dirdos, though?" Versalis asked.

"No idea," Dirdos said, his lips pulled down in a frown.

"Probably sees you as more likely to be able to hold her down," Versalis said. "You're dominant enough to keep her contained, but wouldn't abuse her."

Dirdos blinked at him, brows lifted in surprise.

"He'd just feed her addiction to shiny things," Daemon snipped, grumpy at the whole conversation.

"She is addicted to shiny things?" Dainin asked.

"There's an idea, give her something shiny and sparkly instead of flowers and see how that turns her in your favour," Dirdos said, nodding.

"You give her flowers?" Jason asked.

"We heard her ... in Neah's room. We heard her and didn't do anything," Vincent said, his eyes closed. "We could have saved her within hours of being brought there. But we ignored it and she suffered for months."

"We could have stopped all of that. She lost her baby because of him." Dainin whimpered. "I just want her to know we aren't all monsters."

Jason's face went white, and he looked around at the Hunter, fury burning in him.

"Neah caused her to miscarry? Whose child?"

"Neah got her pregnant, and then beat her," Uzo said in a tiny voice. "Matthew, the human priest, told us. He was angry because she was worried about his hurting the baby when he wanted her. She refused to submit to him, so he threw her up against the wall and hit her, then kicked her when she couldn't stand up any more. He said Neah wouldn't have stopped until she was dead if he didn't say anything. And then he dragged her out. They came back a while later and Neah said the baby was gone, and that he would try again. He was ... trying again ... when Daemon showed up."

"That ... he's evil ..." Jason whispered, horrified.

"And she's married to him," Daemon growled. "We need to destroy him."

"You can't kill the Hunters," Dainin said, shaking his head. "We can't die, Daemon. It's just not possible."

"Then we find a way to keep him down and away from her," Versalis said, looking at Jaia. "You and Kai can come up with something. Some device, when he's back with us."

"Gladly," the furious vampire growled.

Versalis considered the vampire for a moment but then shook his head, turning away as the room fell into an uneasy silence and they all considered what to do.

"How close are we to getting her back?" Versalis asked.

"Oh, right," Jason said with a start. "I got caught up in the conversation. We're almost ready, we just need a bit more time. The men are getting worn out. They don't know why they are trying to get in and it's exhausting work."

"Tell them why we are trying to get in," Versalis said. "Neah was the main concern, but he already knows. There's no need to try and hide it any further."

"Good point. But which part do I tell them?"

Everyone frowned, unsure of what was safe.

"Tell them the woman they all jack off to is in need of their help, and they might see her naked if they get in," Daemon said, snorting.

"Daemon!" Bast cried, indignant.

"No, that would probably work," Vincent said, sighing. "Etani is the stuff of any man's wildest fantasy. To even get a chance to see a flash of her bare wrist would be enough motivation for most of them. These are men who would kill to see a woman that perfect. Imagine what they would do if you hinted that they might be able to touch her, to hold her while she tries to get her body to work again. Just to hold her hand would be enough, but to hold that body while it's naked and trembling?"

"They would literally turn the world upside down for that," Dainin said, grinning.

"You're all disgusting," Bast scolded, though she was smiling a little.

"Tell them... say that the first man into that room will get to hold her hand, and that every man in that room is likely going to see her naked," Daemon said. "Any complaints?" he asked Uzo.

"If it gets her back, I might even permit them to kiss her cheek. Maybe."

"All right, I'll let them know. I assume you will all be staying here for the time being?" Jason asked Vincent, standing.

Vincent nodded, rubbing his eyes and looking exhausted. "Yes, unless you need my assistance."

"No, I can manage for the time being. We'll let you know if we need anything," Jason said, nodding to the others and stepping backward out of reality.

"How was the shower, lover boy?" Daemon taunted. "Get your hormones back under control?"

"Fuck you..." Versalis snapped.

"Gladly," the demon growled, his eyes trailing down over Versalis' frame. "Bring your girlfriend, we'll make it a real party."

"What girlfriend?" Bast asked.

"He and the lovely Aurora have been keeping each other company."

"No, we haven't."

"And whose body were you picturing in the shower?"

"That's enough," Bast snapped, glaring at the demon. "You mind your own business."

"I'll mind Etani's business when her favourite toy gets taken away while she's gone."

Bast growled at him, and Daemon bared his teeth in return.

"I'm not her favourite, nor am I her toy. There is nothing going on between Aurora and I; even if there were, it's none of your business," Versalis said calmly. He wasn't about to get into this with the demon.

"Whatever you say," Daemon said, amused. "But I'm not going to let you use either of those girls. They both deserve better."

Versalis shook his head, turning and leaving the room with Bast calling out after him.

He didn't look back, not wanting to hear any more arguments or explanations, and he was disgusted to find his mind wandering back to Aurora and his immediate thought to go find her.

Why was she plaguing his mind? He really didn't know, and he was ashamed when he found himself wandering into the throne room and there she was, beautiful and soft with a smile that could melt his heart.

She looked up at him and her face lit with pleasure. His heart sank as he met her smile with his own.

What was he doing there? He needed to leave. His heart belonged to Etani, not Aurora. But it was so incredibly hard to turn away from the blonde ice Queen.

She motioned for him to join her as she stood, and the Court bowed to her.

Approaching her, he offered her his arm and she took it, leading the way out of the Court and into a less crowded corridor.

"That was fascinating what you said earlier," the lovely woman said in a delighted voice. "I didn't know any of that. How did you find out?"

"The Hunter Jason figured it out," Versalis said, his thoughts lingering dangerously on the fullness of her frozen rose lips.

"Is that right? I'd love to meet with him some time to see what else he knows. Anything we can do to help our Queen, or Faerie."

She was such a little ball of light that he found himself captivated by her and he felt a sudden, burning urge to know what her lips tasted like, followed by guilt as he thought of Etani.

Throwing caution to the wind, he drew the lovely woman to a stop, and she looked up at him curiously.

"Your Majesty, may I kiss you?" he asked, speaking quickly before his doubt could strike him down as the sinner he was.

She didn't reply, only nodded, hesitant and unsure, but she desired him at least a small amount.

His hand was gentle as he traced his fingers along her jaw, and then curled them around the back of her head to tilt it backward.

Without hesitation, he bowed his head over hers and touched his lips against the coolness of hers. Her eyes fluttered closed, and his followed a moment later, the soft brush increasing only slightly, hesitant.

It was slow, only a touch at first, but increased until his lips moved against hers and his fingers dragged through her hair. She was clutching the front of his shirt, pressing closer to him.

It was delicious, wonderful, and his urge was to request more from her, to know if she desired him the way he desired her, and he thought the answer would be yes, but he didn't know for sure.

A deep clearing of the throat drew them apart and his head lifted, breaking the kiss, and he sighed as he found a smug, hugely grinning Dirdos leaning his shoulder against the wall, his arms and ankles crossed.

"So, apparently this is a thing," the dragon said.

Aurora blushed, looking away from the dragon, and Versalis dropped his hand at her touch, looking back down at her to find her so incredibly lovely with her cheeks flaming.

"Please excuse me, Versalis, Lord Dirdos," she whispered and hurried away to leave him alone with the dragon.

CHAPTER 16
LOVE

"What will you give me to not tell Daemon I found you macking on the Queen?" the dragon asked.

"I won't kill you?" Versalis offered.

"Please, little vampire. I'm more worried about a kitten killing me than you. And here I was thinking you were the pure one of the group."

"Don't tell Daemon; it's none of his business."

"Does the little Aurora know about you and Etani?"

"There is no 'me and Etani.'"

"No? She favours you."

"Because I was there when she needed me. Not because she prefers me over any of you."

"How could you do this to Etani?"

"Etani never has to find out," Versalis growled, unsure why he felt so defensive. Etani was not his wife or even his lover.

"I ... am not entirely confident of your capacity to keep them both, my friend. And I don't think the world would handle those two women finding out."

"I didn't mean it like that. Etani is not my partner, I do not owe her anything."

"You would choose Aurora?" Dirdos asked.

"Would you wait for Etani forever?"

"There is no other woman for me," Dirdos said. "I am all for you deciding to love another woman, but you need to figure it out before she gets back. I will not allow you to hurt her because you're lonely now and want a woman in your bed, but will turn back to her the instant she's back."

"I have no intentions of hurting Etani," Versalis snapped.

"You already have, Versalis. Just don't make it worse."

"Are you going to tell Daemon?"

"If I feel he needs to know. Keep it discreet until you can tell him yourself."

Versalis watched the tall man for several seconds, considering him and what he wanted.

"Would it be so bad if I chose another woman?" he asked, uncertain.

"No, many would be surprised you were capable of choosing another woman, but it would not be bad. I am certain Aurora could make you happy. It would mean you would have to stay here though."

"I don't know, Dirdos ..." Versalis said, desperate for an answer.

"Only you can figure it out. But Etani loves you, and she would very likely give herself to you if you were to ask her for it. That is what you would be giving up."

Versalis shook his head, turning away from him to look back towards the path Aurora had taken.

"Is it possible to love more than one woman?"

"Of course it is. But I do not think it is possible to be in love with more than one. At least not successfully, without everyone being involved and aware. Someone always ends up getting hurt."

Dirdos approached, a heavy hand coming down on Versalis' shoulder.

"You can have the instant gratification and possibly a long, happy life with Aurora. But if you chose her, do not look to Etani again. She will not be yours again, so choose wisely."

"Do I deserve the love of a woman like that?"

"The question isn't if you deserve it. It's if you are worthy of it. However, if what you need is a lover, then make it clear that is all you desire from her. Aurora is a good girl, and deserves better than to be mistreated by a lonely man."

"I wouldn't ever mistreat her."

"No, I don't think you would. At least not intentionally. Figure out where your heart lies and be prepared to break the heart of the other. There's no helping it."

Versalis nodded slowly and rubbed his eyes, wanting very badly to go find Aurora.

Was that answer not enough for him?

"I ... I want to get to know Aurora," he said after a pause.

"Then go get to know her. We will all be happy for you if that is what you want."

"Gleeful, you mean." Versalis sighed.

"That, too, but even with this rivalry we will be happy that another of our ranks found true love. Go on, little vampire, go see if she can captivate you."

Versalis did exactly that, heading after the Queen and finding her lingering a few corridors away, her cheeks still flaming.

Without a word, he trapped her against the wall and his mouth found hers, hot and heavy.

She squeaked in alarm at first, but then her tension melted, and she kissed him back just as eagerly, her body leaning into his as he deepened the kiss, his arms going around her.

"This is improper." She gasped as his lips left hers and trailed along her throat, her skin tasting sweet and delicious.

"You only have to say stop for me to stop," he growled, her little whimper making him chuckle.

She was such a precious, hypnotic creature, and he bit on her earlobe to make her squeak, the sound incredibly endearing.

"Versalis ..." She gasped again as he found her throat and kissed it, teasing her skin with his fangs.

"Yes, Aurora?" he asked, nudging her jaw with his nose.

"I'm afraid," she whispered.

He stopped, leaning back to look down at her. "Afraid of me?" he asked, a little alarmed that he was coming on too heavily for the woman.

"That I may feel more for you than you do for me," she whispered.

"I would never mistreat you so," he said, brushing back a stray hair from her cheek to make her blush. "Now, if you are concerned, we will stop and spend time together, that is all. There is no pressure, lovely Aurora. I am not going to rush you or make you feel like you must do anything."

Cupping his hand around the back of her neck, he drew her forward and kissed her forehead gently, the large pink stone bumping against his chin. "You are precious to me, and I would very much like to get to know you."

"What about Etani? Are you not her love?"

Versalis frowned, letting her go once more.

"Etani ... It is complicated what I feel for Etani. I love her dearly, but she may not be the woman I would like to spend my life with. It may be that it is you I would spend it with, assuming you would have me," he added.

"I would," she breathed, making him pause.

"You flatter me, Aurora, for all I know you may think I smell weird, or not like the way I eat," he teased, making the woman laugh.

"Come along, silly man, let us walk in the garden," she said, taking his arm and pulling him along in her wake. "Before someone catches us and jumps to the wrong conclusion."

"Certainly, we wouldn't want there to be any salacious rumours started."

"Are there rumours that aren't salacious? Last I heard I had three lovers and two husbands I was keeping secret." She sighed. "If these two husbands did exist, then I would very much like to know where they are, because I have plenty of work for them."

"You could have one," he said without thinking, and she looked around at him sharply. "That was inappropriate ... I'm very sorry," he said, backpedalling. He was so used to making comments like that with Etani and the others, it had slipped out.

She stared at him, making him anxious, certain he had made a terrible mistake.

"Perhaps," she said, his tension easing. "With that in mind, perhaps we should get a chaperone," she said.

"That is an exceptionally good idea," he said, utterly ashamed of himself for the comment.

THE CHAPERONE TURNED out to be Lady Karnia, her white-yellow eyes wary of the pair as she followed along several feet behind them.

It made Versalis anxious to be watched so carefully, but he wouldn't risk the lovely Queen's reputation.

"Tell me about yourself," Aurora said, making him smile.

"Well, my name is Versalis, and like many of us, I failed to remember my surname. From what I can tell, only Uzo and Etani have managed to remember theirs. Did you?"

She frowned, squinting into the distance as she tried to recall. "I don't think so. I wonder if that is a natural trait of the species."

"Or perhaps it is so we cannot be trapped. We are very aware of the magic of names and so we intentionally forget."

"That is a very interesting theory, Versalis. How did you come up with it?"

"I don't really know. Just a thought, I suppose."

She nodded, watching while he paused to pick a frozen rose and, bowing gracefully, offered it to the lovely lady. She took it and lifted it to her nose, inhaling the delicate scent. "So, what else?" she asked as they set off again.

"Well, I am a vampire, and I am around three hundred, give or take. I am not entirely sure; I didn't keep track of my years. I was turned when I was thirty-one, a few days after my birthday if I recall correctly. She did not intend to turn me, and I do not know who she was. I felt her die a few decades later. The village I was born in was decimated by her, and as far as I can tell, I was the only one to survive."

"How did you become a King?" she asked after a pause.

"I killed a Queen. Entirely by accident to be honest, but I did kill her," he said, refusing to let the memory surface. "She was a young Queen, only newly-formed, and she came after me. I didn't mean to kill her, she was so little, and so beautiful, but when I shoved her away, she hit a tree and was impaled. I didn't realise it hit her brain and her heart, it got her leg, too, but then I felt her magic just drain out of her and I was so distraught, I just wanted to make her better, but instead, her magic filled me."

Aurora watched him, her eyes wide.

"I haven't told anyone that ... they all think I did it intentionally," he said wryly.

Etani had never asked him, he realised bitterly.

"I'm sorry, Versalis. I didn't have any idea that could happen."

"For all I know, I'm the only one to ever accidentally kill a Queen. They are normally very carefully guarded. She was just on her own. It can happen, but they are normally found within hours of being born. I got the feeling she had been running and thought I was going to attack or capture her. That was about ..." Right about the time he started hunting Etani. "About seventy years ago, maybe ..." He trailed off, trying to wrap his brain around the length of time that was far greater than he originally guessed.

"What's the matter?" Aurora asked, giving his arm a tug.

"Nothing, darling," he said, the endearment making her blush. "Tell me something about you."

"I was born to the Goddess Asherah and a Fae lord; mother refused to tell me his name. He sends me flowers occasionally, though. I was sent to the Court like most of my rank, and had assumed I would be married to a lord at some point, but I was still too young for my mother's liking. I'm still a child in the eyes of the Court, only one hundred and forty-seven." She grinned at him slyly. "Yes, I'm still counting, unlike the rest of you lazy courtiers. Mother believes I must be able to survive on my own before I can marry, and then Etani asked me to be her heir, and now mother is trying to find a suitable husband to keep me in check."

She laughed, sounding sweetly amused by the antics of her mother.

"Do you mind if you are married or not?" he asked.

"Not really, it might be nice to share a home with a husband, but I do not feel any particular rush. We Fae worry too much about the dwindling fertility rates, but so many of us are just impatient."

"Dwindling fertility?" Versalis asked, frowning.

"Yes, fewer and fewer Fae babies are being born. No one knows why," she said sadly. "It seems to be universal amongst the courts, but the Celestrials seem to have been hit first. I believe their fertility is no longer even replacement." She must have seen his confusion. "That is where you have two children to cover yourselves. They are having one child per couple now, which is very bad for all of us."

"I never really thought about it. I just assumed fertility was good because Etani has been pregnant twice."

"Excuse me?" Aurora jerked to a stop, her tone indignant and the dark woman behind them made a soft sound of enquiry. "Where are they? Who has the children?"

"She ... she didn't carry either to term. I'm sorry, I thought you would have known. The first one was taken out of her, and the second ... well, the father gets violent when he is angry."

"Who was the father?" she demanded, horrified.

"The first was to the Lich Prince Epharis, and that was back when she first came to Ayathian, the second was to the Hunter Neah, she lost that perhaps six months before she died."

"Mother, I had no idea ... why didn't she tell me?"

"I don't think she wants to talk about it. She won't talk to any of us about them. I assumed Uzo would have told you."

"No, he didn't. I will have to mention it the next time I see him. That's awful ... But two? In what? Five years of her being alive?"

"Yes, around that. I assumed that sort of thing was normal. But then there were the worlds ... Etani seems to be quite ... well, quite fertile," he said, the word making him cringe. He didn't want to be discussing the woman's personal life like that, but Aurora of all people needed to know. Even if it wasn't his place to discuss the matter.

"As far as I can piece together, Neah could create a world from her every few days, and Dirdos made sure Epharis couldn't create anything from her. Again, she is always fertile, there are no breaks that I can see." He lowered his voice to ensure that Karnia couldn't hear them, wanting to keep the conversation private. "No one said it was abnormal, so I just assumed."

"Perhaps Daemon doesn't want to draw it to her attention?" Aurora asked, fascinated.

"It's entirely possible that the fertility rates have bounced back."

"Not as yet, we've only had two births this season, and it's almost over."

"Two in three months?" Versalis asked, indignant. "There must be, what? Several hundred thousand married women?"

"More so, plus those who are unmarried but wish to have children. There is no reason for it that we can figure out. But she is ... twice?"

"Yes, twice."

"And to a Lich and a Hunter? Wait ... how many times has she been married?"

"Three, now."

She took a step back from him, her face red in anger. "This is intolerable. If she wants to be the Queen, she must tell us these things." She was absolutely adorable when angry, her lips puckering out and her cheeks flushed.

"I don't think she really wants to be Queen as much as she doesn't want to give up Winter. But perhaps you should insist she comes here for a time? Make her be a good girl and run Winter for a few years. She'll love it." He was grinning wickedly.

"Oh, she'll be furious!" Aurora exclaimed, clapping her hands in delight. "As soon as she's back, I'm going to make her come here!"

"Your Majesty? Is everything all right?" Karnia asked.

"Yes, Karnia, we are conspiring against our Queen to make her into an upstanding ruler," Aurora said happily.

"Please don't get yourself in trouble," Karnia said.

"Of course not, Karnia! Wouldn't you like to spend time with our Queen?"

"I would, but she doesn't seem overly interested in spending time with us."

Versalis looked around at the dark-skinned, horned woman.

"That's not true, she has simply been forced to remain away."

Karnia looked at him doubtfully. "That remains to be seen, Your Majesty," she said and turned to look out over the garden while the two conspired against Etani.

CHAPTER 17

CALM BEFORE THE STORM

Eight weeks passed by in a blur as they sat in waiting for the Hunters to move, and Versalis found himself growing less interested in helping free the trapped Goddess and more interested in spending time with the lovely Queen.

It hadn't gone by unnoticed, either, Daemon blowing up into a rage one night and screaming at him that if he didn't love Etani any more then he needed to get out of the council.

It wasn't like he didn't love Etani anymore; it was simply that he had feelings for Aurora as well, and was torn between the two women.

Etani would never stop being important to him; he would love her for an eon, but he cared deeply for Aurora as well, and she captivated him, giving him attention and affection Etani seemed incapable of providing.

"She is afraid," Uzo said when he broke and stressed his fears to the Fae. Uzo seemed to understand, but they had grown distant in the time since. "She is afraid to love you for fear of you leaving her. She is new to love, and she is young in comparison to your experience with love. She hopes you will be able to step up and take over so she can learn what love is from you."

Versalis was ashamed, feeling horribly like he had betrayed her and let her down for the love she entrusted in him, a love he had thrown away when she was no longer there to keep him captivated.

"What do I do?" he begged his friend, the man who he remembered too late had once shoved a teacup through the vampire's eye for daring to touch his niece without her consent.

"Do you love Aurora?"

"Yes, I think so ..."

"Then let Etani go," he said flatly, and Versalis flinched, knowing he had made a mistake in going to Uzo for advice.

"I still love her, Uzo, more than anything."

"More than Aurora?"

Versalis was silent, trying to figure out the answer. "I don't know; it's impossible to know when she's not here."

"Then that's your answer, Versalis. If you can allow another woman into your heart when she is not there, then it is not Etani you love, but her pull. You do not love Etani, you only want her."

Versalis jerked back, staring at his friend who had gone cold against him. He hadn't meant to alienate them all, he had only been looking for advice. "Uzo, I didn't mean to make you angry; I was only looking for your advice."

Uzo closed his eyes and took a deep breath, trying to calm himself while he thought. "Yes, my friend, I know. It is hard to forget how precious she is to me when I feel she is at risk of being hurt. You need to figure this out. If you love her then you love her. If you love Aurora, then you can't tempt Etani anymore. It's that simple. I know it's hard when you are tempted with the simplicity of the love and beauty of Aurora, but is that going to be enough for you? If you leave Etani for Aurora and then get bored of Aurora, Etani would not forgive you."

"I can't leave someone who's not mine, Uzo."

Uzo snarled, slamming his fist down on the table. "You know

perfectly well she was yours! She would have decimated this world for you! She wouldn't let a single man who wasn't either you, me, or Kai anywhere near her, and you have the audacity to say she wasn't yours?!"

Versalis flinched, staring with wide eyes at the man.

"She would have done anything to have you claim her as yours, she couldn't ask you because she was scared this exact situation would happen," Uzo growled, forcing himself to calm. "She was just waiting for you, and you were too blind to see it. And now you've found yourself a replacement because it's too hard to wait for her. You're a coward and you're weak. Letari was wrong, you don't deserve her."

"I didn't know she was waiting for me! I didn't want to press her while she was recovering!" Versalis yelled, his anger and resentment exploding out of him. "I loved that woman to the ends of the earth, but not once did I feel like she wanted me!"

"No ..." Uzo said sarcastically. "No, how dare she not throw herself at you after being raped, impregnated and then having her child beaten out of her! How inconsiderate of her to not beg you to try and love her."

There was that same cold violence in the Fae that had blinded Jaia for a week. The two men stared at each other.

"I did everything I could to make her feel safe, I wanted nothing from her but for her to feel loved and secure so she could process what that bastard had done to her, and start to feel normal again. That's it. I didn't expect anything, I didn't want to ask anything of her. I just wanted her to be safe and feel loved."

"And in the process, you missed her asking for you to want her. You completely ignored all of her attempts, and now you can run off with your sweet, innocent Aurora and leave Etani in our hands. We at least will take care of her."

"That's not fair, Uzo. I made it my life to take care of her."

"What do you want? A medal? A pat on the back? Good job,

Versalis; you took care of a mentally and physically abused woman because you felt like you had to."

"I didn't feel like I had to! I did it because I wanted to help her!"

"And now you just abandon her for something easier!"

Versalis stood up, rage flooding through him.

Uzo jumped to his feet a breath after he did.

"There is nothing easy about this! There is nothing easy about trying to figure out if you are enough to keep her safe! There is nothing easy about loving her!"

That came out in the worst possible way and he screamed a curse.

"No, not for a man like you. The rest of us find it exceptionally easy to love her," Uzo said in a coldly hateful voice. "If you so much as look at Etani again, I will make sure no one ever finds what's left of you. Run along to your new love, Versalis. Stay away from Etani, she's too good for you."

VERSALIS HAD STALKED AWAY and spent the rest of the day with Aurora until Jason had come to find him and he bowed to the young Queen and left, angry and resentful that he would have to face Uzo again.

Uzo didn't so much as look up when he entered the room and stood in the corner, watching the Hunters as they set out the maps with Jaia.

Perhaps Jaia would be the man to talk to? The thought made his stomach turn, but unlike the rest of them, Jaia was the only man who might understand.

"We are almost there; I'd venture at a couple of days at the very most. Tomorrow, if we can push the issue harder. The men are on a rampage, your idea worked perfectly. Any chance to see that woman. What ... what does she look like?" the demon-masked man asked.

"Waist length black hair, huge blue eyes ... Like Jason's eyes but brighter, more vibrant. Full lips, a smoking body," Dirdos growled, making no effort to hide the effect her image had on him.

"Versalis explained it best last time," Daemon said.

"He can just wait until she's back," Versalis said, causing everyone to look up.

"What's wrong with you? You normally love to talk about her," Vincent said, glancing around the room at the sudden hostile anger.

"It's nothing, just worried. Let's get her back and you can stare at her all you like."

Jason appeared impatient as he looked back down, but Versalis saw the exchanged glance between Daemon and Uzo, both angry.

"Let's get her back, then we can all stare at her all we like. Really go full creepy," Vincent said, deciding to ignore the tension.

Jagum laughed. "Just imagine her expression when she walks in and we're all just silent and staring at her. I can already hear that little sound she makes when she gets weirded out."

Bast made a little squeaking sound in her throat and there was a hearty chuckle from the room, barring Versalis, Uzo, and Jason.

"Like the time she found that beetle on the back of the bathroom door and screamed bloody murder. I've never seen anyone so terrified in my life," Jagum said. "That poor door, Daemon almost blew it off the wall."

"Poor bug never saw it coming." Jaia sighed, making a squelching sound that the beetle had ended up as.

"Have you seen her spot a spider before? She climbed Dirdos and was sitting on his shoulders. I have no idea how she got up there, you're what? Three feet taller than her?"

"I don't know how she got there either. One second she was bending over to check the glue, and the next I am bleeding, and she's got her arms and legs around my head screaming in unintelligible Celestrial. I couldn't understand a bloody word she said, she was screaming so fast, and that accent ..."

"Accent?" Jason asked, amused but focused.

"The Celestrials have a weird accent that's really heavy when they get stressed. Think Thor and Loki, only more liquid and lighter, but ten times faster and screeched in your ear by a terrified woman."

"She's not a bug person, huh?"

"Not even slightly. She will happily pick through your intestines for the last strawberry and stitch up a wound, but bugs? Not a chance," Dirdos laughed, the rest of them joining in though Versalis remained silent.

"Gotta love that girl," Uzo said, delighting in the memory.

"She's supposed to be this amazing assassin, isn't she?" Jason asked, looking up from the stuffed map.

"Good enough that we're fielding offers from Alaric's rivals," Uzo said.

"Still?" Jaia asked.

"Yeah, she has a reputation for being particularly ruthless. Especially after what's his name? The one she gutted."

"She gutted someone after her services?"

They stepped out into blinding chaos as figures moved around them. It wasn't the concentrated patches of chaos of the last time where there were. This was wild fighting, and the numbers of those inside were swelling dramatically.

"He wanted her to kill a man's family but leave the man alive. Said he'd pay extra if she also got the infant. She slit him from groin to chin."

"That's what you get for asking a mythical to kill a child," Jason said admiringly.

"That's what you get," Uzo agreed.

"All right, so the plan right now is to flood the field with everyone that's left. Right now, we have about twenty normies on the inside who fell in. You were spot-on with eighty percent of your recommendations, Jaia, after that they went entirely random, and we've just been trying to chase them down and push it to move. It worked fairly well. We now have enough men that no matter where it goes, it'll be taking more of them in and narrowing down the field even further."

"So, hopefully only a few hours?"

"Yes, if things go well, it will be a matter of hours and we will be making a full assault on the place. Again, you will all be required. Get yourselves ready. You have two days at most. At least, two hours. Be prepared."

They dispersed, but Versalis lingered, his eyes on Jaia to the point where Jaia hesitated, looking confused.

"Can we talk?" Versalis asked.

Jaia went on alert but nodded, approaching, and pulling the chair up under him as he sat down.

"About what?" the vampire asked, unsure if he should trust the peace between them.

"I wanted to ask you some questions."

"Look, if this is about what I did ... I'm not going to talk about it, okay?" He made to stand up, but Versalis waved him down.

"It's not about that, Jaia; it's about Selene."

"Selene? Hey, all the more power to you, man. That woman's crazy. Crazy levels of crazy, she tried to burn all my underwear ... not even my clothes, just the underwear and all my black socks ... just the black ones ..."

"No, I ... really? That's weirdly specific."

"I know! I don't know what it was she had against my underwear and black socks, but ... anyway, what did you want to ask?" Jaia looked confused and for a moment, he saw the old, pre-abuse Jaia, no longer bitter and angry at himself.

"What were your thoughts leading up to your relationship with her?"

Jaia blinked at him, black eyes wary before he shrugged. "Is this about Aurora?"

"Partly, yes. Rumour mill working hard, then?"

"No, I overheard Uzo and Dirdos talking the other day. About as subtle as a brick to the face, those two."

Versalis grunted his agreement, frowning at the door.

"Do you want my honest opinion?" Jaia asked, wary and studying him.

"Yes," Versalis said.

"Don't do it." Versalis frowned, but Jaia held up his hands. "Ending up with Selene was my second ... no, third biggest mistake of my life. I get it, you're sad and alone, you don't have her there to light up your universe. You've lost your sun and you don't know what to do without it, and all the flowers are dying. It's horrible, it's devastating, and you're feeling desperate right about now."

Versalis could only nod, fascinated by the man's honesty.

"But the instant that woman comes back into this world, you will forget there is such a thing as a woman that isn't Etani. The very beat your eyes land on her, you will be hers. There are no ifs, no buts, you belong to her." He stabbed his finger down on the table, impressing his point. "The absolute moment you feel her presence, that's it. You are incapable of loving another woman and you will be angry; you will resent her for her perfection. You will do stupid shit, and you will lash out at her for breaking the world you created in her absence. You will blame her for existing and you will hurt her. You will not do what I did, but you will hurt her. Either by falling into Aurora's bed, or yelling at her, or both. And it is not your fault, it's not her fault, it simply is. You cannot *not* love her; it is physically impossible to not love Etani."

Versalis sat stumped, staring at the vampire who had betrayed her and yet was blindingly loyal to her. Jaia would destroy the world for her, it was blatantly clear, and that truth was somehow beautiful in its purity.

"From what I saw of your relationship with her before she died, you could have asked for the moon and she would have clawed it out of the sky and handed it to you on a silver platter. She may not be aware of the passage of time; she may still think we are at the lake. I don't know, it's impossible to tell until she's back. But if you leave her ... you will spend the rest of your existence wishing you could take it all back and do it right. You will wish you could be a decent man for her. But you can't take it back, you can *never* take it back.

"Right now, it might seem like Aurora is easier, something you no longer have to fight for. No longer have to deal with being the last one in the shower and you know why the shower isn't draining because she bent over yesterday. No longer have to deal with ten angry, resentful men who would literally rip you apart to be in your place. But it's not worth it, taking the easy option isn't going to make you happy. Maybe Aurora could, maybe you can go on to spend eternity with her making beautiful children and living happily ever after … But maybe you'll end up alone and never see your sun again, because she will have turned her back on you and be in love with another man who is too stupid to see it."

That last was a little on the bitter side and Versalis smiled, realising he was the other man who was too stupid to see it.

They were quiet for a time, considering their thoughts and staring down at the map without seeing it.

"What was the other biggest regret?" Versalis asked, pushing one of the pins deeper so that it was level with the others.

"Aside from the obvious? My second biggest regret was not begging her to marry me when I had the chance." Jaia sighed. "One day I simply hope she will be able to look me in the eyes again."

"I don't think she hates you. I think she simply doesn't understand," Versalis said, making the man snort in disgust.

"Spare me, Versalis, I'm not an idiot."

"No, you're not. But hear me out. Think about what she has gone through since she came to Ayathian. The men who have stalked her, some literally stalking her. Think about the picture she has in her head. Then there's you, the one she would have clawed the moon out of the sky for before she turned away. You're so caught up in self-pity, you never stopped to simply try and make it up to her."

Jaia's face twisted in anger; Versalis shook his head.

"No, not like Dainin, or begging her or anything like that. But talk to her, she's more animal than human, she'd probably understand more than you realise if you just explain what had happened and why it happened. She understands rage, lust ... she doesn't understand you, though, because you won't give her the chance to understand. You turned your back on her, too, while you curled up into your little ball of self-hatred.

"I mean, all that can happen is she lashes out at you, and you have the scars for a few weeks, but they will be a visible show that you are trying to be the man she once saw you as. She would have ripped all the worlds to shreds for you just to have you look in her direction. Just to have you smile at anything, so long as she could see it. You were the man she chose over everyone else, and you stepped over the line so far that the line was erased. Now you have to see if you can draw it back in the sand and see if she will try and erase it again. You may have your pride, Jaia, but if you set that aside, you might have her look at you again."

Jaia was silent, staring at him with lips turned down into a frown of confusion and pain.

"I will ... I'll try, Versalis. If you truly love Aurora, then it will be like Hunter. You will love her, but you will always keep one eye on Etani, just in case. But you will still love Aurora more."

Versalis nodded, letting out a sigh as Jaia stood, clapped him on the shoulder, and left the room.

He remained sitting for a short time and then stood, following the vampire out and setting about preparing for the fight to bring Etani back from death.

CHAPTER 18
BACK UNDERGROUND

The following day there was no news from the Hunters, and they got ready, all their gear prepared and loaded for when the call came. Now it was just a matter of waiting for that call, and it seemed to be taking forever.

Taking advantage of the time he had left, he hunted down Aurora, and she was delighted to see him, though her delight faded somewhat at his grimness.

He had kept her informed of all that was happening and so she knew what it meant if he came to her looking like that. She excused herself from the Court and they slipped away together, into the garden and the privacy they had been lacking for the whole time he had been there.

As soon as they were alone, he pressed her into a tree and kissed her with a burning passion, ignoring everything Jaia had told him, ignoring the rage that had come from his best friend who now hated him, ignoring his own misgivings, and kissing the beautiful Queen.

"Are you afraid?" she whispered, breaking the kiss only long enough to look up at him, her eyes wide and fearful for him.

"Yes. I do not know if we will all return," he said, and her lip trembled.

To stop it, he kissed her again, and she clung to him, desperate and afraid. He was just as desperate and afraid, crushing the woman to him and he flushed as she felt his passion for her culminating in blood rushing to his groin.

"Apologies," he said gruffly, moving back from her and turning his back on her while he tried to focus on something else.

Her hand was gentle on his shoulder, and he glanced back, her lips parted and glistening with their saliva. "Don't be sorry," she whispered, and to his surprise, she stepped around in front of him, her hand trailing over his shoulder.

He growled when she kissed him, a slow and burning kiss that both scared and aroused him more than he was willing to admit.

This woman was tempting, incredibly so, and he was torn between his desire for the woman before him, and the duty he felt to Etani.

She kissed him like he hadn't been kissed before and he leant into it, hungry and wanting more of the sweet taste of her.

"I want you ..." she whispered, and a bolt of electricity shot through his system, fear, adrenaline, and desire.

Turning her, he pressed her back up against the tree and the kiss grew passionate.

He was afraid, so afraid, and that was his reasoning when he reached down and bundled up the mass of her dress, her cold legs soft under his rough hands.

She shivered when he dragged his fingers up her thighs, her own hands going to his chest and tugging the buttons of his shirt free, though she didn't stop at just his shirt.

"Do you ... right here?" he asked, barely able to form a coherent sentence when she reached down the front of his slacks and grasped him.

"Right here," she demanded, her fingers cool and wonderfully skilled on him.

He didn't stop to think about it, the delicate fabric of her under-garments tearing as he pulled them down and then he gripped the backs of her thighs, lifting her up off the ground.

He was inside her in a matter of seconds, his mouth heavy on hers to smother her beautiful cry of pleasure. She felt like nothing he had ever experienced, and he clutched her to him, her legs tight around his middle and her body moving with him as he thrust into her with a fierce need.

It had been so long since he had touched a woman, been inside a woman, and he revelled in the feeling, relishing every stroke of her insides against him.

He moaned her name, attempting to keep quiet, but it was impossible when she felt so wonderful, her experience making her aware exactly what they both needed to be satisfied, and he found his release too quickly for his liking, panting against her shoulder while she made small, happy little sounds in his ear.

She was so soft, so delicate, and gentle, and he had been a brute to fuck her up against a tree like that. She deserved so much better than that, and yet, she had wanted him just as much as he wanted her. She had agreed, even if it made him feel like a savage.

She untangled herself from him and drew him down onto the frozen ground, his arms protective around her as he settled against the tree with her at his side.

"I may be falling in love with you," she said after a long pause, smirking as he tugged his pants back up into place and tied them, just in case someone were to see them there.

"I already know I am," he said with a slow breath, turning to kiss her startled face.

"Are you teasing me?" she asked.

"Not at all, my darling Aurora," he purred, nuzzling her jaw and tracing kisses along the silken skin. "I love you very deeply."

She gave a sob and he shifted, alarmed that he had said the wrong thing.

"No one... has ever said that to me before," she whimpered, and he pulled her into his lap, hushing her tears with smothering kisses all over her face until she was no longer crying, but instead laughing and trying to twist away from him.

"Well, I love you. I love you, and I think you are wonderful, and beautiful, and perfect," he said, kissing her lips with each part of her he described.

"Will you come back to me?" she whispered, fear filling her once more.

"I will come back to you, when all is said and done, I will be at your side," he said, a twist in his stomach telling him it was likely not going to be that easy.

"I love you, Versalis," she whispered.

"I love you, too, Aurora," he murmured and growled as her small hands reached for his pants, tugging them down and away from him.

It took only a few gentle strokes of her fingers and her mouth on his to have him swelling again and she straddled him, impatient and needy as she lowered herself onto him.

He allowed the beauty to control her own pleasure, her perfect face revealing every tiny emotion that passed through her and he kissed her, greedy for her.

She moved atop him, beautiful and radiant in her pleasure and he tilted his head to trace his lips over the curve of her breasts, intensely focusing on the soft flesh to keep himself from releasing again so soon.

It was half relief, half pleasure when she found her release and he pulled her against him, biting her lower lip gently to make her shiver, and he growled as he released once more inside her.

He knew the risks, of course; their love could lead to unexpected consequences, but right then he didn't care so long as she was happy and he could love her freely.

He could only hope that he could come back to her; he wanted more time with her, more of a chance to love her and be loved by her.

Remaining still for a time, they finally heard the call of 'Your Majesty!' and scrambled to fix their clothes, Aurora grinning wickedly and stuffing her undergarments into his pocket before she ran off, and he couldn't get the thought of her having nothing on under that dress out of his mind.

It was a delicious thought, and it stayed with him all the way back to his room with the others lingering around looking bored.

Dirdos looked at him, eyes narrowed, but Versalis went for the bathroom and took a shower, the undergarments hidden away behind the sink so that he could relish them later.

Washing off her scent, he found himself smiling for the first time in months, a real smile and not one brought on by laughter.

He was in love, and the one he loved was so beautiful and wonderful and kind, and just so ... Aurora.

Sighing, he showered and dressed, stuffing his clothes into the bottom of the hamper to help mask the scent of her skin and pleasure.

It took several hours before the Hunters were ready and then Jason arrived, his shark grin wide as he held out his arms to the group.

They were armed to the teeth, ready for another war against the Gods.

"They're ready for us. If we all make it out, it'll be a miracle," Jason said, and Versalis noted with a start while that the Hunters were immortal, the rest of them weren't quite so fortunate.

"She'll drag us back kicking and screaming," Daemon said, but Versalis exchanged a look with Jaia.

"Right, you, vampire boy, are staying here," Jason said to Jaia.

"Like hell I'm staying here. I am going to help."

"You're breakable and I don't want her to be pissed at me for getting one of you killed."

"I'm not staying."

"Fine, but you all saw me trying to get him to stay." Jason

pointed around at the rest of them. "I tried to make him stay here, but he refused. She can't be angry at me."

"She can, she will, and she'll get over it," Uzo said, looking back down at the map and the rather neat little circle they had made with the placement of the entrance.

"We're going to get her this time. I can feel it," Jason said, leaning both hands on the table.

"What about after we get her out of the chest?"

"We'll figure that out once we have her. I have no way of knowing what he has done to her until I get some real time looking at the heart. Now the problem is, Anubis is going to be angry, so we are going to have to get in and out as fast as possible. Get the heart, get out again. Agreed?"

They all nodded, anxiety growing between them.

No one was tempted enough to think that they would all make it back in one piece, but they hoped it.

"All right, men, same as last time ... don't die," Jason said, and Dirdos snorted, shaking his head before they all linked hand to shoulder and the world vanished.

Versalis was glad he got the chance to farewell the Queen, for as he stepped out onto the deadlands and looked around at the sheer mass of forms around him, he wasn't sure he was going to survive.

There were thousands of them, more. There were at least ten thousand of them, possibly twice that and they were all hooded, all masked and all itching to get moving.

"Say hello to the Hunters," Jason said gleefully, as though he had created every one of them. In a way, he knew them all, given he had created every single mask for them.

Jason's eyes found him, and the man blinked once and then grinned, amused by something he must see, but there was no time to discuss it.

"Ready!" a booming call came out, and they all turned to the single opening several feet ahead of them.

"All right, men! Let's get ourselves a Goddess!" Jason called in response, and someone must have moved because there was a disturbing ripple that flicked across the field, the air warping for a second, and then the ground split in the middle of the open space.

A cheer went out and the mass of beings flooded into the opening, some jumping down into it, others running in while still others vanished. Jason decided to follow the latter and with a wild, feral grin at them, the world vanished once more.

"SNEAKY BASTARDS ... THEY HAVE SOLDIERS," Dirdos said, looking down as a ghoul ran at him.

The dragon stepped forward and kicked the ghoul, sending it flying back into three fellows.

"Clever," Jason said, amused and delighted by the show of power.

Who had called the ghouls was anyone's guess, but there were thousands of them. Drooling, streaking, screaming monsters who ate flesh, usually only dead flesh though.

"What happens if a Hunter gets eaten?" Daemon asked, but Uzo looked around, realisation dawning on him at the question.

"What would happen if Etani ate one of you?"

Jason's smile faded as he contemplated the question, uncertain of the answer.

"I don't know ... I'm sure we can find a volunteer, though," he said, his brows drawn together in a frown.

Shaking his head, he let the subject go for the time being as more and more Hunters flooded into the place, all heading for the temple above.

The only problem was, they didn't get past the first two steps before they were blasted backwards by a ripple of golden light.

"Well, that's inconvenient," Versalis said, looking up as the ripple swirled over the temple and out of sight.

"Is that a shield?" Jason asked.

"Looks that way," Daemon said, unconsciously holding off a ghoul and stabbing it in the skull, all without looking away from the temple.

"Well shit ..." Jason said. "We weren't expecting that."

"Can we get around it?" Versalis asked.

"Oh yeah, it's just going to take time. I'll get the others, stay here."

Jason vanished, and they were left looking around awkwardly, the Hunters ripping into the ghouls, and then having to go back to kill them again.

Men appeared nearby, looking around at them and then heading in the direction of the temple with determined strides.

In total there were nineteen of them, including Jason, Neah, and the demon-masked man. Aside from those three, Versalis could see one with a black cat mask that had white markings and another whose mask split in half at the middle, with huge gold eyes. The rest were too far away to see well. But Versalis noted that unless one didn't see the eyes, it was impossible to tell the magic breakers from the normal Hunters, and the fact disturbed him more than he was willing to admit.

"This might take a while," a voice said from just behind their backs, and Versalis turned to see Hades standing behind them, arms crossed and watching the Hunters work.

"What are you doing here?" Daemon asked.

"Same as you, I want to see her out of there. She's not a pet, she shouldn't be caged up like that. I think we only need to get a deal out of her, one that lasts through death."

"Is it possible to do that?" Jaia asked.

"Yes, you only have to agree to it, or acknowledge past deals. Why were you fighting last time?" Daemon asked.

"Because I want to keep an eye on things from the inside. He has her back up in the tower, but it is booby-trapped to be dumped into the river if the chest is disturbed at all. You will need to get someone either under there, or else you will need to disassemble the trap. If you say you saw me, I will deny it. I'm on the side of the Gods," he said in a flat tone, glaring around at them all before he vanished into a flare of blue fire.

"He's such a cheerful man," Uzo said.

"He wants her out, too? Why?" Versalis asked.

"Who knows with the Gods? They attach to random things all the time. He might simply like her," Daemon said.

THE HOURS TICKED by and the ghouls were annoying, but easy to deal with so long as they damaged the brain. Versalis thought the creatures nothing more than a distraction to keep them busy, and more than anything, they were just getting bored. Sitting around, staring up at the red sky, or around at the red rocks, or down at the blood-stained rocks.

"Should have brought a deck of cards ..." Dirdos sighed, sitting on the ground with his elbows on his knees, staring around aimlessly.

"Are your wars always this boring?" Jagum asked, sharpening the points of his bone claw for the millionth time.

"Generally, yes, there is a lot of standing around waiting," Versalis said, scratching his jaw.

The shield still looked the same, except that it was now blood red instead of gold. Otherwise, there was no change in it at all, still fully intact and stubborn.

"We could go bowling ... use a head to knock down some legs?" Daemon suggested.

There was a pause, then they all moved to scrounge up some legs with the feet still attached, set them up and then start rolling the head.

The head did not like rolling, and after the first few tries, it became a game of seeing who could simply throw the head at the legs, and eventually who could hit a moving ghoul with another's leg.

"Do you think Etani would be disappointed in us?" Versalis asked, taking careful aim at a shambling ghoul with only one foot.

"I think she'd be more ashamed at how bad we are at it ..." Daemon said, the leg missing by about three feet.

"Legs are not aerodynamic," Dirdos complained, picking up a head and throwing it. The ghoul fell over as it was beaned in the head by the other head. "Point to me!"

"That doesn't count, you cheated," Jagum complained, his arms crossed.

Looking around at a sudden screaming sound, they watched as first one, then a second of the magic breakers collapsed into a heap.

Jason and Neah were backing up, waving their hands in front of them as though they had walked into a spider web and were trying to break the threads.

"Has anyone ...?" Dirdos said, and then sighed, rubbing his eyes, and turning so that he was looking sideways at the temple.

Twisting his wrist, Versalis watched as that tiny flame he had once used to transfix Etani bloomed into a raging inferno in his hand, and he took three steps and then threw the flaming ball in an overarm pitch towards the temple.

"Son of a bitch ..." Jason snarled, looking around at Dirdos as the shield exploded.

"Overcomplicating everything ..." Daemon sighed.

There was a pause and then everyone surged for the temple, the ever-silent Sebastian throwing down the leg he had been holding and sprinting towards it.

It took the rest of them a second and then they went after him, running full pelt for the temple doors and shoving their way past the fighting men.

They were inside, finally they were inside, but that only started up a whole new challenge for the Hunters and the men from Ayathian.

CHAPTER 19
THE HEART

The temple had changed, the room that housed the heart the first time, along with the four Gods, was replaced by an enormous pit that plummeted straight down to the river below, which had swollen to the size of a lake.

The chest was suspended by two wires that weren't even attached to the chest, simply looped down under it, and attached to the walls at either end. The wires weren't overly strong either.

Jason growled as he looked up at the thing, twenty feet above them and in the middle of a large room that would likely take twenty paces to cross.

"Where's a telekinetic when you need one?" Jason asked.

There was a ledge of about five feet all around the edge, and it allowed them to pile in, looking around curiously. Across from the entrance Anubis stood, amused, and watched them all as they lined the walls, eyes upturned to the chest that looked as though a brisk breeze would knock it down.

"I want my wife back, dog God," Neah called, angry and glaring.

"Well, if you are incapable of controlling your wife, you should not be married," Anubis said back conversationally.

189

"I don't think there is a man alive who is capable of controlling Etani," Jagum said with an exhale.

"I'd be willing to try," Jason said, making Neah growl.

"Trust me, I'll make sure you never get the chance," Neah snapped back.

"Now, now, boys. There's no need to fight over her, she's not coming back unless we need her," Anubis said.

"What constitutes 'needing her?'" Daemon called out.

"Not sure yet. I'll figure it out, though."

"I'd say good plan, but your plan is just waiting until things get bad enough and then throwing her into it after she's been asleep and raging for a few hundred years. I can see that going oh so well."

"She will be entirely within our control," the dog snapped.

"Will she, though?" Daemon asked, looking up at the chest.

"Yes she will, or she goes into the river."

Looking down into the depths below, Versalis chewed idly on the inside of his cheek as he considered the size of the hole, the God, and the chest above. Odds weren't great that they were going to be able to get to it, but they all knew they had to try. They needed to get her back.

Versalis felt a moment of shame as he realised that his need to get her back was mostly because she was important to the others, and less to do with his own desperate need to be at her side.

It wasn't a proud thought, but it was there.

"How the hell are we going to get that down?" Daemon demanded, staring up at it.

"Can we get mages down there and drop her?" Demon-mask asked.

"I thought that, too, but it's a risk," Jason said, staring upwards.

"We can't lose her..." Dirdos growled.

"We need to keep Anubis occupied; he might just dump her into the river if we get too close. Vincent, we need a grapple," Neah said, his black eyes locked on the chest.

"We'll get the dog. Dirdos," Daemon said.

The dragon nodded and turned to the dog, the same flame appearing in his fingers. Versalis watched as the tall man threw the ball of fire at the God and Anubis ducked, clearly not thinking they would attack him.

Dirdos grinned and went after Anubis with Daemon following after, Versalis looking around as Vincent appeared again.

He hadn't even noticed the man had vanished.

Neah took the enormous crossbow and lifted it, pointing it upwards and frowning before he pulled the trigger.

The grapple shot upwards and thudded hard into the stone above. Neah nodded and unhooked the rope, giving it a hard tug. It seemed to be sturdy enough. Offering the end of the rope to three normies, he hooked his shin around it and climbed up with the three normies digging in their heels and a fourth coming to help keep the rope steady.

"Be careful," Jason called out, but Versalis wasn't at all happy that it was Neah who would be the one to rescue her. Bad enough that it was one of the Hunters at all, but the one who had abused her? She wasn't going to be very happy. At least she would be alive and unhappy.

"Has anyone stopped to think about what is going to happen once you get her out of the chest?" the man with the black cat mask asked, his voice a silken purr and eyes a liquid bronze colour. A shock of blue-black hair was a wild tangle around his head.

"What do you mean?" Jaia asked, his head tilted back to scowl up at Neah.

"Well... What are you going to do with the heart? Do you stab it? Does she regrow from it? Will it vanish? What will you do if she needs to regrow from it? She will be vulnerable. You'll have to get her out of here immediately. Where are you going to hide her? Will you all go with her to protect her? Won't that make it easy to find you all?"

Versalis looked down at the man and Jaia looked around as well, both men frowning as they considered the questions.

"We get her out and take her back to the compound. We can hide her in one of the tunnels until we figure it out. It might be that she will simply reform. If there are no signs of regrowth, we destroy it," Jason said, those eerie blue eyes locked on the chest with a possessiveness that made Versalis frown. Even dead, she had that hold on him?

Neah was just above the chest and he looked down at it, frowning as he wrapped his legs around the rope, ankles twisted together in a way he was certain he had seen Etani do.

Leaning backwards, he smiled faintly as he reached for the first lock.

Versalis felt nothing; she didn't come raging into him or stir at all and Versalis frowned, staring at the chest.

Perhaps Anubis had her under a stronger hold this time; it seemed likely, but still it made him nervous.

The lock snapped free and Neah pulled the chain loose, dropping it, and it plummeted down into the water below. His hands found the second lock and he felt her shifting, a small frown on her lips as she felt the sleep on her melting away.

He could hear the others talking, but he was listening hard to the sound of her, that steady beat starting up as Neah pulled the lock free.

Her eyes opened and she looked at him, confused and content in her warm place.

"Versalis?" she asked through his lips as she reached for him, but as his eyes turned to a soft oaf, her smile was wicked. "Front looks as good as the back," she murmured seductively, Jason's eyebrows lifting.

"Pardon?"

"Hello..." she growled and Versalis could feel a wave of hunger he had never known before. It was more than sexual, it was a mingled bloodlust, sexual tension, and the need to sink his teeth into the man that had blood rushing to his groin.

"Is now really the time?" Jaia snapped, irritated by her carnal interest in the man.

Jason was eyeing him with a keen interest, his head tilted to the side.

"Don't be jealous, Jaia, you had your turn," she said, and her interest shifted as Versalis looked up at a rattle. "Well, well... Wouldn't it be a shame if he fell...?" her grin turned feral. "Quick, someone jiggle the rope."

Neah growled, glaring down at him.

"It's Etani." Jaia sighed, and the two Hunters blinked, and then Neah glared while Jason grinned.

"Where was this attitude when I had you in my rooms?" Neah grumbled as he pulled the chain free and dropped it.

"Where was this ingenuity?" she countered, considering the position of the man.

He grunted a response and reached down to open the locks, opening the chest, and then blinked.

"Umm... It's empty."

"What?" Jason snapped.

Neah grabbed the edge of the chest and tilted it, giving it a rattle, but nothing at all moved; it was indeed empty.

"So, where am I and why can I...?" She cut off as pain rippled through her body, a vivid red slash appearing across her chest. "What is he doing?" She gasped, her hands lifting to touch the slash and coming away scarlet. "How can I bleed here, I'm dead?!"

"Etani?" Jaia asked.

"He's doing something to my heart. I think he's trying to destroy it."

"Where?" Jason demanded, grabbing Versalis' arm and shaking him hard.

"I don't know, I can't—"

Versalis screamed at her pain and a large hole appeared in her chest, his voice cracking, and he would have fallen had Jason not grabbed his arm.

"Where are you, damn it, woman!?" Jason roared and Versalis watched her. Her eyes were unfocused, staring up at nothing.

"Do you think it would hurt to die …?" she asked in a distant voice, her lips parted, and he was horrified to see the hole in her chest spreading.

"You're not dying! Where?!"

"I am underground, in a cave … it's hot and I can hear moving water," she breathed. "I don't want to die …"

"Neah!" Jason yelled, and the Hunter vanished from the rope above them, returning several minutes later.

"I see a few caves that match the description. Let's go, men!" the black-eyed Hunter roared.

"I'm going to find you. Don't you worry," Jason promised, and she looked at him through Versalis' eyes, confused and hurting.

"Hurry … I can't hold on," she whimpered, and the man growled, vanishing from before them. "Versalis, I'm scared …"

"It's going to be okay," Jaia said, and she nodded, wanting so badly to believe him.

VERSALIS STOOD FROZEN, gasping for air as her pain radiated through him, and he couldn't understand how she could be so calm, but then he had to assume she could barely feel anything now, just pain.

"Someone's here," she whispered, her head turning to the side though she couldn't see anything, and she sucked in a breath, her body seeming to squeeze as though she were being crushed inwards.

She reached out for someone, but he couldn't see what it was, she couldn't see what it was, she could only feel something around her, and it was warm and tight.

"I …" She shivered and looked down at her chest as the red mark faded and she looked up at Versalis. "Someone has me!" she cried through his voice.

"Thank you, Mother …" Jaia sighed.

"Not out of the woods yet," Versalis growled as she faded from his awareness to focus on what was happening.

Jason dropped into existence and spun, panting.

"We have to go, now! I can't get her out!" he lifted his hand and in it he held the still thudding heart.

They were all frozen, staring down at it in horrified fascination.

"How ...?" Versalis asked.

"He was getting another pin and while he was looking away, I just snatched it out of his hand and ran for it."

Jaia laughed and looked around as Daemon and Dirdos appeared in the doorway, looking around in confusion.

"We have to hide her here. I can't get her out," Jason yelled at the two.

Daemon growled and looked around at Versalis.

"I have an idea. You come with me. Jaia, you stay here with demon-mask. Vincent, you and Dainin go with them. You can hide her until she has reformed, we can go to the human world and try to draw Anubis to us. We'll come up with something, but we need to split up."

They nodded in agreement and the group split up, Jason handing the heart reluctantly to the demon-masked man and Versalis saw that it had changed, building upon itself, her arteries extending further with each passing second.

"Let's go!" Jason cried, and they all huddled together, only to stagger apart again as the God appeared, his eyes finding Jason.

"Come here, little thief," the God growled, and Jason vanished, his hand stuffed under his shirt as though he had the heart on him still.

Anubis snarled and vanished with him, leaving the rest of them alone again.

"Quickly, go," Daemon said to the demon-masked man, and he nodded, grabbing the others, and the lot of them vanished.

"We should have asked where they were going," Dirdos snarled, anxiety coming off him in waves.

"It's best if we don't. We need to keep Anubis busy once he figures out Jason doesn't have it."

"Where are the other Gods?" Jaia asked.

"Watching to see how things turn out, I expect," Daemon growled. "At this point it's more entertaining to watch rather than get involved."

"Don't they care?" Versalis snapped, her attention focused on what was happening to her heart.

"Yes, but they enjoy the games we are playing. At this point it's likely they will only interfere if they think we are going to fail."

"I'm not sure if I should be glad if they stay away, then, or not ..." Versalis grumbled.

"Come on, you lot, let's go." Dirdos sighed and stepped closer to them, the world vanishing.

CHAPTER 20

THE GODDESS OF DESTRUCTION

Versalis was immensely relieved when they were dumped out onto the field where she had died, though the location wouldn't have been his first choice.

Her blood no longer stained the ground, it had been washed away by the rain, but there was something pained about the area that had nothing to do with their own feelings.

Magic had tainted that place many times now, leaving it marred in some way that they couldn't see as much as simply feel.

He felt her shifting, looking around at him as her focus moved from the events surrounding her heart and where they were, his lungs expanding as she took in the scent of the grass.

"She's awake," Versalis said as she looked around through his eyes, and then reached out for him.

She smiled faintly as she touched his mind and then recoiled so violently that he felt his head tilt sideways and he staggered, nearly falling.

"I see ..." she said through his mouth, and he knew with a terrible sense of dread that she had seen his relationship with Aurora, the love he had for her that overrode the love he had for Etani herself.

She saw it, and he saw the way her eyes changed as she looked at him. She hadn't felt it before, only speaking through him, but now she had seen.

"Etani?" Daemon cried, grabbing his shoulders, and shaking him.

"Yes, Daemon, I'm here," she murmured, her tone guarded and wary.

"What's the matter?" he demanded, glaring down at him.

"Things have changed," she said simply. "It does not matter; do you have me?"

"Yes, but we are trying to buy time for you to reform. We are going to come up with a distraction," Daemon said, and she made a soft sound of agreement.

"Look around, Versalis, where are you?" He obeyed her command, and she made a sound of amusement. "We come full circle so often ... what kind of distraction?"

"Anything. We need to get Anubis up here."

"Very well, I will distract him," she said, and Daemon's face went white.

"No ... no, Etani don't do anything!" he gasped, terrified.

"She's gone," Versalis said, fear flooding him as he felt her looking at him for a long moment, her anger at his betrayal. "I didn't mean to," he whispered, knowing she wouldn't care if it had been intended or not. She turned away from him, reproachful. "I love her."

Daemon hissed, understanding the tone of her voice.

She shook her head, refusing to so much as look at him, and he felt it the instant the thought settled into her mind, the thought of him and Aurora together, their love and passion. Pain ripped through him so violently that he gasped, her pain and his doubling him over until he couldn't breathe but he also felt her rage at his actions and the slowly returning memories of what had happened.

She was growing reckless; wanting to punish, and when Etani wanted to punish, Etani killed.

She didn't kill this time, though, instead she melted down into a liquid state and appeared on the other side of the conjoined worlds of Faerie and the humans, her brows drawn up and her lower lip pulled in as she tried to contain her pain.

Versalis looked up, watching with a horrified fascination as the sky above them shifted.

Clouds parted as her fingers found the surface of the world, pushing the clouds away, and they formed a perfect oval that was her finger dipping in.

To their right the ground buckled as her fingers dug into the ground and everyone screamed. Several miles away, a second oval formed in the clouds to show the clear blue of the sky. She was gripping the world and, with her other hand, she slid her fingertips in under the cover of Faerie.

"Don't do this ..." he pleaded with her, knowing she was angry and hurt, devastated by what she had found in his mind. She had trusted him to be there when she returned, and he belonged to another woman. He had been hers when she left, but now he was Aurora's.

He heard her screaming pain as her rage boiled over and she tore at the two worlds, trying to pry them apart.

THE WORLD SHUDDERED and everyone staggered, Hunters appearing all over the field and looking up at the places where her fingers cleared the sky.

"What is she doing?" Jason yelled over the cries of fear, Versalis not even vaguely aware of when he had arrived.

"Destroying the worlds!" Daemon yelled back. "Because that pig couldn't keep his dick in his pants!"

Versalis growled at the comment, his attention half focused on her as she pulled and tugged at Faerie, and to his utter horror, he saw it coming apart as though glue was separating.

A wave of nausea hit him and he heaved, but nothing came out.

Many Hunters weren't so lucky and several were screaming, clutching their heads.

"Make her stop!" Daemon screamed, but he didn't know how to make her stop. She was going to kill millions because she was jealous and angry at everyone for treating her like a tool.

No, she didn't deserve it, but the reaction was too much.

"You're in control of her magic ..." Anubis growled from behind them and Versalis spun to look up at the God. "Fix it or I will permanently fix it."

"I don't know how to stop her, she's upset."

"That's not my problem."

"It is your problem! You did this to her, too!" Daemon snapped, wiping the bile from his mouth.

"See if you can get her back, we'll talk to her. You're clearly incapable of doing anything right," Uzo said, moving forward with a greenish tinge to his face.

"Etani, Uzo wants to talk to you," he said, but she only shook her head, her face a mixture of anguish and anger. "Etani, please listen. You're hurting everyone."

She looked up at him, her eyes blazing.

"You're the one who hurts me, Versalis!" she screamed through him. "You were supposed to be there for me, but you left!"

"Etani!" Uzo cried, shoving Daemon out of the way to get before Versalis.

"Shut up! You shut up, Uncle! I'm done with this world, and you, Anubis ... I'm going to skin you and make you into a coat!"

"Etania Daewen, you listen to me right now, young lady!" Uzo snapped, and she jerked back, eyes huge at his tone. "You will cut this out right now!"

"You can't tell me what to do, Uzo," she growled, her eyes narrowing on him as he opened his mouth but then shut it again, fuming.

"Etani ... Etani you have to stop," Daemon wheezed, still on the ground.

"Why? Why should I give any of you anything?" she demanded. "All I ever wanted was to live my life, one that *you* decided would be this one. But I can't even do that now! Not unless I separate the worlds and you can all go live in Faerie where you belong!"

"Control her!" Anubis raged.

"Versalis isn't man enough to control me now," she snapped.

Anger burned inside him, and he turned his eyes to Daemon who was glaring up at him.

"Fix it," the demon snarled.

"Etani, stop," Versalis said, and she glared at him, her fingers digging harder into the worlds.

"Go die in a fire, Versalis," she growled back.

"Etani. Stop this right now!" he yelled, and she closed her eyes, her face twitching to the side as she tried to shake his control off her.

It wasn't working; he was crushing her will, and they both knew it. This was what Hades had warned her about, letting another control any aspect of her magic meant they could control her. She had never expected it to end like this, though.

"Let's see how we can deal with you ..." she breathed, and the worlds snapped back together with enough force that their ears popped and Uzo cried out in relief.

She was gone from his mind, pulling up and away from him to leave him empty. He didn't trust it, knew better than to trust it, but had no idea what to expect.

"Where is she?" Uzo asked, and Versalis looked down to see his nose was bleeding.

"I don't know, she's up to something, I just don't know what."

"Jason, go see if the others need help with her heart," Daemon ordered, and the struggling man nodded, stepping sideways out of reality.

IT WAS ONLY A SECOND LATER when the air shimmered a few feet before the group of them, and she was there. It was not the Etani they knew but a different version of her, and she was more dangerous than beautiful.

She looked both different and the exact same, those large, blue eyes wide and glittering, her lips parted in the faintest hint of a smile that was both mischievous and feral, but also amused at his shock.

Her hair floated up around her as though she were under water, shifting and rolling in constant motion, and it took him a moment to realise she was on a level with his eyes, her body curved, and she was floating almost a foot from the grass, her feet crossed at the ankle.

"Etani ..." Daemon breathed in a shocked whisper, all of their eyes turning on her, but she was focused on Versalis.

She wore a tight black dress that trailed up over her right shoulder in a twist, flowing down her like liquid to just below her knees. It didn't look like any fabric he had ever seen.

"Hello." She sighed, her eyes trailing down his face to his lips and then down to his chest before she peeked over her shoulder to the demon who had whispered her name.

The Demon moved unconsciously, wanting nothing more than to go to her, but her eyes had already left him and returned to Versalis, focusing on his lips before her face shifted in irritation and her eyes met his.

"You are trying to control me," she said, her tone suggesting it was a stupid, wasted effort.

"You need to be stopped," he said, watching as her face flickered with anger and then settled into a teasing, seductive smile.

He could almost see the thoughts as she hid her anger and turned on the charm to convince him to let her do what she wanted, and had he not been scared out of his mind, he would have found it endearing.

"Versalis ... why?" she asked him, her voice revealing her petulance more than her pouting lips. "Why won't you let me be happy?"

"Will destroying the worlds make you happy?" he asked, and he was fascinated when the emotions flashed over her face. She had never been so easy to read before.

"You both need to be punished," she hissed, her eyes lighting with righteous anger and her hair flowing upwards around her, seeming to respond to her fury.

"I know, but you will kill millions to punish the few."

She didn't like that he was making sense, and her lips turned down, eyelids lowering as she planned her next tactic.

"You love me, don't you?" she asked in a little girl's voice, the sound of it sending a jolt through him. He wanted so badly to give her what she wanted, even if it meant the end of the world.

"You know I do," he said, his insides quivering as he tried to resist the need to do whatever it was she wanted.

"Then give me this," she demanded.

"Etani, what are you doing?" Dirdos growled, and her face darkened, her head rolling in his direction, and he saw her anger that was gone in a flash.

"Shut up," she said.

Eyes returning to Versalis, she lifted up higher from the ground, her face only an inch from his.

"Versalis ... I want this," she whispered.

It was so hard to fight the urge to give her whatever it was she wanted. He wanted to give in, and only part of that was her trying to force him into submission.

"No, Etani," Versalis said. "You need to stop this now and come back to us."

"Why?" she asked, her tone suggesting she was actually uncertain, even if she was smiling at him.

"We need you back," he said.

Her brows lifted and her lips parted to speak, but then she looked annoyed. "You don't need me back, Versalis, I no longer matter to you," she said, her words stinging his heart.

"You matter to the others," he said, and she looked first at Daemon, and then at Uzo.

"Is Letari screaming?" she asked quietly, the Fae's face darkening in his pain.

"Yes, her and Kai. Hunter is with them."

"Did they marry yet?" she asked. "He and Letari?"

"No, they wanted to wait for you," Versalis forced out, drawing her eyes back to him.

"That is nice. Do you think they will have babies?"

"Yes, probably."

"They would make pretty babies ..." she murmured as she turned away from him. "Do you think we would have had babies?"

Versalis jerked around to face her, shock flooding his system back into motion. She wasn't looking at him, but out over the lake where it had all begun.

"Us?" he demanded.

Those glorious eyes turned on him and she smiled faintly, just a tiny twitch of her lips. "I had dreamt about it, before all of this," she whispered, making both Daemon and Uzo growl. "I had dreamt of a beautiful wedding, one I wanted. The only husband I asked for, and pretty babies to fill the Court in Winter. Little half vampires with pale lavender eyes."

"Etani ..." Uzo said in a pained voice, unable to bear her sadness.

"We would have made pretty babies," she breathed, lost in her imaginings.

"Very pretty," he agreed, trying not to feel like a monster, but it was hard when she spoke like that.

She looked at him once more, her face twisting with pain. "I suppose you will have pretty babies with Aurora now," she said, and he could see the physical effort she made to keep from showing the full extent of her pain.

"Why did you love me?" he asked after a pause, her eyes searching his.

"That day in the bathroom ... I cut your face. But you didn't get angry or upset. You didn't leave when you could have, and I wouldn't have blamed you. You were in pain and suffering, but you stayed for me. You never left my side after that, even after I woke up screaming and fighting, or when I got angry, or was crying. You were always there to calm me down again. I knew you would stay for me if I needed it."

"I would never have left you," he said.

"You did leave," she countered as though she was expecting his words. "All men leave eventually. Women are but a fleeting fancy to them," her eyes turned on Dirdos. "Eventually they all move on to another love."

Dirdos glared at her, but her eyes had already moved on to Daemon. Versalis didn't think she resented them for their love affair, but it had hurt her in a way she didn't fully understand.

Her eyes swept the crowd of Hunters, and she seemed to only just notice their existence.

"The Hunters are her—" She cut off as her eyes found Neah. "Neah ..." she breathed in a delighted, feral voice.

The Hunter jerked in alarm as she was before him. No liquid, no movements, just there before him and her eyes were enormous, gleeful and promising violence.

"Hello, husband," she purred, her lips pulling up into a wide, dangerous smile.

"Hello, wife," he said, his face wary.

"Where's your mask?"

"It got broken."

"What a shame ..." she said, and then she lifted her hand and her fingers splayed out over his face.

The black liquid spread down her arm and onto his face and she watched with a clinical fascination as he struggled to get it off, clawing at it, but after a minute he was on his knees, blood coating his face where he tried to claw it free.

Another minute passed, and he was on his side. She had suffocated him, though they all knew it wasn't a viable way to kill the Hunters.

Shifting to sit cross legged in the air, she waved her hand and the liquid melted away into the grass, her head cocked to the side as she watched him. They all watched him and waited to see what would happen.

After only a few seconds he gasped in air and coughed; her face showed her disappointment, but then she smiled and a boulder appeared out of nowhere, crushing him.

"Etani ..." Daemon sighed, rubbing his eyes as she made the boulder disappear and with elbows on knees, she watched the Hunter repairing before her eyes.

"No, she's earnt this much," Uzo said. "And if she's busy killing him, she's too busy to destroy the world," he added in a whisper.

"What do we do?" Daemon murmured, all of them watching her.

"I don't know ..."

"We just keep her distracted until her body is formed and then Versalis orders her back into it."

"You think I can order her back into her body?" Versalis asked.

"You got her to stop, and she seems ... less rational in this state. She wouldn't normally be this easy to distract from a goal, or am I seeing this wrong?" Daemon said.

"No, normally she has more focus. I don't know what's going on with her brain, but if we can take advantage of it, it might just save our lives," Uzo hissed.

After Neah had woken, she materialised a crossbow and shot him in the face, her head turning to look at them over her shoulder.

"What are you whispering about?" she asked.

"We're not whispering, darling. Might I suggest fire?" Uzo said, and for a moment her eyes narrowed, but then she smiled and turned back to her husband.

She did exactly that, attempting fire, drowning, explosives, and then lightning, but nothing worked to keep the Hunter down for very long. At least she seemed to be entertained by the task.

CHAPTER 21

HOW TO THROW A TANTRUM IN THREE EASY STEPS

It was quite some time later when she got bored and turned to look at them all, standing with an enormous axe in her arms. The axe would have looked more suited for Anubis, given the thing was taller than her by a good foot. But she used it to cut the Hunter straight down the middle and then threw it aside, her eyes sweeping the group.

"Where is Malik?" she asked, more curious than alarmed. "Is he with my body? I'm going to be annoyed if you left him unprotected in the underworld ..."

There was a sudden tension, and she sensed it, her body turning towards him slowly, dangerously slowly. Anubis, however, vanished with a growl, realising she was still somewhere in the underworld.

"Where is my Malik, Versalis?"

"Etani ..." he said, terrified.

"Where is he?" she screamed, the world around them shivering with the force of her anger and she lifted off the ground once more, her hair floating and shifting as her rage levelled on him.

"He's dead," Dirdos said.

She turned on the dragon and there was a terrible silence as she

207

processed that information. "Dead?" she asked, and Versalis knew with a terrible certainty that Dirdos did not want to repeat that word. He did not want to confirm that fact.

"Yes, Etani," the man said slowly, wary, and somehow surprised that she had set her attention on him.

She moved, her body pulling inwards on itself, and then she was gone, except that none of them could move, their legs frozen to the ground.

"Odds on us all being brutally murdered?" Uzo asked.

"Fifty-fifty," Daemon said.

"I'd say more along the lines of ninety-ten," Versalis muttered.

"In our favour?" Uzo asked.

"No, not in our favour."

She returned after only a few minutes, rising out of the darkness of Dirdos' shadow and the man spun, all eyes turning to her as she floated up, hovering a mere inch from his face. Why he was allowed to move when the rest of them weren't was beyond Versalis, and more than a little unfair.

"He's not there," she said in a quiet whisper. "Why did you lie to me?"

"He's not where?" Dirdos asked.

"Where the dead are," she growled.

"Vampires don't go to where the dead are," Daemon said, and her eyes turned on him.

"Where do they go?" she asked.

"To where the human dead go."

Fear flashed across her face, but then she turned, moving away from the dragon.

"Hades," she called out in a singsong voice, a wicked grin on her face as she turned to look at them all. "I want Malik back."

Hades evidently chose to ignore her because she smiled.

"Hades, don't make me bring you here," she cooed.

Flames burst up behind her and her eyes lowered, a vicious smile on her face that vanished in just a moment as she tilted her head, her spine bending back just enough to look up at him as he loomed over her.

"Hades, my love ..." she purred, their faces only a few inches apart.

"What is this?" he demanded, but Versalis could see him drinking her in just as greedily as the rest of them had. He was not immune to her.

"I want Malik back," she said, and he frowned, considering her carefully.

"Who is Malik?" Anger flashed across her face and her eyes narrowed up at him, still locked in that staring contest with him.

"My scion. My height, brown hair, vampire, *mine*." She was angry, and they could all see her struggle to contain her rage.

"Never heard of him," Hades said, and her head lifted.

He had never seen that homicidal intent on her face before, her expression blank and eyes wide, but he saw it now.

She moved, melting into liquid that moved around him and up until she was hovering before him, his head jerking up at her fluid form, and his eyes were wide as she floated just an inch above him, her legs tucked up under her as though she were kneeling.

"Give him back!" she raged, her eyes sliding shut as she worked to contain her fury. "Please ..."

Hades looked down at the empty air below her, and then around at them all, his normally stony face confused.

"Anubis?" he asked, but Daemon shook his head.

"Look at me!" she screamed, and he did, but not before he saw the world shivering under the force of her fury. "Give me back my Malik."

"Etani, he is dead," he said slowly, carefully.

"He is in your care. Return him." She was working hard to contain herself and Versalis shifted, ready to reign her in if the need arose.

"He is a dead human. They don't come back."

It was the wrong thing to say.

She screamed her rage, the sky flashing to a pale white-grey as her fingers reflexively contracted around the world and they all felt it as reality squeezed in on them.

"Etani!" Versalis yelled, and she spun on him, her eyes blazing white.

"Shut up, Versalis!" she snarled, and something slammed into his face like a slap. "Shut up right now!"

It was wet and cold, his hands lifting to pull at the black liquid that felt like tar on his mouth.

"Etani ... what are you doing?" the God asked, very wary of her now.

"I want ... my Malik back," she said, still glaring at Versalis though she was speaking to Hades.

"Anubis?" he called, and she turned to look at him, furious anew.

"Why do you refuse me?" she demanded.

Anubis stepped into reality, followed by no less than eight others. Sobek, Poseidon, Amun, Hel, Thor, Loki, Mara, and Eile.

The world seemed to ripple around their magic and Etani sighed, turning to look at them all. "Is this a party?" she asked innocently, though her eyes had locked on Anubis.

The God was livid, but she was happy.

"Etani?" Eile asked, but Etani ignored her, entirely focused on the God.

"Good doggy ..." she purred, her hair floating up around her as she sank down and her feet touched the grass, seeming so very small beside them all.

"What is going on?" Amun asked.

Her eyes flicked to the man and her smile faded a little as she considered him, knowing his power, and Versalis knew she respected the man.

"I want my scion," she said in a petulant tone.

"I told you, he's dead," Hades growled.

"Then go to the underworld and get him," she said with a false smile, her tone clipped as though she were dealing with a particularly dense person.

"He's not coming back. Ever," Hades snapped.

The God vanished with a suddenness that made them all flinch, and their ears popped, though she was still looking at Amun, her smile vacant.

"Where ... where did he go?" Sobek asked.

"Swimming," Etani said.

No one got it, their faces confused.

"Swimming where?" Daemon asked.

"In a river," she said evasively.

Hel got it first, and she was indignant. "Did you put him in the Styx?" she snarled, taking two steps toward the tiny Goddess.

"Do you want to join him?" Etani threatened, forcing the woman to stop dead in her tracks.

"Etani, stop this," Amun said in a gentle voice, causing her to pause, lips parted and eyes locked on his.

Versalis didn't think she was trying to push her will onto him, she was wary of him. He was stronger than her, and she didn't want to make him angry or risk him trying to stop her.

"You didn't tell them to stop when they were binding me," she said, sounding almost hurt. "Did you?" she wanted so badly to think he would try to protect her.

"No, sweetheart, I didn't tell them that," he said, and her face fell. "I should have... I should have protected you."

She had turned away from him, bitter and hurting that so many of the Gods had abandoned her when she needed them.

"Bring him back," Hel demanded, but Etani only shook her head.

"Not until he finds Malik," she said quietly, not fully focused on them.

Versalis glanced around and he realised that more and more people were stepping out onto the field, Gods and the higher up Fae, powerful and dangerous beings that were being drawn to the explosive magic being thrown up by the angry woman.

"Etani..." Daemon said, drawing her attention to him.

She melted and reformed before him, small, with her chin lifted.

"Daemon... why are you all so set on controlling me?" she asked, that high voice drawing them in, sounding so young and helpless.

"Look at what you're doing to this world," he said, and she frowned, turning away from him to look around as he suggested.

Versalis watched the expressions on that perfect face, taking in the disturbing warp of reality.

She frowned, frustrated, and not wanting to admit that she was having doubts about her actions.

It took her a moment to realise so many others had come to join the show and she tilted her head warily, watching them all as they craned to see her. She didn't know how to respond to the attention and it was making her a little anxious, he could tell by the way she shifted, the way her lips pressed together.

Her eyes lifted back to sky, those perfect shapes of her fingers that were parting the clouds, and he saw she was chewing on her tongue, considering.

"Etani, you need to put things back," Amun said, moving closer to her and extending his hand to place it on her shoulder.

"Why?" she asked the sky. "Why shouldn't I put an end to it?"

"Because you will kill us all."

"You can all go and live in Faerie."

"You know we won't all be able to survive in Faerie."

"Does it matter?"

The man frowned, stepping around her to force himself into her line of vision.

She looked up at him reluctantly, searching his white eyes for something Versalis could only guess at.

"If it didn't matter, then you wouldn't have worked so hard to save us all."

"Yes, but last time I did that I was punished. You all punished me for saving you."

"I know, but this time we will do better."

"Because you are afraid of me," she said.

"No, because doing what we did was a mistake, and we will never attempt to bind you again. You deserve better than that ... so long as you promise to not do this again."

She turned to look up at the God, his face stern like a father scolding his daughter. "After everything, you're going to ask me to agree to a deal?" she demanded, anger seeming to radiate off her.

"Yes, sweetheart. Because we need to be able to trust you. If you are one of us, then we will need that promise."

"I didn't even intend to use my magic. I didn't mean for any of this to happen!" She gasped, moving away from him. "You just keep pushing me and pushing me but then blame me when I push back. Like I'm the bad person for not wanting to be hurt, or abused," she snarled, the last directed at the white-haired man with bolts of lightning in a quiver. He lifted his chin slightly, eyes blazing.

"Zeus, go," Amun said coldly.

"I will protect the others."

Amun only sighed and rubbed his eyes, but Etani was moving away from him, her eyes sweeping the field, and then she swore at top volume as Hades burst into reality.

He was soaked and withered-looking, wheezing and hacking up water even as she grabbed the front of his robes and pulled him up off the ground.

"Where is Malik?" she demanded.

"I ... He's not there," Hades hacked, confused and unsure of what was happening.

Letting go of him, she turned on Versalis, Daemon, and Dirdos as they stood frozen, her rage turned on them.

"Why didn't you keep him safe?"

"He died before you, love," Dirdos said, and she frowned.

213

"What do you mean?" she asked, her eyes going distant as she tried to remember.

"He died trying to protect you ... from Anubis."

The field went silent as she took that in and then turned towards the canine God.

"It wasn't intentional," Anubis said.

"Etani ... don't do anything rash," Amun said, but she didn't listen. She was starting forward for the God, her right hand extending, and Versalis saw the blade, black and seeming to move on its own.

"Stop her!" Daemon yelled.

Etani lunged for the dog, but Amun got to her first, wrapping one arm around her middle and the other hand around her wrist, forcing her still even as she screamed and raged against the dog.

She did, however, manage to score a brutal kick to the groin and drop him.

Every man on the field cringed with sympathy.

"I'll kill you, you bastard!" she screamed, tears glistening silver on her cheeks as she thrashed in Amun's arms. "I'll kill you just like you killed him! He was mine! He was the only thing I could call mine, and you took him!"

Amun held her tight to himself, not trying to calm her or silence her. Instead, he let her scream herself out until she had deteriorated to tears and the blade melted away into the grass, leaving her hanging limp in the God's arms.

THE TINY GODDESS WAS SILENT, tears streaming down her face as she tried to come to terms with being unable to get revenge, and the loss of something so precious to her.

He felt something changing, and he twitched slightly, confused, until he realised she was pulling magic to herself, drawing on it from the world around her and from Faerie.

"What is she doing ...?" Versalis asked slowly, uncertain of what she might be up to.

"What? I don't see anything," Daemon snapped.

"She's pulling magic to her, at least I think so."

"Why?" Uzo asked, frowning.

"She just realised she lost her scion ..." Versalis said. Didn't they understand what that was like to a vampire? He didn't think so, they weren't vampires, and it was different for them, but he wouldn't be surprised if she went on a rampage as so many others in her position had before her. She was simply more powerful than most.

"How is she even doing it?" Daemon asked.

"She's in The Nameless Place, she can do whatever she likes."

Amun was gazing down at her, her fragile-looking body limp in his grip as he held her off the ground and against his chest.

Her head was bowed, and with her hair hanging around her face like that, she looked more like a child in his arms, or even a porcelain doll. She looked helpless, over a foot shorter than the God, and pale against his coppery skin and gold armour.

"What is she doing?" Uzo asked, all three of them watching her though there seemed to be no physical change in her.

"Still pulling ... what could she possibly be planning?" Versalis asked.

"Your guess is as good as mine," Daemon muttered, his golden eyes narrowed on the woman.

Everyone moved just slightly as her hair lifted, their skin tingling and hair standing on end as they felt something none of them could understand. It was like a whispered scream just behind their ear, like someone was whispering something but they couldn't quite hear it and the keening sound was both terrible and beautiful.

Her body melted into the grass, and she reformed several feet away.

She changed before them as her hands lifted at her sides, palms facing upwards. She was growing taller, her already long hair growing longer, and her dress changed into a flowing black skirt that trailed out behind her, though it was entirely see-through. Her clothing consisted of little more than undergarments interconnected with long strips of fabric and black chains that clung to that exquisite body like a second skin. A large pendant at her chest resembled that of Versalis' chest, trailing down her front in a complex web of silver and black metal that held the fabric together around her, a similar twisting shape curling up around her arms and calves.

She was no longer the tiny creature they had all come to know; she was taller than Anubis, graceful and elegant as she moved towards the lake, and those Hunters who stood between her and her goal fell. They didn't show any signs of injury, they simply collapsed into a heap on the ground.

It only took three for the rest to back away from her, knowing better, and her chin lifted, eyes turning skyward as her arms extended out at her sides.

Above them the sky darkened, her hair floating up around her and she smiled, terrible and dangerous as she called on whatever magic she needed to do whatever task it was she had planned.

The world shuddered around them to the point where they were staggering to stay upright and he saw in his mind her lifting the world, holding it up before her eyes in The Nameless Place and considering it carefully, deciding what to do and where to plan her next attack.

"Can't you do something?" Amun growled, and Versalis jumped, the God having moved up beside him, and he hadn't noticed.

Looking up at the God, Versalis could only shrug.

"Like what? She's lost her scion, she's angry at having her heart ripped out and put in a box ..."

"And at having the man she loves abandon her," Daemon added.

Amun made a soft sound as he looked around at her, standing still and smiling as she worked on her next course of attack.

The others dared not move for fear of drawing her attention onto them; he couldn't blame them in the slightest, he was terrified, but he also knew he was their best chance at survival. She would destroy the world in her thirst for vengeance, and after everything they had done to her, could any one of them blame her? She had been abused, raped again, and again, caged, and beaten. Then after all that, they had betrayed her for the last time.

She was fury and fire; she was the Goddess of Destruction.

"What happens when you piss off the Goddess of Destruction ...? She destroys ..." Versalis said gently a moment before she dug her fingers in under Faerie on one side and the other hand in under the human world.

"Etani, stop!" Daemon screamed as Uzo swayed, eyes wide as she pulled, and then he collapsed to the ground, blood flowing anew from his nose and ears. "Do something, you worthless fucking vampire!" He turned on Versalis, but Versalis didn't know what to do.

The Gods were screaming, the Hunters were screaming, but Daemon was refusing to scream, blood dripping down the sides of his face from his ears, but he refused to give in.

"Stop her!"

"How?" Versalis yelled back.

"Use the magic she has in you! How stupid are you?!"

Versalis growled at the insult, angry and trying to figure out what to do. Hades had said that he could control her from a distance, but that hadn't worked. She had shaken off his control. So, what happened if he touched her?

Letting out a snarl of frustration, he ran for the Goddess, tall and beautiful, standing there with her eyes closed.

The world shuddered and the Hunters fell as one, limp and unmoving as she pried away the surface of Faerie.

The Gods had stopped screaming; they stood frozen and vacant-eyed. They would likely die instantly if she succeeded, the Hunters would most likely survive, but not the Gods, and not the Fae who were in the human world.

She seemed to sense him as her arms lowered and she turned to look at him out of the corner of her eye, more curious than alarmed by his coming for her.

A faint hint of a smile, and he saw the ground buckling, rising up before him, but he twisted, spinning around it and sprinting forward for her. She looked annoyed, but she wasn't about to give up that easily.

Her hand lifted, and she twitched her middle finger down, another pillar of stone shooting up in front of him. When he ducked around it her head tilted, and he knew she was going to make a game out of it.

He wasn't wrong, and as she turned towards him, more pillars flew up and he dodged around them, over them when she was too slow, and he frowned as she made him circle around her. She was only half paying attention or she likely would have beaten him already. He was no match for a Goddess, but she was so focused on trying to pry the worlds apart that only part of her was focused on him.

HER SKIN WAS cool as he wrapped his arms around her waist, twisting his arms so that he gripped his own wrists. She wasn't the same level of coldness he had known her to be in person, and he had to assume that this was only a replication of her former self.

"Stop! Right now!" he screamed, calling on that part of himself that slumbered peacefully until she needed it. His chest burnt as the magic that she had given him rose inside him and he felt as though he were going to explode.

He didn't know how she could possibly exist with so much magic, but she was born to contain it. He was not, and his teeth ached as it flooded his body and reached out for her.

It found her through his skin, and she screamed as it flooded into her and crushed her magic, forcing it down.

Her body seemed to disappear, though she was still in his arms, the magic that had changed her reverting back, and she collapsed into his chest.

As he wrapped his arms around her she squirmed to get free of him, and he felt those around him beginning to move as the worlds snapped back together. It was at least good that whatever glue held the two worlds together adhered again, and she was forced to start over, or they might not be there to be glad for it.

"Stop fighting me," he snarled, struggling to keep her still.

"Don't you ever touch me again!" she screamed, writhing like a wildcat in his arms, but he refused to let her go.

He understood why she didn't want his arms around her. She was angry and hurt that he had chosen another woman, but that didn't mean he was going to let her destroy the world because she felt scorned.

"Promise to never destroy the worlds!" he yelled, having no idea what else to say to her. "You're going to kill Uzo if you do! You'll kill Dirdos, Daemon, all the Gods... what about Letari?"

That got her, and she went still, panting and straining to look around over his shoulder towards the others.

Uzo was on his hands and knees, struggling to get back to his feet with Dirdos sitting in a daze, eyes unfocused and staring at nothing. Daemon was one of the only people still standing, though it looked as though he was standing purely out of locking his muscles in place.

"I don't care!" she said, turning away from them all.

"Yes, you do, you love them," he said, her struggles stilling, but he refused to let her go.

"No, I don't!" she cried, but he knew she was lying. She was trying to shut herself down to escape the pain, but he wasn't about to let her do that. If she didn't love them, then there was nothing keeping her from obliterating them all.

"Yes, Etani, you can deny it all you want but you love them all. We found the box in the wall."

She froze, her lips pressing together as she took in first the invasion of her privacy, then the evidence of her true feelings for them all.

"We saw what was in there. All the little things you've found or taken from us."

"No, you didn't …" she whispered, her face pale.

"My ribbon, Kai's glove, Jaia's button, Uzo's stone … Daemon's chain, the rock you gave Dirdos … all of it."

She stared blindly at the water, angry and scared of what they were going to do with the information now that they had it.

"You're so damned distant all the time we all thought you simply tolerated us. None of them knew you even cared about them." He was getting angry now, resenting her for not being like Aurora and making her desires clear, but that wasn't fair. She didn't deserve to be compared to Aurora, they had very different circumstances and were very different beings.

"Let me go," she pleaded, her voice quivering with her efforts to keep from crying.

"Not until you promise. The Gods will stop trying to contain you if you promise."

"No, they won't, they're liars!" she screamed at the Gods, and Versalis saw Amun flinch at her words. He was creeping closer, trying to get near to her without her noticing.

"Promise, Etani, promise so that it sticks even after death. Promise you won't try to destroy the worlds again," he said. Amun's intense look was making him nervous, and he wanted to move her further away from him, but that would alert her to his presence, and she would likely retaliate to defend herself.

"No, let me go," she whimpered, but he could hear her resolve breaking; she was not a stupid woman, she was simply scared.

"If the Gods promise never to do this to you again, will you promise?"

She bit her lip, staring out over the water, but then she nodded.

"Amun, will you come over here?" he called out, knowing the God was mere feet behind them, but it was best to have her think he was not about to get to her.

Amun paused for a moment and then approached, his eyes narrowed at Versalis. "What?" he demanded, playing along, but he was near her now, he could easily reach out and touch her if he needed to.

"Will you promise that the Gods will not try to control her again? If you do, she will promise not to destroy the worlds ..." Versalis asked.

"I can't promise that I have no control over the actions of the others ..." He paused, squinting down at her. "However, I will promise to punish any who try, and ensure she is returned. That should be enough of a threat to deter them."

She looked up at the God, her face showing her doubt, though neither of them could blame her for doubting him. The Gods had all abused her in one way or another, Zeus most of all, but none of them had done anything to punish him for what he had done to her.

Amun looked down at her for a second before he shifted, lowering himself onto his knees and taking her hands. Her nails were bloody, but he didn't remember her using her nails on him. She must have done it at some point though; it was his blood.

Kneeling before her, Amun lifted her hands to his face and kissed them both, his normally hard face tender with his understanding.

"I promise to keep you safe from the Gods, and I promise to punish those who try to, or succeed to hurt you or bind you," he said, twisting her hand so that her palm was pressed to his cheek. "I will not let you down again, you are precious to us all and we will look after you."

She watched him, her face guarded and reserved as she tried to figure out where the lie was, where the trick was that would get him out of the deal before she made her own promise.

"No tricks. I will place you under my personal protection," the man said, and she hissed, along with several others. To be under the protection of Amun would almost guarantee her safety from the Gods.

"I promise I will not attempt to destroy the worlds so long as you uphold your side of the deal, excluding your lack of knowledge," she said, unsure, but wanting so badly to trust him.

"Will you make me another promise? A personal one?" he asked, and she frowned. "Will you promise to try and fix our worlds? To make Faerie what it was intended to be?"

Her lips parted and then closed again as she considered that. "I promise to try," she said slowly. "I will not promise to succeed, but I will try."

Versalis doubted she wouldn't be able to do it, but she seemed to.

"Thank you," Amun breathed, and turned his head to kiss her wrist.

She shivered and when he let her go, she pulled her hands away from him as though she were nervous of touching him.

CHAPTER 22
TEMPTING FATE

When it seemed that the worst of it was over, Versalis let go of her and she turned on him, shoving him away from her.

He staggered back, glaring but not able to say anything against her.

If she wanted to act like a child, then she would. Again, he felt a slash of guilt when he realised how young and inexperienced she was when it came to an actual relationship, and it was unfair of him to think so badly of her, but it was hard when he was still bitter at her for her own actions.

If she had only shown him that she loved him, things might have turned out differently. All it would have taken was a hint from her and this might have ended with a better story. But she hadn't and now it didn't matter.

She glared right back at him, and they looked up as her grip on the world released, the ground moving weirdly to fill in the space like wet sand, leaving the world perfect once more as though she hadn't been digging her fingers into it.

"Creepy ..." they heard Vincent say, and they looked around just in time to see Uzo running for her. His arms went around her before she could react and he snatched her up off the ground, crushing her to his chest, even as she squeaked like someone had trodden on a mouse.

She struggled valiantly, reaching for Amun, but he only shrugged as the Fae hoisted her up over his shoulder and carried her back towards the others.

"He's not a God," Amun said calmly, and she swore at him, making the man smirk. "She's such a lady."

She obviously heard him because her middle finger came up, but then she vanished as she was dumped into the arms of Daemon. A moment later, she shrieked as Dirdos attacked the three of them.

There was a yell from the group as she melted and reformed several feet from them, pink-cheeked and glaring at them all. She had never been able to escape them before and now she could.

When he turned to look up at the roiling sky there was an odd rippling behind her, and Anubis appeared, eyes narrowed, an enormous axe raised.

She tilted her head back in time to see the axe coming down, the crowd yelling for him to stop, but it was too late. Her expression changed from one of confusion to one of utter delight as the axe swiped through her, her body parting and re-joining again like water. She looked utterly ecstatic that he had tried to kill her again. The God trying to kill her was the best thing to ever happen.

Her body melted down into a puddle of black that moved between the God's feet, and she reformed behind him, her grin savagely gleeful.

"Oh, Anubis ..." She sighed and as he turned, her fingers closed around a knife that had not been there a second before.

She drove the knife up into his gut, ripped it out and drove it up again, and again, and again.

Five or six by his count, and the God dropped to his knees before her, looking up at her and she looked back with a smile as she bowed over him and her fingers found his muzzle.

"Etani ..." Versalis warned. Her eyes snapped up to him and she went from lover to child who had been caught stealing.

"Versalis ..." she mimicked his tone, her lower lip thrust out in a pout.

"No," he said, and her eyes narrowed. He didn't dare break the staring contest with the Goddess and he felt her trying to dominate him, trying to crush his will down so she could have what she wanted. But he had her magic, and the seconds ticked past, their eyes never wavering.

Finally, her head turned, and she broke the contact, irritated that he wouldn't let her do whatever it was she wanted, and Anubis whimpered in relief, so very close to death.

With a wave of her hand the God was gone and Versalis frowned. "Where is he?"

With her head bowed and her hands linked behind her back, she peeked at him sideways through the curtain of her hair, her smile sly and mischievous.

"Somewhere safe. In a box like he put me in," she said, a little girl who was unashamed of being caught doing wrong.

"Etani, he needs help," Versalis scolded.

"You all need help," she countered, refusing to give him what he demanded.

"Bring him back right now."

"No, Versalis. I do not want him back," she said, still watching him with that same sly smile.

"Etani, bring him back now!"

Her smile faded and she was gone, melting only to reform right before him. He wanted to jerk back but he didn't dare move, her hair flowing up around her as she rose, her feet lifting off the ground to make her taller than him, her face furiously cold.

"No," she whispered, a challenge if ever he heard one.

His chin lifted to meet her eyes, refusing again to back down as she tried to force her will onto him. "Now," he growled.

Her eyes widened as she tried to again crush his will, and again, he refused. She hissed and turned away from him, her hand flicking out and with that same black liquid, the God was thrust up from the earth and she turned her back to Versalis, arms crossed.

Looking to the God, his brows lifted as he saw the box she had stuck him in. She wasn't a Goddess of Creation for nothing. She had created a wooden cage, elaborate and decorated, with no doors or top or bottom; it was simply a cube of wood bars with the God stuffed inside.

The God only fit due to the sheer force of her will, back curved and shoulders pushing against the bars, head bowed down between knees that were pressed against his chest.

What could he say to that? She had given him what he wanted, hadn't she? He wasn't dead, not yet anyway.

"Let no one say she isn't creative ..." Amun said slowly, wary of her. "He was not aware of the deal."

She waved him off, turning away as she dismissed the attempt to kill her as meaning little. People tried to kill her all the time; her friends had all tried to kill her at least once, it wasn't like death meant much to her.

Versalis watched as Amun headed for Anubis to explain the situation and the caged dog nodded, at least as much as he could in that space.

"Etani, my dear, would you mind letting him out?" Amun called out.

"No," she said back, looking at the sheer number of Hunters, though she was pointedly ignoring Neah. He hadn't moved an inch, either, evidently hoping she would forget he existed while in that state. He would likely be after her again when she was back in her body ...

Versalis blinked, realising he had forgotten about her body being regrown in the underworld and the more he thought about it, the more he realised that it wasn't going to be that much longer before she was able to return to it.

He headed for the others while she beelined for the nearest

Hunter, who looked about ready to wet himself at her stalking approach. He leant in close to the three sulking men.

"She's almost fully formed. It would appear to be happening at a faster rate when it's her own body, or maybe because it's such a vital part of her body? I don't know, but it'll only be an hour or two more."

"That's not long," Uzo said quietly, watching her with such a desperate longing that it hurt to look at.

"That's forever," Daemon whined. "Who's with her?"

"Jason, if he found them, Dainin, and Jaia plus the demon-mask guy to keep their magic masked."

"She's going to be so thrilled to find out that Jaia was looking out for her body," Dirdos said happily. "Maybe she'll be so excited by it she'll hug his head right off his body."

"Wishful thinking," Daemon said with a sigh.

"Bet you a round that she at least punches him," Uzo said.

"I think it'll be more than that, more like a special kiss," Daemon growled.

"I reckon she'll either stab him or drown him in the river," Dirdos said.

"Okay, I think she'll just hit him. You're all on."

The others nodded and looked around at a furious growl as Amun struggled with the cage.

Etani was distracted by the Hunter, having dragged him down to sit on the grass with her, talking to him about who knew what.

"She's such a weird girl ..." Dirdos said.

"The whole species is weird," Daemon added, and then grunted as Uzo punched his stomach.

Etani looked around at them, but Uzo only waved at her, smiling widely.

"What is it about her that looks so ... creepy?" the Fae asked.

"I don't know ... I thought that, too. It's her but it's different somehow," Versalis murmured.

Dirdos nodded his agreement, all of them watching as she looked up at another Hunter who had crept over to her like a puppy, joining the first on the grass before her.

"Back to being a lure, I see," Dirdos said.

"I don't think it's her magic, I think they are just fascinated by how pretty she is," Uzo said, frowning. "I don't feel any pull towards her, do you?"

"No, not at all," Dirdos said "It's like she's a normal woman for once. Ravishing, but normal."

"And slightly creepy ..." Versalis said.

"On that note, you need to go back to Winter," Daemon said, turning on Versalis.

"What? Why?" Versalis demanded, annoyed by the demand.

"Because as soon as you see her in her body, you will forget all about Aurora and she will own you again. You made your choice, now you can go be with your love."

Versalis frowned at them, glancing around as Vincent joined them, looking curious at their conversation.

"What's going on? Are we just waiting now?" the Hunter asked.

"Yes, for now. We can't move until she's reformed. Versalis said it should only be a couple more hours," Daemon said, unable to tear his eyes off her. "You should take Versalis to Faerie."

"Why?" Vincent sounded surprised, looking back to them where his eyes had drifted to the Goddess.

"Versalis has decided to be with Aurora," Dirdos said before Daemon could say something nasty.

"Really?" Vincent asked, and there was a weird expression on the man's face.

Versalis had to wonder if the man had put himself in the race for Etani's love.

"Why does that mean he has to go to Winter?"

"Because he shouldn't be around for her pull to kick in," Uzo said, still staring at her.

"Shouldn't that be irrelevant? Hunter manages it just fine."

"You'd think," Dirdos said slowly, wary.

"Versalis will fall for her instantly. He doesn't think so, but we all know it, and then he'll leave Aurora and go running back to Etani. She'll immediately forgive him because she loves him and wants to be with him even if he hurts her ..." Daemon smirked. "All we need now is you to rape her and it'll be an exact repeat of what Jaia did."

They all flinched, but it was what the demon had wanted.

"That's harsh ..." Dirdos scolded.

"No, what's harsh is him. He makes her fall in love with him but then the second she's gone he's onto another woman. But he knows that she will pine after him and long for him, so he can come back at any point and when he gets bored of Aurora, he'll get Etani back," Daemon snapped. "But I'll be dead and gone before I let you do that to her. She deserves better than you."

"Who does she deserve, Daemon? You?" Versalis growled.

"She deserves better than all of us," the demon grumbled.

"Yes, she does," Uzo said.

There was an awkward pause as they all turned inward.

"Who would be good enough for her?" Vincent asked.

"Kai," Daemon and Uzo said together and exchanged a wary glance.

"Why Kai? Isn't he too ... soft for her?"

"He might seem it, but I think he is more like Jaia than we think. Strong, capable, and more dominating than you'd expect. She needs a mate who can keep one paw on her to keep her grounded but isn't going to crush her," Uzo said. "Plus, she finds a dominant man appealing."

"I wonder why that is ... Isn't that usually a symptom of having a dominating parent?" Dirdos asked, and Versalis shook his head in the direction of their conversation.

"She is strong and powerful, she knows not many men can withstand or even tolerate that in a partner, so she finds men who can both withstand and outdo her appealing. In some ways that pull to her is a blessing. The stronger the male, the stronger the pull towards her," Daemon said, shrugging. "Look at Dirdos, would literally burn the world down to make her smile. Versalis, the only Vampire King, the twins are both super intelligent, Epharis the Lich, Alaric the titan, even Galad doubted his existence when faced with her. The more power you have, the more you would rip the worlds apart to get to her. Then there's also the physical aspect. The Hunters and Sebastian, they all look like they could rip you apart, and they can. Dirdos is physically intimidating. Every man she has taken a liking to has something about him that triggers that part in her that is more animal than woman."

"We shouldn't talk about her like this," Uzo said, irritated with their conversation and his own part in it.

"What about Kai?" Vincent asked.

"I think she sees him as soft and gentle," Daemon explained. "I don't know that she has really seen him as what he can be and he's very controlled, I'd be surprised if she has seen him for what he is outside of the stoic gentleman."

"Then why not encourage him to break that if you want him and them to be together?" Dirdos asked, his mood souring.

"He would see it as manipulating her."

"Are you sure he likes her, though?" Vincent asked, and there was a pause before Daemon snorted.

"Have you seen the way that boy watches her? Have you seen his jaw whenever someone else touches her? I'm surprised he has any teeth left from how often he's grinding them," the demon snickered.

THEY FELL silent and watched the Goddess and the others considered their own thoughts. Versalis considered the lot of them, and then the woman herself, wondering if she might know they were talking about her. She seemed oblivious to them, but she was growing tense, her movements becoming somewhat abrupt as though her body didn't want to cooperate with her and finally, she went still, her hand frozen in the air.

"Vincent!" the man called out, and they all looked around in alarm as she sat perfectly still for a second, her fingers slowly, oh so slowly, clenched into a fist, and then she collapsed.

The Hunter at her side caught her as she slumped into him and he looked up in terror, though Versalis wasn't sure if it was because he was holding that glorious form, or because she had collapsed. Possibly both.

They were all moving but Versalis frowned, considering her body.

"It's okay, her body is reformed!" he called out.

Her body melted into that same black liquid and the Hunter looked up in horror as though he had broken her, but Versalis could feel her pulled back fully to The Nameless Place, blinking and looking around in confusion.

"Your body is reformed," he told her, and understanding came over her face as she made the connection and she looked up, but there was no lightning bug.

Frowning, she turned, searching for the escape, but there seemed to be nothing for her to reach for.

Pivoting back to him, she lifted her hands in a questioning gesture.

"She can't find the way out," he told the others, and they were on him in a second, their fear making him anxious. "We'll figure it out, everyone calm down," he told them all, including the Goddess, though she only looked annoyed.

"What do we do?" Daemon demanded, but she was looking around again, looking irritated, and then she rolled her eyes, and he felt her flooding into him.

"Try and call me, I don't think I can get out without you," she sighed through him.

"Oh ... right," Daemon said, his face flaming at his panic. "Do you think anyone can call you, or does it have to be Versalis?"

She blinked, looking at them all through his eyes. "I don't know, why don't you try it?"

They had caught her attention, but she was still bothered by the fact that she couldn't get out without them.

"What do I say?" Daemon asked, and she shrugged, forgetting that they couldn't see her.

"Call out my name," she suggested.

Looking at the others, he shrugged and lifted his eyes to the sky. "Etani!"

She shivered, her eyes widening and her lips parting.

"I heard you ..." she whispered, relieved, but when she looked around, she couldn't see an escape. "It didn't work."

"Maybe you're just not enough for her, Daemon," Dirdos teased, and the demon growled.

"You try, then," Daemon snapped.

"Etani!" Dirdos cried out, and she tilted her head back at a flickering above her.

"Wait a moment, I saw that ... Daemon, try again."

He did, and she saw it again, that flicker of light from above her.

"Interesting, you can call to me, but it goes away after a second. What does that mean?"

"Maybe one isn't enough?" Dirdos asked.

"Try it," she said, seemingly quite content to keep trying.

"Etani!" they called out together, and she looked up, seeing it. She floated up towards it, curious to see if it was going to stay.

It disappeared after twenty seconds or so and she tilted her head. "Interesting, the more of you that call, the longer it stays?"

"I wonder what would happen if everyone here called to you?" Dirdos asked.

"An experiment for another day," Uzo said.

"When are we ever going to have this opportunity again?" Daemon said.

"Come back now," Uzo ordered.

"Yes uncle ..." she said, and Daemon snorted his amusement.

"Only man in any world who she would listen to," Daemon muttered.

"Don't be jealous," Uzo said. "Just because she loves me more than you …"

"Oh, shots fired," Dirdos said.

"Now, young lady," Uzo said.

"Please call me before I get into trouble." She sighed.

Daemon and Dirdos exchanged an amused grin before their voices called out in unison.

She reached up for the flash of white, her fingers closing on it, and her awareness vanished from The Nameless Place.

CHAPTER 23
RETURN OF THE QUEEN

T hey stared at him until he nodded, and they all sighed, glad to have her back and yet there was still the issue of getting her out of the underworld.

Jason appeared only a few seconds later, and he looked around at them all in alarm.

"She's not here?" he asked.

"No, she's back in her body."

Jason got a weird, almost anxious, look on his face, but then he nodded, looking around them.

"So ... where are the other two from the underworld? The green guy and the woman?"

There was a moment of confusion as all their eyes first turned on the tall man, then on the surrounding Gods. Even the Gods looked around, confused and worried.

"They ... don't know about the deal, do they ...?" Versalis said.

"No, but they can't find them, Cyle is with them."

"Who is Cyle?"

"Demon-mask," Jason said.

"Oh, we've just been calling him 'demon-mask guy,'" Daemon said.

"That works, too."

"Demon-mask has a name?" Dirdos asked, looking surprised.

"Yes Dirdos, we have names," Jason said, squinting.

There was a moment of amused silence as they relaxed. There didn't seem to be any real reason for their fear if Cyle was with them.

Versalis, however, was not convinced, and he tilted his head slightly as he felt a sudden flash of fear coming from her.

"Something wrong," he said, squinting as he tried to figure out what it was. "She's afraid."

"She just got dumped into the underworld, wouldn't you be afraid?" Dirdos asked, but he wasn't looking quite as certain as he sounded.

A flash of terror shot through him and then blinding pain, her soul being ripped at. She screamed, though she couldn't get air to breathe. It wasn't like water, but it also was exactly like water, filling her lungs and suffocating her when water had never done that before.

Versalis turned on Vincent, grabbing the man by the shirt and dragging him closer.

"She's in danger! Take me there! Now!" he screamed in the man's face, not caring what he thought.

Vincent didn't even hesitate, grabbing him, and the world vanished around them, dumping them out onto the rocky outcropping several yards away from the temple base.

Spinning at a screaming voice, he turned to see Jaia clawing his way out of the greenish river, a limp and exceptionally pale form in his arms.

He was coughing, wheezing, but he dragged the limp body from the water, turning on it and then slamming his linked fists down onto its chest.

"Etani!" Vincent roared, grabbing Versalis and dragging him

through reality to burst out on the bank. She wasn't moving, her lips an odd green-blue colour and skin almost transparent with how pale it was.

Jaia bent over her, his mouth on hers, and Versalis watched as her chest rose, but she didn't respond.

Vincent moved to help, pulling her feet out of the water and linking his fingers to press down on her chest while Jaia forced air into her lungs, the two falling into a quick pattern in the attempt to restore her back to life.

Versalis couldn't move, staring down at her in a horrified fascination. He couldn't look away; he couldn't feel her mind. She was gone, the true gone, and there was no pull towards her, just a dull emptiness in him.

Pain ripped through his body, and he screamed just as her body moved, clenching in on itself and the two men rolled her onto her side, Jaia hitting her back to help expel the water that was blocking her airways.

He had been so sure she was gone, so certain that he felt tears streaming down his face as the feeling of her flooded him once more, her pain and her confusion.

"Oh, Sweet Mother..." Vincent cried, dragging her up off the rocks and hugging her to his chest.

She whimpered, her exquisite face tensed in pain as she turned her head towards him, inhaling the scent and then latching onto him.

Reaching for Jaia, the Hunter pulled him in, but Jaia twisted away, panting and confused, as he leant forward onto his hands, gasping and shuddering.

"Jaia?" Versalis asked.

Jaia looked up and Versalis jerked bac;, the man's eyes had turned a liquid silver, and he looked terrified, but then she made a sound and his eyes snapped to her.

He knew in that instant as his eyes found her that Jaia had been right, that Daemon had been right. In that moment he almost forgot about Aurora as the magic that was Etani ensnared him. He couldn't think when she was there; he could never love another woman, and he belonged to her.

"She's okay?" he gasped, voice jagged.

Vincent nodded, refusing to look up as she pressed her face into his chest, breathing him in as much as she could.

"You're okay, sweetheart. We're here, we've got you," Vincent gasped, his eyes glistening with tears.

"Vincent?" she whimpered, her voice sounding just as jagged as Versalis' had.

"Yes, love, I'm here," the Hunter said, his hand shaking as he stroked back her dripping hair.

Versalis shook himself and stripped out of his shirt, working it over her arms and wrapping it tightly around her.

"I can't see," she said softly, her eyes open wide but unfocused.

"What?" Jaia snarled, grabbing her face and turning her head to him. She blinked, confused, as he stared intently into her eyes, only an inch from her face.

"Jaia?" she asked, uncertain by the roughness of his voice. "Jaia, where are we?"

"How did you end up in the water?" Vincent asked, trying to draw her attention back to him.

"Osiris pushed her in," Jaia growled.

"Jaia!" someone called, and they turned to see Dainin running for them, his face pale and eyes huge. "Oh, thank Mother, you got her out!" Cyle was only a few paces behind him, his mask bloody and the lower half of the jaw shattered off.

"Where's Osiris?" Jaia snarled, releasing her to struggle to his feet.

"He left... he just vanished after she went into the water. I was so sure she was gone! I... you..." He broke off when Jaia shook his head, tilting it in Etani's direction.

Dainin frowned, confused, but kept his mouth shut, stepping backwards and then appearing at their side.

Cyle was panting hard, turning and sweeping the area to ensure they were safe, and then he too joined them on that side of the bank, scanning for threats, but there seemed to be nothing.

"I can't believe she's back," Dainin whispered, and she looked up, reaching blindly for him.

"She can't see," Versalis said.

"Why not?" Dainin asked, but Versalis didn't know. He took her hand as she reached for him and pressed his lips to her palm, her face seeming to relax at his touch.

"We need to get her out of here, just in case they try again," Jaia said. "I'm not keen to go swimming again."

Versalis grabbed the vampire by the wrist and then Vincent by the shoulder, the world going dark and then blindingly bright.

"Etani!" Bast screamed, throwing Dirdos off her and ripping the small frame from Vincent's arms.

"Bast? Bast I can't see anything... why can't I see?" Etani pleaded, clinging to the Goddess desperately.

Bast looked up, but it was Hades who spoke.

"She was in the water? How did she get out?" the God asked in a horrified voice.

Vincent, Versalis and Dainin all looked at Jaia, the vampire rubbing his streaming eyes.

"You... you pulled her out of the water?" Hades asked, sweeping forward to grab the vampire, and forcing his head up. Hades sneered and after only a second shoved him away. "He jumped in after her."

"What?" Bast gasped, looking up from her quiet crooning.

"He's a hero, look at his eyes."

Everyone turned to look at Jaia, the vampire looking angry and still dripping water.

"You sacrificed yourself for her?" Bast asked, Etani's head lifting to look around, but she couldn't see him.

"Jaia?" she asked, her tone confused.

"It wasn't like that..." Jaia growled.

"Don't bother lying. Your eyes are enough proof. Little shit was willing to die for her. Her vision will return in a few hours," Hades snarled before stalking away from the lot of them.

"What is he talking about?" Versalis demanded.

"He's ... he's like a God, just without the worshippers. He willingly gave up his life to save hers," Bast whispered.

"I knew I wouldn't die," Jaia snapped.

"No, you didn't. You thought you would die," Versalis said, reading the man. "You hoped you would die. You gave up your life for her."

There was silence as they all took that in, staring at the vampire.

"I didn't want Kai to be sad," Jaia lied, angry at them all. "I'm not a hero, I'm a selfish monster. Don't forget that."

Versalis looked around for Etani once more and caught sight of Jason, frozen and staring at the group with wide blue eyes. He seemed unable to bring himself to move.

"Take her up to the castle and get her cleaned up," Dirdos said.

"I smell like a dead swamp," she said, looking around, but she was still frowning.

"We weren't going to say anything," Daemon teased, and when she scowled, he kissed her hard on the forehead.

"I'll take her," Vincent said, and she moved easily into his arms, clutching herself to his chest.

"You stink, too," she said, the man laughing, but his tears still fell.

"I'll go with them to make sure he doesn't blubber all over her," Uzo said, putting on a brave face, but they all saw his desperate hunger to be near her.

He was gone before they could say a thing and Versalis dropped onto his arse, his head falling into his hands.

"Mother ... I was so sure she was gone," he said, his eyes stinging.

"I couldn't feel her at all, I was so completely sure she was completely gone."

Bast wrapped her arms around him and he clung to her while she stroked his hair.

"Shh, it's okay. She's back now, and she's safe," Bast murmured, rocking him gently.

"She's back …" Daemon whispered. "She's fucking back!" he cheered, his hands on his head and his face alight. "She's back!" he screamed to the sky.

Dirdos was rubbing his eyes, shaking his head in his relief, and the two Hunters were hugging tightly.

"Did you see her?" Dainin asked.

"No, not yet," Jason said, his eyes going to the castle in the distance.

"Go on, man, you haven't lived until you've seen her."

"You think I should?" the blue-eyed man asked.

"Yeah, she's already seen you, you should go see her. Go on, she'll want to meet you," Daemon said. "We should all go up there anyway, she'll want us there when she can see again, then she can yell at us all for taking so long to get her back."

Dirdos took over the transport, grinning widely at Jason as they vanished from the world. "Prepare to have your mind blown."

They landed in the living room that no longer smelt of her as much as it once did, and there was gentle talking coming from the bathroom, the door shut.

It was another hour before the door opened and Uzo headed for the bedroom to grab her clothes, looking around at them with a slight nod.

"Her vision is coming back. You, get in the bathroom," he said to Jaia, who frowned but obeyed.

Another hour passed, and the door opened once more, Jaia

looking somewhat scared, but also relaxed, glancing at them all before he headed off to find Kai, a bag of blood clutched in his hand.

Uzo led her out and Versalis had never seen anything so beautiful in his life. Her skin glowed with youth, her perfect face smooth and unblemished. Her arms were raised, hands in her silken hair, bundling it all up, and there was a faint hint of a smile on those full lips that would drive even the holiest man to sin as she slid a long, silver pin into her hair to keep it all piled up.

"Sweet Mother ..." Jason whispered from the corner of the room, and he jerked when she looked up at the sound of his voice, the man completely floored by her. It wasn't surprising, everyone reacted the same when faced with her for the first time.

"Jason ..." she said, that voice both innocent and wicked enough to make a succubus jealous.

He could only nod, his eyes locked on her and unable to turn away or even blink.

She smiled and the world lit up with it, radiant and wonderful, but then her attention was captured by Daemon as he reached for her.

She wrapped her arms tightly around his neck, pulling him down to her level until he picked her up and crushed her to him, and she laughed, the sound making his heart race.

"I missed you so much." The demon gasped, bent back with her lithe body squished against him only to have her stolen by Dirdos.

"I missed you, too," she said, allowing herself to be bundled up into the dragon's arms and squeezed.

She made a happy sound in her throat that made Jason turn red.

"Spontaneous erections are forgiven," Versalis whispered, then smiled when she looked in his direction.

"What are you whispering about?" she asked.

"Nothing, come here!" he demanded, and she untangled Dirdos' arms from her and she was in his, the world righting itself as he clung to her.

Burying his face in her hair, her arms crushed him, but he loved the pain, clinging to her just as hard and inhaling the scent of her. He caught the glance between Uzo and Daemon, their anger at his actions, but he didn't care; he was desperate to feel her pressed to him, even if there was a certain coolness to her embrace. It was a full ten minutes before he was forced to relinquish her to Jagum, who refused to let go of her again for twenty but then she wriggled herself free and almost tackled Dainin, her eyes lingering on Jason over the Hunter's shoulder.

Finally, free of them all, she approached the tall man warily, her expression guarded as she reached for him. He couldn't move, muscles locked and rigid until her fingers found his cheek and his eyes slid shut.

Drawing him down, she pressed a soft kiss to his cheek, and the man shuddered. "You are the one who got me free?"

"We all did," Jason growled, unable to move.

"I owe you my life," she whispered, her arms snaking up around his neck and his went slowly, hesitantly, around her waist as though he was afraid to mar her perfection.

"You don't owe me anything," he murmured, his muscles clenching as he hugged her.

THE DOOR SLAMMED and there was a feral scream that made Jason snatch her out of the way, and Versalis exchanged a wary glance with Dirdos at the man's immediate reaction being to protect her.

Letari was in the doorway, her eyes wild as they found her sister.

"Etani!" she screamed.

Etani reached for her twin and Jason released her, watching with wide eyes as the two women hugged with a violent force.

Kai came skidding into the room, blood still on his mouth, and tackled the two women, all three landing in a heap on the carpet as he growled and crushed them both under the force of his affection. Kai kissed Etani's face over and over, ignoring her squirming attempts to get free and then growling in protest when her hand flung out for help and Dirdos yanked her free.

Looking around the room, she took in everyone and everything with an expression of relief, making sure she had the chance to touch all of them, but then her head tilted and she narrowed her eyes.

"Malik?" she asked, and everyone tensed.

"Don't you remember?" Daemon asked.

Her eyes found the pile of clothes and the chain sitting on top, her face showing her confusion before her eyes filled with tears. "Hades ... Hades will give him back, right?" she asked, turning to look at Daemon, and then Bast.

"I don't think he can," Bast said.

Her eyes turned on Versalis and he swallowed, unable to bear her pain. "Give me my magic, I will go find him," she said, reaching for him.

"No, love, you can't bring him back. Not this time," Daemon murmured, pain washing over his face.

"Please, Versalis, you have to let me find him," she pleaded, her begging destroying his soul.

"Etani I can't ... the humans don't come back," he whispered, knowing he was going to destroy her.

"He's not a human, he's my scion. He's a vampire!" she cried, turning away when he tried to wipe away her tears.

"He's only a modified human. We go to the underworld when we die ..."

"Daemon! Daemon tell him ... Tell him I can get Malik back," she pleaded, turning on the demon who could only look at her helplessly.

Versalis looked up and frowned as he saw Letari and Jason staring at each other, the crazy woman looking confused, her lips parted as she seemed to be trying to understand something he was saying, though he hadn't spoken a word. Jason was almost glaring at her in response.

Sensing Etani's distress, Letari turned away from him and headed straight for her twin.

"Daemon you have to … please!" she cried, the sound of her agonised voice destroying them all. "Hades!"

No one expected the blue flames to appear, and the God looked around at them all, cold and irritable. "What?" he snapped, his face softening slightly as he found her. "What's the matter with you?"

She stumbled into his arms and he caught her easily, Versalis blinking as he saw the finger guards and realised who the one in the box belonged to in an instant. "Hades … Malik?" she whimpered, his dark eyes softening.

"No, child, he's already gone," Hades said, his fingers gentle on her face as he brushed away her tears. "I looked, but he wasn't there."

Daemon cocked his head to the side but remained silent, watching the two as was everyone else.

"Hades please … please," she begged.

His eyes closed, pulling her against him even as she broke down, her body trembling with her sobs. "I'm sorry, Etani, I can't bring him back. I would if I could, but I can't return him to you," the God said gently, his face showing his anguish.

She couldn't hear him, broken again by the loss of something so precious to her, and he could only hold her, hoisting her up into his arms and stepping in front of the couch, sitting down in one graceful motion.

Setting her down in his lap, he looked around at the lot of them, the enormous man looking incredibly odd in the warmth and brightness of the room.

"One of you get her a blanket or something," he snapped, and Kai jerked, heading into the bedroom, and dragging the blanket off the bed. Hades wrapped her up in it, but Versalis didn't think she was overly aware of what was happening around her.

Settling her back on his lap, he wrapped his arms hard around her and set his cheek down on top of her head, the whole string of events looking determined, and then he was still, glaring at the wall while she cried herself out against his chest.

The others only moved enough to settle themselves, curled up on the floor or crammed into chairs, their faces distressed and yet still relieved now that she was with them again.

It was hard to be truly upset when they had her back, though her pain was hurting them all.

CHAPTER 24

HOMICIDE NEVER LOOKED SO GOOD

Over an hour they shared in the quiet misery of the woman they all loved, her body still, and Hades shifted, motioning for Versalis to come.

As it turned out, she had fallen asleep as her grief and the events of the day had worn her out.

Moving forward, he lifted her up and nodded to the God, taking her into the bedroom with Kai close on his heels. The vampire grunted a soft agreement and settled onto the bed, arms out for her.

Laying her down with him, Kai wrapped himself around her and made a motion for Versalis to leave, which he obeyed immediately, stepping out and closing the door quietly behind him.

"How do you endure that?" Jason murmured, his face white as snow with wide eyes and trembling hands. "How can you be around that much magic? I feel all jittery..."

"You get used to it," Daemon said.

"Is she aware of how much she affects those around her?"

"Not as far as we can tell." Uzo sighed, rubbing his eyes. "She appears to be entirely oblivious of the magic she puts off, as well as the emotional effects."

Daemon looked around at him and there was a brief pause before the demon grabbed Versalis by the shirtfront and dragged him away from the door, slamming him down onto the carpet.

"If you so much as *hint* to that girl that you are back under her spell, I will kill you ... You are to stay as far away from her as you can be," the demon snarled, fury radiating off him. "You are going to go to Winter and play house with Aurora. I don't care what it takes, you are *not* going back to Etani."

"Get off me!" Versalis growled, squirming to get himself free of the demon, but Uzo and Dirdos were moving to grab him. Hades watched from the doorway to the bedroom, tracing his index finger down the door.

"She shouldn't be able to hear. What's this about?" the God asked.

"This piece of shit went off and fucked Aurora while Etani was dead. Now she's back and I'm betting you've forgotten all about your little Princess, haven't you ..."

Versalis could only shake his head, struggling as Dirdos and Uzo grabbed his arms, Jagum stepping forward to grip his ankles.

"Is that right?" Hades asked, and Versalis saw the fury in the man's face.

Jaia was looking at him with wide eyes, fearful for him and what was going to happen.

"You were involved with her before?" Hades asked.

"No, but it was only a matter of time, same with the other vampire idiot," Daemon snapped, nodding towards Jaia. "Both of them ... she dies, and they run off to the first pair of legs they can find."

"At least this one knows what 'no' means," Uzo growled, and Hades' brows lifted.

"Implying he does not?" Hades asked, those terrible eyes turning on Jaia.

"Please, you're one to talk, Hades," Daemon snapped. "If I recall correctly, your wife didn't exactly want to go with you, either."

"I was a younger man then. Stupid, blind," Hades said with a growl. "Persephone and I no longer have issues."

"That only took a few thousand years. There you go, Jaia, just wait her out. She'll eventually forgive you."

Jaia glared at them all, shaking his head and inching away. "I ..."

"If you say you didn't mean to do it, I will obliterate you ..." Uzo snarled.

"I wasn't going to ..."

Hades was looking at Jaia with a weird expression on his face, and then reached for him, grabbing the vampire by the neck, and the two vanished.

"Well, Jaia's dead," Dirdos said, looking back down at Versalis.

He didn't seem overly concerned by the fact; none of them did, really.

"Shame, that," Uzo said as he too looked down at Versalis. "Now, what do we do with this one?"

"Castration sounds good," Daemon said, and Versalis moved to protect his groin, but he couldn't get his arms free of the two men.

"I won't try anything!" he gasped, looking up at the three of them.

"You can't try anything if we castrate you ..." Daemon said reasonably, reaching down to his belt and unsheathing a long, stiletto blade.

"I will go to Winter!" he said quickly, eyes wide.

"Yes, you will go to Winter. You will say goodbye and you will leave, and you will never come back," Daemon growled, lifting the blade above them. "You will disappear and if she ever comes looking for you, you will refuse to speak to her. You will tell her whatever it takes to ensure she can move on from you. Understand?"

"Yes," Versalis said, fear flooded through him. They let him go, and he sat up quickly, looking up at the four men who were so prepared to mutilate him for her. But then again, he would have been one of them holding the man down if he was on their side.

WHEN SHE WOKE, she looked groggy and irritable, her hair a tangled mess and her cheek imprinted with the buttons of Kai's shirt from where she had been sleeping on his chest.

Kai looked just as bad, wiping drool from his cheek as he followed her out of the bedroom. They had both slept like the dead, her out of exhaustion, and him out of stress.

She headed for the shower, dragging Kai along by the index finger and he followed her, looking at them all warily before he yawned.

Kai left the door partly open to make it clear of their intentions, and they heard the thump of someone's forehead against the tiles after the water started running.

Daemon was smiling, Dirdos was tilting sideways to see who it was.

"That was Kai's head," he said. "Etani's sitting on the floor looking like she would drown herself in the drain."

"They're such elegant morning people," Uzo said with his eyes on his tea, trying to fish out a leaf that was floating in it.

There was a low murmur of conversation from the bathroom and the sound of someone dropping a bottle though it didn't sound like it had broken.

"You'd think out of a Fae and a vampire, they'd have at least an ounce of coordination between them," Jagum said as he stood and headed for the bathroom.

"Not a chance," Vincent said in a whisper.

It was weird how easily things settled back in, though the new additions of Cyle and Jason were still a little odd.

"Who stole all the towels?" Kai called out, and all eyes turned on Daemon.

"What?" Daemon asked.

"You're usually the towel thief."

Jagum growled as he stalked back out of the room, whacking the back of Daemon's head, but Etani had followed him out, looking confused and still dripping water.

"Someone stole my towel ..." she said sleepily, squinting. "You ... towel thief. I need one."

"I'm not the towel thief!" Daemon snapped.

Versalis heard a choking sound and tilted his head slightly to see both Jason and Cyle staring with open mouths at the naked woman, though they could only see her from the side.

The rest of them were so used to seeing each other naked that it was surprising that anyone had an issue with it, but the two Hunters rarely saw women, let alone naked women.

"Who are you?" she asked, looking around at the demon-masked man.

"Cyle ..." He whimpered, and she closed one eye, squinting at him for a second before she looked away again. She didn't have the energy to be nice that early in the morning.

Jagum arrived after several minutes of the two dripping water onto the carpet, one towel hitting Kai in the face and the two Etani needed handed to her.

Wrapping one around her body and the other around her hair, she looked around, spotted Dirdos, and headed for him. She crawled into his lap while he simply lifted his book, still reading with it above his head while she settled herself. Then his arms dropped around her with the book rested against her thigh and her head rested against his chest.

"How did we not see what Jagum said?" Daemon asked, irritated.

"No idea," Versalis said.

"You're all blind idiots," Jagum said.

"What are you talking about?" she mumbled, not bothering to open her eyes.

"Nothing dear, get some more rest," Dirdos rumbled.

"I don't think I can sleep anymore," she sighed. "Anyone hungry?"

"Yes," the room rumbled as one. They were all always hungry.

"Good, go get food."

"Let no one say you don't know how to give commands," Dirdos said, kissing her forehead.

"Shut up," she mumbled half-heartedly. "Fine, I'll get food," she grumbled and wriggled free of his arms. "Kai, come for a walk?"

Kai was back on his feet, heading to the bathroom to get dressed while she went to the bedroom.

She came out a few minutes later, tugging her shirt down over her pants, and scowled when she found them all looking at her. "I need new clothes ... I can't find mine."

"What do you mean you can't find them?" Daemon asked.

"They aren't in the wardrobe, they're gone. Can someone send a message out to Valerie? I'll go get food. Don't tell her to go off Epharis' measurements."

"Will do," Dirdos said, watching her in those devious black cotton pants that drew all eyes.

She nodded and Kai took her hand, the two heading out of the room.

"Are you going to change the measurements?" Daemon asked.

"Not a chance. Those pants are the best thing in existence."

"Good, I was going to be angry if you did."

"I think I blacked out, what happened?" Jason asked after a moment.

"They went for food," Daemon said.

"Was it when she came out in the pants?" Dirdos asked.

"No, when she was naked ..." Jason replied, Cyle nodding his agreement.

"Yeah, she doesn't like wearing clothes unless she has to. You'll get used to it."

"How do you get used to that?" Cyle asked, indignant.

"Jerk off, a lot," Vincent said from the corner where he was carefully cutting feathers for his crossbow bolts.

The others nodded their agreement, amused, but Jason and Cyle exchanged a glance.

WHEN THE TWO returned the smell of meat arrived a good ten seconds before the guard was asked to open the door, and it was the most glorious sight he had ever seen.

Her eyes were lowered, an enormous silver platter of food in her grip. Her long hair was still damp and sticking to the side of her throat, enchanting him more than it should.

With that slight smile on her lips she looked even more heavenly, and she looked up at them as Kai followed her in with a second platter, a maid following along behind them with plates and cutlery in her arms.

"Is there anything else we can get you, Your Highness?" the lady asked, and there was a pause as they all were brought back to the situation in Ayathian.

"No, thank you for your help," Etani said, placing the platter down on the table between the couches. "Let's hope these savages actually remember to use their utensils."

Those savages were all staring at her arse as she bent over in those pants, oblivious to their intensity. The maid noticed, though, and she glared at them all. She was human, but she was an older woman and she very likely saw them as the pervy giant young men they all looked like.

"You all behave yourselves," she scolded.

"Yes, ma'am," Dirdos said with a straight face.

They all nodded their agreement, and she left.

It took only a second and then they lunged for the food, ignoring the utensils and racing to grab the biggest pieces of meat.

Letari and Hunter arrived not long after, the smell of food drawing them in, and Etani turned on her sister, her mouth full and eyes wide. She pointed between the two of them with her fork accusingly, her scowl making it clear that she didn't approve of their having their own room.

"Oh, stop being such a baby. It would be awkward if we started having sex with you lot around," Letari said, and Etani looked disgusted, her homicidal glare turning on Hunter, who moved around so that Letari was between him and Etani.

Swallowing hard, she picked up her knife, but Vincent plucked it out of her hand before she could use it on the man.

"Stop trying to kill my fiancé," Letari said without looking up.

"What if you end up pregnant before you're married?" Etani asked, indignant.

"What if?" Letari asked, looking up at her sister.

Etani was furious, though she seemed to be blaming Hunter and not her sister.

"Epharis gave us some of ..." He trailed off as death blazed in those amazing blue eyes.

"Don't make me do it," Letari warned, and Etani turned on her sister, fuming.

"You wouldn't dare," Etani snapped back, furious.

"Etania Vellorie Daewen, you cut this out right now!"

Etani jerked back and everyone was on high alert as the name was used, all of their predatory instincts triggered by that tiny flash of magic that shot between the two of them. It was far from a full name, but it was one of her names that none of them knew.

Etani stared at her sister, lips parted. "Why would you tell them that?" she whispered.

"You need to be nice," Letari growled.

They saw Etani's struggle, the want to retaliate, but her need to protect her sister made it impossible for her to return the shot.

"Vellorie?" Daemon asked. "That's not one of your grandmothers ... How many names do you have?"

"It's none of your business," Etani snapped.

"She has seven," Letari said, picking out several pieces of food.

"Seven?" Uzo asked.

"I have five," Letari said.

"Me, too," Uzo said, fascinated. "Seven is really unusual."

Etani only shrugged, glaring at her sister.

"How many do you know?" Dirdos asked.

"Five now," Daemon said, and Etani looked around at him in alarm.

"How?" Uzo demanded.

"One from each grandmother, one from the mother, and her first and last," Daemon replied, watching her.

There was no helping the drive in them all to have that level of control over her; it was absolute. But it didn't matter who the control was over; it could be anyone, the urge to own another like that was strong in all of them.

"Which ones do you know?" she asked in a small voice, his eyes narrowing for a moment before he moved to her side and whispered in her ear. She looked absolutely terrified, turning to look up at him as he moved away, smug at his success.

"You know she'll kill you if you get any closer ..." Uzo warned.

"I know," Daemon said, gripping her jaw and lifting her chin to better look at her face. "But not if I get it all first, then she can't."

She couldn't move, the fear and anger burning in her that he was so close. He kissed her forehead, and she watched him go, looking down finally to see that she had crushed the fork in her grip, the metal twisted and warped.

Setting down her plate, she headed into the bedroom and closed the door firmly behind her, making it very clear she wanted to be alone.

SEVERAL HOURS LATER, Kai slipped into the room and Versalis sighed, rubbing his eyes.

"You need to talk to her," Daemon said, and Versalis nodded, knowing the odds were that he wasn't going to be allowed to see her again after that. Not only that, but Aurora would be waiting for him. He had promised to go back to her and there was an odd urge in him to follow that promise.

It was incredibly painful to think that he was going to leave Etani, possibly forever. But he had the deal, and he had agreed to their conditions.

Kai returned after a few hours and Daemon pointed Versalis towards the door, all eyes turning to look at what was happening.

"What are you doing?" Kai demanded, defensive.

"I need to talk to her," he said.

"About what?"

Versalis frowned, his eyes going to Daemon, whose brows had lifted. It was the first time they had really seen Kai so protective of her against all of them, but there was no blaming him after what she had gone through.

"It's private," Daemon snapped.

"I'm going to be with Aurora," Versalis said.

"No, you're not," her voice came from the doorway, eyes narrowed on the lot of them.

"Yes, he is," Daemon growled back.

Her eyes turned on Daemon and the two glared at each other for several long seconds.

"He is going to stay right here, Daemon. None of you are going anywhere." There was an intensely possessive note to her voice that made them all shift in response, and a desperate hunger started up in his stomach.

"He is going back where he belongs," Uzo said.

"He belongs here with me. None of you are leaving, end of discussion. Excluding you two if you wish to leave," she said to Jason and Cyle. "Versalis is staying here, that's it. I don't care what your opinion is, I don't care what you agreed to, he's staying here."

"Etani ..." Daemon growled.

"He's staying here!" she yelled, making them all jump. Her eyes slid shut as she tried to control herself, exhaling slowly.

Kai was at her side in an instant and she turned into his chest without opening her eyes, sensing his presence. He murmured something in her ear and she nodded, Versalis' brows pulling together at what was going on.

"Etani?" Uzo asked.

"She's fine," Kai said, touching her chin with his thumb, and she smiled faintly.

"He's staying here. I'm not losing any more of you," she said, resting her forehead against Kai's chest. His arms went around her protectively.

"Where's Jaia?" Kai asked when no one spoke out against her command.

"Hades took him," Daemon said.

Etani looked up at them, her eyes narrowing before she sighed. "Hades!" she called, her hand sliding into Kai's.

Versalis didn't understand her sudden attachment to the vampire, but it might have something to do with his kindness and gentle nature that she needed so badly. Her life was in turmoil, and he wasn't sure just how much of it she was able to deal with at once.

"No," Hades said, and they all turned to find the man standing there, arms crossed.

"Yes," she said.

"No," he repeated.

"Now, Hades."

"He abused you."

Her eyes flicked to Daemon and then Uzo and Dirdos.

"Return him," she said simply.

"No."

"Now."

"Etani ..."

"Now!" she snapped, the air seeming to crackle around her, and she turned into Kai.

Hades watched her carefully, his eyes narrowing in consideration. "What's wrong with her?" he asked Daemon.

"Your guess is as good as mine," Daemon said.

"It's fine, just return my brother," Kai said, his fingers in her hair

256

and holding her head against his chest while the other splayed against her back.

"He's a rapist," Hades growled.

"Yes, but he needs to be here," Kai said.

Hades glared at them all, shaking his head.

"You're all insane," he snapped, and flames burst up in the corner of the room.

Jaia was naked, bleeding, and bruised with his left hand missing entirely.

"Jaia!" Kai cried, letting go of Etani and moving to his brother, and for a second Versalis could see the fear on her face before she masked it, turning to look at Jaia on the rug.

Hades moved for her while Kai was distracted and she looked up at him as he lifted her jaw, forcing her head back to meet his eyes.

They seemed to be communicating silently as he held her gaze, his face going dark before he nodded and bent down to murmur in her ear.

She nodded, her face carefully blank. She looked up at Versalis as he stared at her, confused and worried about what was happening.

She asked Hades something and he shook his head. Her shoulders slumped slightly, but when he spoke again, her eyes turned from Versalis to Dirdos. Glancing at Dirdos, the dragon was watching her as well, his brows pulled together in a frown.

Hades motioned for Dirdos and ushered the two of them into the bedroom, Dirdos silent as a ghost, though most were paying attention to Jaia, anyway.

Daemon was looking gleefully at Jaia, but Uzo saw the interaction and his lips pressed into a hard line, but he didn't interfere with them.

CHAPTER 25
KINGS AND QUEENS

They didn't find out what it was she needed from Dirdos, the dragon refusing to answer their questions, and she wouldn't even open her mouth when asked. She would simply look as though she didn't understand the question.

The conversations about Aurora and Versalis were not brought up again, but he could feel the death glare on him from Daemon. He ignored it, given Daemon was easier to ignore than Etani, but after the first few outbursts she seemed to calm down, her mood considerably more relaxed, as though nothing had happened at all.

They knew better than to bring it up again; instead they all pretended it didn't happen and after the first day, Hades left with a warning glare at Jaia who didn't appear to be healing at all.

It was decided that when human blood didn't work, Etani would supply him the blood, and she held out her wrist to him without a word, her eyes still on the bowl of fruit that had been brought up. She was digging through it for chunks of strawberry while Dirdos and Uzo stole the bits she ignored.

The vampire went for her arm with an eagerness Versalis didn't like, but he kept his opinion to himself, and she didn't so much as flinch as his teeth sank into her soft skin.

He looked ragged, part of his face burnt, lacking his hand, his body broken in multiple places, but after he fed from her, his body had repaired within a matter of hours and his hand had regrown by the next morning.

Afterwards she made an effort to almost drain herself of blood in order to ensure both of them had enough to keep them going, and she fell asleep in Dirdos' lap, purring faintly at the warmth of the man.

It wasn't unusual to see Jagum nearby in those moments, his ears twisted to the sound of her quiet purring, or even holding her hand while she slept.

Dirdos became increasingly protective, wary of those around her whom he no longer trusted and, much to his own disgust, Versalis had come to rely on Jaia for advice. They were the odd men out now, though Versalis wasn't keen to associate himself with the man.

A few days after they had arrived Alaric learnt of their return when he stumbled upon Versalis and Jaia in the hallway, the giant man looking surprised by their appearance.

"When did you get back?" Alaric demanded.

"Three days ago," Versalis said.

Alaric appeared annoyed, looking them over before he turned to a guard.

"Arrest them," he said simply, and Jaia yelled as they were jumped on.

Cuffs and muzzles were quickly applied, and they were left flattened to the ground, looking up at Alaric's feet.

"I'm sure Helena will be happy to see you," Alaric said happily. "Welcome to the world of political prisonership."

Versalis and Jaia looked at each other, deciding that no, they weren't going to enlighten the man on the current presence of a Queen of Faerie in his castle, a wry smile on Jaia's face telling him it was going to be funnier when Alaric found out on his own.

With the help of two men, Versalis climbed to his feet and smiled up at Alaric, amused even though he was very aware that the King already had the muzzle on him, as though he had expected to find them. It was possible the thought was true, given how things had ended with them last time.

Versalis smiled when he looked up at a scuff and found Dirdos watching them from the end of the hall, head tilted to the side and looking bemused.

Giving a little wave, Dirdos shook his head and turned, walking away down the hall. No doubt he was off to inform Etani of their capture.

"Going to be pissed," Versalis said.

"Like someone stole the last strawberry," Jaia replied. "And ate it in front of her."

Alaric didn't hear their words, instead he ordered them be taken to the war council room, and he stopped a maid, asking that someone be sent to inform the vampiress of Versalis' return.

Forced into a chair, Versalis shifted and settled himself with a curious look at Jaia, who mostly just looked bored, his silver eyes sweeping the room.

"You should have told me you were back. We would have thrown a party," the giant man boomed out as he came into the room, delighted by his capture. "Winter not to your liking?"

"We had other matters to attend to," Jaia said, looking up as the woman entered and blinking hard.

There wasn't much else one could do when faced with a Vampire Queen. They were exquisite creatures by nature and the sexual tension they radiated only made it worse.

"Versalis!" she cried, sweeping down on him and kissing his cheek. "How are you? I haven't seen you in a terribly long time ... Who's your friend?"

"Jaia, he works for Alaric."

"Not anymore," Alaric said, and Jaia flinched. "There's a twin as well, Kai."

Her brows lifted, fascinated by them. "Twin vampires? Alaric you've been holding out on me," she teased. "We have so many arrangements to make."

"I'm afraid I'm not going to be able to do that," Versalis said as he felt that screaming rage coming in the back of his mind. Etani had just found out what happened.

"I don't think you have much of a choice, my darling. What do you say, Alaric? Do we have a deal?"

"You might want to waylay that," Jaia said with a slight smirk.

THE DOOR EXPLODED inwards with such force that it splintered down the middle and both Alaric and Helena spun around.

Etani stood in the doorframe, her hair wild and eyes blazing. She was glorious in her anger, the air around her seeming to shimmer and warp. "Alaric ..." she growled, that voice dripping both sex and violence in equal measures.

"Etani?" Alaric sputtered, not at all expecting her.

"This is your Goddess? She's tiny ..." Helena scoffed.

"Dinner says she's dead," Jaia said.

"You're on," Versalis said.

Etani's eyes moved from Alaric to Helena, and there was no longer sex in that glare, only violence.

"Who the fuck are you?" Etani snarled and Versalis looked down to see that the marble under her pretty feet was frosting over.

"Helena of the Lamia Clan," the vampiress said. "Who are you?"

Etani didn't look overly impressed by the woman's boasts. "Etania Daewen, Queen of Winter, Goddess of Destruction, Princess of Ayathian, Creator, Death ..." Etani said, Versalis' next breath forming mist in the air.

"You? You look like an overdeveloped child," Helena said, amused.

"Damn," Versalis muttered, fairly certain he had just lost the bet.

"Three …" Jaia said slowly as Etani's cheeks flushed.

"Two …" Versalis muttered, her hair lifting up off her shoulders.

"One," they said together, and she moved.

Taking three steps, she closed the distance to the Vampire Queen and with a movement so fast he couldn't see it, she drove her foot into Helena's side and the vampire vanished, a hole appearing in the side of the castle.

Etani looked out of the hole at the Queen and then turned back to Alaric, her eyes glowing an ominous white.

"If you ever attempt to take a member of my Court prisoner again, I will bring the full force of the Court down upon your head. Do we understand each other?" she spoke in a deadly calm voice.

"You can't threaten me," he said, and she smiled, a very dangerous smile.

"Very well, we will continue this conversation shortly, please excuse me for a moment."

Etani vanished, streaking out of the hole in the wall.

Dirdos and Daemon appeared in the doorway and looked at the destruction before they sighed and moved to release the two vampires, all of them crowding the hole to see.

Etani was standing on Helena's back, gripping the woman's arms, and was heaving backwards. They watched with fascination as she ripped the arms free of the woman's body and threw one, stepping off the woman's back, and when Helena scrambled to her feet, Etani took aim and stepped into it, using the arm like a bat, the vampire's head snapping back.

Dirdos started laughing, Daemon was grinning and Jaia whistled.

"Didn't expect her head to stay on…."

"No … we need to stop her," Versalis said as Etani grabbed the woman's hair and, placing one foot against her back, started pulling to rip the woman's head off.

"Etani, stop!" Daemon yelled as he realised it at the same instant as the rest of them.

Leaping out of the hole, she looked up at him just as he slammed into her, ripping her arms free with the rest of them right on his heels. She didn't try to fight them, her hands up in the position of surrender.

"Why?" she asked, unsure of what was happening, but she trusted them enough to know they wouldn't have stopped her without reason.

"You can't kill a Queen; you'll have her whole clan on you," Jaia called out. "Normally it wouldn't matter, but we don't know if you will end up like Versalis, taking her magic. You don't want to end up a Queen in control of that clan."

She looked up at Jaia for several seconds and then nodded. "Okay," she said simply, her agreement surprising them all.

"You're just going to listen?" he asked.

"You wouldn't make that up," she said.

"Where did you put the real Etani?" he asked.

"Shut up before I change my mind," she snapped.

Daemon let her go, and she turned on the vampiress. "If you ever touch Versalis, or one of my people, or try to take him again, I will personally hunt you down and put a stake through your heart," Etani promised, the Queen whimpering.

There were more of them at the hole in the wall and she looked up as Kai appeared, making her way back towards the castle as he leapt down.

"Are you okay?" he asked, clutching her face and drawing her close.

"Yes, I'm fine. Did you know there was a Vampire Queen here?"

Kai blinked at her, looking past her to the others and then shaking his head.

She was visibly relieved by that but then her head tilted and she squinted up at the hole.

"Excuse me ..." she muttered and bit into her index finger.

"Etani, no!" Jaia cried, but she was already gone.

"She's going to talk some sense into Alaric," Versalis said to Daemon.

"Oh, that will certainly end well," Dirdos said, seemingly unconcerned by the threat.

Daemon growled and vanished, Dirdos grinning at them all. "Group hug!" he called out, and they all moved closer to him, vanishing in an explosion of fire to leave Helena on her own, though her vampires would be joining her soon enough.

THEY STEPPED out into the room above and they all froze, seeing Daemon with his hands in his pockets and Etani sitting calmly on Alaric's chest while six guards stood over her with spears pointing down towards her. The problem was, all six guards were frozen solid and there was snow falling from the ceiling.

"You do realise that if I kill you, Epharis and I will rule Ayathian, yes?" she asked conversationally, the big man either too scared to move or otherwise deciding it was in his best interest to stay still while she was in a violent mood.

"I am aware of that. But my people will never follow you."

"That's perfectly okay with me. I can get my own people. We can be the counterbalance to Istralis, they are almost exclusively human, and we can be almost exclusively mythical. It'd be a wonderful balance."

Versalis didn't think she was serious, but it was hard to tell with her sometimes.

"Etani, stop playing with the little King and come back to the rooms," Dirdos said in an affected, bored voice.

"Maybe it's best if we vacated Ayathian for good," Daemon said slowly. Versalis thought the demon had seen the same calculating look on the King's face as the man looked up at her that he had seen. It wasn't ever a good thing when Alaric was scheming.

"Back to Winter?" Uzo asked, casting a glance in his direction.

"Possibly."

Etani was watching them all with her head tilted to the side, more curious than alarmed now that they were discussing tactics.

"You think we should leave?" she asked, her expression going thoughtful. "What about husband number one?"

Daemon frowned, his lips pressing together at her casual mention of the Lich.

"Bring him along if you want. But it's not safe here for you."

"Me?" she asked, surprised and more than a little confused.

"Yes, you," the demon sighed, offering his hand to her. She took it and he pulled her to her feet, tapping her nose. "Keep in mind, my little Etani, that you are the Queen of Winter, and a Creator, among other things. That makes you an exceptionally valuable target for kidnapping, assassination, and the like."

She blinked at him, her mouth opening then closing, opening again and then closing again as she tried to come up with an argument, but he had stumped her. It was rather adorable to see her flounder for an argument.

"I have all of you to keep me safe," she said.

"And look how well that has turned out," Kai muttered.

"Oh, you shut up," she snapped, the vampire smirking at her in amusement.

"Oh how terribly rude of me, I shouldn't have told the truth. It's not like you were dead for several months. Oh wait... Ow!" She punched his arm, glaring up at him.

"That's enough sarcasm out of you!"

"Yes, ma'am," the vampire said, rubbing his bruised arm.

HEADING BACK TO HER ROOMS, Etani threw one last look at Alaric who glared at her, the guards around him only just starting to defrost as the snow stopped falling.

"You know he's likely going to retaliate …" Daemon said, falling into step beside the tiny woman.

"I know, but let's see what he comes up with. What about the vampires?"

"Definitely, we're spiteful creatures," Versalis said, ignoring the snort from Daemon and Uzo.

"Oh right … the husband …" she said and looked to the door that belonged to the Lich. "Hold on."

She headed to the door and banged on it; her head cocked to the side as she considered the sounds coming from inside. Her eyes narrowed and she took a step back from the door, lifted her foot and slammed the heel down on the wood a few inches above the handle.

"Epharis!" she snarled, stalking inside.

Versalis looked around at the others and then shrugged, following after her and peeking around the doorframe.

"Oh, you're back," the Lich said, his pants around his ankles and a young woman looking a little flustered on her knees before him.

"You know … no, you know what? You can stay here," she snapped and stalked back out of the room. "Stay here with your psychotic brother and this whole city of weirdos, I'm going to Winter."

"Etani come back here," the Lich growled, pulling his pants back up and sighing. "It's really not what it looked like."

"Looked pretty obvious to us," Daemon said, amused that the man had been busted with another woman.

"Etani!" he roared, but she was already gone to her room.

The young woman stood, her hands on her hips and looking irritated, but the Lich had gone after his wife.

Daemon took one look at the rest of them and then ran for the suite where they could already hear the two shouting.

"You'd think she'd be thrilled if she didn't want to be married to the man …" Kai said, following along behind them all as they streamed back towards the room.

"Get out!" she screamed.

"Don't raise your voice at me! You are my wife, and you will behave as such!"

"This whole city brings new light to the term 'dysfunction.'" Versalis sighed.

"You were just in there with another woman! And you had no pants on, while she was on her knees!"

"Well, it's not like you're ever in that position," the Lich muttered and then ducked, a knife lodging in the wall. "Stop throwing things and calm down. I was not engaged in intercourse with her."

"That wasn't intercourse Epharis, that was oral!" she snarled, throwing another knife at him which he also ducked.

"It wasn't oral either," he said, frustrated but calm enough.

"Epharis I don't want to hear what weird things you are doing with random women. I'm going back to Faerie, and you can stay here."

"You're not going anywhere without my say-so."

Daemon snorted his amusement at that and the rest of them groaned in sympathy.

"Excuse me?" she asked, that tone suggesting violence was only a matter of seconds from erupting.

"You're staying here."

"Do you think she'll just try and stab him?" Dirdos asked, leaning against the wall with an amused expression.

"Probably not, I think she's past the stabbing stage," Daemon murmured.

"What makes you think I'm going to listen to you?"

"You will do as you're told."

"Castration is still an option, though ..." Daemon said into the silence.

It wasn't an option, she didn't castrate him; instead, she kicked him through the wall and into the hallway with them.

They all looked down at the Lich, his face livid, and he didn't seem capable of seeing them at all, glaring at her as he dragged himself back to his feet and stalked back in after her.

"Come here!" he snarled.

"Do we interfere?" Dirdos asked.

"Do we interrupt her chance to become a widow?"

"Black widow ..." Jaia muttered, all of them listening as the Lich yelled in pain. Evidently, she had stabbed him.

The Lich had her by the hair and she twisted on him, driving her knee up into his groin. The Lich collapsed onto the floor, dragging her down with him.

"Let go of me!" she screamed, but he refused and Versalis tilted his head to see around the edge of the doorframe. He had his arms wrapped around her, pinning her arms to her sides, and was hoisting her up off the ground, growling when she squirmed.

"You're not going anywhere. You belong at my side, and in my bed."

"I belong in Winter!" she yelled, looking up at a huff from the door.

Etani's brows lifted, and she looked around, smiling when she found something.

The woman had appeared in the doorway, completely ignoring the group of men eavesdropping on the conversation.

Using her foot, she pitched a chunk of broken wood up into the air and then kicked it towards the woman, the chunk of wood scoring her right on the forehead, snapping her head back.

"Good shot ..." Dirdos said with a clap.

The woman wasn't overly injured, though she was bleeding.

"What is wrong with you people!?" she screamed, the two of them freezing in place.

"Nothing, this is my wife. Etani, this is my doctor, Evelyn."

Etani blinked, staring at the woman, and then tilting her head back to look up at Epharis. "What do you need a doctor for? You're dead ..."

"He was deteriorating somewhat after the magical anomalies that happened," the woman said, brushing her forehead.

"Yes ... about those ..." Epharis growled, and she shrugged.

"And you needed to do that with your pants off?"

"Most of the damage was around his trunk, however there was some damage to his left thigh, just below his groin. I was merely inspecting the area."

"Inspecting ..." Etani sneered.

"Unlike some, I have no interest in being with a Lich," Evelyn snapped.

"No one wants to be with a Lich, they're bastards," Etani snapped right back at the woman.

"Enough. You are clearly well enough to be fighting, what else are you well enough for?" he growled, and she went still.

"If you intend to go to Faerie, then you will recover faster. However, you appear to be recovering fine now, ensure you continue at the current volume and then reduce when the damage is repaired," the woman said, glaring at them. "I'll be charging double," she stalked away, Etani looking at Daemon and Versalis then, realising they were watching.

"You all thought the same thing," she said.

"No doubt about it," Daemon said with a sigh. "Put her down, Epharis."

Epharis set her down on her feet and she turned on him, glaring.

"I didn't know you would get so jealous," the Lich sneered.

"Shove it," she snapped, sweeping past him and into her bedroom. "Seriously?" After a moment she came back out, looking around. "Where are all my things going? Which one of you is stealing it all?"

"Stealing what?" Uzo asked, the lot of them filing into the room.

"First my clothes and now my stock in the panel in the wardrobe..." She swept the room with her eyes. "The necklace ... where's the necklace?"

Versalis turned to see that the little bowl holding the cat necklace was gone.

"Daemon, where's Letari's necklace?" the tiny woman gasped, reaching for him in a panic.

"I don't know, none of us would take it."

"Someone has been stealing from your rooms? A staff member, maybe?" Kai asked.

"We need to get that back! Where's Letari? Maybe she took it?"

"I'll go find her," Dirdos said, sweeping from the room.

"Who would steal from here?" Daemon asked.

"Anyone looking for a quick bit of money? We should have been able to smell them, though." Versalis shook his head, unable to smell anything out of the ordinary.

CHAPTER 26

THIEVES

After a pause she turned on them and ordered them all out, and they obeyed her orders though Epharis refused to leave and they heard the sound of the chair being moved, a soft scuff of the panel and Epharis growling a question at her. She didn't answer, a soft tinkling sound and a thud.

She was apparently satisfied and Epharis called them all back in, the panel replaced, and the box hidden away once more.

"I don't think anything else has been taken," she said, chewing on the nail of her index finger as she swept around the room.

"Did you know there was a panel in the wardrobe?" Daemon asked.

"No," Versalis muttered back, somewhat annoyed by the missed opportunity.

"None of you took any of it?" she asked, her eyes hopeful. "I won't be mad."

"No love, we didn't take anything," Daemon said gently.

She searched his face before her eyes turned on the rest of them, wanting to find one of them lying, but none of them were.

Letari, Hunter, and Dirdos appeared a few minutes later and the lovely green-eyed woman went to Etani.

"What's the matter?" Letari demanded, seeing the stress in her twin's face.

"Someone stole my things ... the necklace ... your necklace," Etani whimpered.

"Hey, it's just a necklace, silly. Don't stress so much."

"But ... you died in it," she whispered and Letari blinked.

"I'm not dead now."

Etani frowned, unable to fault that logic, but it didn't seem to make her feel any better.

"What has been going missing?" Epharis asked.

"My clothes mostly ..." she said, looking around at the man.

"Someone's stealing your clothes?" Hunter asked, looking around the room and then heading into the bedroom to sniff around.

"What?" Letari asked, frowning after the man.

"That's really odd behaviour ... I mean it could be harmless, but in this city? It could be someone who's obsessed with you."

"Who isn't obsessed with Etani?" Daemon asked.

Versalis watched Etani's reaction, her frown, and the way she turned away from the man. She didn't like that people were so addicted to her.

"Well, it won't matter if we're in Faerie," Dirdos said.

"We're going to Faerie?" Letari asked.

"We had planned to," Etani said. "At least for the time being."

"Etani needs to be more closely guarded. We can't do that here," Daemon growled.

"Is Faerie going to be safer?" Hunter asked.

"Is there anywhere better?"

"I can think of a few places."

"Such as?" Etani asked.

"My clan can protect you."

There was a total silence as they all looked at the man, frowning and uncertain.

"Your clan? You mean there is actually a clan like you? I assumed you were kidding," Dirdos said.

"No, there are more like me. The Queen of Winter and my soon to be sister-in-law? They'll be glad to have you."

Etani's eye twitched at the mention of her soon-to-be-relationship to the man but she only nodded slowly, uncertain. "What do you think?" she asked Daemon, the demon scowling at Hunter.

"I would need to see this place first."

"You can't. You can only go there if you plan to stay."

Etani watched Hunter, chewing idly on her nail before her eyes turned on Letari and the two seemed to be communicating silently.

"All right," Etani said. "But we need to be able to leave when we want."

"That's fine. But you also have to swear to not speak of what you see to anyone," Hunter countered.

"Deal," she said.

Daemon growled his anger, but everyone was already moving in preparation for the at least temporary departure from the city, Etani still watching Hunter before she turned away and headed for her room to pack what was left of her belongings.

Versalis let out a soft sigh, and they followed the others out to get his own things packed.

By the time they returned the room had been dismantled and Versalis was fascinated to see the sheer number of places Etani had managed to hide things from them in there. Trick drawers were opened, hidden compartments, walls that she could pop out and back in. A panel of marble that lifted up on the floor.

"How is it possible that you could do all of this without us noticing?" he demanded.

"You're all oblivious sometimes," she replied, packing it all into a series of large leather cases.

"You're taking all that?" Daemon demanded when he appeared, looking at the pile of luggage she had collected.

"Yes," she said, her eyes a blatant challenge.

"You're going to need a pack mule."

She looked at Dirdos, who had apparently been beaten into submission.

"Dirdos said he'd do it," she said.

"Dirdos said he would do it so she would stop hitting him," Dirdos said grumpily.

"Dirdos knows better than to argue," she said, smiling.

"Is Jagum going to be okay in the werewolf compound?" Letari asked, dragging along several large chests all piled neatly on top of each other.

"She's just as bad as Etani ..." Dirdos complained.

"Dirdos!" Letari cried.

"Get your own pack mule," Etani snipped.

"I'm not coming to the clan," Jagum said. "I need to go back to my own clan."

Etani spun around to look at Jagum, her eyes huge in her fear. "What do you mean you're not coming?" she whimpered.

"I have to go back, darling, I'm needed there," he said, scooping her up into his arms. "Plus, werewolves and werecats don't go well together."

"We can go somewhere else," she said, clinging to him.

"No, you need to be safe, and they can look after you."

"We can go to Winter and be safe there. All of us together," she pleaded, her arms tight around his neck.

"Etani, sweetheart ... you have to let me go," he growled. "I've been here too long, they need me."

She shook her head, that perfect face anguished. "Jagum, we can go with you," she said, terrified to lose even one of them though she wasn't actually losing him.

He seemed to realise the same thing Versalis did, and he frowned at her, his large paws soft on her face as he cupped her cheeks and rubbed his nose on hers. "You're not losing me, sweetheart, I'm still here. I just need to be apart from you for a while. But I'll come back to you," he promised, his claw gently brushing her hair away from her face. "I won't even be gone all that long."

"You can't go ..." she whimpered, but he smiled.

"Silly girl, don't stress. You'll have a whole heap of stupid dogs to keep you company. You can see how many you can kill and make my job easier."

She laughed, but it was a teary laugh, tugging him down and nuzzling her face against his. "Promise you'll come back to me?" she whispered, and he growled, crushing her against him as he nuzzled her right back, determined to leave his scent all over her even as she squirmed.

"You can't actually get rid of me, I'm like a bad smell. It goes away for a little while, but it always comes back."

"Okay ..." she whispered, all the more beautiful for her tears and suffering. "I love you."

"I love you, too, crazy kitten," he said, licking her cheek before he let her go.

"I'll take you," Daemon said, ruffling her hair before he wrapped an arm around Jagum's shoulders.

"Appreciate that," the cat said, looking down at her hungrily for a moment before he smiled and waved, the two of them stepping through the tear in reality and away to where the werecat lived.

There was a warmth that filled the room, the warm scent of rainforest and greenery.

"Everyone's leaving," she whimpered, looking so small and fragile.

"No, they're not, we're not going anywhere," Dirdos said, taking her hand and pulling her close to him.

"We're never going anywhere," Uzo murmured, watching her, and smiling when she looked at him.

"I suppose he'll have to come in for the wedding," Hunter grumbled, looking around at Letari, who nodded.

"Pardon?" Etani said, looking around at him.

"Where did you think we would get married?" Letari asked.

"Winter," Etani said immediately, the two looking confused.

"Why Winter?" Hunter asked.

"Because you're the birth heir to the throne. You should be married there."

There was a sudden silence as they took in the fact that they all seemed to have overlooked.

"What?" Uzo gasped, looking genuinely alarmed.

"Oh right, second born ..." Letari said. "Would you be offended if I murdered you?"

"Only a little bit ..." Etani said, shaking her head. "How did none of you realise that Letari was next in line?"

"None of us really thought about it," Daemon said, just as horrified as Uzo.

"Well, let's hope I don't die any time soon then, huh?"

"So, what do we do? The clan or Winter?" Hunter asked.

"Depends how soon you want to get married," Etani said, her eyes sweeping the room for any compartments or weapons she might have missed.

"Right away!" Letari cried.

"Then Winter," Etani said absently, her head tilting as she looked at her room.

Versalis swallowed as he realised just how much trouble he was going to be in once they got to Winter. He was going to have to deal with Aurora, who was certain to know he had reneged on his promise to her. He didn't know, but he could only hope she wasn't going to be too angry.

Collecting the last of their supplies, Etani did one final sweep of the room and nodded in agreement, deciding that she likely did have everything she owned.

Etani looked up at Dirdos and smiled, the dragon frustrated, but when she slipped her arms around his middle he smiled, her touch enough to calm the beast.

"Come on then, we can all go at once," the dragon grumbled, suckered in by her charm.

They all shuffled in, bags piled high and looking more like a supply train than anything else.

Those like Vincent, Dainin and Sebastian all stood back, grinning at them. They would get there on their own.

Dirdos looked down at Etani and smiled, her eyes turned upwards to meet his gaze, and Versalis was suddenly certain that there was something they weren't telling the rest of them. He would have to find out what it was one day.

They were dumped out in the royal suite and Etani looked around, her lip curling at the pastel colouring of the room. She was very adamant about the rooms not being in pastel colours, but at least this one didn't seem to be as disturbing as the one in Alaric's suites. It was mostly blues and purples, but still.

Etani changed almost immediately, silver seeping down her hair as though water were being dripped onto her head, her skin paling just slightly and those same odd, lovely markings burning their way into existence.

Her hair pulled up into elaborate braids, twisting and knotting before their eyes with little pearls blooming, linked with a silver chain.

Her eyes lowered, the same dark pigment seemingly flowing up to her skin like blood, enhancing the shocking blue of her eyes.

Her dress started at her shoulders and flowed down around her with an odd appearance of ice crystals that darkened to a deep silvery-grey, wrapping around her arms and flowing down around her in soft layers. It wasn't bulky like they wore in Ayathian but soft, elegant, and smooth with a short train and elaborate vine-like embroidery down her back in pure white.

She lifted her hand, touching her hair, and her smile was devastating, fond as though welcoming a lover back to her. Versalis didn't understand her connection to Winter, but they seemed a lot closer than they should be.

"Letari!" Hunter cried, and they all looked around in alarm.

Letari had changed as well, though she looked at least mostly the same. She had an elaborate marking over her brow and her short, black hair had turned a sweet silver, her already white skin seeming to glitter as Winter greeted her.

Her dress was considerably shorter, coming to a stop just under her knees, and she wore little shoes with ribbons that curled up around her calves. The dress was a deep grey-black and left her shoulders and back bare, though it curled up around her throat in an exotic, almost fiery lace pattern.

Etani smiled at her sister, warm and adoring. "Welcome to my home, Letari Daewen," she murmured, her face oddly still and curious as she studied her sister.

"Etani?" Versalis asked, but Etani only looked at him, her eyes trailing down his form before turning back to Letari.

"I am sorry I never got to meet you before, but you have yet to visit my land while I was alert. Regardless, I am glad to finally have you here," she spoke in a formal, almost clipped voice that was very much not her own, her face barely moving and her hands linking before her.

"Thank you," Letari said in a small, terrified voice.

"Do not be alarmed, I only asked to speak with you for a few moments. Etania is perfectly fine, I am what you call the magic of Winter. Etania is the first one to speak to me in eons, but she is also one of the few who were born to wield me, as you are as well. However, I do not believe your mind would be capable, meaning no disrespect."

Letari only shrugged and smiled sheepishly, looking around at the rest of them all for help.

"Etania wishes to come back now, I am sorry if I alarmed you all. Please be kind to her, she is suffering more than she is willing to admit. She will need your help if she is to survive intact. I do not think it will take much to cause her mind to shatter like yours and she is too powerful to be contained," she turned to look at Dirdos, eyes narrowing, before looking again at Versalis. "Good luck. I will be watching."

Etani blinked hard, her hand lifting to her head, and she made a soft sound of distress. She reached for Versalis, and after a moment of surprise, he took her hand and allowed her to lean against him. He hadn't expected her to reach for him of all people.

"I feel like I have ice in my brain," she said, his arms going around her to help support her. Her bodice was oddly hard, and he had to wonder if it was a corset like the ones they wore in Ayathian. She wasn't going to be very happy about that.

"It will pass," Versalis said, reaching up to rub her temple gently, and he was surprised that the kohl and markings didn't smudge at all.

"We need to go to the Court, they will know you're here," Uzo said, and she nodded, her head bowed as she touched his hands, pressing them to her cheeks. He revelled in her touch but then her eyes snapped up and she pulled away from him, seemingly remembering what had happened between them.

"Yes, you're right." She sighed, doing a doubletake as she looked at Letari.

"Lee, you look so pretty!" she gasped, smiling at her twin.

"So do you!" Letari cried back.

NONE of them seemed willing to discuss the matters that Winter had mentioned, and it appeared that she was unaware of what had been said. It was probably for the best, but it was still concerning.

Hugging her sister, Etani took her by the hand and led the way out of the room, the guards jerking around as the doors to the royal suite opened.

Evidently, they had thought they were empty.

"Good evening," Etani said, and the two guards bowed deeply to her.

She moved past them and Versalis snorted when both guards turned their heads in unison to stare after her, stunned into silence as she moved away.

The doors to the throne room opened of their own accord as she approached and the hall turned to see her, looking only slightly pained, but if one didn't know her, it wouldn't be possible to tell.

A whisper started out and then a cheer went out as she headed for the throne. Aurora stood with a huge smile, stepped down, and the two embraced.

"You owe me dinner," Uzo muttered to Daemon, and Dirdos snorted.

"Really? On this?" the dragon asked.

"Aurora stole her love; I'd expect some reaction."

"She wants to rip her throat out," Letari said, watching the two. "There is so much rage it's blinding. But she needs Aurora, so she will be what we all expect her to be."

Versalis glanced at the woman and when he looked back, Aurora was watching him over the Queen's shoulder, her eyes burning.

Etani drew back from the taller woman and Aurora turned with her, guiding the Queen up onto the dais, and as Etani turned, Aurora dropped into a deep curtsy, almost kneeling before the radiant woman.

The Court followed suit, bowing to their Queen, and Etani sat down, the throne lighting up behind her with a deep, warm, blue-white glow.

It was odd to outsiders, but the Fae were so completely obsessed with formality that even their magic responded to it.

A cheer started somewhere, and the room exploded with noise, drawing others into the hall until there was barely room to move.

The celebration started almost on its own, someone with a violin playing a merry tune and the Court going into full celebration mode, dancing and laughing as Etani turned to Aurora and the two spoke quietly.

Aurora looked annoyed for a moment but then nodded, kissing Etani's hand and stepping down from the dais.

Etani looked around as a tall man approached her and she accepted his offer to dance, a soft rumble starting up behind them.

"Keep an eye on her," Hades growled. "No one is to take their eyes off her, understood?"

Dirdos nodded once and moved to position himself at the exit to the hall, his crimson eyes locked on her as though magnetised. Versalis hadn't noticed the God arrive, but the others didn't seem surprised by the appearance.

"What's going on?" Daemon asked.

"Nothing, but this is a good opportunity to cause havoc. She's also vulnerable in a moment like this."

"You need to go deal with your lover," Daemon snapped, looking around at Versalis.

"I need to stay here and help."

"The Gods are coming; she will be safe. Go," Daemon snapped.

Versalis sighed and moved to follow after the small blonde woman. He could feel Etani's eyes on him and her burning rage, but he ignored it as he made his way after Aurora.

She sat against the wall, her head bowed and arms wrapped around herself. "You are going back to her, aren't you," she said, not a question as much as a statement of fact. "I don't blame you; everyone immediately loves her."

He stopped and looked at her, beautiful and tragic with her sad face and lovely eyes.

"No one can help but love her," he said, moving towards her. "But I love you as well," he said, knowing it was a different love now. It wasn't the blinding, desperate, lust-filled love he had felt for her before; it was softer now.

"But you will follow after her again. Is that why she came back? To taunt me?"

"No, for Letari. She plans to leave again after the wedding."

Aurora nodded, staring at him with pained eyes.

"Why did you love me if you were only going to go back to her?"

"I love you, and I am greedy. I wanted you... I still want you."

"Then stay with me," she hissed.

"I belong to her."

Aurora bit her lower lip and shook her head, turning away from him.

"It's not her fault, she can't turn it off."

"Would she?"

"I think so. I think she doubts we really care about her and feels we are only there for her magic pull."

"You probably are," Aurora whimpered. "You loved me when she was gone."

"That didn't stop because she's back."

"Then love me," she demanded.

Versalis frowned, considering her for a moment before he moved forward, and he took her jaw in his hand. His head bowed and his lips met hers gently.

The kiss was both the same and entirely different. It was Aurora, and she was so soft and gentle that he knew he could easily fall back into their short relationship, but there was still that pull towards Etani. It was strong and demanding and he wondered if Hunter had been through this exact moment, kissing Letari and turning his back on the pull towards the Goddess.

He deepened the kiss and she clung to him, drawing him down harder against her. He groaned, feeling a sudden fraying of his connection to Etani and he knew he could break it. It would be easy to break it and it would be over, but did he want it to be over?

Did he want to turn his back on Etani?

No.

He drew back from Aurora, looking down at her pained face as she turned away from him. "I'm sorry. Blame me for being weak. I am not enough of a man for you," he said, releasing her and moving away.

"I suppose not …" She gasped, turning and fleeing down the hallway.

Versalis rested his head against the wall, jerking back as he heard a scream coming from the hall.

CHAPTER 27
ETANI

Versalis turned and sprinted for the throne room, but there appeared to be nothing out of sorts, Etani was dancing with a man with purple hair and Letari had been stolen away from her fiancé by a satyr who seemed to be deeply regretting his choice to flirt with her. She was grinning maniacally and he was looking more than a little scared, but it was only a few minutes more before the green-eyed woman was stolen away by Dirdos, whose eyes had tracked them both very carefully. Etani might be his priority, but he wasn't about to let anything happen to Letari, either.

The scream had drawn some attention, but it appeared to have been a happy scream and not a scared one, his eyes tracking the small group of apparently intoxicated revellers.

Glad there was no danger, he headed for the hallway back towards the royal suite, but then paused, knowing his absence would be noticed by the others. It was best if he just stuck around to play bodyguard, and then escaped when it was suitable to do so.

Settling himself in a chair by the edge of the party, he studied those who frequented the Court. The Fae were definitely the most common, but there was still a large variety of beings, everything from Gods to a little pixie who was singing a rude rendition of a love song at top volume.

As before, the three vampires were garnering a lot of attention and a young woman was slowly inching closer to him where he sat, Jaia and Kai having already been kidnapped onto the dance floor.

He wasn't in the mood to party, but trying to explain that to a member of the Court seemed impossible. They would grasp onto any excuse at all to have fun.

The woman appeared to be a human at first glance, though unusually perfect. But the more he watched her out of the corner of his eye the more he doubted she could be. Humans didn't have that level of perfect grace and beauty.

The lady never got the chance to ask him to dance as Letari found him first, all smiles and bright green eyes that were both mischievous and innocent at once. She didn't so much ask as demand that he go with her and he sighed, allowing the woman to draw him up off the chair and onto the dance floor.

He had never had much to do with the woman, Hunter always close by and fiercely protective of her, but he looked at her then, taking in all the details of her lovely face.

She didn't look her age, but she also didn't look as young as her twin. Perhaps thirty, but also only twenty. It was never possible to tell the age of a mythical but unless one looked, she appeared young. There were the first hints of lines at the corners of those exquisite eyes, laugh lines, and as he watched her, he noticed a spattering of pale freckles across her cheeks.

She was a woman, painfully beautiful, with thick wavy hair that had been cut short around her ears and stuck out to give her a wild look. She was almost a mirror of Etani, oval face and big, slightly creepy eyes, a small nose, and full lips. She was less voluptuous than Etani, but it gave her a more proportionate look while Etani was a sex Goddess, all curves in all the right places and a full chest. Letari was also softer looking, her limbs feminine and rounded while Etani's were hardened with centuries of training. It didn't make her any less feminine, but it gave her a more angled appearance compared to Letari.

Letari had a fondness for brighter colours, which suited her well, even if she was wearing a dark dress that Winter had given her.

"You look tense," she said, and Versalis blinked, realising he had almost been glaring at her in his intense scrutiny of the beauty before him.

"It has been a trying time," he said, unable to help a smile in response to hers.

Letari might not have the pull Etani had, but she was naturally charismatic and sweet, prone to random giggling and happiness. It made her addictive in a totally different way, her nature making her deeply enjoyable to be around.

"Yes, I imagine it was. I wanted to thank you for helping to return Etani," she said, and Versalis was surprised by just how alert she was.

"You don't need to thank me," he said, reaching up to brush her hair back from where it was tickling her cheek.

"I also want to warn you... If you touch Etani I will remove your balls and feed them to you," she said in a perfectly cheerful, perfectly happy tone.

His stomach dropped and he stopped moving, looking down at her with a wary frown. "What do you mean?" he asked, knowing already, but he wanted her to say it.

"I know you want her, almost as much as she wants you. But I will not sit by and let you manipulate her into being your plaything. She's not your toy, you can't just use and discard her then decide you want your old toy back when your new one isn't to your liking."

Versalis was stumped on what to say. She hadn't raised her voice or sound hostile, but the sweetness only made her words more threatening. "I have no intentions of hurting her."

"Perhaps not, but you want her back."

"You can't want something back that was never yours to begin with."

"Don't play word games with me, Versalis. I'm crazy, not stupid. You can't have her, and you need to stay away from her. If you try, I will tell Daemon and Uzo. They meant their threats; they will castrate you."

"I'm not going to do anything," he growled.

"Don't do, or say, anything. Don't forget that she trained me, I can kill you just as easily as she can. Do you understand me?"

"Yes, Letari," he said, smiling, and she smiled back, content with her threats.

He wasn't going to listen to them, though. He wouldn't push Etani, of course, but he refused to give up that small shred of hope that she would forgive him.

He knew now that she had wanted to be with him; maybe he could find a way to make it up to her.

Bowing deeply to the green-eyed vixen, he turned, and his stomach jumped up into his throat as he found Etani herself behind him, her head tilted to the side and her eyes a challenge.

Without missing a beat, he snatched her hand up and pulled her into the steps of the dance, though he was careful to keep a respectful distance between them, his eyes lingering just above her head.

"Do I offend you so much?" she asked with an amused, only slightly hostile tone.

"You do not offend me at all," he said to the air, his eyes stinging with the need to look down at that devastatingly beautiful face.

"Things not go well with the girlfriend?" Her head turned and he could tell she was no longer looking in his direction, taking the advantage to glance down at her. She looked calm but the muscles in her jaw were tensed, giving away anger she was trying to hide.

"We were never officially in a relationship, and now we will not ever be in one," he said, not entirely sure what his relationship had been with the woman. Perhaps if they had more time together, it would have been different.

She looked up at him and their eyes met for an instant. He was certain in that moment that there was a hopeful hint to hers, but she looked away again.

Daemon and Uzo had been right, she would forgive him in a heartbeat if he asked for it, and he understood Letari's threats. She knew better than anyone what her twin was thinking.

"You gave up a good thing," she said, and her tone was odd, strained as though she were forcing herself to say it.

"It was not meant to be, my heart belongs to another."

Her breath froze in her chest and her eyes found his. He drank her in, all that perfection and ferocity. She was so much more than just a woman, she was everything, and he was a selfish bastard who didn't deserve something as perfect as her, but he was selfish and greedy, and so he pulled her closer, gratified by the way her eyes widened in fear.

"I want you to be mine, and I yours, if you will have me," he growled, throwing off all hints of caution, all the warning bells going off in his mind. He couldn't resist her, he had to have her. It didn't matter if she was immeasurably better than him in every way, it didn't matter if he would never, ever be good enough for her. He had the chance to be with her and he reached for it.

She froze, their dance stopped as she stared up at him. Even her breath had locked in her chest as she tried to process what he wanted from her. "I... I don't know if I can... what you did with Aurora... not yet..." She gasped, terror radiating off her in waves.

He could have laughed in relief as the reason for her hesitation came to light and he lifted his hand to cup her cheek, his thumb feeling rough against that feather-soft skin.

"I am a patient man. I will wait for an eternity, and if that eternity comes and you are still not ready, then I will wait another and another. You are worth waiting for."

It seemed as though her mind had gone blank, and she could

only stare at him for a long time, but then those odd, black tears swelled in her eyes, and she bit her lower lip. Mother, it was the most tempting thing he had ever seen.

"You'll wait?" she whimpered, that terrified little sound, and when he nodded, she made a broken little sound and she released his hand and he found himself in her arms, her body chilly against his.

"You'll be mine?" he gasped, clutching her to him.

"Yes," she breathed, and his eyes slid shut, crushing her to him. Turning to her, he pressed his lips hard against her hair and the smell of her flooded his system, rich and warm.

"I love you," he said, trying his best to keep his voice from breaking, but it didn't work.

"I love you, too, Versalis," she whispered, her fingers tangling in his hair and using that as leverage, she turned his face to hers and kissed him hard, deliciously hard.

He kissed her back just as hard, his body craving her touch even as she clung to him. He had never been able to adequately imagine what her lips would taste like and even if he had, it would have been nothing compared to the real thing.

She had kissed him before, of course, but it was nothing to the burning, passionate pressure he felt then.

A LOW GROWL started up to their side, but they ignored it, her lips moving against his and his arms went around her waist, squeezing her as he returned the kiss, deep and desperately hungry for her.

"That's enough of that," Dirdos growled as he gripped Versalis' head and pried it backwards.

Etani looked up at Dirdos in anger, the dragon glaring right back at her.

"Don't be stupid, Etani," the dragon snapped, and her eyes narrowed as a pair of hands found her shoulders and drew her back from him, but she refused to budge, muscles tensing as she clung to him.

"Let go," she demanded, pulling herself free of her sister's grip and looking around at the green eyed, furious young woman.

"Etani no, not him," Letari cried, trying to coax her sister away, but Etani was having none of it.

Versalis looked up at Dirdos and growled in warning, taking Etani's hand and leading her away from the two.

"Dirdos, do something!" Letari cried, and those around them seemed to notice what was happening.

The dragon glared at Versalis but Etani caught the dragon's wrist before he could grab Versalis' shirt, and she moved between them.

"This is my choice, Dirdos, not yours," she said, and the man's crimson eyes flared red.

"You're making the wrong choice," Dirdos said, his face dark, but he was unable to be furious with her. It was Versalis he blamed.

"Etani, what's going on?" Daemon said as he approached.

"That bastard did exactly what you said he'd do, she is right back in his arms," Dirdos snarled, furious and yet struggling to find fault with her. They all saw her as a helpless victim of Versalis'.

"Etani!" Daemon snapped, his fingers curling around her wrist.

"Let go," she said in a low, dangerous voice.

"You stupid girl."

He didn't get the chance to say anything else, his hand flying off her and the man staggering back as her fist smacked into his chest and ice bloomed across his clothes.

"Do not speak to me like I am a child, Daemon. I am not a child, and I am fully capable of making my own decisions."

"You're making the wrong ones!" Letari cried, her eyes filling with tears.

"How would you know?" Etani snapped.

"I can read his thoughts!"

Etani scoffed and turned away from them, Dirdos grabbing

Daemon's shoulder to melt the ice that had locked his lungs and was turning him blue.

She was so lovely when she was angry and he took her hand, her anger melting away as she looked up at him.

"Let's go somewhere private," she murmured, Daemon and Dirdos both snarling. "Not like that, you perverts!" she cried and practically dragged him from the hallway with those around her parting to allow their Queen access, though he could see others of their group closing in on them.

She led him out onto the deck, and while he was glad for the chance to be alone with her, he was still a little worried about her safety. Hades had been right; she was already vulnerable in that situation, and he wasn't going to be able to do much against some of the Fae.

Stepping out onto the balcony, she closed the doors in their faces and let out a huff of frustration before she eyed him and then smiled, taking his hand once more and guiding him to a small bench.

It was growing dark as the sky above deepened to grey, and he had to wonder if Winter was reacting to her dark mood, though she looked relieved when they were alone.

"You'd think they'd at least pretend to be happy," she said as she sat and he joined her, taking both of her hands and gripping them.

"They're just worried," he replied, lifting her small hands to his lips and kissing her knuckles.

"I suppose so. Should they be worried?" she asked, her face somewhat confused as she studied him.

"No, I have no intentions to hurt you in any way, in fact I will do whatever it takes to make you happy," he watched her face, the uncertainty, and then the relief as she curled her fingers around his and drew him closer.

There were bright, multi-coloured pixies fluttering around in the garden and their light shone dimly on her pale face, only adding to the exquisite magic of her beauty.

Her eyes fluttered shut as he leant down and his lips met hers in a slow, teasing kiss.

He never imagined he would ever be in that situation, though he had fantasised about it more than once when he was alone. A part of him had always doubted that she would ever end up in his arms but there she was, almost off the seat as she pressed up into the kiss, and his fingers traced along her jaw.

She shivered and he growled, a playful sound at her delight and he pressed down on her mouth, hungry and burning, but he would not push her. He would only go as far as she was ready for, and as he had told her, he would wait an eternity for her.

THE DOORS BURST open with an explosion of glass and her lips stilled against his, her eyes still closed when his opened. A small crease of irritation had formed between his brows.

"No," Uzo snarled, stalking across the deck towards his niece and she sighed, the sweet coolness of her breath washing across his cheek as she turned to look at the angry Fae. "No. This is not happening, not ever."

"Uncle, this isn't any of your business," she said, looking irritated by his anger.

"You are my niece and that makes it my business. This ..." He pointed between the two of them, still close and their fingers interlocked. "This is not going to happen. I forbid it."

That set her off, and she dropped his hand to stand, toe to toe with her uncle who was a full foot taller than her. "You can't tell me who I can and can't be with," she said softly, the quiet of her tone drawing out the others who had clearly been listening in.

"You are clearly incapable of figuring it out on your own. First Neah, and now him?" Uzo dodged back when she took a swing at him, eyes narrowed. "Did you want to try that again, little girl?"

She did, and he ducked back, eyes blazing.

"Try that again, Etani, and see what happens."

Apparently, she was keen to see what happened, and she scored, slugging the man with brutal force on his jaw, and he staggered back.

Versalis grabbed her before Uzo could, and he dragged her back, writhing and hissing, but she fell still when she realised who had her. "That's enough," Versalis growled. "You can't control her, Uzo."

"Shut up, scum. You've already hurt her once, why are you so determined to do it again?"

"I won't ever hurt her again."

Uzo snorted, rubbing his jaw and glaring down at Etani, her eyes defiant.

"Fine. If you are so keen to have this man break you, then go ahead. But I'm not sticking around to watch it," the Fae snapped.

She went rigid, gasping, and reaching desperately for the Fae as he gave one last hiss at her and disappeared.

"Uzo!" she screamed, ripping herself free of Versalis' arms but the Fae was already gone, her fingers curling in empty air. "No! Uzo, no! Come back!"

He didn't come back, and that lovely face broke as the realisation dawned on her that she had lost him. "Uzo!" she wailed, her voice a terrible scream of agony that broke all of their hearts and when Letari reached for her, Etani jerked away, staggering back from them with panicked eyes and cheeks already streaked with black.

"Etani, don't ..." Letari gasped, but Etani picked up the hem of her skirt and ran, streaking across the deck and down into the gardens.

"Kai, go!" Daemon snapped, and the vampire nodded, sprinting after her and leaving Versalis alone with the group.

"You ..." Dirdos growled. "You selfish little bastard!"

Versalis jerked back from the dragon as the tall man reached for him, refusing to let him set hand on any part of his person. It was likely the dragon would set him on fire at that level of anger. "It's not my fault she loves me," Versalis snapped, knowing he shouldn't prod the beast. "She will never forgive you if you do anything to me."

"If she never finds the body, she won't know you're dead," Daemon hissed, and Dirdos nodded, Letari glaring with just as much furious hunger.

"Of course she will know you did it. She's not an idiot."

"No, she's just naïve about dangerous men," Letari snapped.

"I'm not going to hurt her."

"Of course you are," Jaia said, previously quiet and glaring at him furiously. "You know you can never be with her, you'll explode."

Versalis scowled, their private conversation out in the open.

"What does that mean?" Dirdos said, turning on the silver-eyed vampire.

"They are like oil and a flame; they've known it since the beginning. He sets her destructive side off and she sets off the vampire."

"That was private," Versalis snarled, and Jaia shook his head.

"You can't be with her, not ever. People will die."

"It's none of your business, traitor."

Jaia's eyes narrowed, but Dirdos and Daemon were looking at each other and Letari was scowling, unsure of this new development.

"Let her love me and then grow bored of me," Versalis said coldly, hating himself for it, but if it meant they would all go away and leave them alone, he didn't care. "It's only a matter of time until she realises I'm not enough and moves on. Until then at least I can help her heal."

Dirdos was fuming, his skin steaming in the cold air. "And you think you're capable of helping her heal?"

"Are you capable of waiting for her until she's ready to be touched?" Versalis snapped back.

Dirdos frowned, his mouth opening and then closing again as he considered that.

"Exactly. None of you would be able to wait for her. But I am, I can give her the love she needs without the expectations."

Daemon was livid, but they couldn't argue with the logic. Their needs were so much more carnal than his own. Yes, he would literally kill to make love to her, but he could wait longer than the others and they all knew it.

"Fine. But it's on your head," Daemon snapped, stalking back inside.

The others followed but Versalis waited, turning to look out over the gardens where he could see Kai and Etani, the vampire clutching her with enough force to bruise her, and he had a terrible, agonised look on his face.

CHAPTER 28
DRINK

E tani returned after two hours of sitting in the garden with Kai, though whether she needed the space or was simply waiting in hopes that Uzo would return wasn't clear.

Whatever the reason, he waited for her, and she threw herself into his arms as she approached.

He wrapped his arms around her tightly, lips pressing hard against the top of her head, and he sighed, her body still trembling and lovely eyes looking puffy with tears.

"Hey, it's okay, he'll come back," Versalis murmured, and he did a double take as he met Kai's eyes. He looked weird, his eyes wide and both vacant and homicidal at the same time, like he was seriously contemplating murder. He had never seen that look on the man's face before, and he immediately had to wonder if Daemon had been right about the vampire. He might very well be in love with her.

It wasn't like it was hard to love Etani, one only had to meet her to love her. The expression was gone in an instant and had Versalis not looked up when he did, he wouldn't have seen it at all.

"I didn't mean it ..." she cried, clinging to him in desperation.

"I know, love, he is only angry right now. He will come back, he loves you too much to be away from you," Versalis said.

"I can't lose him, too!"

"You won't, he'll be back before you know it."

Kai kissed her hard on the side of the head and headed inside to give them privacy, his posture stiff and angry. Leading her to the bench, he sat down with her pressed close to his side and she whimpered, her heart broken as the man she loved the most left her.

"Give him a few days and he'll be back. He can't be away from you for too long," he said, and she nodded.

They sat in silence for a while, her pain settling down into a steady burn that she crushed down with all the other pain she felt. She was remarkably good at hiding her suffering once she calmed down, and he hated it. He didn't want her to silence it, he wanted her to deal with it in a healthy way, but now wasn't the time to lecture her.

Standing slowly, he drew her up and kissed the tip of her nose, giving her a small smile. "Now put on your brave face for the savages and let's go finish this night in style," he said, watching as she collected herself and wiped the tears from her cheeks.

Her mask rose, and she was that same calm, collected beauty he knew so well. Leading her back inside, there was a moment of hesitation as they searched her for signs of distress, but she smiled, and the party continued.

They might want to party, but she was still their Queen, and they worried about her. Once their fears were waylaid, they were back into it.

She was pulled away almost, and she laughed as someone teased her, accepting the mug, and taking a cautious sip before downing the entire thing. Versalis frowned as he saw the delicate pink to her cheeks.

He had never seen Etani drink before, and he wasn't sure she ever had in her life. Judging by her curious look into the cup, she likely hadn't.

"Someone is feeding her alcohol," he said to Daemon, who had come to stand at his side, watching her.

"Has she ever had alcohol before?"

"I don't think so."

Daemon growled, glancing around the room. "Damn Fae, where did he run off to ...?"

"No idea, do we get her out?"

"Give her a chance to burn off some steam, then get her out. Just watch her very carefully," Daemon muttered before stalking away to sweep the room for Uzo, who wasn't there.

Versalis watched her like a hawk, lips pressed together as he watched her giving in to her brethren, and they seemed to be all the happier for her letting go of her tension, the dance becoming wilder, and it was only after one man's arm went around her middle and jerked her against him that he decided it was time to retrieve her.

"Etani, come on, it's time to go," he said, and she turned to him, her eyelids heavy and lips pulled up at the corners.

She was very clearly drunk, her cheeks a flushed pink, and the man looked irritated.

"Who are you? Her father?" The man was a satyr and Versalis wasn't very impressed by his possessive tone.

"I am her mate. Hands off."

"Versalis, what is this stuff? It's great!" she gasped, and the man reluctantly released her to Versalis, his arms going around her protectively. He took the cup and sniffed it warily, but he didn't know what it was.

"Alcohol," he said, and she scowled, looking around for Letari.

"I don't drink that stuff, it's bad for you," she lectured with a faint hint of a slur that would have been adorable had it not been alarming. "Letari! I had alcohol!" she cried when her twin seemed to materialise out of nowhere.

"I see that," Letari said, taking the empty cup and sniffing it. "Why did you let her have this?"

"She had already drunk it before I noticed and Daemon said it would be alright so long as we watched her," Versalis said.

"Daemon doesn't know what alcohol does to our kind. She's going to puke on everything."

"Oh great ... Last time I listen to him."

"If you can't look after her then leave her to us," Letari snapped.

"It's fine, I'll get her to her room."

Etani was looking at them both with a pretty pout on her lips and she lifted up onto the balls of her feet to whisper in his ear.

"You know ... we could go back to my room and get to know each other very ... intimately," she said and giggled.

He flushed and pulled back from her, both very turned on and alarmed by her reaction.

She had made it clear that she wasn't ready to be intimate, but here? Her inhibitions were gone, and he sighed, turning and slipping his arm up under her legs.

She shrieked as he hoisted her up off the floor and she latched onto his neck with painful force, her eyes huge as she tried to figure out what was happening. "Lee! I want more of that!" she called out as Versalis carried her down the hallway for her room.

"Okay!" Letari called back, but he very much doubted that was going to happen.

Etani clearly did not tolerate the liquid very well.

THE GUARD OPENED the door for him and watched as she stared at him upside down, her head hanging limply over his arm.

"Hi ..." she said in a sinfully suggestive tone, and the guard blushed before he pulled the door shut, his motions jerky and only slightly alarmed.

Setting her down on her feet once they were in the bathroom, he looked her over, but there were no outward signs of damage to her person, and when he was satisfied, he turned away to run the bath for her.

Turning back, he jerked to find her right behind him, her dress pulled down to expose the upper curve of those beautiful, perfect breasts.

Her eyes were wicked, and he swallowed hard, trying not to stare as more skin was revealed.

"Help me get this off?" she asked.

He squinted, unsure of her intentions, but then he nodded and stepped around her to pull the buttons of her dress free.

She shoved it down and groaned, long pink lines on her torso showing the bones of the corset that had been digging into her flesh.

Regardless, she looked magnificent standing there with her breasts free and those deviously little underwear that showed off almost half of her backside and fit snugly against her hips.

He had never seen the style before, and he was captivated by those long legs and the roundness of her backside as she moved, her hips swaying as she hummed and reached back to release her hair.

It would be easy to take advantage of her in that situation, and he frowned as he watched her, so beautiful and relaxed with the alcohol coursing through her system.

Bending down, he picked up the mass of her dress and moved it away from the bath to avoid it getting wet and turned back to find her watching him, long strands of hair falling down around her as she released the braids.

He would have given anything to throw her to the floor and have his way with her right then, his eyes dragging down her body, but she was in no condition to decide if she wanted him or not. He was not Jaia, he wouldn't take what she didn't want to give.

She smirked as she saw his hungry stare, hair falling down around her in waves from the braids and she reached for him, slender fingers curling in his shirt as she pulled herself to him.

"You want me, don't you?" she whispered, and he growled, blood rushing to his groin as she bit her lower lip and her eyes lowered.

She had no idea just how devastating she was when she looked like that. Or perhaps she did, because she grinned at him wickedly.

"I think you do ..." she said playfully, her smile growing wider.

It was so incredibly hard to resist her, and it was even worse when she reached down and cupped him through his pants.

She made a soft moaning sound that sent a shudder through his body, and she squeezed him, stroking him.

"Stop, Etani," he almost begged her. He knew it was only a result of the alcohol but *Mother* ... it was so hard to hold on to his resolve. "This is not what you want."

"You don't want me?" she asked, sounding almost hurt, even as she grasped him and stroked him. He groaned softly, helpless as she worked him, and it was all he could go to reach down and pull her hand off his erection.

"You would regret this in the morning, and I want our first time together to be something you cherish," he said, but she didn't look happy about it.

"Don't you love me?" she whispered, reaching for him once more, but he caught her wrist, pushing it away from him and holding them both behind her back in a firm grip. "I didn't know you were into that sort of thing," she said, and he growled, frustrated, and incredibly aroused.

"Let's get you in the bath," he said, and she nodded, eyeing him.

He shook his head and reached down, tugging off her underwear and throwing them aside as he guided her to the bath.

She stepped down into it without fighting him and eyed him when he didn't join her, pointing at him and then the water in a silent demand as she stood naked and thigh deep in the warm liquid.

"Not with you in this state," he said, and she scowled, her hand shooting out and unceremoniously yanking him into the water.

Still fully dressed, and almost falling in face first.

He staggered in with her and sighed, frustrated but also somewhat amused by her attitude when drunk. She was so different, happy, and playful, sexual, and with all her guards down.

"Now, you be a good girl," he teased.

She looked up at him with narrowed eyes, considering him and then she grabbed him, dragging him closer. Her chin lifted, and he lent down into her, his kiss hungry and deep.

Wrapping her arms around his neck, she leant into him, but he was very aware of how close they were getting, the reaction his body was having on her attention. He wasn't going to let her get him so worked up that he forgot what she had said when she was sober.

When he drew back from her she scowled and there was no warning. She tucked her foot in behind his and jerked his foot out from under him, his body dropping down onto his backside with a splash.

She was on him in the next beat, straddling his lap and her fingers tangled in the length of his hair, dragging his head down to meet her lips.

It was so incredibly hard to resist her then, feeling her so close and so eager. But drunk Etani wasn't the same. He kissed her back, but when she reached down between them to tug at his pants, he caught her wrist and pushed her hand behind her back.

"You stop that," he scolded, his eyes narrowing as she gave him a sly smile.

"But I want you," she countered, and a thrill of excitement went through him, taunting him with what he knew would be a very bad choice.

"You want me right now, but probably not as much when you're not coursing with chemicals," he said, keeping his grip firm when she tried to twist her wrist free.

"Versalis let go," she whined, but he shook his head and with his free hand, he grabbed a bottle, offering it to her. She scowled, but her eyes focused with only a little difficulty on the bottle, using her free hand to remove the cork.

She made a face at the smell and he popped the cork back in.

The next one was more to her liking, and he gave her a warning look before he poured a measure onto his hand and then began to work it into her hair.

She froze, her eyes wide at the delicious sensation, and she almost melted when he used his nails. He understood, it was a sinfully wonderful feeling and while he wasn't Bast, his nails still felt good.

She remained still while he did what he needed to, and she seemed to understand that he was not going to sleep with her right then, her expression sulky, but she didn't push the issue any further.

When he was satisfied with his work, he pulled her out of the bath and wrapped her up in a towel, scrubbing her hair and laughing when she squirmed.

"You're all wet still," he said, ignoring her attempts to escape, and she was still again, growling moodily while he dried her off and pulled a night dress down over her head.

Stripping out of his wet clothes, he smirked as he found her eyes on him, almost as though her stare was a physical touch on his skin. It was a little embarrassing, but also it made him feel good to have that beautiful woman watching him that way.

Drying off quickly, he pulled on a pair of pants and tugged her out onto the empty bedroom.

Her eyes found the bed and then turned on him with a wicked gleam and she reached for him, her arms snaking up around his neck.

He eyed her, but he couldn't resist the lure of her kiss and so he leant into it, unconscious of her slowly inching him toward the bed until she shoved him down onto it and she was back on his lap before he could process where he was.

His hands went to her hips to keep her from falling and she growled, her mouth on his and when she ground against him, he shuddered with a sudden, blinding need.

She was evil, pure evil, and she took advantage of his arousal to deepen the kiss, pressing him backwards onto the bed and leaning over him. Her kiss grew more demanding, and her hand was on him, stroking him through his pants.

Torn on what to do, he groaned when her fingers left him only to slide down under the band and her bare fingers curled around his erection, squeezing him firmly.

No, he had to stop her, or he was going to lose control. He could already feel his resolve slipping as she stroked him, and pleasure washed through his system.

A plan started up in his mind and he pressed her back, her face wary until he rolled her onto her back, and he pressed down on her, her eyes burning with hunger.

Reaching down with one hand to drag his fingers up her inner thigh, he used the other to grab the heavy blanket.

In a second, she shrieked and then he jumped back, his beautiful love wrapped up like a swaddled baby tight enough that she couldn't move her arms.

She glared, squirming and wriggling, but when he saw she was working herself free, he wrapped his arms around her and then his legs and she huffed, a little Etani burrito with pink cheeks and a scowl.

Thankfully, he thought the effects of the toxin in her system seemed to be fading and finally she fell asleep, the warmth of the blanket and him lulling her to sleep, and he could finally relax.

She was a devious little monster, and he didn't for a second think he was safe, but she was sleeping and after an hour he dozed off as well, the smell and quiet sound of her breathing soothing him into slumber.

WHEN HE WOKE, he wasn't surprised to see the room had filled with the others, piled onto any available surface or asleep on the floor, though there was still one form missing.

He was surprised to see a large bin at her side, however.

Looking at it curiously, he wondered what it was for as it hadn't been there when he had fallen asleep. He figured it out an hour or so later when Etani stirred.

It took only a minute for her pale face to turn green and he reached for the bin, shoving it under her chin, ten seconds later the sound of her retching woke the others, and they yawned, looking around in confusion.

Helping her to untangle herself from the blanket enough to hold the bin herself, she moaned pitifully, but at least she could expel it all, there was only the alcohol and stomach acid as it had been some time since she had eaten anything.

"That's what you get for drinking," Daemon said from the corner where he was propped up against Dirdos, who was scowling grumpily.

She called him something rude, and then heaved again, clinging to the bin like it was the only thing keeping her together. "I didn't know it was alcohol," she moaned, resting her cheek against the cool metal to sooth her face.

"Don't drink strange liquids from those you don't know," Dirdos said, yawning and shoving Daemon off his shoulder.

She decided to ignore them, eyes closed as she contemplated her life and then wriggled herself free of the blankets and padded into the bathroom.

Versalis sighed, rubbing his eyes, and looked around in confusion. The room had changed, the pastel colours deepened to rich, warm hues and even some black. It was like it wasn't even the same room anymore and he had to wonder how much Winter really had control over. Was the entire palace simply a part of it? He didn't know, but it was a curious theory.

"Poor Etani." Letari sighed, stretching out on top of Hunter, and thumping her head back down into his stomach to make him grunt in pain. "You'd think she would have tried it by now. It's not like she's a baby anymore." A weird look crossed her face then, and they all watched her curiously. "Guess she missed a lot of experiences."

"Why is that?" Daemon asked as he stretched out, shoving Dirdos' hands out of the way and using the man's lap as a pillow.

"She was always out and about. She said it was to keep us safe, but I don't know."

"Cain," Etani said from the doorway, her head bowed and rubbing her eyes. "I was trying to keep Cain away."

Versalis stood and moved to her side, her face pale and sweaty.

"Who?" Letari asked.

"The one who got you and Ava. He was hunting us since we left."

Letari looked deeply confused, her face twisted in anger and confusion.

"Why didn't you ever tell me?" the woman demanded.

"That was up to Ava."

Etani squinted up at him, but she smiled when he bowed his head and kissed her forehead.

"That whole time?" Letari demanded.

Etani shrugged, leaning into his chest for support. "I assumed you knew."

"No. What else are you hiding from me?"

"I didn't hide anything. Ava said she would tell you."

Letari growled, but Etani ignored her, arms sliding around his middle.

He hugged her, his fingers stroking through her silken hair while she tried to survive the hangover.

CHAPTER 29
LOVERS

Even looking so irritable she was exquisite, and he traced his thumb along her jaw, loving the feel of her skin against his and when she smiled, cheeks turning a delicate pink at his attention, he couldn't believe his luck. How was it possible something so perfect was his? How was it possible that *she* was his? He didn't know, and didn't care so long as he got to be with her, touching her like he never had before, perhaps even being able to love her as she deserved one day.

His thoughts were turning somewhat less wholesome as he watched her eyes lowering, long eyelashes brushing her pale cheeks, and he thought of all the devious things he would like to do to her when they were alone.

"Are you feeling any better?" he asked, and she shook her head, making a pitiful face.

"Good, you'll never do it again," Daemon said as he stood, annoyed at Dirdos trying to shove him away, and she looked over, her eyes narrowed as she slipped out of the bed with an intent stare.

The demon's face went wary as she approached, but it was

Dirdos she was after and he held his arms out for her, to which she settled in with a soft whining mewl.

"Now, now don't sulk," the giant man scolded as he pressed her head down against his chest, his fingers light in her hair.

"I need all the hugs in the world," she whined, and he laughed, hugging her with enough force to make her squeak, but she was content in his lap, and she was smug when she found Versalis glaring at her, wanting her back in his arms. He wasn't going to deny her comfort, though, even if he wanted all of her attention to himself.

"Your boyfriend is jealous," Dirdos teased, and she growled, both of them looking over at Versalis.

"Good, keeps him interested," she mumbled and Dirdos snorted in amusement, though there was something pained in his face as he looked down at her, her eyes focused on Versalis.

They were all suffering from her choosing him and not them. He would have been suffering too had she chosen any of them, so he couldn't blame them for their resentment. They all desired her, but she wanted him, and he wasn't about to give her up for anything.

Smiling at the grumpy looking woman, he glanced around at the lot of them and then focused on Letari, who was wrapped in Hunter's arms.

"Who are you going to get to do the wedding, or are you doing it all yourself?"

Letari opened her stunning green eyes and looked at him curiously for a moment before she tilted her head back to look up at Hunter, who shrugged.

"No idea, I don't know anything about the Court. We may have to ask around."

"Uzo would know," Etani said, her voice sounding broken as she mentioned his name.

"Don't worry, he'll be back when he's over his tantrum," Dirdos said, stroking her hair. "Until then, we will make enquiries."

"Yeah, I'll see what I can find out," Daemon said, and stretched as he headed into the bathroom and started the water. "I miss the shower already."

"Winter will give us one before too much longer." Etani yawned, nuzzling her face into Dirdos' chest, and within a matter of minutes, she was asleep again.

"Winter?" Dirdos asked, his head turning slightly to rest his cheek against her hair.

"Winter seems to respond to her." Versalis frowned, watching her as she slept. "Like it's trying to keep her happy."

"It's weird how it responds to her," Hunter said, all eyes on the slumbering Queen.

"I don't think it's malicious, maybe it's just been lonely for so long it's doing everything it can to keep her? Maybe it's afraid she'll leave."

"You think so?" Jaia asked, him and Kai squished into a chair together. It had been exceptionally hard to tell them apart before, but now it was easy with Jaia's silver eyes and, oddly, it seemed to give him more humanity while black eyes had given him the look of a shark.

"It would make sense, if she's the only one to ever speak to it. It would get attached to her almost instantly, even if her magic had no effect on it, it would still love her simply for listening," Kai said thoughtfully, his lips pulled down into a frown, and he was staring at her with such a naked longing that it almost hurt to see. "Wouldn't you love something that was the first being to ever be able to communicate with you?"

"Yeah, I suppose so," Versalis said.

THEY WERE QUIET FOR A TIME, simply watching her sleeping, and Daemon returned, his head covered with a towel.

"There's a shower in the bathroom now ..." he said, looking baffled.

"Well, that proves it then, doesn't it? Winter is trying to make her happy," Dirdos said, and she shifted, her cheek rubbing against his chest. They all went still as she sighed the dragon's name, warm and content while the man himself turned a bright red at the sound.

"What?" Daemon asked, watching the two.

"We were wondering if Winter was responding to her needs. She mentioned hating the room, the room changed. It was mentioned that we wanted a shower and there's suddenly a shower. She wanted things to be more beautiful for her ball, the garden changed. It's responding to her," Versalis said.

"Why would it do that?"

"We thought perhaps it is trying to please her," Letari said quietly. "If she's happy she'll stay. I thought maybe it just wants her to be here with it, together."

"You don't think it will try and keep her here?" Hunter asked.

"I don't think so, it might just be happier with her here where they can be together all the time, close and content. She's further away in the human world and it's harder for Winter to be with her. Here, it's in constant contact with her so it can love her all the time."

They were all silent as they considered the sleeping woman, uncertain and worried.

"It has never been known to be destructive unless ordered to be," Daemon said, his frown clear.

"I think it's more like a child," Letari began. "Clinging to her because she is listening. If the others listened, it might not be so attached to her, but she's the first one, and it's happy it has her to talk to. Or maybe it loves her for the same reason all of you love her. We won't know until we can talk to it."

"You're surprisingly lucid," Daemon said to the woman.

"Oh, shut up, this is my sister we're talking about. I don't care about any of you, she was mine before any of you came along and she will be mine long after you're all gone again," she snapped, making them all scowl.

"Stop talking …" Etani groaned and Dirdos growled at the lot of them for disturbing her as her eyes opened and she blinked slowly, drowsy and unimpressed. "What are you all complaining about?"

"Nothing, love, go back to sleep," Dirdos said, and she mumbled something, turning her face into his chest and sighing at the warmth of the giant man.

"We should let her rest, we can go talk to some people," Daemon said,

The others nodded but Versalis wasn't keen to leave her alone, Dirdos lifting her up and carrying her to the bed. Settling her down on the mattress, he tugged the blankets up around her and she whined, reaching for him.

"I'll be back soon; I'm going to help them and then bring back food. You rest," Dirdos said, kissing her forehead.

Etani sighed, nodding as her eyes slid shut and she was asleep again before they left the room.

"Come on, lover boy, you're coming along," Daemon said and grabbed Versalis by the back of the shirt, dragging him out even as he stared at Etani. He wanted to go back to her, he wanted to be in her arms and nuzzling her jaw until she squirmed in disgust at his obnoxious affections, but no, he had to go find a stupid wedding planner with the other idiots in her life rather than revelling in the affection of his love.

Sighing, he followed along behind Daemon, Dirdos, Jaia, Kai, Hunter, and Letari. Sebastian and the Hunters hadn't bothered to arrive yet, but they would when they were ready. She was safer here, so Sebastian at least was able to take a break.

The others might well have gone back to the compound anyway, they had their lives that were separate from that of Etani.

A cry made Daemon stop and take two steps backwards, his grin going wicked as he found a radiant woman with gold skin and silver hair with her arms in the air, stark naked and screaming like she hadn't seen him in eons.

"Star!" Daemon cried, shoving Versalis on after the others while he headed for the golden woman.

"Oh yeah, vital work," Versalis complained. "He leaves at the first pretty girl he comes across."

"Well, you can leave at the first pretty girl you come across," Dirdos said, his hands in his pockets as he led the group along, though he didn't seem to really know where he was going. "You could always ask your ex."

"She'd probably kill him if he mentioned marriage," Hunter said in an amused tone.

"I wouldn't be overly opposed to that," Dirdos said, his brows lifting as they stumbled out into the dregs of the party from hours before.

"Me either," Letari muttered, glaring at him, and Kai snorted his amusement, wrapping his arm around the woman's shoulders.

"You, too?" Versalis snapped, glaring at the normally friendly man.

"You are going to destroy her," Kai said in a quiet, angry voice. "You'll destroy her, and she'll blame herself, she'll never want to love again because you're selfish."

They all went still, freezing in place as Kai of all people spoke out against anyone loving Etani.

"Kai?" Jaia asked, but Kai only shook his head, glaring at Versalis.

"You will be responsible for everything that happens to her. You will be responsible for the people you kill when you two explode, and you will be responsible for what happens to her after it's over."

Versalis stared at Kai, the man who had been one of the few who would always smile and be happy, but not now. He was angry, fuming, and glaring at Versalis.

"Do you love her, Kai?" Versalis asked.

"Everyone loves her," Kai snapped.

"No ... are you in love with her?"

Kai only glared at him, furious that he would dare ask that question, but they were right, Kai wanted her just like the rest of them. Kai would kill for her, and the worst part was, he would probably smile while he did it.

"Let's go," Dirdos growled when the silence stretched on, the two vampires staring each other down.

THEY HEADED into the throne room to find the least hungover person. That turned out to be a giant werecat with fluffy, silver and grey fur, her pale golden eyes squinting at them as she lifted her arm off her eyes. She wore a lovely black velvet dress, though there wasn't really anything for her to hide given her species.

"No Jagum this time?" she asked, her attention flicking over them all one at a time. "I hope the Queen is well."

"Moody and homicidal as always," Dirdos said in a cheerful voice that made the woman turn her eyes on him in consideration. "But no, Jagum went back to his clan for the time being. They had need of him. He will be joining us in a few weeks or so."

The woman gave a low growl of agreement, her arm draping back over her eyes.

Turning away from the conversation, he looked over the hall and jerked to find Aurora was watching him from across the room, tilting her head in the direction of the deck.

He followed after her, curious to know what it was she might need from him.

"How is she?" Aurora asked.

"Hungover and irritable, but otherwise fine."

"That's good, the Court was beside themselves to find out she was with us. They don't get to see her very often, with her living in the human world."

The conversation was stilted and Versalis nodded. He had noticed their marked mood increase with her around.

"Is there something you wished to talk about?"

"There is a rumour that Etani now has a lover," she said bluntly.

"Etani has three husbands," he said.

"Aside from them. A vampire. It's you, isn't it? You and Etani are together?"

The silence stretched between them and he really didn't want to give her an answer. He cared deeply for Aurora and a part of him still loved her, but his heart belonged to Etani.

"I need to know, Versalis. As the heir, I need to be informed of these things. If she is to produce an heir..."

"We have not, and likely will not for a long time, be intimate. Etani has no wish to give herself to anyone in the near future."

"She won't have much of a choice in the matter, the Court will demand an heir. Either from you or one of them. They will expect her to at least try."

"She has time. They don't need one right now, they have you."

"What of the sister?"

"Letari is not a viable heir, Winter has recognised that she should never be granted access."

"What? Winter can talk to you?" she demanded.

"Winter is constantly talking to Etani, and she gave it permission to speak through her to greet Letari."

"I've never heard of anyone speaking to Winter..."

"According to Winter, no one has ever thought to try, and so it has latched onto her as the first one to do so. It loves her with an incredible depth and is insanely jealous. She was forced to surrender her Creator magic to Dirdos as a result, Winter didn't want to share her with any other magic."

Aurora scowled, trying to take in all the information.

"Okay, so let me get this all straight. Etani is no longer a Creator by giving her magic to *Dirdos* of all people, the most dangerous and oldest dragon in known existence, and she refuses to produce an heir. Winter is sentient and talks to her, and has spoken to you."

"She is still a Creator, she has made Dirdos her bearer. As far as we can tell, he cannot access her magic, only hold on to it. I didn't know that about Dirdos, and she is simply not ready to try again."

"All right…" she said with a heavy exhale of breath. "Is that everything?"

"As far as I can remember. You should speak to her."

Aurora looked up at him with narrowed eyes, jealousy radiating off her in waves.

"I'll take that under advisement," she said, glaring at him.

Versalis opened his mouth but then shut it again, deciding it was best not to shove his foot any deeper down his throat.

"How have you been? Did you join in on the party?

"No, I had other matters to attend to. I'll keep the Court running while she enjoys herself and gets to know her people," she spoke coldly still and Versalis sighed, rubbing the back of his neck as he tried to think of what he could say to help cheer her up. "Here, we can have our own celebration," she said suddenly. Pulling a small, elaborate silver flask out from a pocket, she unscrewed the cap. "To the Queen, long may she reign."

Lifting it to her nose, she sniffed and then took a hearty swing, smiling as she wiped the rim free of her saliva and offering it to him, giving it a little shake when he hesitated.

He repeated her sentiment before he took a drink, and she seemed happy. It was an odd drink, almost like fruit juice with a tangy aftertaste he couldn't place.

"Would you like to go for a walk?" he asked, looking out at the gardens.

"I would enjoy that," she said, and he offered her his arm.

She linked hers with his and he led the way out onto the path, heading away from the palace and away from where they had enjoyed each other's bodies.

"Tell me, have you ever had the palace respond to your desires?" Versalis asked, the thought that the palace might obey anyone else coming to mind.

"What do you mean?" she asked, and they paused so Versalis could pick her a frozen lavender rose, offering it to her. She took it, her eyes confused as she looked up at him.

"We noticed some things when..." He thought it best not to mention the Queen herself. "When there was a desire. For example, the room changed colour, a shower appeared in the room when Daemon asked for one. Things change to suit the needs, but maybe it's only the Queen's suite?"

"I assume everything was heard in the vicinity of the Queen?" she asked, and when he nodded, she nodded as well. "The palace responds to the needs and desires of the Queen. If she wants something and it can provide, it will give it to her, or in this case, all of you if you bring it up."

"That's really interesting... I didn't know anything about that."

"From all accounts, Summer does the same, though we have no information on the other two courts. It could be that their magic doesn't respond to them at all now, given the nature of succession. There are no familial ties in Ceress, whoever kills the Queen becomes the ruler if they are female, but if the killer is male, then it will go to the closest eligible woman."

"That's fascinating... is Summer and the Celestrial magic sentient?"

"I don't know, it seems logical that if ours is then theirs would be as well."

"Makes sense... at least as much as sentient magic can make sense," he said with a laugh, and the woman smiled.

"It's entirely logical, if you assume there are no rules and anything is possible," she said with an amused smile.

"I like that. No rules and anything is possible." Versalis grinned, pulling her along to a frozen water fountain whose water sprayed up in an exquisite arch to form a sort of umbrella around the base.

"This place really is beautiful." He sighed, touching the ice that seemed to hum.

"Yes, Winter is lovely, though I hear Summer is quite lovely as well."

Versalis nodded, turning to look down at the lovely lady, his smile fading as he saw her unhappy face.

"Aurora..." He frowned, not knowing what to say to her. There was nothing he could do to make it better.

"Don't say anything," she was almost angry, staring up at him with a deep longing.

Without warning, she grabbed him and pulled him down into a hard, deep kiss, and he froze. She was so soft and warmer than Etani, eager and wanting him.

His body responded to her touch, his longing to be touched that drove him wild and went unfulfilled by his mate. His hesitation made her deepen the kiss, and he wrapped his arms around her, his fingers tangling in her hair. He knew it was stupid, he knew it made him weak and unworthy of either of them, but the desire she had for him made him feel remarkably good and he longed for a woman.

When her hand moved down between them, he shuddered as her hand cupped his groin, her smile wicked as she felt his erection.

CHAPTER 30
DRUGS

Forcing himself back from her, he gasped for air and shook his head, half angry and half hungry for the beauty before him. But she wasn't Etani, and while he loved Aurora, he wanted Etani.

She reached for him, but he turned and walked away from her, his need driving him into a reckless abandon that pushed him forward along the path with one thought in his mind.

Heading back into the palace, he ignored the calls of the others as he headed straight for the royal suite and shoved the door open.

She was alone, and she looked around, holding up two heavy looking dresses and making that same face she always made when she didn't want to get dressed. All the better, because she wore nothing but a skimpy pair of underwear.

His eyes blazed, and he closed the door behind him, her brows drawing together in a frown as she heard the lock click.

Stalking across the room to her, he gripped her arms and her back hit the wall with a loud thud, his mouth demanding on hers. It was rough, hungry, and angry, but he couldn't hold it back, he wanted her more than anything.

She hesitated for a second but then she kissed him back, confused and wary, but she didn't try to push him away, unsure but eager to meet his hunger.

Growling her name, he bit down hard on her lower lip, and she shuddered, her breath hitching in, and a low whimper escaped her throat.

He could feel the vampire rising, the need to savage her, body and soul, and leave her his toy, but he forced it back down, his mouth hard enough to bruise her soft lips as he struggled with himself, the vampire coy and knowing as it dodged his attempts to tame it. It wanted her, too, every part of him wanted her.

Why couldn't she be a normal woman? He'd be pounding out his frustration on her body already if she was a normal woman. He could have had a normal woman in Aurora, but he had chosen Etani instead: beautiful and perfect, but damaged.

His hand went to his shirt, and he jerked it off, his arms demanding as he pulled her against him, and he growled at the feeling of her soft, bare breasts against his chest.

He wanted to hold her down and violate her, to claim her again and again and leave his scent all over her so they would know he had fucked her. He wanted his mate to submit to him.

Deepening the kiss, he pressed into her, and she hesitated as she felt his erection, unsure of his intent. When she drew away from him, he lost his grip on himself and the vampire rose in him, screaming its triumph, and he growled, his hand lifting to grip a fistful of that feather soft hair.

Her cry of pain was heavenly, and he dragged her to the table, forcing her small frame down onto the top of it, her body bent at the hips in a way that made him smile savagely.

"Versalis!" she cried, her voice terrified, and her body writhing and brushing against him.

He closed his eyes, keeping her down with his grip on her hair and revelling in the feel of her struggles. He was going to do terrible things to her, the thoughts flicking through his mind to make his groin ache with need.

"Please! Stop!"

He ignored her, reaching down to grip the band of her underwear, and jerking them down her thighs to bunch at her knees. Gripping her backside, he squeezed the soft skin and smiled savagely, his need burning through him, and he leant down to lick her jaw. Crimson from his eyes shone off her pale skin and he smiled when he saw her tears, smelt her fear. He was going to enjoy fucking her.

"Scream for me," he growled in her ear, a soft whimper escaping her.

"Please, Versalis, please stop!" she cried, but he only moved back enough to pull the ties of his pants free.

"You are my mate, and I will have what's mine," he growled, the knot of his pants pulled tight in his eagerness to be inside her.

He could feel the temperature of the room dropping, but he didn't care, he needed her. She could fight if she wanted to, but he would beat her into submission and take what he wanted.

Struggling with the ties was infuriating, and he snarled, gripping her wrist and jerking her hand down to use her sharp nails on the fabric, the frustration lifting when the tie was cut, and his pants hung loose on his hips.

"You have no idea how much I've wanted to do this," he said hungrily, taking in the perfection of her form. "How many times I've fantasised about this exact moment,"

She didn't reply, her body tense and her eyes clenched shut.

He knew she would go elsewhere, but that didn't matter; he could have her mind later, he only wanted her body right then.

THE DOOR SLAMMED open and he looked up just in time to see fire before he was blown back into the wall and sank down into a heap on the ground, smouldering and smoking with his head spinning.

Dirdos reached Etani and pulled her from the table, his arms going around her protectively as she worked to pull her underwear back up. Her body was tiny against the dragon's giant mass.

"If you ever touch her again, I'll leave nothing but ash!" Dirdos screamed as Daemon came stumbling into the room, tousled with his shirt buttons done up wrong.

"What's going on?" Daemon asked, a near perfect imprint of lips just under his left ear.

"That bastard was holding her down trying to get his pants off."

"Isn't that normal for a couple?"

"Not when she almost killed Dirdos screaming for help," Kai snarled.

Dirdos growled, looking down at Etani as she clung to him, her body trembling.

Versalis looked around but then his eyes found her, and need flooded his system. Twisting onto his hands and knees, he jerked himself up and started for her, not caring if they stayed or not, he was going to have her.

"What has gotten into you?" Daemon snapped as he moved to intercept the vampire, shoving him back as Dirdos backed away, pulling Etani towards the door.

Kai tugged off his shirt and pulled it down over her head, at least covering her nudity, though it didn't do much else to cover her and Versalis growled, his eyes on her thighs.

If the fucking demon got out of the way he could sink his teeth into those thighs, drink from her and keep her as his own personal pleasure and blood doll.

The thought had his groin aching with need, his eyes burning into her back as the dragon pulled her to the door and then out, Kai's posture defensive.

"She's mine!" Versalis snarled, trying to shove the demon out of the way, but he and the other vampire gripped his arms and dragged him backwards.

He could only think about burying himself inside her, hearing her screams as he fucked and fed from her, he wouldn't stop until he was satisfied, or he killed her and then he would do it again. His eyes slid shut as he heard her screaming, her body writhing under him as he drove himself into her with a brutality she had never known before.

His eyes opened, and he found Daemon staring hard into them, but there was someone else, Uzo's face confused as he stood in the doorway.

"What happened? Where's Etani?"

Daemon whipped around at the sound of Uzo's voice.

"He was going to force himself on her," Daemon snarled.

Uzo's eyes found Daemon, and he stalked forward, the promise of death in his eyes.

"How did you find out?"

"Etani somehow communicated it to Dirdos, and he got here in time."

"Where were you? Why weren't you here?"

"I have a life."

"Your job is to protect her!" Uzo snapped, grabbing Versalis by the face and forcing him to look up.

"You are the one who threw a tantrum and left," Daemon shot back.

Versalis couldn't look away from those blue eyes, though his mind was still lingering on Etani's naked, broken body as he took her again, not caring that it hurt her, he only wanted to take what was his.

"He's been dosed," Uzo said, shoving Versalis' head back. "What have you been eating?"

"Dosed with what?" Daemon asked, looking at Versalis.

"Get the fuck out of my way," Versalis snapped, furious at the lot of them for coming between him and his goal, but the more he struggled, the more they clung to him to keep him still.

"What have you been doing?" Daemon snapped.

"He went off with Aurora while we were in the throne room, then he came back here," Jaia said, quiet from his left.

"Aurora?" Uzo asked, his eyes narrowing in suspicion. "Did she give you anything to eat? Did she stab you?"

Versalis shook his head, glaring at the Fae as he tried to pull himself free.

"What about a drink? Did she give you anything to drink?"

"We had a toast to Etani," he snapped, the name coming out as a feral, hungry growl of need.

"Stupid, idiot man." Uzo sighed, rubbing his eyes.

"She drugged him?" Daemon asked, baffled by the suggestion.

"Tie him up, I need to see that my niece is okay. Make sure he can't get out."

The vampire and demon nodded, pulling him backwards towards the chair, and he writhed madly as he tried to fight them off, straining, and when Daemon got too close, Versalis turned on him and sank fangs into his arm.

Daemon yelled in pain, smacking his face back, but it was too late; Versalis had gotten a taste and he licked greedily at his lips, staring hungrily up at the demon as he was dragged into the chair and they used a series of clothing, curtain ties, robe ties, and other things to bind him down to the chair from neck to ankles and wrists.

Versalis watched Daemon, hungry for blood, though she was still in his mind, his groin demanding his attention, but he couldn't move or get to her and so he could do nothing but endure the pain.

"What happened to him?" Daemon asked, tilting his head to look into Versalis' eyes properly. "That's not him, at least not a side of him I've ever seen."

"The vampire," Jaia said, sitting down on his heels with his arms resting against his thighs, ready to move at any moment.

"That's a real thing? I thought that was just an excuse for you lot to go savage."

"No, it's a bit like the werewolves. They have their wolf; we have our vampire. It's the savage, feral nature we all suppress as we mature. It wants what it wants, and it will kill, rape and torture to get to it. In this case his want is Etani."

"Is that …" Daemon asked, looking down at Jaia.

"It doesn't matter," Jaia said, his silver eyes turned to Versalis. "The important part is we stopped him before he could hurt her. At least this time we could protect her."

"I'm sure she will be glad for that," Daemon said, his expression thoughtful.

Versalis sighed at their conversation, straining at the ties, but they had done their job well, ensuring he couldn't move any part of his person.

"I'll share her with you if you let me go," Versalis said in a wheedling voice, both men turning to look at him curiously. "You can fuck her as much as you want, but I get her first."

Neither man said anything, their eyes wary and though they wanted her, they weren't going to abuse her.

"Pussies," he snorted, dropping his head back.

It was a solid hour later before Uzo returned, looking at the three of them with narrowed eyes before he nodded and approached Versalis. Gripping a fistful of hair, the Fae jerked his head back and studied his eyes.

"It's going to be a few hours before he comes down," Uzo said, angry, but at least not trying to kill him.

"What was it?" Daemon asked.

"No idea, something strong that targeted his libido."

"Jaia said it set off the vampire."

"He's likely right. Whatever it was, it was incredibly strong. All inhibitions gone, just his need."

"Aurora wouldn't do that," Versalis said, refusing to believe the woman would do anything against him.

"Of course she would, you idiot! Etani has something she wants and what's the best way to get you? To break you two up! If you wouldn't betray Etani to fuck her, then at least you'd be frustrated and angry enough that you would go and force yourself on her when she wasn't ready. These are the Fae, Versalis. These are creatures who have few morals. Stay away from Aurora," Uzo snapped. "Etani would never have forgiven you if you had gotten the chance to finish. Then Aurora can sweep in and comfort you, then she wins. Don't be fooled by the pretty face and the glamour, Versalis, these are predators who are expert manipulators."

"I didn't think she would go that far," Daemon said, frowning.

"She wants him, she'll do whatever it takes. Even if it means setting him loose on Etani when he's mad with lust and not willing to listen to her wants. He would have destroyed her."

"That's insane, why would she put her Queen's life at risk?" Jaia asked, running his hands through his hair for the millionth time, still crouched and wary.

"Etani's life wouldn't be at risk. A vampire couldn't kill her, he could rape her for an eternity and drain her a million times, but she would always come back."

"So just her sanity, then," Daemon growled.

"Aurora would only see it as getting what she wants." Uzo sighed. "Shouldn't have left her in your hands, you're clearly incapable of keeping her safe. You smell like a whorehouse, go bathe."

Daemon grunted and sniffed himself, frowning before he stalked away to leave Uzo and Jaia to monitor Versalis.

"Will she forgive me?" Versalis asked, pale and feeling like he wanted to jump off a cliff as the vampire realised he had been manipulated and slunk back, leaving Versalis to deal with the mess.

"I spoke to her first. I explained what happened, she is waiting for you."

Jaia snorted as he stood, his knees popping.

"You stay where you are, I need to talk to you," Uzo snapped before turning back to Versalis. "Don't let your dick do your thinking for you. These people will destroy you if you let them. Do not under any circumstance trust a single one of them. I suggest we leave Faerie for now; the wedding doesn't have to be here, and we can go to the hybrids to hide out."

Jaia nodded once, moving to help free Versalis, and he was out of the chair in an instant, the door slamming against the wall as he streaked out of it.

She was standing in silence with Dirdos, the man's large hand clutched in both of hers as she looked up at him, the two communicating without a word being spoken.

It was odd to see, the way their bodies leaned in towards each other, their faces intent and staring into each other's eyes. Trying to ignore a stab of jealousy, he approached the pair and Etani turned to look at him, her eyes wary.

Dirdos was tense enough to shatter, but he allowed her to move away and approach him, her pale face uncertain and scared.

"I'm so sorry, Etani ... I didn't know that would happen," he whispered, wanting nothing more than to grab her and hold her to him but he remained still, allowing her to move to him if she desired it.

"Aurora drugged you?" she asked, and he was pleased to see her lips pressing down into a frown, her eyes tightening in her jealousy. "Why were you in that situation?"

"I was hoping to patch things up, so she at least didn't hate us. I never imagined she would try something like that. I never for a second thought anyone would try that."

"These are the Fae, idiot. They aren't the petty saboteurs of Ayathian, these people don't do anything halfway," Dirdos snapped, furious and wanting Versalis gone.

Etani frowned, her lips parting, but then she shut her mouth again, torn and confused before she seemed to come to a decision. "I … I don't want you to talk to her anymore," she said, hesitant and uncertain.

He could see her struggling with the situation and her lack of knowledge meant she didn't know what she could and couldn't request of him.

"I won't, not unless I absolutely have to. I'm sorry, love, this is all my fault."

He lifted his arms for her to come to him and she looked up into his face for a long moment before she closed the distance to him and he closed his eyes, the coolness of her body feeling blissfully wonderful against him. He had been terrified that his actions would have turned her away from him and he wouldn't have blamed her, but she didn't run, and she was back in his arms.

Tilting his head, he pressed a hard kiss against her forehead, the scent of her hair strong in his nose.

"Are you okay?" he whispered.

"You're lucky she didn't rip you apart …" Dirdos said, glaring.

He wasn't wrong, she had every right to obliterate him when he went for her, but she hadn't.

"Why didn't you? You should have destroyed me right then and there."

"I couldn't hurt you, Versalis … I love you," she whispered, and his stomach dropped. It was the same reason she hadn't killed Jaia when he had succeeded in forcing himself on her. She had frozen, unable to bring herself to hurt him because of her feelings for him.

"No, Etani, you can't ever do that," he said, gripping her arms and pulling her back from him. "It doesn't matter who it is, you always defend yourself. Even if it's me, you have to protect yourself."

She looked up at him, confused and scared, but he couldn't give in to the need to hold her.

"Promise you will always defend yourself. Never hesitate," he demanded.

Biting down on her lower lip, she searched his face and then nodded once. Relief flooded through him as he pulled her against him, holding her head against his chest and kissing her hair.

"You're the most precious thing in the world, Etani, you need to be safe, even from those who would protect you." He sighed, her arms wrapping around his ribs and her hands splayed against his back.

"Next time don't do a warning shot," he said to Dirdos. The dragon glared, but then nodded. He knew the man would kill him in an instant, but that was better than Etani being hurt.

"I love you, Etani, I love you so much …" He sighed, revelling in the feeling of her against him.

"I love you, too," she whispered, his heart skipping a beat at the soft words.

CHAPTER 31
HYBRIDS

When told that they would be leaving for the hybrids, Etani nodded and they headed back, Dirdos fuming as he followed along behind the two of them.

A sudden fear filled him as he recalled the look they had exchanged, and he had a terrible vision of her leaving him for the giant man. Dirdos was certainly more suitable for her, and the thought made him nervous, especially with this new connection between them. Dirdos had become a very viable threat to his future, and the man only made it worse when Etani headed off ahead to Daemon, his grin wide as he reached for her.

"The instant you drop your guard I'm taking her," Dirdos said, his face carefully neutral as they watched the small woman being crushed by the demon. "The very instant you look away I will steal her away. You don't deserve her, and I will make sure you don't have her for long."

"You think you deserve her?" Versalis asked, fear washing through him.

"No, but at least I will do a better job at keeping her safe."

"I'm not going to look away. Not ever," Versalis hissed, but

Dirdos only smiled, glancing down at him and back up when she turned back and called for them to hurry up.

They did so, moving quickly to join her and Daemon, Jaia lurking back further with Uzo standing beside him.

Etani spotted her uncle and shrieked, shoving Daemon out of the way, and threw herself into his arms. Daemon looked both irritated and amused as she latched onto the Fae and he embraced her, murmuring in her ear as she whimpered. "Don't ever do that again!" she cried, dragging him down to kiss his cheek hard. "I forbid it!"

"Yes, my Queen," he said playfully, kissing her cheek, and with his arms clamped around her ribs, he hitched her up and carried her dangling from his arms into her room, Etani giggling the whole time like a little girl.

It was endearing to see her so happy, and they all smiled as they watched her, Uzo scooping her up into his arms as he swept into the royal suite and plopped down onto the edge of the bed.

"We're leaving," Uzo said in a matter-of-fact tone while setting Etani down into his lap where she wiggled herself closer to him and smirked at them all in smug pleasure, content and secure in the man's arms while the rest of them went without.

Versalis was quite content without, but she clearly thought they were missing out.

Letari stormed into the room with Hunter trailing along behind her, smiling in amusement as the crazy woman scanned the room for her sister.

Etani's eyes narrowed on her twin when Letari looked at her, then Uzo, then back again with a considering look, and Letari moved forward, Etani's foot coming up to press against her twin's stomach as Letari strained to get into Uzo's arms. "No, get your own," Etani snapped, Letari hissing back as she tried to dodge around Etani's attempts to keep her way.

"There's plenty of room for the both of you." Uzo sighed, looking down at the two.

"Don't be a selfish bitch!" Letari whined, shoving Etani's foot out of the way and then shoving her sister sideways, forcing herself into Uzo's lap.

Etani hissed, frustrated at having to share the man, the two glaring at each other while Uzo winced at the struggles.

"See? Don't be a bitch."

Etani shoved her sister off Uzo's lap without so much as a hint of her intentions and Dirdos burst out laughing.

"You'd think they were kids." Daemon sighed.

"They are. They're not even a thousand yet," Uzo grumbled, helping Letari up and tugging her back onto his lap next to a pouting Etani.

"Suppose they are fairly young still," Daemon sighed.

"You smell like a wet dog," Etani muttered, and Letari grinned in response.

"That's because Hunter knows what his lady likes."

Etani made a face and turned away with a muttered "Gross ..."

"You'd know if your vampire got off his butt and did something," Letari growled.

THE ROOM FROZE and Letari looked around, sensing the shift.

"What happened?" she demanded, her eyes going to Hunter as an immediate means of stability.

"Don't worry about it," Etani muttered, sitting sideways with her back against Letari's arm, her body leaning into Uzo's with her cheek resting against his chest, his arm clutched in her hands as though she was afraid he was going to vanish.

Letari searched their faces, and they all became suddenly very interested in the items in the room, focusing their minds on something to keep her out.

"Tell me!" Letari screamed, and Hunter moved forward immediately, ignoring her attempt to slap his hands away and pulling her from Uzo's arms to soothe her, his fingers combing through her short hair and murmuring softly in her ear.

"Aurora drugged Versalis, and he attacked Etani. We are leaving for the hybrid compound as soon as possible," Daemon said, making it clear that Versalis wasn't to blame but his eyes still dropped when she turned to look at him.

It didn't matter that he had been drugged, he had hurt her, and he hated himself for it. His hormones were still raging but now that the vampire was down, he could keep himself calm and his hands to himself.

"Did you hurt her?" Letari asked, her eyes wary.

"Not physically," Versalis said; at least he hoped not.

"I'm fine," Etani said as she stood, pulling Uzo to his feet as she made her way around the room, throwing things one-handed onto the bed while refusing to let go of the man.

"Etani, I'm not going anywhere," Uzo said.

"No, you're not. Especially when I'm holding onto you," she said, pulling him across to the closet and bundling up her clothes against her body, dumping them at the edge of the bed, shoving them back towards the middle and looking around.

"I swear I brought more than this …" She sighed, glancing around before she pulled Uzo into the bathroom with her to collect everything in there, too.

"My people will be glad to have us," Hunter said as he kissed Letari's hair, the woman still staring at Versalis with a small frown on her lips.

"It will certainly be interesting," Daemon agreed, reaching under the bed to pull out some of the cases. She hadn't had the chance to unpack much before they were planning to leave again and so they were all prepared to leave again within an hour, Etani never once letting go of her uncle and the man looking resigned to his fate of being pulled along like a toy on a string. But Versalis thought the man was secretly loving it.

The two didn't really get that much time to spend together and while Etani loved him with a ferocity bordering on obsession, she was still terrified to lose him again and that translated into her being wary of getting close to him.

But she had him back now, and she wasn't about to let go.

Once they were settled into a small group surrounded by bags, Etani looked around and frowned but didn't speak, her mind on something that Versalis couldn't even guess at. "Someone will need to tell Sebastian and the Hunters where we're going," she said, her eyes going to one of the cases before she looked up at Dirdos.

"They'll be able to find us. Maybe. Why not make them all sweat for a bit? It'll be good for them," Daemon said, grinning wickedly.

"You're such a jerk," Hunter said in amusement as he leant in to whisper something to Dirdos and the giant man nodded once, the world around them melting into a smear of red.

Etani's eyes flicked around the room once more before the world was gone, something bothering her.

He would have to ask her about it when they got the chance.

THEY STEPPED out into a large clearing and moved apart, looking around at what seemed to be nothing but dense forest on all sides; a little odd but they didn't want to criticize.

"Trap," Etani said, and they all froze, Hunter grinning.

"Buzzkill," he growled and slid his foot to the side.

The enormous net shot up around them and they all yelled as they were yanked up into the air, bouncing a few times before settling with a steady stream of leaves and twigs falling down as they all struggled to right themselves.

"That's not funny!" Letari shrieked.

"How did you know?" Hunter asked Etani, who was standing on Dirdos' back and holding onto the wall of the net.

"You are really bad at covering it," she said as she looked up and around. She reached out and her nails made quick work of two of the ropes, allowing her to wiggle her small frame out.

"Don't do it. It's not worth it," Dirdos growled as Daemon reached out for her backside as she wiggled her way free.

Daemon opted to ignore the warning, and his fingers closed on her, squeezing the soft flesh.

Etani flipped herself onto her back and her foot slammed into the side of his face, sending him flying into the side of the net where he groaned.

"Worth it ..." He whimpered as she pulled herself up and out onto the outside of the net.

"You look like a spider," Versalis teased, and he grinned when she stuck her hand back into the cavity, her middle finger raised. "Love you, too, honey."

Climbing her way up, the net swayed as every man inside the net tilted to see up her dress as she moved, appreciating the view of those seemingly endless long legs.

"Morning," a cheerful voice called out, and they all turned to look down at the ground below, a tall man with a thick brown beard and equally thick brown hair standing a few feet away, leaning on a spear and looking up at them with interest.

"Morning," Etani said back, eyeing the man as her nails worked on the net. "Nice day, isn't it?"

"Very nice. Perfect weather for a stroll."

"Indeed, it is. Where might we be taking a stroll to?"

The entire situation was bizarre as Versalis found himself almost crushed under the squirming mass of men all trying to get themselves upright, and then the net began to give way at one side though it was far from freeing them.

"Why don't you come down here and we can talk?" the man asked.

"While I appreciate the offer, I must politely decline."

There was a soft whistle, and the net jerked as Etani looked around.

"I'm afraid you don't really have much choice in the matter," the man said.

"Son of a bitch ..." Etani growled, pulling a small dart out of her thigh.

"Literally," the man said with a wide grin. "Who are you, girl?"

"Etani," she called back, and his smile faltered.

"Ah shit," he said, his eyes going to the net. "Hunter?"

"Hi, Dad ..." Hunter said, his tone amused.

"We just darted the Queen of Winter, didn't we?"

"Sure did."

Etani wrapped her arm around the main rope and her smile was almost tipsy as she threw caution to the wind and her nails slashed through the ropes.

There was a yell of alarm as the net released and dumped them all out onto the ground in a tangled mess, Etani hanging to the net with her feet hooked into the rungs.

She blinked hard as she looked down at them, trying to focus.

"Dirdos?" she asked, her tone confused.

Dirdos was on his feet in an instant, his eyes skyward as he moved to stand below her and she let go of the net, falling neatly into his arms.

The dragon turned with her and Versalis stood, going to her side. With a gentle hand, he pulled at her eyelid to see her pupil.

"They have fun drugs," she said in a slurred voice.

"It'll wear off in an hour," the bearded man said, approaching the group and looking at Etani curiously.

"Did you have to dart her?" Daemon asked as her head dropped back, still conscious, but her neck seemed to no longer want to support her head.

"She had climbed the net, we had to make sure she didn't get you all free. But I didn't see a knife."

Versalis took her hand and lifted it, showing the man those delicate fingers and the short, perfectly oval nails that could shred metal.

"Interesting creature," the man said.

The man and Hunter exchanged a hard hug and then the man grabbed Letari, crushing her in a bear hug as Etani sighed, her eyes sliding shut, and she was unconscious.

"Not even a full six months," Daemon growled and held up a coin, Uzo snatching it out of his fingers with a grin.

"Told you." Uzo laughed.

"This is my dad, Yak," Hunter said.

"Yak?" Versalis asked, amused.

"You'll get used to the weird names. Here we have Letari, Uzo, Daemon, the big guy is Dirdos, Jaia, Kai, and Etani. Stay out of arm's reach of her when she wakes up, she is violent," Hunter said as he pointed to each person in turn.

"She looks like a child," Yak said doubtfully.

"Lucky she's unconscious," Uzo snorted.

"Yeah, don't mention the height if you want to live."

"Right-o. Come on then, you lot, let's go."

The man turned, and much to their surprise, he walked to the wall of ferns and brushed them aside, as though they were a curtain and as they all passed through, their eyes widened.

On the other side of the curtain was a fully flourishing town, massive and certainly not there when they had been in the net.

"Mage magic keeps us hidden," Hunter said as they made their way down into the main street.

There were at least a thousand people living in the village, all of them tall and attractive like Hunter with that feral wildness that they associated with Hunter. The women were exquisite, the men wildly handsome and the whole place had the weird sense of wild abandon and ferocious territorialism at once.

"So, this is your wife to be?" Yak asked, watching the crazy woman warily.

"Letari," Letari said, her eyes just as wary of the bearded man. "What kind of name is Yak?"

Hunter snorted and Versalis slowed to walk beside Dirdos, watching the sleeping form of Etani carefully. She was still out cold.

"It's a perfectly respectable name. Hunter is the exception here, his mother insisted on giving him an improper name."

"Yak is a proper name?" Daemon asked, looking at the man.

"Yak is perfectly good. My cousins are named Bur and Pur. Non-identical twins."

Letari snorted at the names, trying to keep a straight face, but it wasn't happening.

"Ever stop to think you have a weird name?" Yak demanded.

"Letari is Fae, her name was given to her by whatever magic names all the Fae and most of those born to Faerie."

"It is generally believed that either the magic of the Court chooses the name, Winter in this case, or The Great Mother chooses it. We don't really know," Uzo said, voice quiet.

"They weren't Winter Court, though," Daemon said.

"No, but their father was, and given that his mother was a Winter Queen, it's likely that Winter would have claimed them unless they decided otherwise."

"I didn't know that could happen," Versalis said.

"It's only a theory, we would have to ask Winter to find out for sure, but it makes sense if you think about it. It's not often a Queen is born to one of the Queens."

"Why is that?" Yak asked.

"Aurora said that the overall fertility of Faerie is dwindling," Versalis said.

"What?" Daemon demanded, outraged.

"With each generation there are fewer children. There are people working on it, but no one really knows why. No one knows if it's the men or women, or even if it's just the magic of Faerie that is the result. The less magic, the less children."

"Faerie is fading?"

"It was, but it seems that Etani is fixing it. It's just another theory, but it goes hand in hand with what Jason said. Etani is creating magic, it radiates off her, and Faerie is taking what isn't absorbed by us."

"Do you feel stronger being near her?" Daemon asked Yak, the bearded man scowling.

"No, but my wolf is getting restless."

"That happened to me. I thought it was just the pheromones she put out that were triggering my wolf, but it's also her magic making it stronger while she calls to it," Hunter said. "Just be careful, if you think the pack is territorial, we have nothing on this lot if they think you're hunting her."

All eyes turned on Yak in consideration, each of them weighing up the man as a potential threat to their own claims on Etani.

"Don't worry, I'm happily married. I have no interest in your girl," Yak said, glancing down at Etani before he turned away and they made their way down to a large home with two floors and a large garden attached to the side filled to overflowing with vegetables and fruit trees.

"We'll let her sleep it off inside and we can talk. I'm curious to meet this girl," Yak said as he opened the door. The woman standing in the doorway was tall, buxom, and scowling at her husband, the man ducking his head in an amusingly submissive posture. Her hair was a bright flaming red, and she had large green eyes, vivid compared to his dark browns. Earth and fire.

"What is this, Yak?" the woman demanded, looking them over, but then she found her son and she cried out, snatching the man off the ground and into the house, hugging him with the ferocity of a mother.

Daemon grinned at the irritated man who was trying to detach himself from the woman, but she was having none of it.

"Bring your friends inside, I'll put the kettle on," she said, but then dragged Hunter away, the man looking remarkably like a cub being carried off by a she-wolf.

They followed him in, smirking at the new taunts they could use against him.

"Where have you been all this time?" the woman demanded.

"Ayathian. I got captured by the King and then got involved in that lot," Hunter said grumpily, forced into a chair. His face lit up as a plate of food was set before him.

Versalis' attention locked on the meat hungrily, but there was more than enough for all of them, and they at least attempted courtesy, thanking the woman politely before stuffing the food into their faces.

"What happened to her?" the woman asked as she spied the unconscious woman, Dirdos sitting in the corner of the room with her clutched to his chest, his eyes wary.

"Dad darted her," Hunter said.

"I didn't dart her!" Yak cried when his wife turned on him. "She was climbing the net and one of the men got her."

The woman approached Dirdos, brushing Etani's hair back to get a better look at that exquisite face.

"Who is she?" the woman asked.

"Etani, the Winter Queen," Dirdos said.

The woman drew back, eyes wide as she turned on her husband. "If you bring the Court down on us, I'll personally hand you over."

"The Court won't be coming, it's okay, mum."

"Oh, right, everyone this is Bee, my wife and Hunter's mother."

There was a low growl of greeting from men too focused on eating to pay much attention.

"That's Etani with Dirdos, Daemon, Uzo, Jaia, and Kai. This is my fiancé, Letari; we're here to get married."

Bee froze, eyes on her son and then the woman in question, then moving between Letari and Etani before returning to Hunter. "Well, I suppose it's about time you got settled down."

Letari grinned and almost tackled the woman, and Bee hugged her tightly in return.

It was a solid hour and a half before Etani stirred, and she groaned, face tensed, but then she sat up, looking around with wide, alert eyes. "Where are we?" she demanded, making Uzo and Daemon jerk up from where they had been lounging by the fire, full and sleepy.

"In the hybrid town," Dirdos said to calm her while she studied the room and the two frozen strangers.

She took them both in warily before her attention turned on Letari and then Versalis, his smile warm and comforting. "Someone darted me," she said, uncertain of the course of events. "And Hunter set us down into a trap, right?"

"Right," Dirdos said, stroking her hair.

Etani nodded, her attention moving between the men in her life, and then when she was satisfied that they were all safe, she relaxed.

"Etani, this is my father Yak and my mother Bee," Hunter said.

Etani's eyes snapped onto the woman and an odd, slightly confused expression came over her face.

"Mother?" Etani asked, unable to tear her eyes off the woman.

"It's an honour to meet you," Yak said. "You are welcome in our home, Your Majesty."

"Etani," she corrected, her lips slightly parted, still staring at Bee.

"It's okay, love," Versalis said, and coaxed her attention around him with a gentle touch on the cheek. "We have food."

That caught her attention, and she turned on him, her eyes narrowing suspiciously, but she stood willingly enough, allowing him to draw her towards the table.

Dirdos sighed, rubbing his eyes and resting his head back against the wall, relaxed now that she was awake again.

Picking up two plates, she loaded them both up and stuffed a small roll in her mouth before she padded back to Dirdos, the giant man smiling at the offered plate.

"Stop staring at her, she's mostly nice," Hunter said, and they all looked around to find not only the parents watching her, but another man who had come down the stairs, remarkably similar to Hunter, though his hair was tinted red and he had no scars on his face.

"My brother, Marsden," Hunter said with an irritated look.

"How did you get involved with the Court?" Yak demanded, Etani's eyes on Marsden as she chewed the roll.

"Etani was in Ayathian when I was there, at least most of the time," he said in amusement.

"I was captured, too," Etani said, her attention back on Bee with an unnerving intensity. "Not much of a choice in the matter," she added, licking her lips before giving a small green vegetable a wary sniff and then offering it to Dirdos.

"Try it," Dirdos growled, and she looked at him, frowning. His brows lifted in challenge and her eyes narrowed in irritation. Finally, she stuffed it into her mouth and stalked away from him to Versalis' side.

It seemed that Yak and Bee didn't know what to say to that, and Etani was content to just eat, leaning into his side when he wrapped his arm around her shoulders.

"Daemon?" Etani said in a sweet voice after she had finished eating, and the man's head snapped up in alarm, looking at her as she smiled at him.

The demon seemed to vanish, the door bursting open as he bolted, but she was on his heels in an instant.

Filing out of the room as the demon screamed, Versalis watched his love as she sat on the man's back and, using a knife she had evidently stolen from the dinner table, she sawed off first one hand, and then the other.

When she was done, she calmly lifted the bloody knife above her head and stabbed it into his back, aiming it to miss all of his vital organs. Lifting her hand, she beat the knife in until the handle no longer protruded from his back. She then smiled, getting up and heading back into the house.

CHAPTER 32
STATE OF EMERGENCY

The days passed by in the hybrid town, relaxed and eating the happy parents out of house and home, but they seemed content to have the house full of young-looking people who inhaled every scrap of food put before them.

Etani had become obsessed with Bee, watching her and following her absently around the house while trying to look like she was in the same room for another reason that wasn't stalking Hunter's mother.

"What's her deal?" Yak asked as they watched Etani following Bee, a large basket in her hands and those large blue eyes wider still as Bee spoke in a motherly tone, trying to teach the starstruck Queen about gardening.

"I don't think Etani has ever seen a normal mother before," Dirdos said, his eyes locked on the small woman as she looked down, somewhat surprised that Bee was taking a tiny shovel out of the basket and then looking back up again, silent and hypnotised by the taller hybrid woman.

"They lost their mother at a young age. No maternal figure has ever shown an interest in her before Bast, and now Bee. She's a little starved for female affection that isn't her sister, and on top of that, she probably finds Bee fascinating given how few mothers she's been around," Uzo said, his smile soft and sad.

"Big bold assassin looking for a mummy," Daemon said with a fond smile.

"Please, you'd be clinging to her skirt too if she paid you even a hint of attention," Dirdos snapped.

"True. Most of us probably have mummy issues."

"Why is it she isn't attached to Yak as well?" Jaia asked.

"She has Uzo for the paternal figure. It's mother she's lacking. You should get married, Uzo, then you can give her a mum."

Uzo jerked and looked around at him. "Why don't one of you get married and give it to her?"

"She can't be her own mum," Dirdos said and Versalis looked around at the man while Daemon snorted.

"In your dreams, dragon boy, she's not going to marry you," Daemon snapped.

"No? Says who?"

"Me," Versalis growled, the crimson stare of the dragon turning on him.

"You think you're getting that far?" Dirdos growled, darkly amused.

"None of you are marrying her. Well, except Kai, maybe," Uzo muttered.

Kai's head jerked up, his eyes wide in alarm and his mouth full.

"Me? Why me?"

"You're probably the only one I'd approve of out of this group."

Kai's face twisted, and then pleasure before his eyes turned on her with a sad longing that had them all watching him warily.

"Etani doesn't see him that way," Versalis snapped.

"Because she hadn't really tried. I bet you, if he put even an ounce of attempt into it, she would drop you like she found a spider on your head."

Jaia looked at his brother with a scowl and Kai dropped his eyes from her.

Etani looked away from Bee to the group of men, and she gave them a happy smile that made his heart leap. She looked so content for the first time, though her smile faded as Bee moved away and she hurried after the woman, the basket clutched to her chest.

"How's the wedding preparations going?" Versalis asked Yak, the man watching Etani with a fascinated stare.

"I expect it'll be another week or so; Bee is insisting on a lot of things that we have to get imported."

"Could always get Dirdos to do it, he makes for a good pack mule," Daemon said, grinning.

Yak only snorted. "I'm not giving you our location, so stop trying,"

Daemon's face fell, and he glared at the man, grumpy that his umpteenth attempt to get Yak to reveal their location had failed.

Dirdos only shrugged, not caring all that much.

Their eyes lifted as Etani stared up at Bee, confused and unhappy about something, but then she nodded and set down the basket, dusting off her hands, and when that didn't work, she headed for a pump while Bee headed in their direction.

"She's such a strange creature," the woman said, pink cheeked and flustered.

"Don't worry, she'll adjust," Uzo said, picking up the teapot and refilling Yak's cup when the man nodded in acceptance.

"Adjust to what?" Bee asked, eyeing the men with irritation.

"To having a mother for the first time in her life. She idolises you," Versalis said, watching the woman in question as she scrubbed her hands clean.

"Oh, I didn't realise," Bee said, her face melting into distress. "And I've been short with her..."

"Don't worry, love, she's a big girl, she can handle it," Yak said, touching the woman's shoulder.

"I've never seen her this happy, just let her follow you around and give her things to do. She might look delicate, but she's strong, and she's eager to help. She just wants your affection," Uzo said quietly. "She did the same to me at first, too, following me around like a puppy and getting in the way. But if you give her things to do that help you out, she'll be happy and out from under your feet."

"What happened to her mother?" Bee asked, turning to watch the small woman as she cupped the water in her hands and drank from it.

"Died in childbirth. She's been the mother to her sisters since, so she never got the chance to be the child after the first ten years or so."

Bee made a distressed sound and Etani looked up, her eyes wary and alert, but when she decided nothing was wrong, she turned away again to finish drinking.

"Don't get us wrong, she is dangerous and volatile. She is an assassin and mercenary by trade, but under all that she just wants someone to comfort and protect her. She could probably kill everyone in this town in under an hour, but she's still very young and I think she's more lonely than she lets on." Uzo's voice was low and sad, Versalis watching the woman as she picked up a bucket and carried it to the garden, poured it onto the soil around the trees, her attention flicking between them before she looked around.

"Where's Letari?" she asked as she approached, her cheeks flushed and clothes dirty.

Bee looked like she was going to cry, Etani's eyes widening as she met the distressed woman's face.

"I think she went with Hunter. Probably showing off the hut," Yak said.

"The hut?" Etani asked, her hand lifting but then settling back at her side, wanting to touch Bee but afraid of the potential rejection.

"Hunter built a hut before he left, no doubt he'll be there trying to convince her that he's a decent builder. It's traditional to build the first home together."

Etani nodded, still watching Bee. "Where is it?"

"Down the path," he said, pointing down a narrow path between the garden and the next house, a small wooden house standing alone near the garden wall.

Etani glanced down the path and then offered Bee a smile before she headed off in the direction Yak had indicated, her braid swaying down her back as she went.

"She's an incredibly attractive woman. How is it that she has no husband?"

Daemon snorted in amusement, chewing on a piece of steak.

"She has three, and that's the boyfriend," Uzo said, jerking his thumb in Versalis' direction.

Hunter and Bee exchanged a glance.

"The Queens of Faerie are generally encouraged to have multiple husbands and lovers in order to produce an heir. Illegitimate children do not exist, if the child is female, she is a viable heir regardless of the status of the father," Uzo explained.

"Strange concept," Yak said, frowning at his wife.

"The Fae are not overly fertile, the more men, the better the chance at an heir," Daemon said finally. "If the Fae had the fertility of the hybrid for example, then they would likely take a different stance on marriage, but generally we don't tend to bother with it. The Queens do so only out of tradition."

A SUDDEN, horrified scream had them all jumping to their feet, recognising the voice that made it, and they headed down the path Etani had taken, alert and ready, but there seemed to be no threat.

Etani was staggering back from the door to the hut, her hands over her eyes. "I can't unsee that! Don't you people believe in locking doors?!" she screamed.

"Don't you believe in knocking?" Letari screamed back as she staggered out of the hut, pulling her dress back down and the neckline back up over her chest while Hunter followed, pulling his pants back up.

"I did knock! Twice!"

"Then what are you doing barging inside when no one answered?!"

Relaxing, the group of men and Bee watched the scene unfold.

Etani stumbled away, hands covering her face as though something had stuck them there, the rest of them amused by the scene. "They said you were in there with Hunter! I didn't think you'd be...!" she shrieked again.

"She's not what I expected," Yak said, watching Etani as she rubbed at her eyes as though she could rub the image of her sister and Hunter out of her brain.

"What is wrong with you people?" Etani cried.

"Stop being so dramatic; we were only having sex. It's not like we were doing anything weird!"

"In what way?" Uzo asked, watching the two women with an amused smile.

"I was expecting this... I don't know, a Queen. Regal and calm."

"She would have been had she been raised in the courts, but she wasn't," Uzo replied.

"No?"

"No, they are half breeds, expelled by their own people at around twenty and left to fend for themselves."

"That's, what? Two years ago?" Yak didn't seem overly impressed.

"The twins are nine hundred and a bit. The Fae don't age."

Yak looked around at Uzo and then back at the twins as Letari tried to pry Etani's hands away from her face.

"However, by comparison, they are little more than teenagers. Very young. Very wise, but very young,"

"How old are you lot?" Yak asked.

"I don't know really, I'd venture a guess at about five thousand," Uzo said.

"I've been here since the birth of Faerie," Daemon said, making Yak choke.

"Me, too, around the same time, maybe a decade younger," Dirdos murmured, his eyes on Etani as she stumbled away from her sister and Hunter joined the rest of them, flustered and red faced.

"You all look like you're less than thirty."

"Flatterer," Daemon said with a grin.

"You need to learn to lock doors," Yak said, amused. "Did she see much?"

"We were... almost done," Hunter said and scowled when they all laughed. "I didn't think she would just walk in."

"I'm sure she'll see worse before the end of this," Uzo said, smirking.

"What is it about her? It's hard to look directly at her but it's impossible to not look," Yak said.

"Etani is a magical lure. Think of it like a siren song given flesh, she calls to you, so you want to go to her," Daemon said quietly.

"What happens if you go to her?"

"Usually she would eat you. Etani consumes souls, human mostly, but mythical, too, sometimes. Wasn't intended that she could eat us but there you have it."

"Really? I figured that had been planned like the rest of it," Kai said, perking up at the conversation.

"No, was meant to be just humans, but it didn't go that way."

"You talk like you created her..." Yak said, frowning at the demon.

"Daemon has been working on her for millennia, sculpting her through picking and choosing each new generation and manipulating the children into marrying who he wanted. Fifty generations." Kai supplied, ever eager to discuss the matter.

"Why? I mean, I can see why now, but why spend so much time doing that?"

"Prophecy," Daemon said. "First oracle in existence predicted her. All the Gods tried; I was the only one to stick to it."

Yak stared at the demon; lips pressed into a hard line as he considered the golden-eyed man.

"I'm sorry, did you just say you were a God?"

"She's one, too," Hunter said, looking at the twins as Etani kept her back to her sister, her smile telling them all she was no longer distraught but teasing her sister. Etani might be cold, but she loved it when Letari paid attention to her.

"Letari or the Queen?" Yak asked, watching the two.

"Etani. You don't have to call her a Queen, she's just Etani."

"Etani the Queen of Winter, and Goddess," Yak muttered, the woman in question looking around as though the man had called her name.

"Death, a Creator, the most exquisitely beautiful creature in existence..." Daemon said with a sigh.

Etani watched them, her head tilted to the side but then her attention was captured by Letari and she glared, swiping for the taller woman.

"How can she be all that? And why didn't you go for her?" he demanded of his son.

"Letari and I just happened."

"You're scared of her," Yak said knowingly.

"I'm terrified of her," Hunter agreed.

"Well, at least you will have her ear."

"Assuming she doesn't chew my face off. She doesn't like me much."

"Etani is extremely protective of Letari," Daemon said in response to Yak's curious look.

"Ah, well don't fuck it up. She's a valuable ally if we ever need it."

"Yes, Dad..." Hunter sighed. They all looked up as Letari approached, Etani following after her though her attention was focused elsewhere, her eyes searching the houses.

Dirdos was at her side in an instant, capturing her attention with a gentle brush against her jaw with his fingers.

"What's bothering you, kitten?" he asked, frowning when her eyes turned away from him again.

"Something's wrong," she said, taking Dirdos' hand in hers as she stared around.

"What's wrong?" Daemon asked, his eyes narrowing as he, too, started looking around.

"The magic is being disturbed. Like it's warping."

Yak looked up and Hunter growled, his eyes going to Letari.

"Get them inside and into the basement," Yak demanded of Hunter, who nodded and grabbed both Letari and Bee by the arms and dragged them for the house.

The air rippled eerily a few feet above the top of a house and Yak swore.

"Attack!" he bellowed; the call spread quickly through the town.

People were running, eerily silent children who were standing calmly still being scooped up by the nearest adults and thrown into houses. The men were quickly armed, and behind them were their equally well-armed wives.

Turning on Etani, he found her watching him as she drew two long knives from the folds of her dress, and he had to wonder how she had managed to slip those past them all.

Versalis snatched up one of the knives from the table, the others already carrying weapons as was normal for them.

Letari struggled to get herself free, her arm outstretched for Etani, but Etani's eyes had lifted, her lips set into a grim line as the air seemed to explode outwards with a mass of people, all of them hooting and screaming their joy as they got through to the town.

Without a word, Etani scooped up a handful of forks, and with her knife between her teeth, she flicked the first fork up, caught it by the tip of the handle and turned, throwing the fork with expert precision.

The first form fell, blood pouring out of his eye where the fork had sunk in almost halfway.

Three more fell before the intruders knew what was happening and she was out, the forms turning out to be a large number of snow-white men in black clothing, their crimson eyes announcing them to be vampires in the throes of bloodlust.

He wanted desperately to drag her into the basement with her sister, but he knew she would never let him. She was not a woman who needed protection like that, and she would not thank him for trying it.

The vampires turned on them and their battle cry was deafening as they ran for the growing group.

TURNING one last glance to his love, he found her staring at him in equal fear, but then she growled and turned away, darting forward to meet the vampires an instant before Uzo, the twins, and Daemon started forward. Dirdos stood back, that little ball of fire starting up in his hand as he took aim. Versalis lunged forward with the rest of the fighters, and he was into the fight, slashing at the screaming face before him.

A call went out and stakes were tossed from fighter to fighter. Versalis caught his and turned on the vampire as the vampire struggled back to his feet, his face bloody and ripped. Driving the stake into the chest, the vampire's scream joined that of the others and he collapsed, Versalis ripping the stake out before turning on the next.

He could still see her nearby, her face calm as she hacked and slashed her way through the group and left a path of destruction for others to finish off while the vampires were still down.

She was a cyclone of destruction, and when her knife got lodged, she tugged only twice before abandoning it in the skull of the vampire and with her next step the temperature dropped as she called on Winter to join her.

Silver streaked down her hair, those lovely markings burning into existence as the ground around her began to frost over.

He had never seen her use magic outside of a blind rage before and it was hypnotic to watch, her eyes a solid glowing white as the first vampire to reach her staggered, his feet freezing to the ice, and she turned to him, her hand lifting.

The air warped as though it were pulling inwards towards her hand, and she closed her fingers around the icicle as it formed, using it to drive into the vampire's chest.

Sucking in a breath as he spotted a new contender creeping up on her, she didn't even look up as her hand flicked and the man simply froze in place, sweat on his skin showing that she had completely frozen the liquid in his body.

Moving on from the two, she systematically froze or skewered target after target, her path clear by the frozen grass and frost.

Hunter yelled, but Versalis didn't have time to look around, his attention drawn by the vampire before him, both of them frozen as they watched the Queen moving, hypnotised by her. But they forced themselves back into action and Versalis blocked a punch with his forearm, driving the stake into the man's chest.

It was odd how easy it was to dismantle the attackers, but they would worry about that later.

The vampires seemed to see that they were outmatched and had retreated, only to find the grimly smiling face of Winter blocking their path. They didn't seem game enough to try to take her on; instead they bolted, and the guards went after them in a rush.

One decided he would try his luck, and when she didn't attack him, he grew bolder, slinking closer while those remaining watched in fascination at what she was going to do.

"Hello, pretty," he cooed, and her head tilted, her lips turning up into a smile.

"I'll make a deal with you," she said, her voice echoing slightly as though she was repeating the words only a fraction of a second after the initial words were spoken. "I kiss you, and you kiss me."

The guards looked confused and alarmed by the suggestion, but Daemon only smirked, Versalis' shoulders relaxing slightly.

"And then you let me go," he countered, and she nodded once.

"I get to kiss you first, though," she said, and he nodded.

Daemon was doing his best not to laugh as the vampire approached her, his hunger clear in his movements.

He reached for her, and his skin steamed at the contact, but he didn't let her go and she lifted her chin. He seemed to be triumphant, as though he had won a prize, but the moment their lips touched, his body stiffened and her hair flashed to black, the markings on her skin flickering out like a candle.

Yak stepped forward, his mouth hanging open as he watched the scene, but then the vampire fell and she stood still, eyes black as sin. "What the hell?"

Versalis smacked his arm and murmured a soft, "Don't draw attention to yourself."

Her head had turned in their direction and Dirdos hissed a warning as she seemed to almost float forward, her movements liquid and feline.

Stopping before Yak, she leant forward and inhaled the scent of him, her smile seductive, but then something caught her attention and her head snapped away to the right, her eyes narrowing on Dirdos who had moved intentionally to draw her attention away from Yak.

"Dirdos ..." she purred in a way that had every man shifting uncomfortably, aroused by the suggestive tone of her voice.

Dirdos watched her as she approached him, her fingers curling in his shirt and drawing him down. He looked down at her, eyes glowing a solid crimson as her magic worked on him. The need was beginning to wear off as she came down from the high, her feline movements becoming more natural and less seductive, her face showing a faint hint of confusion as she dragged him down towards her. He bent down, need warring with self-preservation, but a shout made her head snap around, the name hitting in her mind as the black of her eyes sucked inwards towards her pupils.

Hunter was calling for Letari and Etani was alert enough to register it. She let go of Dirdos and the men around her were suddenly able to breathe again, hostile and irritable towards each other.

"Hunter?" Etani called out, and the man came skidding around the corner, eyes wild.

"She ran off and I can't find her!" the man yelled.

Versalis growled, fear for the crazy woman flooding through him. "Spread out, find her."

CHAPTER 33

ANGER

"Letari!" Etani screamed, but there was no response and she growled, stalking away from the group.

Versalis followed after her, watchful for any of the vampires that may have escaped, but she was gone in only a second and he cursed, running along the street to locate her again.

She seemed to have vanished into nothingness and he wondered if she had indeed simply left, but she wouldn't leave if she thought Letari needed her. She had to be around there somewhere; it was just a case of hunting her down.

He could hear fighting and he wanted so badly to go help, but his priority was finding his mate and he focused on that.

A terrible screaming started up and he spun, recognising the sound and the implication was terrifying.

Sprinting in the direction of her scream, he came into a wide street with five dead men.

Etani had been in the middle of three men when she clutched her head, her fingers digging into her scalp as she keened in a way that made everyone she knew run for cover, their hands over their ears and grabbing anyone they could to drag them away. Versalis was alone and so he turned and streaked back the way he had come, hands clamped over his ears. Even with the distance and his hands, he could still hear her.

The wail ripped free of her chest, her eyes clenched shut as she curled in on herself, her body bent and agonised as she screamed as only a banshee could.

She wouldn't have used it there, not willingly. Not when so many innocent people could have been killed as the vampires around her suddenly were.

"Letari!" Hunter yelled, and Versalis understood. He waited until the keening cry had stopped and he ran for her, snatching her small, trembling body up off the ground and crushing her to him, his hand clamping down over her mouth.

"Etani! Etani, it's going to be okay! We can get her back!" he yelled, unsure if she could hear him but he had to try, he had to make her listen to him or she might start screaming again.

Hunter's terrible cry of anguish tore through Versalis, and he felt her turning, responding to the cry, but he turned her face into his chest, his eyes finding the man and the limp, broken body of his love in the distance. She had been a matter of seconds from reaching her sister, but it was too late.

Uzo reached the man before the vampire that had been creeping up on him could strike, and the Fae moved so fast Versalis couldn't see it, the vampire headless in a spray of blood.

"She can be revived, Hunter! Etani will bring her back!" Uzo yelled, trying to get the man to focus, and finally, he grabbed the hybrid off the ground and dragged him away as Letari's body shattered into a million shards of dried clay upon impact.

"Letari!" Etani wailed through his hand over her mouth, her face anguished, but she didn't seem to be able to cry, too horrified and stunned by the sight of the broken shell that had been the host of her sister.

The others joined them after a few seconds and Dirdos unceremoniously grabbed Etani and yanked her into his arms, crushing her to him as he started back towards the house.

"Come on!" he snarled at Versalis, whose arms were empty and mind blank on what to do.

Versalis hurried to catch up to the tall man, his face white as he stalked towards Yak who was pale, blood smeared on his neck.

"What was that?" the bearded man demanded, but Dirdos ignored the question.

"Why are vampires attacking your town?" the furious dragon boomed, making Versalis and several others jump.

"Hunter!" Bee cried as she found him being dragged along by Uzo as he wept.

Etani pulled herself free of Dirdos' arms and looked around for Hunter, stumbling forward for him, but he was being engulfed in the arms of his mother and she stopped, her face broken and, when she couldn't reach him, her tears fell.

"What happened?" Yak asked, horrified by the sight of his howling son.

"Letari's dead," Versalis said in a low murmur to avoid Etani hearing.

"Oh Gods ..." He gasped, turning to look at his son and the tiny, shivering Queen.

"Why were the vampires attacking?" Dirdos demanded again, Etani turning to look at them in desperation.

"Versalis..." she whimpered, and as she reached for him, he wrapped his arms around her and held her against him, rocking her gently as she cried.

"You can get her back," he whispered. "You just have to go find her."

"What if I can't? What if she's really gone?" she whimpered.

He hushed her, stroking her hair. "She's too stubborn to die. She'll be there waiting for you," he said gently, trying his best to soothe her.

"I can't feel her. I can't feel her at all, Versalis ..." she whimpered, terror in her voice.

"They have been attacking for years, we don't know why," Yak said, hurrying past Dirdos to get to his son, but Hunter had turned on Etani.

"Bring her back! You have to bring her back!" he cried, Etani looking around at him as Yak and Bee tried to hold him back.

"I can't feel her." Etani gasped, clinging to Versalis.

"Bring her back!" he screamed, and she jerked back, alarmed by his fury.

"Hunter! You can't do that ..." Bee said, trying to soothe him. "I'm sorry, love ... she's gone ..."

"She's death! She can bring Letari back, she did it once before! She brought Uzo back from the dead!" Hunter ripped himself free of his parents and rushed forward, gripping Etani's arm and dragging her closer. "You can bring her back!" He gasped.

Dirdos moved forward to pull the man off her but he refused to let go, terror in his face.

"I ..." Etani gasped, trying to pull her arm free of him. "I can't feel her, Hunter, she's not there yet!"

He growled in frustration, squeezing her arm until she cried out in pain, and Dirdos grabbed the man, wrapping an arm around his neck and cutting off his air.

"Calm yourself, Hunter, you're hurting Etani. Let go or we will make you let go," Dirdos growled, and the man's eyes widened, his face slowly turning red as he stared at her, anguished and terrified.

"Please ..." he whimpered, letting her go finally. Etani pressed herself into Versalis' chest and he hugged her, looking down to see the bruise on her arm.

"Versalis?" she whispered.

"You don't need to go right this second," he growled, anxious for her.

"I have to look for her."

"Hunter, what has gotten into you?! You can't bring the dead back to life ..." Yak said, dragging his son back as soon as Dirdos released him.

"Etani can, she can bring back any mythical," Hunter whimpered, drawing the attention of Etani.

"I will go ..." she said softly, and Hunter gasped out a sob of relief.

"Etani, no ... not right away," Dirdos said, reaching for her and running his hand across her hair. "You need time to recover."

"I have to try," she said. "Versalis, I need my magic."

Versalis looked down at her, her jaw set and face hard as she met his stare and he sighed.

"Okay, love. Everyone move back."

The group of guards and stragglers, plus their friends, moved back.

He turned her to better position her for when her wings would form, and looked down at her. Lifting her chin, he kissed her hard before he took her hand and pressed it to his chest.

Reaching down into himself, he called for the magic, and it flowed up in him, eager and wanting to return to her. He saw the magic as it left him and moved into her, black ink that poured into her hand and spilled down to form at her wrist.

She sucked in a deep breath and her eyes slid shut, her body shuddering as her wings seemed to melt into reality like dripping wax, huddled close to her body and then stretching out as though she should have been yawning with it. The large headdress forming over her head and reaching back behind her melted down into that oddly liquid-looking dress.

YAK GASPED, seeing the massive span of those wings and the vision of death.

Her head turned and she found first Uzo, and then Kai, as though they were calling to her, and she smiled lovingly to the two of them, her slender arms reaching for them.

"I missed you two." She sighed, her voice sounding huskier than ever. The two men were in her arms in a second, clinging to her while she kissed their cheeks and stroked their faces as though she hadn't seen them in years. That part of her likely hadn't, given it had been housed in Versalis for so long.

"Etani..." Hunter growled, and her head turned, relaxed and unconcerned by his anger.

"Hush, pup. I want time with my children. Letari is not yet ready to be reborn."

"Why not?" he demanded, her smile adoring as she cupped Kai's face and drew him down to kiss his forehead while Uzo looked annoyed.

"Dying is quite a shock to the soul," she told Hunter, though her eyes were still on Kai, his face blissful at her affection. Her eyes turned to Uzo and she made a distressed sound at his pouting, and he eagerly bent down to accept her gentle kiss against his forehead. "It will take her a little while to recover and then I will find her. Do not fret, I will bring you back your mate."

Hunter stared at her in desperate hope and naked longing, though she wasn't paying any attention to him, her focus on the two men before her as they vied for her attention.

She looked relaxed and calm, though what did death have to worry about?

"Who is she?" Yak demanded, and she looked around, her eyes black and seemingly soulless.

"I am death," she said as though it were the most obvious thing in the world, and it was, really. She looked quite similar to how many worshiping sects depicted death, dark and beautiful, welcoming but also cold. Death loved you for dying and joining her; she would welcome you with open arms and a loving smile.

"That's impossible," Yak said, taking a step back from her, but she wasn't paying attention to him anymore, her eyes drawn back to Uzo as he tugged at her hair, a child trying to get his mother's attention. He lit up when she turned back to him, exhilarated that he could be so close to her and touching her.

"What's wrong with them?" Bee asked, her eyes hypnotised by the winged figure.

"She brought them back, they adore her for it, and she loves them. From what they've said it's like being inside her heart, you can feel how deeply she loves you, and it makes you love her in return," Daemon said.

Versalis nodded, watching the three of them. He didn't feel jealous; their love for her in that moment was not sexual, she was their mother in that state, but it still bothered him that she had completely forgotten about him.

"Once she is back to normal it will pass," Dirdos said, captivated by the trio.

"Can't you go look for her?" Hunter pleaded, reaching for the woman, but she drew away.

"You mustn't touch me if you have not already died," she said, her unfathomable eyes turned on Hunter though she was running her fingers through both Kai's and Uzo's hair, the two men looking both smug and like they were going to melt. "If it will make you happy, I will look. But she will not be there," she said after studying his face for several long seconds. "You must learn patience if you wish to be with Letari, little wolf vampire."

Hunter scowled but refused to give in and she sighed, turning back to Uzo and Kai.

"I must go away for a little while, my darlings. You behave and I will be back soon."

"No, don't go..." Uzo pleaded, and she smiled, drawing him down to rest her forehead against his.

"You can keep an eye on all of them for me. Keep everyone safe, and keep my darlings safe. I will be back before you know it."

Uzo turned a furious glare on Hunter while Etani gently pulled Kai's fingers off her dress and kissed the tip of his nose. He refused to move away and Dirdos stepped forward, drawing the distraught vampire away.

"Thank you, Dragon King," she said, her longing almost painful to see as she looked between Uzo and Kai, but then her eyes turned to Hunter and she exhaled gently.

Versalis wanted to call to her, but he knew better; she didn't belong to him in that state, she belonged to the dead.

Stepping back from the group, she shifted her dress and her eyes slid shut, those massive wings moving forward and wrapping protectively around her delicate frame, and as they joined again behind her, her body vanished into a shimmering black mist.

"What is going on?" Yak yelled once she was gone, turning on his son. "What did you bring into my town?"

"Etani is many things. So long as you do not cross her then she is a very powerful ally. If you cross her then you will have a very dangerous and entirely ruthless enemy," Daemon said. "You will also have the strength of the Winter Court on your side. It doesn't matter what she is, it only matters what she can do."

"Tell me what she is," Yak cried, panicked even as his wife tried to calm him.

"Etani is death, a Creator, the Queen of Winter... She is one of the Gods and the daughter of several of the Gods, she is a magical lure and an assassin. She's also the Princess of Ayathian due to her marriage to Epharis. Did I miss anything?" Dirdos said calmly.

"Don't think so," Daemon said, frowning.

"She's also part Lich and part vampire," Jaia added. "Epharis tried to turn her, and then we tried."

"Oh yeah, forgot about those two," Daemon said, shrugging.

"How long do you think she will be gone?" Hunter demanded, ignoring his father's spluttering.

"Could be a few minutes or a few days," Dirdos said, wrapping an arm around Uzo's shoulders, the Fae looking incredibly distraught. "Try not to stress."

"You try not to stress! The love of my life is dead!"

"The love of my life was dead for three years, I'm sure you can handle a few days," Dirdos snapped.

Hunter jerked back and Versalis growled in warning, but Dirdos ignored him, instead dragging the anxious Fae towards the residence with the suggestion that they all eat.

Jaia pulled Kai along while the frustrated vampire stared longingly at the place in which she had vanished.

IT WAS a full three days before they heard the quiet murmur of voices and Versalis threw the chair out of the way as he lunged for the door.

Etani stood looking up at the tall, armoured form of Hades, and she tilted her head, lips pursed as she considered something he had said.

Her black eyes turned on them, Hades still staring at her face with an odd intensity.

"Who is that?" Bee asked, fear written all over her face.

"Hades, God of the Underworld. One of them, anyway," Versalis said as he approached, her eyes lingering on him with a slight frown.

"Bearer," she greeted him, and though she was polite, she was wary of him.

The way she said it had it clicking in his mind as to why she had been mostly ignoring him. Her magic didn't like being inside him, it wanted to be in her. Understanding flooded through him and he felt an immediate sense of relief.

Bowing to her politely, he saw her purse her lips but then she looked back to Hades.

"You shouldn't allow yourself to be persuaded by the whims of a dog," Hades said, his eyes narrowing as she shrugged.

"If it calms his mind, then it is no trouble."

"You are not the tool of these men," he said irritably.

"Careful, Hades, someone might think you actually cared about something," she purred back, her smile playful as she patted his arm. "Do not fret, all is well."

Hades looked annoyed but mollified by her touch, and when she turned away, he looked down at his arm where she had touched him.

"Uzo, Kai," she cried as they practically tackled her, her wings stretching to keep her upright.

"Where is she?" Hunter demanded, stopping dead in his tracks to stand before a stumped Bee and horrified Yak.

"There's a God on my lawn..." Yak whimpered.

"There's three of them," Jaia corrected as Daemon stalked forward to harass Hades while Etani focused her attention on the two clinging to her.

"She is slumbering still, she will wake soon," Etani said to Hunter, smiling up at the doting men.

"How long?" Hunter demanded.

"Mind who you are talking to, pup," Hades snapped, glaring at Hunter, but Hunter couldn't tear his eyes off Etani.

"She will wake when she wakes," Etani said. "I am tired, I must rest now. Bearer?"

Versalis swallowed hard and focused his thoughts on trying to pull her magic back to him. It was the oddest sensation, like he was reaching out with his mind for her, and death was glaring at him, both wanting to stay with her and wanting to return to him for rest. Finally, he felt it reaching for him and his body swayed as he pulled the magic from her, the feeling very similar to peeling glue away from his skin.

Her wings exploded, and with them her dress and headdress melted away, the black of her eyes swirling inward.

Hades swept forward and when Kai reached for her, the God slapped his arms out of the way and wrapped her up in his cloak, lifting her seemingly tiny body against his chest and sweeping inside the house.

"That's a God..." Yak whimpered, still frozen beside the door.

Uzo and Kai followed close on the God's heels, the rest of them trailing in after him to find the God sitting comfortably on the tiny couch with a sleepy-looking Etani in his arms.

"I will fetch her when she's awake," she murmured to Hunter before he could say a thing.

He glared at her, but she was either too tired to notice, or otherwise ignored him.

Versalis slunk forward and she looked up at him, smiling. He had missed her terribly over the time she was absent and when he leant down to kiss her, her chin lifted to meet him.

They both ignored Hades growling in irritation, simply revelling in the moment of being reunited.

"Why are you here?" Daemon asked of Hades, Versalis' eyes locked on hers though hers were beginning to droop.

"I felt her wandering around and decided to go see what she was up to. Didn't have anything else to do at the time," the God said, his eyes intent on Etani.

"There's a God in my house," Yak whimpered; clearly, he had lost the ability to function normally.

Hades gave the man the most contemptible look possible, and Yak shrank back in fear.

Looking back down at Etani, he found that she had fallen asleep, her head resting against Hades' chest, her soft purring filling the awkward silence that followed the hostility radiating off the God.

CHAPTER 34
SISTER

She didn't wake until the following evening, and she was moody when she woke, crawling her way out of Hades' arms and blatantly ignoring Hunter when he tried to talk to her. At least until he stepped in front of her attempt to get to the kitchen.

Looking ruffled and irritable, she lifted her eyes from his chest up to his face and glared at him silently.

"Move, or I'll stab you," she said, her voice a husky growl.

"Is Letari awake yet?" he asked, his eyes hostile.

She didn't reply and when she tried to step around him, he moved in front of her again and she closed her eyes, a deep breath suggesting her attempt to calm herself.

"Is she awake?" he demanded.

"Move..." she hissed.

He reached for her and then yelled in pain, the others jerking awake and the smell of blood making Versalis' mouth water, but he was amused; the idiot hybrid had it coming.

Etani moved past him and Versalis saw the knife she had stuck in his stomach, only the hilt remaining outside his person.

"What happened?" Daemon asked.

"She stabbed me!" Hunter yelled.

"You refused to get out of the way," Versalis argued.

Versalis stood and headed into the kitchen after her and smiled as he found her standing at the sink, downing a mug of water from the tap. Sidling up behind her, he wrapped his arms around her middle and kissed her hair, her half-hearted growl making him laugh. "Now, don't be grumpy," he murmured in her ear and tilted his head, nuzzling his cheek against her hair.

She swatted at him, but he growled playfully and nuzzled harder, her beautiful face screwing up in protest.

Turning her to him, he rubbed his face against hers and she made a pitiful mewling sound that he adored. It was always difficult to resist her when she made that sound, but he continued, his arms trapping her against him until she laughed and squirmed, the delicious sound of her laughter finally making him stop.

Looking down at her, he smiled warmly as she met his eyes and then lifted herself up to kiss him.

Tightening his grip on her, he kissed her back and met her growl with his own, leaning into the kiss. Her arms draped around his neck and he shivered at the soft touch of her fingers against the back of his neck, dipping down into the back of his shirt and splaying against his skin, the coolness of her touch making him quiver inside. He wanted her terribly, but knew he had to be careful with her; he didn't want to push her too far and send her into a state of shutdown or panic.

Reaching down, he gripped her backside and hoisted her up onto the counter and his lips turned up into a smile as she wrapped her legs around his middle, her feet crossed at the ankle to trap him against her. She felt so incredibly wonderful, cold and soft against his body, and her lips dancing against his, her breaths coming in uneven huffs and when his fingers slid around to her hips, up her waist and then traced around the underside of her breasts, her breath hitched.

Breaking the kiss, he nudged her nose with his own and growled, her eyes still shut and lips parted. Finally, those glorious eyes opened and she looked up at him, her tongue darting out to trace over her lips before she drew him down, using his shoulders to pull herself up into the kiss.

The low murmur of voices alerted him to the fact that the others were only a room away and he considered the options, deciding to take her outside and into the garden where they could have some privacy.

Gripping her backside once more, he hoisted her up higher and she squeaked, tightening her grip on him with arms and legs. With one hand still gripping her, he opened the back door and stepped out, grinning as she eyed him, suspicious of what he had planned.

His plan was simply for privacy, though he was more than a little eager to take things further with her. He wasn't stupid; he knew she was afraid, but that didn't mean he wasn't going to show her just how much he desired her.

HEADING down the path into the garden, he spotted the table and chairs and unceremoniously plopped down into the chair, allowing her to drop down onto his lap, and her smug smile suggested she was pleased with his choice.

Her wriggling around to settle herself did nothing to help his desire, and he growled in warning at her, her eyes widening before they flicked down and then back up at his face, narrowing, and then a wicked grin came over her face.

Panic flooded through him as she curled her fingers in his hair and yanked his head down to hers in a heavy, passionate kiss while at the same time her hips rolled forward against him.

His entire body shuddered at the sensation of her grinding against him, and he clutched at her, pressing down on her hips to apply more pressure to his groin until he groaned against her lips.

Her voice was low and guttural as she sighed his name and he revelled in the sound, hunger almost dripping from it. He would have given anything to have her right there, to hear her cries of pleasure as he took her, but he worked hard to keep himself calm.

Tilting his head, he traced his lips along her jaw and down to her throat, her head turning away from his, and he felt her shiver as he teased her, grazing his fangs against the delicate skin. He couldn't bite her, that wouldn't end well for either of them, but it was incredibly tempting.

Turning his head back to hers, he kissed her and she met his demanding kiss in equal measure, her slow movements against him driving him wild, yet she always held back just enough to keep him from losing control or finding release. How she knew, he would never know, but she was skilled at reading his body and he revelled in the game, his trying to get more from her and her denying him over and over.

Deciding to throw caution to the wind, he lifted her up from his lap and, taking two steps, he laid her down on a small patch of thick grass that served as a centrepiece for the garden, almost perfectly round and big enough for her to lie on comfortably. Settling his weight on top of her, he pressed his lips into hers and with a wicked grin, he pressed his erection against her, her gasp making him growl in pleasure. He could be a tease, too.

Rocking against her, he broke the kiss to watch her face as his movements rubbed against her, her cheeks flushing, and her lower lip crushed between her teeth as she tried to remain silent and not alert the others to what they were doing.

It was a sinfully wonderful feeling, the coldness of her body pressed against him, her thighs pressed against his hips and her whimpered gasps loud in his ears, though she was remaining quiet enough that no one nearby would be able to hear.

Unlike her, he was merciless, and he was desperate to please her, to see her face as she released and to feel her body quivering against him. It would have been better were he inside her, but he would take anything he could get.

Reaching up, she cupped the back of his neck and drew him down to meet her lips, her free hand going to the small of his back and pressing down with each rolling motion of his hips against hers, encouraging him to press harder. He did so, and she jerked away from his lips, burying her face in his neck as the addictive sound of her moan broke free of her control.

He wanted to hear it again, and he pressed himself hard against her. Her teeth sank into his throat with a suddenness that shocked him, grunting in pain and jerking, but he recovered quickly, the pain of her bite urging him on until he heard that delicious sound again.

Her moans were so soft, as though she were afraid to make a noise, but he wanted more of them, he wanted them louder. He didn't know if she was embarrassed, or simply didn't want the others to hear; whatever the reason, he had to get more of them.

His own soft groans of pleasure were low and deep, trying to remain quiet so they could be alone without the other men in her life interfering. He wanted her all to himself and so he kept quiet and revelled in the peace and the sensation of moving against her.

When he felt the build of his release, he forced his mind elsewhere to picture grass waving in the wind, mundane but pretty, and he was relieved when the building eased somewhat, though it refused to go away entirely. He couldn't find satisfaction until after she did, it wouldn't be the same if he was no longer aroused.

She hadn't been drinking from him, she had only bitten and latched onto him, her moans muffled, and he smiled as he realised that had been her purpose, if only in part.

Giving in to his need, he pressed against her hungrily while his hand slid down over her shoulder and he cupped her breast through her shirt, squeezing the soft flesh, and she hissed as his fingers found the small nipple, pinching it playfully.

Her breathing had grown ragged, her moans higher pitched, and he knew she was getting closer; he tilted his head with the devious intention of biting her ear when a soft cough alerted them to company.

Versalis growled, a feral sound of warning as his instincts to protect his mate kicked in with full force.

Whipping his head around, his eyes glowed in the darkness as he found the amused-looking guard leaning on the fence.

"If you wanted privacy, you should be doing that inside," the guard said in a voice that was nearly a laugh.

Etani groaned in frustration, dropping back onto the grass, and staring up at the sky above.

"Besides, it's past curfew," the man added, more amused than anything. "Time to head back inside or I will be forced to raise the alarm and then you'll both be in trouble."

Versalis sighed in frustration, his erection feeling as though it were on fire as the pleasure stopped and he was unable to find release.

Standing, the guard seemed surprised that his pants were done up, her dress still lowered, and he shook his head.

"If I had a woman like that ..." He sighed wistfully, his eyes lingering on Etani as she sat up and glared at him.

"We only needed five more minutes," she complained, and the guard laughed.

"Sorry, sweetheart, I don't make the rules, I only enforce them. Off you go."

Dragging himself to his feet, he pulled her up after him and kissed her hard, her lips turned down into a frown as they headed back up the path and slipped inside once more, their hands linked tight.

"Where have you two been off to?" Uzo demanded, his eyes narrowed on them as they were caught sneaking in the door. He had been getting a drink.

"Talking," Etani said, Uzo's eyebrows lifting as he dragged his eyes over her mussed hair and crumpled dress.

"Sure you were. It's hard to talk with your mouths glued together." Uzo moved closer and touched Etani's cheek, lifting her face to look up at him but his head tilted, and he glanced between the two of them. "Did something happen?"

"Interrupted," Versalis grumbled and Uzo laughed, kissing Etani's cheek before he turned and headed back into the sitting room with the others.

"He's such a jerk," Etani muttered, but Versalis was smiling. At least he hadn't been threatened. Kissing her hair gently, he tugged his shirt down further to hide the front of his pants and headed for the bathroom, his thoughts turning devious as he went to the shower.

At least he had a bit of time to himself, able to finish the job in peace, though he would have preferred that the sultry vixen were there with him. But it was her image he brought up in his mind and with all that sexual tension, he was at least mostly satisfied in just a few minutes.

HEADING BACK out after he finished showering, he found they had started eating without him but when he started for the dwindling table Etani caught his eye, and she was holding a plate for him. This was why he loved that woman; she was perfect.

Taking the plate, he kissed her hard and started eating, almost inhaling the delicious meat, and when he saw the pile of vegetables and eyed her plate, he scowled.

"You know..." he started, trailing off when she turned those big, innocent eyes on him with her cheeks bulging. He frowned at her in frustration, unable to be angry at that face. She knew perfectly well how to use her charm against them when the need arose, like when she gave him all of her vegetables in exchange for more venison. It wasn't like she needed to eat the vegetables -- they did very little for her nutritionally, if anything at all -- but it still did the same thing for her as it did for the rest of them, preserving her energy until her next proper meal, and given they were amongst allies, eating one of them wasn't a good idea. At least she had eaten the vampire who attacked them; that would keep her going for a while.

She smiled when he backed down, returning to her food. If it wasn't for Bee force-feeding them the vegetables they wouldn't have bothered, but no one had the heart to tell her the meat was better for them all, except maybe Daemon and Dirdos.

Hunter turned on Etani as soon as she had finished eating and he scowled when she tried to use her charm on him, the man brushing it off easily.

"Nice try. Where's Letari?" he growled, and her face fell, disappointed that she couldn't get him to go away. It had stopped working as soon as he fell in love with Letari.

"I still can't—" She broke off, her head turning away from him towards Dirdos, who froze. "Did you say something?" she asked, her expression confused.

"No, love, I didn't say anything," he said, glancing around at the others near to him, but they all shook their heads in denial.

"I could have sworn…" She trailed off, but then shook her head and looked back to Hunter, then turned to Dirdos fully.

"I swear I didn't say anything," he said.

"Someone keeps whispering my name…" she complained, glaring at the twins, Dirdos, and Yak.

"No one has said anything," Kai said, concern radiating off him.

"Could it be Letari?" Hunter asked, but she shook her head, tilting an ear as though that would help her hear better.

"It's male," she said, turning her head to try to find the sound again.

"A worshipper?" the low growl of Hades sounded and Versalis jumped, forgetting the man had been there.

"I don't know. It's not prayer, it's just my name. Over and over again, like a chant."

"Someone is trying to summon you? They can't do that without your summoning name," Daemon said, and Etani glanced at him.

"It's not even my full first name, it's just 'Etani.' Don't they know me as 'Etania?'"

"Yes, true," Daemon said thoughtfully. "It must be someone you know. That could literally be anyone."

Etani scowled and then looked down, her left hand lifting, and they all saw in the same instant that the normally pale shadow of her wedding ring had gone pitch black.

Versalis scowled as he saw both rings, Epharis' and Neah's, but it was the Lich's band that had changed.

It remained black for a solid minute before she scowled, the band starting to turn brown and then red.

"It's getting hot..." she said, baffled, and when it glowed red, she whimpered, shaking her hand to try to get it to cool down again.

"The Lich is using it to call you back," Daemon said, scowling as he gripped her wrist and turned her, shoving her hand into the water pitcher.

It hissed, and after only a minute, the water bubbled.

Etani never made a sound, though she was almost gnawing off her lip and tears were streaming down her cheeks, her lovely face twisted in pain.

"How do we make it stop?" Kai cried.

"Kill the Lich?" Dirdos suggested, a suggestion Versalis liked.

"He wants her to go back," Uzo said. "Let's go see what he wants, then we reconsider murder."

Seeing Etani's distress, he turned to Bee and Yak, both just as distressed by her pain as they would have had it been their hand burning.

"Thank you for your hospitality, we must leave. We will be back for our things in a few days."

Bee nodded, Yak's face anguished as Etani made a mewling cry, Daemon pulling her hand free of the water to see the band had turned white, glowing and shimmering with heat.

The men all moved forward to circle the tiny woman, and the world vanished into a smear of crimson as Dirdos transported them back to Ayathian.

CHAPTER 35
LICH

They spilled out into the cramped room, knocking books over and sending scrolls and maps tumbling, but Epharis only looked amused by the appearance of them all, their faces dark with anger.

"Welcome home, gentlemen. Where's my wife?"

Kai and Jaia stepped aside and Etani was revealed to him, her eyes pained as she cradled her left hand against her chest, the band still burning white, though it didn't seem to be affecting the other ring at all.

"Was it really necessary to do that to her?" Daemon snapped, prying her hand away from her chest to see the band had cooled.

"How else am I going to get her to come back?" Epharis asked, eyes locked on Etani with a fierce hunger that made Versalis' stomach clench in fear for her.

"How did you even do it?" Uzo asked, looking at her hand over her shoulder.

"Magic," Epharis said sarcastically, though it wasn't entirely untrue. "You can all leave now, my wife and I need to talk."

Versalis opened his mouth to argue, only to have Kai elbow him, eyes narrowed.

Hissing in anger, they filed out of the room and as soon as the door closed, he turned on Kai.

"What?" he snapped.

"Don't anger him. He just found out that he can call her back to him, imagine what else he might try if he is angry. Just let them talk and then we can leave again."

Versalis hated it but he knew Kai was right and it was hard to resist going back in there when he heard the Lich's voice raised in anger.

"We need to go," Daemon said suddenly, his eyes wide as he gripped Dirdos by the arm, but Dirdos refused to move, eyes narrowed on the door.

Versalis tensed as he heard the unmistakable sound of flesh on flesh and Etani's cry of pain, then another.

"Go," Daemon demanded, but they had all frozen, horrified by the sounds.

It was only a moment later before the sound of wood grinding on stone reached them, rhythmic and accompanied after a moment by masculine groans joined by feminine whimpers.

Versalis' eyes slid shut, realising why Daemon had wanted them to leave. He had known what Epharis wanted from her and had been trying to spare them. But they hadn't been able to leave, and they all stood frozen, listening to the terrible sounds and finally, the cry of the Lich finding his release on his wife.

Dirdos had gone white, his eyes blazing with fire while Jaia was hugging a trembling Kai to his chest. Daemon was staring at the window in the distance, unfocused and vacant.

Versalis couldn't breathe, his mind drawing up images of her under the man, her eyes unfocused like Daemon's, her body crushed against him as he took what he wanted.

It was another several minutes before the door opened and Epharis blinked at them, looking ruffled but satisfied.

"What are you lot doing out here? Eavesdropping? If I had known you were interested, I would have let you watch... Did you enjoy the sound?" He was smirking, but Versalis looked away from Epharis to find Etani, standing against the table with her head bowed, her dress creased at the back.

Pushing past Epharis, he nearly gagged on the scent but ignored it, moving to her side and touching her hand. She jerked back on impulse and looked up at him, her moment of alarm melting into shame as she turned away from him.

"No, don't do that," he growled. Her lower lip had been split and blood trickled down her jaw. He turned her back to him gently and wiped at the blood, her eyes focused on his left shoulder.

Behind them the Lich was laughing, but he didn't look around, focused on her until the scent of Kai joined them and he growled softly at the sight of her lip though it was healing well.

After several minutes of argument, Dirdos joined them and Daemon stood fuming, the Lich calmly walking away from his rooms.

"Why?" Kai whimpered.

"The oracle who foretold the prophecy that Alaric has been obsessed with has been found alive and well. Meaning it can still come true. Both he and Alaric are fighting to fulfil it. Epharis isn't the King, though..."

"Part of the deal to give me his magic was to depose Alaric," Etani said quietly, her hand going to her lip and touching it, then looking down at the tiny trace of crimson.

"He made you reinstate it?" Kai asked, her nod the only answer.

Versalis frowned as a thought popped up into his head and he looked at Uzo, the man's eyes narrowing on her.

"You can't just reinstate one deal, can you?" Versalis asked.

"No, it's all or none, unless he made a new one," Uzo said.

"All of them?" Dirdos asked, perking up.

"All of them," Etani said gently, her eyes going to Versalis, wide and afraid.

Reaching for her, she moved willingly into his arms and closed her eyes, Kai's hand gripping hers tightly, desperate and afraid.

"It'll be okay," Daemon said, but Dirdos was grinning, deeply satisfied by something.

They pulled Etani from the room and back into her own which had oddly been preserved as though they had only left the day before, not a speck of dust or piece of furniture out of place.

Dropping onto the couch, he pulled her into his lap, and she moved easily, nuzzling her head under his chin and sighing as she got comfortable. Dirdos approached hesitantly, offering her the small mug of foul-smelling potion; she looked at it and then up at the dragon.

The room was silent for a long moment, but then she accepted it and downed its contents in one go, making a face at the taste of it and when Dirdos took the mug back, she nuzzled herself into Versalis' chest.

"What are we going to do now?" Uzo asked, settling himself down on the floor with his side pressed against Etani's legs, his head on her knees.

"Wait for Letari and then back to Winter," Etani said.

Hunter had been entirely silent the whole time, his face pale and eyes wide as he stared at Etani as though he had never seen her before, but the rest of them were ignoring him.

Versalis watched her face as she pulled up her mask to protect herself and those around her from suffering along with her. She was a lot stronger than any of them gave her credit for.

Turning his head, he kissed her hair, and she gave a little growl that made him smile just slightly, glad she was at least still her feisty self.

"How do you endure that?" Hunter asked thirty minutes later, Etani almost asleep against his chest and Uzo snoring quietly. It seemed as though Hunter, he, and Etani were the only ones still awake.

"What would you have me do?" she asked, her eyes still closed.

"How can you just submit to him?"

Her eyes opened and she looked at the hybrid, her lips turned down into a frown. "He is my husband," she said as though that were the most obvious thing in the world.

"He is abusive."

"So are most men," she countered, Hunter's face twisting in frustration.

"You need to fight back."

"A husband has a basic right to his wife's body for copulation for the purpose of procreation and pleasure."

"You're not a whore!" Hunter yelled and Uzo jerked upright, alarmed, along with everyone else in the room. "You don't owe him or any of them anything! They don't own you!"

Etani looked up at the man with a slight frown on her lips, considering him. "Perhaps it is so in your culture. Perhaps your men see their women as more than property, but it is not so in others. I do belong to my husband."

"No, you don't!" he cried and jerked forward, Uzo growling a warning, but Etani didn't seem alarmed, allowing him to reach out and take her face into his hands. "You are a Goddess, you're Etani!"

"I'm also a wife, Hunter," she said quietly, her fingers touching the backs of his hands. "It is my duty to submit."

Hunter swore, stepping back from her and staring at her intently, furious at the way she saw the world.

"You're not going to change her mind," Daemon said, yawning and stretching. "You were raised one way, she learnt things another. Just be glad we can keep her safe."

"Letting that monster abuse her on a regular basis is not keeping her safe!" Hunter yelled.

Etani frowned, looking up at Versalis, their eyes meeting for an instant.

"What about you? Would you do that to her if she refused you after you get married?" Hunter demanded of him, and he jerked.

"No," Versalis said, honest.

"No, exactly! That's not what happens in a marriage! This is not normal!"

"What about my entire existence is normal, Hunter?" Etani snapped, getting frustrated, though her eyes had narrowed in consideration on Versalis. "I was born only because a God decided I needed to exist, based on a story a drugged girl told him. I am so powerful that I am incapable of holding my own magic or I'll explode, and I eat people. My sister is dead and I'm waiting for her to wake up so I can bring her back to life. Nothing about this is, or will ever be, normal!"

Her cheeks had turned pink, and she glared at the man, his face pale.

"Etani ..." he said, but she cut him off.

"No. You listen to me, dog boy. I don't know what has gotten into you, but you need to mind your own business."

"We heard," Uzo said, and her teeth clicked as she shut her mouth, looking down at the Fae. "We were right outside the door and heard everything."

Etani swallowed, looking around at them all before she frowned and pushed herself off Versalis' lap. "I'm going to get something to eat," she said curtly and left the room, ignoring their attempts to reach for her or bring her back. Instead, Kai ran after her.

"I just ... I can't see her getting hurt like that and just accepting it as normal ..." Hunter said softly.

"None of us can, but we have all tried to convince her otherwise, she just can't hear it," Uzo said. "I think at this point it's just a case of kill all the husbands and start over."

"I agree," Daemon said.

"I say we just kill anyone who has touched her without her

permission," Dirdos chimed in and Jaia shifted, inching towards the door.

"You're fine, silver eyes," Uzo said, and Versalis jerked.

"He's fine?" Versalis demanded.

"He and I have come to an understanding," Uzo said.

"Does Etani know?" Dirdos demanded, glaring at the vampire.

"She does not, and you're not going to tell her until she is ready to know."

"What are you talking about?" Dirdos snapped.

"You remember what happened with Versalis, only no one was there to stop Jaia," Uzo said, glancing at the scared looking vampire. "He lost control."

Versalis stared at Uzo, half refusing to accept that answer and half terrified of what it would mean for his relationship to Etani if it were true. They all knew part of her was still attached to the man, she wouldn't allow him near her if she wasn't, but how would she react when she found out?

There was silence in the room for a solid minute as they tried to take in the new information and what it would mean for the future.

"She can't know," Versalis said finally, a vicious possessiveness coming over him.

"She has to know, eventually," Uzo said calmly.

DIRDOS SWORE and turned on Jaia, who backed away quickly, but there was no time for violence as Etani's voice reached their ears and they all went still, confused and afraid of what to do.

In a breath they were all settled again, experts at hiding everything from the woman. When she entered the room she was carrying a large platter with Kai following close behind her, almost drooling on her shoulder, and trying to reach around her but she was keeping the food out of his range, his games leaving a smile on her face that told them she hadn't heard a thing.

Setting the platter down, she turned, and without warning, tackled Kai and cried, "Go!"

The others were on the food while Kai struggled to get himself free of her, yelling in distress and trying to wriggle himself free, the platter mostly depleted by the time he got free and sat up, rolling onto his knees and crawling to the table, eyes wide and hands reaching.

Etani was laughing, lying on the floor where he had shoved her off him and she sat up, watching him as he grabbed as much food as he could hold and glared at her while stuffing his face.

"They got all the good bits," he complained, referring to the extra toasted edges of the meat that they all loved.

"Well, you shouldn't have been trying to steal," she said, an adoring smile plastered over her face.

Pushing up onto her feet, she watched as Kai shuffled away, still on his knees and looking mutinous, cheeks bulging and shoulders slumped in defeat.

Picking out food for herself, she looked at the lot of them and tilted her head, curious at something she saw but decided not to comment, instead looking between Versalis and Dirdos, unable to decide who she wanted to be with, so instead she went for Daemon.

The demon wrapped his arms around her as she settled into his lap and leant back against his chest.

It was odd to see the two of them so close, as their relationship was somewhat cold as of late, but the instant they were back together, their tension was forgotten, and everything was back to normal.

Daemon stole a piece of her food and she elbowed him in the gut, grunting, and when he froze, she bit the chunk of meat out of his fingers, leaving only a small edge.

He glared at her but she only smiled and stuck out her tongue, holding the rest of it out so he couldn't get to it, except that left it open for Uzo, who took full advantage.

Etani snarled and when she tried to move after the Fae, Daemon wrapped his arms around her and she squirmed, watching in disgust as her uncle stuffed the meat into his mouth and swallowed it.

They had numbers on their side, and she huffed, glaring at Uzo while Dirdos inched his way up from her other side, and before she noticed him, he had her wrist and stole the last of the food, seeming to inhale it like he didn't need to chew.

Her retaliation was to try to kick him, but he had been expecting it and jumped back, grinning wickedly.

"I hate you all!" she cried, flopping back against Daemon and glaring petulantly.

"You love us," Uzo said, grinning.

She glared back, her lower lip stuck out in a pout.

"Don't look at me like that, it's not going to work."

She continued to look up at him with that pitiful face and pouting lips, the Fae's resolve beginning to melt, and finally he threw up his hands and picked out the last few pieces that Kai and Jaia had been eyeing off and giving them to her.

She didn't even hesitate before she stuffed them in her mouth and chewed, all the while glaring up at Uzo and then Dirdos and back again, almost daring them to try again.

There was no denying how much they all adored her and wanted nothing more than to make her happy, all of them trying to help her recover herself after the events with the Lich, though they were all wary of the possibility that the Lich would be coming back for her again soon enough.

His concern that the Lich would return for her wasn't wrong; the man stalked into the room, looked at her, and then stalked back out again.

Etani sighed, her eyes lowered, but she stood from Daemon's lap and shuffled out of the room, looking dejected and helpless.

They all waited in silence, unable to hear the goings-on in the next room, and by the time she returned the next evening, she looked exhausted.

Without a word, she headed straight for her bed and collapsed onto it. Versalis followed her in and settled down at her side, dragging her over and curling himself up around her, his face buried in her hair.

She murmured, her slender fingers curling around his wrists to hold him in place, and she fell asleep almost instantly.

"We need to fix that ring," Uzo said in a quiet voice from the next room, their voices low but with the door open he could hear them relatively well.

"How are we going to do that if Epharis is still alive?" Daemon asked, Versalis pacing every time he passed by the open door and glanced in at the two of them on the bed.

"We may have to find ourselves another Lich," Uzo replied, his tone thoughtful. "We might be able to *convince* him to help us, and if he refuses, we kill him and find the next one."

"We still have the deal to worry about," Dirdos said.

"Good point. Do we have any options aside from killing the man?" Uzo asked. "A war between us and Alaric isn't desirable at this time."

"Get rid of Alaric first?" Hunter suggested.

"He has that witch as well. I don't know how loyal she is to him."

"If she's looking to get to the throne, then likely very," Daemon reasoned. "We can put her down if we need to."

"So, we'll have an empty throne in one of the biggest Kingdoms in current existence. What do we do with it?" Uzo asked.

"Stick someone else on it," Daemon said. "That part isn't as important as simply getting rid of Epharis."

"Stick Etani on it and keep her out of trouble for a few centuries," Dirdos suggested with an amused tone, but there was silence as they all considered that. "Oh, come on, she'd kill you all if she had to deal with another throne."

"Maybe, but it would keep her occupied for a time. It's not like she isn't up to the challenge," Uzo said. "Something to focus on and ground her."

"It's an appealing idea. Do we suggest it to her?" Hunter asked.

"No, don't give her a choice to refuse," Uzo said.

"Bastards ..." Etani whispered and Versalis snorted in amusement, kissing her hair. She must have woken up to their low voices and had been listening.

"Get used to it, love, when you are adored by so many, they are all determined to look after you, whether it's good for you or not," he said in a low whisper, his eyes meeting hers as she rolled over to look up at him.

"I love you, Versalis," she said, her face showing a hint of frustration.

"What's the matter, love?" he asked, raising his hand free to touch her cheek.

"There aren't words to describe my feelings right now," she said after a brief pause. "I am afraid to love you, afraid that you will think I am... despoiled ... I am afraid I will not be enough for you, and I am afraid that if I let you in, you will hurt me, or that I will hurt you," she trailed off, biting her lower lip as she spoke the truth of her inner self, something that was so rare for the private woman.

"I do not see you that way, nor will I ever. There is nothing in this world that could happen to you that would ever make me think any less of you. I believe I am the one who would not be enough for you, you are so much more than everyone," he kissed her cheek softly, lovingly. "You are beautiful and brilliant; you are everything a man could ever dream to be near, and you are so much more. You are the envy of the world," he kissed her other cheek gently. "I've never met a woman more cunning, intelligent, careful, loving, or protective. Nor any person as skilled and capable as you. There is no being in the world stronger and more reliant than you." He kissed her nose to make her smile, though there were tears in her eyes, staring up at him. "You are something words cannot adequately describe, and I love you more than anything in this world."

Tears trailed down her cheeks and a tiny sob escaped her as she rolled into his chest and clutched him to her. He held her tightly, silent and relieved that he had finally, finally been able to tell her what he truly felt about her, what they all saw in her, and he glanced at the door to find the rest of them lurking, watching with sad faces. They remained silent while she cried herself out and fell asleep clinging to him, her face buried in his chest and her vice-like grip never once releasing.

CHAPTER 36

SORROW

It was three days later when Vincent and Dainin turned up and looked around in confusion, not expecting to find them there lounging around as though nothing at all had changed. Vincent jerked back as the tiny black-haired ball streaked across the room at him and slammed him to the floor with a shriek.

Dainin took one look at the tiny woman attacking Vincent with her affection then jumped on the two of them with a yell that made Vincent grunt in pain at the weight.

"Hello ..." Vincent said quietly, both alarmed and pleased by the attention she forced on him, and the two men hugged her tightly, nuzzling and stroking her hair affectionately.

Versalis looked around at Daemon and Uzo, who were eyeing the Hunters warily, but they seemed pleased for her happiness. It was hard to be angry when she was in such a good mood and they had been enjoying it since she awoke, her mood seeming to have lifted and her wary affection shifting to a more outward form. There was no denying each and every one of them was basking in it, greedily trying to coax more attention out of her.

The two Hunters were almost glowing when she let them go, her attention caught by a low growl and she growled back, stalking after the feline that had finally been returned to her by the greedy Bast, who had learnt about their return and arrived the day before with the annoyed feline in her arms.

Etani had stolen the feline straightaway and Cat had been mostly ignoring her, occasionally hissing, and giving the impression of being resentful.

He swiped at her when she reached for him and she hissed as her blood was drawn, but she still grabbed him and snuggled him, ignoring his attempts to wriggle free, but then he settled into her arms and glared around at the rest of them smugly.

Versalis smiled as she sank down onto the floor, cooing to the feline who yowled back occasionally, the two seemingly having a whole conversation while the others watched. "How long have you been back?" Vincent asked.

"Four days, I think, they're blending together," Daemon said as he belched, ducking Bast's attempt to swat the back of his head for being rude while he lounged, looking full from the massive meal they had finished not long before.

"Why didn't anyone let us know?" Dainin said, heading over to sit cross legged in front of Etani. Cat hissed, but allowed him to rub those massive ears.

"How exactly are we supposed to contact you lot?" Daemon asked. "It's not like I can just call your name to get you to come over for tea and biscuits."

"True, you could always let me bite you," Vincent said with a mischievous grin.

"Fat chance, I'm not letting you have any control over me."

"How did you know to come back?" Uzo asked, his eyes on Etani and Dainin as he sipped his tea.

"We've been checking back every five days or so, just in case," Dainin said happily, his fingers working Cat's chin, and the feline seemed to be nearly catatonic with pleasure.

"Stalkers," Dirdos said in an amused tone.

"You wish I was interested in you enough to stalk you," Vincent said, slinking over to Etani and settling himself at her side, his leg pressed against hers. Etani's arm shot out, wrapping around his shoulders and pulling him against her, her head tilting to rest against his.

The man's tension seemed to melt away and he sighed, his fingers curling around her hand that hung over his shoulder.

"I'm crushed," Dirdos said. "I thought we were soulmates!" The man flopped dramatically over the arm of the chair, his arm over his eyes.

"You should be, I'm awesome," Vincent said, Etani's laugh brightening the room.

"So, what has been happening?" Dainin asked. "We haven't been able to locate any of you."

"We have been travelling a bit, all over the place," Etani said, smiling as Cat turned in a circle in her lap and settled himself down to nap.

"I thought you were going to call us for the wedding," Dainin complained.

"It hasn't happened yet. Letari's dead," Hunter growled from the corner where he regularly sulked.

"Is she coming back?" Dainin asked.

"She's not ready to come back just yet, but once she is, I'll get her. Sometimes it takes a little time to get over the shock of dying," Etani said, her attention focused on Cat.

"Oh, sorry," Vincent said, turning to kiss her cheek.

"It's my fault, I should have been watching her. She was supposed to be in the house, but she ran out again," Hunter said.

"Probably to find Etani," Dainin said.

"Why would she be looking for me?" Etani asked.

"She loves you and thinks you need protection," Vincent said, sadly amused by her cluelessness.

"She's not that stupid," Etani said, shaking her head.

"Not stupid, she just loves you," Vincent said, taking up the end of her hair and using it to tap her nose.

Etani growled in frustration, but it wasn't like the answer was unlikely. Letari would do anything for her twin, just as Etani would.

"Do you think it will be much longer?" Dainin asked, reaching out to take her free hand now that Cat was asleep.

"I don't think so, she's just resting," Etani sighed.

"Does Alaric know you're back?" Vincent asked and Etani smiled.

"Apparently not, or if he does, he's ignoring us for the time being. And I'm quite happy for him to continue doing that. He's becoming tiresome, perhaps we should consider Epharis' plan?"

The room tensed, but Versalis smiled to himself, knowing she had heard the conversation between the rest of them.

"What did you have in mind?" Uzo said slowly, wary.

"Exile," Etani said, looking sideways at Vincent as he teased her neck with the piece of hair.

"On what grounds?" Dainin asked, frowning in consideration.

"Ordering the forced abortion of his own niece or nephew under the belief that it would supersede him," she said, the Fae's face going pale at the mention. They all knew about it, but it was hard to hear her talking about it. She hadn't wanted to be pregnant to the Lich, but she had cherished that child.

"That should do it," Vincent said, his face just as white as hers.

Dainin, however, looked like he wanted to vomit. Apparently not all of them were aware of the story.

"What do you mean 'forced abortion?'" Dainin snarled, making the rest of them look at him.

"You don't have to tell him anything," Uzo said, but Etani only looked at Dainin, her lips turned into a frown.

"Alaric ordered Drizdan to capture Epharis and myself. I was fairly far along by that point, and we were in the dungeons," she started. Versalis was captivated just like the rest of them, horrified and trapped by the story. "We were both locked in with iron and gold, and couldn't get out, we were too far apart to reach each other, and Epharis was dazed but alert enough. Drizdan came in a while later and we put up a struggle, but bound we didn't get very far, and the bastard decided he was going to play a game called 'choice.' Drizdan would put two choices to Epharis and whichever Epharis chose would be removed. Finger or tongue, Epharis chose my finger and Drizdan ..." She held up her hands and using her index finger and middle finger of her right hand, indicated cutting off her left ring finger.

Dainin looked ill, and he stared at her with his mouth hanging open, the rest of them unable to so much as suck in a breath.

"Etani ..." Uzo said in a strangled voice, and she looked around at him, her eyes wide. "You don't have to relive that."

"It's okay, uncle, it isn't as hard as it once was," she said, and Uzo closed his eyes, resigned to listening. "Next was my eye or my foot. He chose eye, and it makes sense, I can fight if I have my legs, and so he cut out my eye. He said he didn't like that my eye had changed and so he ..." She shrugged. "After that he offered the final choice, either he would kill me using a soul blade, or he would destroy our child. Epharis chose the baby, and his men held me down. I screamed and when they moved away, I ripped out the throat of one of them, but there were more of them. I don't know how many men he brought with him. I don't know if the other survived, probably not. I almost ripped the chains out of the wall, but he smashed my knee with a hammer, and they held me down.

"At the time Letari and I were sharing a body, and she had managed to change my physiology to protect my womb, I never asked her how she did it, but she had forced my body to grow muscle around it, keeping it safe from a lot. But it was no good ..." Her voice sounded strained. "It could sense us, and it was so happy just to feel us nearby. It hummed, like a child." Her voice broke and she swallowed hard, tears swimming in her eyes. "I could see it for a long time and then, when we were trying to protect it, I could hear it, it sounded so happy ... and then he ... he just drove the knife into it, and it was gone." She didn't try to brush away the tears that rolled down her cheeks, Dainin's face already glistening as he stared at her. "I wanted to die and had planned to sever my connection to life. But he wouldn't let me die, he had vampire blood and used it to heal me back up. He had taken my womb entirely, and then fed me blood to ensure I would survive because he wasn't done playing his game."

Dainin's face twisted but she didn't stop, too lost to the memories.

"He got to keep me in repayment for his work and he had wanted me for a long time, had threatened to rape me over and over. So, he took me into the next cell and injected me with something to keep me awake and alert so he could have his fun while I was aware of it. He wanted to rape me, but he wanted to wait for marriage, so he pleasured himself while touching me, and he left when he was done, but he hadn't bound me properly so I got up, and when he came back ... I nearly killed him, but his men stopped me, and he took me back into the cell with Epharis. We spent the better part of three days together, Drizdan returning regularly to beat and torture me, threatened to do worse and promised that he would rape me to death as soon as he got the chance. He told Kai where we were, and he came to free us. I tried to kill Epharis the moment I was free, for choosing to save me over the life of our child, but Kai stopped me, and he thought he had hurt the baby when he managed to get me down." Her eyes turned to meet Versalis' and there was a pained, pale smile on her face. "I think they still had you in the box at that point, didn't they?"

Versalis nodded, forcing a warped smile onto his face. "Jaia had gone too long without her blood and had succumbed to insanity. But Etani fed him."

"And then Jaia ..." Etani trailed off, looking around at the silver-eyed vampire who stood rigid, frozen as he remembered the sight of her. "He did something ... a little metal device ... it made sure I wasn't going to fall pregnant to Drizdan. I couldn't say he hadn't ... I could barely think. That was the first time I suffered a panic attack and my scream set Versalis free, he knew what to do and they looked after me, the three of them."

Kai was crying silently, eyes closed and lips set in a hard line.

"You saw her in the dungeon?" Dainin asked, his voice cracking.

"She was just sitting there, waiting for him to come back and abuse her again. I've never seen something so sad before, he had broken her," Kai whimpered, his eyes opening to land on her.

"But you helped fix me," she said, reaching out to wipe Dainin's cheeks free of tears. "And here we are. My grandmother forced me to marry Drizdan in exchange for his returning me to Winter. I was a valuable Princess who had been lost for nine hundred years and they wanted me back."

Kai had crossed the room and dropped to his knees behind her, arms wrapping around her shoulders to hug her tightly to himself and she leant back against him, turning her head to kiss his arm gently. "I want to kill Drizdan, but I don't know where he is. I assume the Heathen Court, but I don't know. Every time I get near him ..." She trailed off, shaking her head in fear.

"We will find him and hold him down for you," Dirdos growled.

"Do you promise?" Etani asked, half smiling as she traced her fingers up and down Kai's arm.

"If you ask us to, we will find him," Vincent growled.

"I can do that?" she asked.

"Of course you can; anyone can ask us. You just have to give us something in exchange."

"What would one exchange for the capture and transport of a drow and King of Winter?"

Vincent frowned, looking at her for several seconds as he considered that.

"Drow don't have magic, so you won't need one of the magic breakers." Vincent glanced at Dainin, but Dainin appeared to be struggling with his own thoughts and incapable of speech.

"You just want us to contain and bring him to you?"

"Yes, alive," Dirdos growled. "Guaranteed alive."

"For you, an alliance between the Hunters and the Court. We had one with Tatialia, but it was broken with her death. And a personal favour."

"Do you have a favour in mind?" she asked.

"Not as yet. I will come up with something," he said.

Etani glanced back at the others and Uzo nodded, Dirdos looking pleased.

"Deal," she said, and Vincent smiled, kissing her cheek hard.

"We'll get the bastard for you."

THE ROOM WAS silent after that, Etani leaning back against Kai, her fingers linked with both Vincent's and Dainin's though the latter didn't seem like he was going to be capable of speech any time soon. Versalis could only watch the suffering woman, and not for the first time, wonder how she had survived all that time. She didn't move until Cat decided to go looking for a more interesting venture, allowing her to stretch her legs for the first time in an hour.

Looking up at Kai, she smiled while he bent down and kissed her forehead, her eyes closed and at peace with her friends there to keep her company; even if they had failed to keep her safe for so long, she still loved them.

Finally getting to her feet, she looked down as Dainin clung to her hand and she ruffled his hair gently, bending down to kiss the top of his head.

"Do not worry, Dainin, everything will turn out right in the end," she said The man looked distraught, but she pulled her fingers free and moved away from him though Versalis could only stare after her and then she looked at Vincent, something passing between them.

Etani approached him on the couch and Versalis smiled, opening his arms for her but she shook her head and instead took his hand, giving it a gentle tug.

He stood and waved a goodbye to the others over his shoulder as he followed her out of the room, his fingers linked with hers. A sudden joy filled him that she wanted to be alone with him instead of Uzo or Kai.

They moved through the halls, not wanting to tempt fate that Alaric would either find out about them or lose his mind if he found them just wandering around the castle.

He had no idea where she was taking him, but they came to the private little room after only a few minutes and she pressed the door quietly closed behind them, her ear against it.

"What are we doing here?" he asked.

She turned on him, leaning against the door for a moment, and then moved forward, arms snaking around his neck, and pulled him down into a tight, almost painful hug.

He wrapped his arms around her middle and squeezed her tightly, eyes sliding shut as he inhaled the scent of her hair.

"Privacy ..." she whispered. "We've had almost none for so long."

He smiled, straightening up and lifting her off the ground to make her squeak as he squeezed her. Her laugh was heavenly in his ears, and he could feel her tension melting away, their simple pleasure at being together easing their stress.

Turning his head, he kissed her cheek gently and set her back down on her feet.

"Feels like it's been ages since we've been alone," he said, leaning back just enough to look down into those glorious eyes.

She nodded as her fingers combed through his hair, tangling in the long strands, and she used that to tug him down while she lifted herself up to meet his lips halfway.

His insides melted as his lips met hers and he clutched her tighter, revelling in the taste of her and feel of her cool body pressed against his. Nothing could compare to the feeling of her being close or the way she made him feel just by giving her attention.

The kiss was gentle and tentative, exploring the taste of him while he revelled in the taste of her, his fingers splayed out against the small of her back to try to get as much contact with her as he possibly could.

Drawing back from her after several minutes, he coaxed her over to the bed and pulled her down with him. He had no intentions to seduce her, not after the pain she had re-lived. Instead, he wanted to hold her.

She moved willingly and settled herself down, pressing as close as she could into his side with her head resting against his shoulder while his arm wrapped around her, and he used the tip of her hair to tickle her arm.

"Do you think we would ever get to have a normal life?" she asked, her finger drawing small circles and spirals against his chest.

"What's normal?" he asked, making her smile.

"Normal for us," she said.

Versalis nodded and kissed her forehead, smiling when she lifted her chin to press a gentle kiss against his lips.

Her palm pressed against his jaw and he leant into the kiss, his lips moving against hers. She shifted up closer, her head tilting to deepen the kiss and she growled, moving too fast for him to see.

She straddled his hips, her body curved down to kiss him almost roughly, fingers tangling in his hair. His hands found her thighs and trailed up over her hips to her backside and she growled as he gripped the soft flesh, but then a devious thought came into his mind and he reached up to curl his fingers in her long hair.

Jerking her head back, he sat up, and with one arm around her middle, he used her hair to pull her head back enough to expose her throat, his tongue dragging from the base to the tip of her chin.

She shuddered, her breath quivering as she exhaled. Clenching her hip with his free hand, he pressed her down against him, her lips tilting up at the corners as she realised what he intended.

She rolled her hips against him and he groaned, the pressure of her moving against him driving him wild.

Releasing her hair, her head lifted, and she kissed him with a fierce abandon, her movements liquid and slow as she rocked against him. She reached down and with one fluid movement her dress was gone and fluttering to the floor, his head tilting down to kiss and tease her bare breasts.

She was still wearing her underwear, and the thought that he was so close to being inside her made him dizzy with need, but he wasn't about to push her too far.

The soft groans of her pleasure were quiet, almost hesitant as though she were afraid of the sound, yet she didn't stop her movements.

He bit her breast, ever careful not to break the skin, but it was enough to send a shudder through her body, her back arching to give him more access, and he took full advantage. Turning his head, he caught the peak of her breast in his mouth and sucked, teasing her with his tongue and nibbling on her until she was quivering, her breaths ragged and panting.

Shifting his position, he growled as he pressed her back and rolled on top of her, grinding himself against her to make her moan, the sound delicious and sinful.

Cursing, she reached down between them and, with trembling fingers, she tugged at his pants, trying to pull them free, and his mind went blank for an instant.

Was she really wanting that? Did she really want him?

"Versalis ..." she whined when she could only get the knot to tighten and he growled, his hand joining hers to pull the ties free, but they stubbornly refused to let go.

The door opened before they could get any further and the brightness of the hallway outside reached them.

Both looking up, they found the amused face of Hades looking in at them, leaning against the doorframe.

"Oh, don't let me stop you," he said when they remained frozen, watching the giant man.

Etani sighed, flopping back onto the bed, and staring up at the ceiling in irritation. "What do you want, Hades?"

"You are being summoned back to your rooms," the God said,

slinking into the room, pretending to give them privacy while Versalis rolled off her and searched for her dress, but it was Hades who picked it up. He didn't bother trying to hide his admiration of her chest as she sat up and pulled her dress back on, glaring up at Hades as he grinned.

"You have a wife," she said.

"And you have three husbands, isn't stopping you," Hades countered.

"Who needs me?" she asked, pushing herself off the bed.

"No one. I just wanted to ruin the mood," Hades said, and without a backwards glance, he swept from the room, leaving them to look after him.

"Son of a bitch ..." Versalis growled. But he was right, the mood had been entirely ruined.

CHAPTER 37

RETURN

They headed back to her rooms and she ignored them as she stalked into the bathroom, grumbling under her breath, but he followed after her.

"Leave the door open," Uzo called out, ignoring Versalis' angry growl, but he left it open as ordered. It was never a good idea to ignore what Uzo told you to do.

Stripping out of his clothes, he stalked her into the shower and as she turned to him, he shoved her into the wall and his mouth pressed hard into hers, demanding and hungry.

She was surprised at first but then she kissed him back. He could tell she wasn't as eager to be with him as she had been before, so he eased back on the intensity.

Breaking the kiss, she glanced at the door and then pulled the divider out further to give them a little more privacy before she grinned at him wickedly. Her fingers found his erection and he froze, his eyes wide as the chill of her skin and her boldness blanked his mind.

"Don't make a sound," she whispered, and he nodded, bowing

his head and it was her lips that muffled his low growl of pleasure as she stroked him.

She wasn't overly confident, but it didn't take much for her to turn him on and he revelled in the feeling of her hand on him, stroking him.

He had imagined her hand on him so many times that it was hard to wrap his mind around the fact that she was holding him in her fingers, her soft skin gliding over his shaft in a way that left him trembling, wanting to throw her down and bury himself inside her but he kept still, muscles locked in place to keep himself frozen.

He groaned against her mouth, and he was more than a little embarrassed when he found his release after only a few minutes, gasping for air and biting his tongue to keep from making a sound.

Bowing his head over her, he watched her as she rubbed her fingers together and lifted them to her lips.

His heart skipped a beat as her tongue touched the tips of her fingers, experimentally tasting his seed. It was possibly the most arousing thing he had ever seen, and yet it was entirely innocent at the same time. She didn't pull a face, only looked down at her hands as though the taste was unexpected.

Looking up at him, she smiled, and he leant down to kiss her, hungry and wanting more, but they weren't alone and her bringing him to release was more than he had ever expected.

Thankfully, they were at least reasonably separated, their lips meeting in a gentle brush when the partition was jerked back and Uzo glared at them.

"The point of leaving the door open was so you two couldn't get up to anything," he growled, eyeing them suspiciously.

"Nothing happened, uncle," Etani lied, resting her head against Versalis' chest. "I am allowed to kiss him, aren't I?"

"So long as it's above the belt," Uzo growled, glaring at her and then him.

"Yes, uncle," Etani said, but Versalis was laughing inside. Apparently, Hades hadn't told him what they had been up to, and he wasn't aware of her pleasuring him only moments before.

Uzo stood glaring for a few more seconds and then stalked away; Etani turned to smirk up at him as he stepped away from her, shaking his head.

She was such a devious little thing, but he wasn't about to complain, and he reached for her favourite soap and oil, offering them to her and watching as she cleaned herself. He was unable to take his eyes off her, unashamedly jealous of that soap that was able to rub over her skin when he couldn't.

The oil came next, and he accepted the soap, setting it back and picking out his own, setting the oil back when she had tipped out enough to rub over her skin and hair.

Washing himself, he kept his eyes on her, not wanting to miss a second of her routine.

Finally finished, she shut off the water and rocked up onto the balls of her feet, her body straining. He closed the distance and kissed her gently, warm and loving, before she moved away to get her towel.

Accepting his as she offered it to him, he watched her backside as she turned away to dry herself off, grinning as he appreciated the perfection of that well-shaped rear.

Once she was dry, she pulled on a clean pair of underwear and then pants, turning back to find him ogling her with his mouth slightly open.

"Stop staring," she said, but he couldn't really process her words, his eyes on her chest now.

Her cheeks flamed red and she moved, but he could only see the movements of her breasts with each step she took, right up until she used the towel to flick his leg and he jerked back, eyes wide and looking down at the red welt that formed.

"Ow!" he complained.

"That's what you get for staring," she growled, and he smirked.

"That's what you get for being so gorgeous," he countered.

She scowled at him and turned away, pulling her brassiere on, and rearranging her breasts in it before tugging on a shirt and glaring at him.

"Get dressed," she said, and he looked down to find that he was stark naked and had been holding the towel against his navel to hide his erection.

He watched her go, and once she was out he closed the door and sat down with his head in his hands as he tried to focus on something that wasn't the sight of her bent over like that and the things it was doing to him. The thought of just gripping her hips and driving himself into her was a feral need in him, but he swallowed it and took in a deep breath, forcing himself to calm down.

IT WAS a good five minutes before he was able to get dressed and the swelling at his groin had gone down, heading back out to find the room full of those who had positioned themselves around Etani. They were all ignoring him as the woman herself sat on the floor against Bast's legs, one arm wrapped around the slender shin of the Goddess with her head resting on her knee. Bast was stroking her hair, those dangerous nails working against Etani's scalp and sending her into a nearly catatonic state, her lips slightly parted and eyes barely open.

The rest of them were sitting around doing whatever it was they normally did, though Vincent and Dainin were preparing for their hunt of the drow.

Looking up at him, both men gave him cold glances, though they weren't entirely hostile. It wasn't uncommon for them to give him that look since Etani had chosen him as her mate and he didn't take it personally, instead turning to look around for a place to settle down.

He didn't get to take even a single step before he jerked, pain ripping through his body as a large, wooden bolt thudded into his shoulder.

Looking down at it, then up in alarm, the entire room had tensed, but it was Vincent who spoke.

"Oh, sorry ... finger slipped," the Hunter said, his face blank as he saw where he had struck Versalis.

There was a moment of silence as they all took in the situation, the wooden bolt would have ended Versalis in a second had it struck his heart, and none of them were overly good at hiding their hostility towards him, but none of them had tried to actually kill him yet.

Etani stood and her hand smacked into the back of Vincent's head as she approached Versalis.

"Be more careful, Vince, not everyone here is immortal." She sighed and Versalis glared at the man who had jerked at the casual use of a nickname for him, his expression smug that he was the only one who got a nickname from her.

She didn't see the incident as the assassination attempt it was, and she smiled as she jerked the bolt out, eyeing it for a moment. It seemed to disappear as she wrapped her arms around his neck, and he bent down to meet her kiss.

He kissed her back, his fingers finding her jaw and moving down over her neck.

"It was an accident," Vincent lied, and she made a dismissive sound, leaning back slightly to kiss his cheek gently and moving away again, the bolt gone.

He could only assume it was going to join her box of treasures with the other one.

Vincent looked at Versalis, his hands, and then Etani as he realised the bolt had vanished with her and he scowled, annoyed at the loss, but it was his own fault.

There was a moment of silence as she closed the door and all eyes turned on Vincent, watching the man warily as Versalis' shoulder healed.

"What? I didn't do it on purpose," Vincent said.

"Oh, please, we're not stupid," Daemon said, more amused than anything.

Vincent scowled at them all but before he could respond, a scream came from Etani's room.

"Dirdos!" she screamed, the dragon looking up suddenly and his eyes were wide with alarm.

It was a furious scream, and all eyes turned on him, seeing his fear.

"What did I do?" he demanded, knowing he was in trouble for something.

"Bet you dinner she found the ruby missing," Uzo said, flipping the page of his book.

The door slammed, and the dragon jumped, all heads turning to see the furious woman, her eyes glowing a rich blue in her fury.

"Give," she growled, seemingly too angry to come up with a coherent sentence. "Give now."

"Whatever is the matter, Etani?" the dragon asked and Versalis had to admire his bravery in the face of her fury.

"Give. Ruby. Now!" She was trembling and everyone else in the room scattered, ready for the explosion, with Bast grabbing Cat and slinking out onto the balcony.

"You steal from me, I steal right back," Dirdos said.

"Give ..."

Versalis swallowed at her guttural snarl, realising right then what the sound of death was. It was that voice; that, coupled with the flames they saw in her wide eyes. She was ready to burn him.

"It's mine now," he said.

"Burn," she said in a hungry voice.

"Burn my belongings and I'll take you to replace it all," Dirdos said.

She seemed to be weighing the pros and cons of that for an instant but then shook her head.

"Give!" she snarled.

"If you want it, go get it," the dragon said, and her eyes narrowed at the challenge. "I won't stop you from trying."

She bared her teeth at him, the threat of those razor-sharp fangs real when she was angry. They might be small, but they could shred skin like wet paper.

"You know the deal, little girl. One a fortnight."

"Month," she growled.

"Fortnight."

"Month!"

"Fortnight, or I bury it and neither of us can have it."

She growled, and then deteriorated into cursing him in her native tongue at such a speed that none of them could keep up, eyebrows lifting while Dirdos smiled at her, delighted by her foul mouth, and she screamed, "Fine!"

"Save it for pillow talk," he purred, and she lifted her hand, middle finger extended, and stalked from the room.

"Where will you take her?" Uzo asked conversationally after several seconds of silence that made the rest of them creep back.

"Back to the cavern probably, I'll keep you informed."

A sudden crash sounded, and a man screamed as she swore at him.

"What is it about short people that makes them so angry?" Dirdos asked, his eyes back on his sword.

"Closer to Hades," Uzo muttered, licking his finger, and turning the page. He hadn't once looked up from his book.

"Is it actually in the cave?" Versalis asked as he crept back to his seat.

"No," the dragon said, lifting the red gem out of his pocket and putting it back again.

"That's cheating."

"I never said I'd put it in the cave. Only that she could go look for it."

Uzo and Daemon laughed, but Versalis was frowning at the man warily. That was two now; two days he got to be with her alone plus a whole month each year. He didn't like that at all.

SHE DIDN'T RETURN for a couple of hours but when she did, she was glaring at Dirdos, the dragon only smiling at her, which enraged her further. She stalked into her room, growling something about men and castration.

"Promises, promises." He sighed.

"She's going to kill you one day," Uzo said.

"She can try," Dirdos said in an amused tone, sliding the sword back into its sheath and setting it aside to start working on a series of small daggers he had procured, his intentions to practice knife throwing.

Versalis stood and followed her into her room, finding her sitting on the bed with her measly supply of weaponry. It seemed to be dwindling somewhat, and she was getting frustrated, most of it either lost to another group who had taken her, or stolen by one of them. Some had been broken, and some had simply vanished into the ether.

"You can't go right now," Versalis said, approaching her and sitting down beside her.

"Preparing," she snapped, still too angry to come up with a real sentence.

Reaching for one of her knives, she froze and her eyes unfocused, staring at the door though he didn't think she saw it.

"Letari ..." she whispered.

"Hunter!" Versalis called out as she sat frozen, listening, or watching whatever it was she was seeing or hearing.

Hunter rushed into the room, followed by the others. They watched her warily as she withdrew her hand and her other hand reached out for Versalis.

Accepting it, he drew her off the bed and turned her around, her movements automatic and unresisting as he guided her around.

"Letari's awake," he said in explanation, Hunter's face relieved as they all moved to give her space.

She murmured something in a language none of them seemed to be able to understand, and Versalis glanced around at Hades, who was watching her from the doorway.

"The language of death. She's comforting Letari, your girl is in a panic," he said in a relaxed voice. "Go on, Etani, before she breaks something."

Etani nodded and Versalis pressed her hand to his chest while reaching down into himself for the magic that rose in him like a wave, eager and greedy to get back to her.

Uzo and Kai reacted, but Jaia and Daemon held them back as her wings stretched out and she sighed, her lips tilting up in relief.

"Don't go anywhere," she murmured to the group, and Versalis stepped back quickly, giving her room to wrap her wings around herself, and she vanished into mist.

"She's such an interesting little monster," Hades said.

"Don't get any ideas, Hades; you know what happened to the last woman you took an interest in that wasn't Persephone," Daemon said, half amused and half territorial.

"She's not quite so jealous anymore," Hades reasoned. "Besides, Etani can hold her own."

"You're not touching my niece," Uzo growled.

"No promises," Hades said, smirking at Uzo when the Fae turned on him. "Come on then, Fae, I will rip you apart."

"That's enough. Hades, keep your hands off her. She has enough issues without another God chasing after her, and you two aren't fighting. We are going to all sit down and behave until Etani gets back," Daemon growled, watching the spot where she had vanished.

"You can't stop me from pursuing her," Hades said, smiling at them all.

"Exactly what she needs, another megalomaniac trying to get his hands on her," Kai muttered.

"She's my partner," Versalis snapped.

"Yes, but you two haven't even slept together yet, so you don't count," Hades said in an amused, cruel voice.

Versalis' face went pale and he glared at the man, turning when Kai gasped, his eyes on the spot where Etani had reformed.

SHE STOOD FROZEN, her wings still wrapped around the two of them, but Letari seemed to be struggling, and when the wings parted, they found Letari, clinging to Etani, who was covered in bites and scratches from the frenzied woman.

Green eyes swung on them all and then locked on Hunter. With a shriek, she lunged for the man, and he caught her, wrapping his arms and then his jacket around her slender, naked form, but it was only a moment before she went limp, unconscious in his arms.

"She just needs to sleep," Uzo said when Hunter looked up, terrified, but then he nodded and he scooped her up, carrying her from the room.

Kai was already on Etani and she looked up, dazed and reaching for him.

He caught her easily, wrapping his arms around her as her wings melted away and she was left trembling, her face paler than ever.

Uzo joined them and he stroked her hair, pressing against her bleeding abdomen where Letari had tried to gore her in her frenzied panic.

"She was disorientated, she didn't know what was happening," Etani explained, sounding breathless and weak.

"Hunter took her to rest, you should rest, too," Uzo said, stroking back her hair.

Resting her head against Kai's chest, she mumbled, leaning into him as she clung to consciousness.

Versalis moved forward and she seemed to sense him, tilting her head, but Kai refused to give her up, even as she growled that low, feral sound of hunger.

"Kai …" Versalis warned, but he shook his head, clutching her harder to him.

She turned on him, her teeth sinking into his throat, and he jerked as she bit again and again and then latched onto him, drawing hard on him.

He grunted in pain but refused to let go, his eyes going unfocused as she fed with a wild need of one who was starving.

Her eyes were clenched shut, and she clutched him to her; even as his arms fell from around her, she refused to let go.

"Swap out," Jaia snapped at Versalis, who nodded, and Uzo moved behind her, sliding one arm around her neck and the other gripping her hair, forcing her head back.

She snarled, struggling to cling to the unconscious man, but then Versalis was before her and her arms snapped around him, her teeth sinking painfully, deliciously deep into his neck.

The rest of them filed out except for Uzo, his eyes wary as he monitored the situation, but she was slowing down, satiated but greedily taking more just because she could until she drew back from him.

Blood smeared her face and dribbled down her chin and neck, her frenzy driving her to carelessness and waste, but he didn't care.

He smiled, feeling a little woozy himself.

"Into bed," Uzo said and Etani moved obediently, full but exhausted.

Versalis flopped onto the bed at her side and they were both asleep in a matter of minutes, their fingers linked and clinging to each other.

His dreams were flooded with her, the scent of her and the feel of her skin on his, the feeling of what it would be like to make love to her. That thought alone was enough to keep him happy, and he slept peacefully, the imagined pleasure soothing his thoughts.

CHAPTER 38

NEVER MESS WITH THE SISTER

After that day, things were quiet, and they were all grateful for that chance. They waited for the two women to regain their strength before their planned trip back to Winter.

Sitting at the table on the balcony of his room after he had fed, he took in a deep breath and closed his eyes, simply enjoying the peace and quiet with the knowledge that his love wasn't far away.

There was a terrible, gut-wrenching scream from somewhere in the castle and his head snapped up, alert, and when he felt her panic, the name that was screamed, he was immediately on his feet and out the door.

He wasn't the only one who reacted to the scream; guards and others of their group were all heading in the same direction, but he reached her first even though the terrible pitch of that scream made his teeth ache and his ears bleed. She was incensed; beyond that, she was so enraged that she was in a state of perfect calm when they got to her, the room a flurry of snow, and her hair was drifting up around her, shifting as though under water once more.

Dirdos headed for her first as the rest of them stood in the doorway, pained and struggling with the aftereffects of her scream.

It was like someone had injected acid into their brains and it was trying to escape out of their ears.

The dragon reached for her, but he jerked back and when Versalis looked down, the dragon's hand was red, raw and blistering from the temperature of her skin, but he didn't look at all disturbed by the events.

"We are going to Winter," she snarled and turned on the lot of them, murderous intent in her eyes. None of them were about to deny her or risk being left behind, and so they all moved forward.

Taking her hand, Versalis saw the giant man's jaw tense in pain, but he refused to let go of her as the world around them vanished into a smear of crimson and they stepped out into the coolness of the Winter Court.

Glancing at the pale beauty, he saw those same changes in her that were always evident when they arrived in Faerie, but she didn't so much as pause, turning to look around at the damage that had been caused.

Blood was sprayed up the walls and frozen on the floor, but she ignored it all, stepping over limp forms and heading for the hallway.

She screamed the drow's name and was met with a cold laugh from further down the hall. She set off that way, fury radiating off her in waves.

They stepped into the throne room and froze in place, staring at the sight.

Drizdan, the drow they hadn't seen in who knew how long, had somehow changed, though it was hard to place how. He was still tall with dark, predatory eyes and dark hair that matched his dark skin. He had that same hungry gaze when his eyes found Etani, that same curl of his lips that promised pain and suffering. He was a sexual sadist and rapist. He wanted nothing more than to hear her scream in agony and brutalise her. Owning her, being her husband and her magic, were all secondary to his need to mutilate her beauty. It made him somewhat uncommon, able to find release through simply hurting her just as much as actually penetrating her.

Kai was the only one of them to truly see what that man was capable of, and the vampire would never speak of the events that had left him mentally scarred and would likely never heal.

"I have never seen something so innocent being destroyed so completely," he had said, the only thing he would ever say if asked. They decided it was best never to ask him again and Etani had only asked if they really wanted to know what had happened.

No, they had not really wanted to know, because they were all terrified of finding out what he had done to her.

The scene before them was incredibly odd, with a happily swinging Letari hanging from the ceiling, her cage swaying back and forth as though she were on a swing and her grin enormous as she looked down. She waved when she found them all looking up at her. The other oddity was Aurora, bound to the throne using that same gold chain that worked on them all. In the middle of the dais sat a very large, very ornate gold throne that, evidently, Drizdan had brought himself.

Aurora evidently didn't seem to be enjoying herself as much as Letari was, and while both women had shadows of bruises on their faces, they seemed to be otherwise unharmed.

The whole group took three steps into the throne room and unconsciously spread out to form a semi-circle with Etani before them. The twitch of Daemon's finger informed them to attack at any moment was shattered when Drizdan glanced back at Aurora and a wave of cold rippled over them.

Versalis looked down; ice crept up his legs, and he frowned as he met Aurora's terrified stare, her lower lip quivering. She wouldn't have done that without good reason, and the poor beauty was putting on an excellent show of calm, but he could see her fear. He was going to try to get to her and get her free. Even if things might be tense between them, he still cared about her, and her fear was hurting him. He needed to fix it.

"IF YOU TOUCHED EITHER OF THEM …" Etani threatened, but the man's face twisted in irritation, his predatory eyes sweeping over all of them.

"I tried, but she's protected by Winter …" the man said, jerking his head towards Aurora. "And your sister…" He looked up, confused and annoyed. "Did you know she could set herself on fire?"

None of them knew that, and when they all looked up, the crazy woman laughed.

"No matter, I have you now. I had hoped to simply take you and beat you into submission, but I got the wrong sister, and this works just as well. Now I have all three of you and I'll make you submit to me this way instead, and I can't wait to see their fury as I fuck you right here on the floor."

Versalis' stomach twisted at those words, glancing sideways to see Dirdos was looking down and tiny rivulets of water were trickling down from the ice containing his legs.

Daemon looked about ready to set the world on fire and Kai looked like he was going to vomit, his face green and eyes huge as he stared at his precious Etani in reach of the man.

"I see you haven't gotten any class since we last spoke," Etani said, her voice and manners relaxed, but he could see her fingers clenching in the folds of her dress, furious.

"Keep it up, Etani. I'll be glad for the opportunity to shut that smart mouth of yours for you," Drizdan growled back, his grin massive as he looked her over, hungry and wanting.

"I'm going to rip you in half," she promised, but the man only grinned wider.

"Pillow talk already, love? Isn't it my job to rip you in half from the groin up?" His lecherous stare went down to her hips and back up again, suggestively lingering on the fullness of her partially exposed chest before landing on her eyes.

"How about we take this outside?" Etani suggested.

"No, love, I want them all to see you beaten and submitting to me. They'll love seeing you on your knees and screaming in pleasure."

"I don't think you've ever had me screaming in pleasure."

"No, not yet. It's always been screaming in pain ..." The man's pants were growing tight as he thought over the times he had made her scream. "But we can always fix that," he added when she sighed in exhaustion at his antics.

"Are you even capable of having a woman screaming in pleasure?" she asked, her head tilting to the side.

"Just because you've never experienced it doesn't mean it's not possible," he said snippily and Letari shrugged when Etani looked up, her pale legs swinging back and forth to make the cage swing faster.

"Is she always like that?" the man asked.

"Yes, pretty much," Etani replied, watching the cage, and then he grunted in exasperation, the two sharing a resigned glance. "How many guards was she responsible for?"

"Most of them ..." the man grumbled.

"I figured as much."

"Come here." His tone changed, and her head turned in his direction. Versalis could imagine her narrowed eyes at the demand. "I have something to show you," he said, tweaking at her curiosity.

She moved forward and Daemon growled, hating that she was even closer to the man who had hurt her so many times.

The man pointed up and she frowned, her pretty face confused as she squinted at her sister's back, unsure of what she was looking at.

Drizdan's hand dropped, and his eyes turned on Etani, lips parting as he studied her profile with an intensity that confused Versalis. It wasn't love or the need to destroy, it was possessive to a whole new level none of them had seen before.

"What is that?" she demanded, turning to look at him.

He spoke quietly and they all strained to listen but it was impossible to hear what they were saying from across the room, and over the obnoxious squeaking of the cage above them, but judging by

Etani's face, she was disgusted by what he was saying. Letari was frowning down at the two of them, then twisting around to try to see what it was Drizdan had been pointing to.

When she turned, Dirdos hissed, and they all frowned up at the green-eyed beauty, seeing a large black mark on her skin.

"What is that...?" Daemon asked, keeping a close eye on the pair on the dais but also trying to see what was happening to Letari.

"Death magic... how the fuck does he have access to death magic? Isn't he just a drow?" Dirdos growled, staring up at it.

"Can we remove it?" Kai asked, his eyes locked on Etani and unable to even glance up at Letari.

"If I can get to her, I can burn off the poison, but I need to be able to touch her."

"How long?"

"Five minutes at least. We need to keep him distracted." Dirdos glanced down at the ice, the outside of it still relatively intact, but he was standing in a pool of water inside the blocks, able to at least move somewhat, but not entirely.

"I'll kill you!" Letari screamed, all eyes going up to her, but when they looked back down again, Drizdan had closed the distance to Etani and he jerked her arm up above her head, his free arm going around her waist to pull her up against himself. His head tilted to trace his nose up the length of her throat, inhaling deeply while her eyes went to Dirdos, who held up five fingers.

Her lips pressed together and she looked back at Drizdan, who appeared furious.

"Where is all your magic?" he demanded, clenching her delicate wrist hard enough to leave bruises.

"It has been dispersed," she said, uncertain.

"Dispersed where?" the angry man snapped. "Why?"

"So I do not explode. It's too much magic."

"You were born to hold that much magic, idiot girl. This is inconvenient ..."

"How so?"

415

"I can't use your magic if you don't have access to it."

"Well, I'm sure if you ask really nicely, they'll let you borrow it."

Versalis frowned and saw Dirdos scowling out of the corner of his eye, and he realised what had changed between him and Etani, confirming his suspicions. Dirdos was like Versalis, he was indeed holding her magic for her.

"Who?" Drizdan snarled.

"It's a secret," she taunted.

"You're a difficult, little bitch, aren't you ...?"

"Are you this sweet to all your ladies, or am I just special?" she asked, and he jerked her roughly against him, his face furious.

A soft squeal of protesting ice made them all glance at Dirdos though Drizdan seemed too intent on his prize to have noticed.

Dirdos scowled, but four fingers twitched down and Etani frowned, knowing they were running out of time, and she gasped as Drizdan snarled to get her attention back on him.

"Jealous?" she asked, her tone amused.

"Perhaps ... How many of them are you enjoying?" he demanded, angry and scornful.

"Probably less than you've been enjoying."

"I haven't had any, my darling girl."

Her exquisite voice rang out in a laugh of disbelief but then her head tilted and she frowned at him. "None?"

"Once you go, Etani, there's nothing else that can satisfy your lust," he growled.

"How terribly frustrating for you."

His eyes narrowed in response and he squeezed her wrist and ribs until she flinched, and he pulled her arm further back so that her chest was pressed against his, his nose tracing her jaw.

She asked him something, but the others could only hear a faint growling voice, the cage above them still as Letari tried to set the man on fire with the force of her glare.

The argument escalated and Drizdan stepped back, jerking her so that she fell to her knees before him, her face strained with the pain.

"I will not be denied!" the man raged, and she flinched back from him, unable to escape.

Kai heaved, that terrible voice and her terror triggering memories in the vampire that nearly made him pass out.

The rest of them were growling in warning, every one of them ready to rip the drow to shreds the second they got their hands on him.

"Your collection of men love you, do they not?" he asked in a low, dangerous voice.

"Yes ..." she said.

"And it's safe to assume they all desire you," he said, staring down at her kneeling before him.

"You'd have to ask them," she said, her fingers turning an agonised purple colour as his grip cut off circulation to her hand.

"I can feel their want, I don't need to ask. Every man here would kill for you, kill to be inside you."

She frowned, glancing at them, and they all did their best not to make direct eye contact with her. She was in total denial that they were all so in love with her and their embarrassment made her blush.

"That's what I thought," Drizdan said smugly. "You will satisfy me here, or your sister and your heir will die."

"I'm death, Drizdan. I will drag them back kicking and scream-ing," Etani countered.

"Yes, but what if they have no souls to bring back?" he purred, bending at the waist until his face was a mere inch from hers, smug against her disgust.

LETARI SCREAMED her rage at the man and that seemed to only confirm his words. His face twisted in triumph and glee as her eyes slid shut,

417

terror for her sister and Aurora setting in.

"Satisfy my needs and you can have them back, but I want my wife at my side."

Shaking her head, she opened her eyes and looked up at him. "I will not surrender to you. I will not give you my magic."

"Satisfy me and you can have your heir, surrender entirely and your sister will be free to live a long, happy life."

"Why couldn't you just find yourself a nice girl who would love you?" Etani asked quietly.

"Because you are mine and I will have what's mine," Drizdan growled softly.

"If I satisfy you, you will let them both go," she said, biting her lower lip when he shook his head. "After that we can discuss a possible surrender."

"Very well, Etani, but I'm not removing the curse from them. In order to keep you here at my side, they will need to return frequently for their antidote. Forever, if we cannot come to a favourable agreement."

"You're a bastard..." she whimpered, his voice booming out in a delighted laugh.

"Good girl," he purred happily, letting go of her.

He moved away from her and settled himself into the golden throne, his finger crooked for her to come to him, and she did so, standing slowly and moving before him, her shoulders tense as she stood between his spread knees.

"Undo your hair, you look so much better with it down," he demanded, and she shifted slightly, confused. "Now." There was no amusement in his tone then, her hesitation only promising violence.

Moving slowly, she lifted her hands to the coils of braid and undid them all, her long hair falling in waves down her back, and Versalis couldn't help but note that it almost reached her thighs now.

When she was done he pointed down, and she lowered herself slowly to her knees before him.

Versalis felt much like Kai as he watched the terrible scene, his stomach clenching in fear and Daemon growled furiously, rage burning off him.

"You know what to do," Drizdan growled, but she only gave a tiny shake of her head and Versalis glanced at the others, just as confused as Drizdan. She had never done that before, and the idea of her first time being with that man made him feel ill. "None of them showed you?" he asked and when she shook his head, he laughed happily. "Well, this will be even more fun for me. Pants first."

Versalis wanted to look away, to give her at least some semblance of privacy, but it was like seeing a dead thing, he couldn't look away and he found the others were all staring, forgetting their attempts to escape as the horror unfolded.

She was releasing the buttons of his pants, her pale fingers slow and hesitant, and when she pulled the fabric down to expose him, she looked away, embarrassed and ashamed.

"If you bite me, I will kill them both in an instant," he growled, grasping himself and easing his erection out of his pants, his free hand going to the back of her head. "Open."

Looking around, he found a small bin and grabbed it, handing it quickly to Kai who snatched it up and vomited into it as they heard the man's first groan of pleasure, his head tilting back against the backrest of the throne and his fingers tight in her hair, guiding her movements.

Tears had sprung up in his eyes as he watched, none of them able to look away from the tragic sight.

She was so small before him, her body tensed like a bowstring, the beautiful Queen in her exquisite gown forced to kneel and orally pleasure her abusive, rapist husband before all of those who loved her most.

How many of them had imagined her doing that for them? Probably all of them, but this wasn't what they had imagined, this was disgusting, humiliating, and that was the whole point. He wanted to torment her and leave her broken.

He glanced at Dirdos; the dragon's entire body quivered in rage, eyes glowing a solid crimson as he stared, furious and impotent, as the woman he loved was forced into that position.

He hissed softly at the dragon and that furious glare turned on him. He visibly shook himself and glanced down, focusing on the task at hand, and they all tried to block out the monster's groans that were growing faster and louder.

IT WAS ONLY a few minutes before the growl of "Swallow," had them all tensing in anguish, and she tried to jerk back, her body straining to be free of him, but his grip on her hair was tight and they saw her flinch when he released inside her mouth.

"Mm, don't cry ..." he growled as her body clenched in a heave but she managed to keep it all down. He stroked her cheek, but then his eyes lifted to the rest of them, and a sadistic grin came over his face. "Here you are, gentlemen, your precious Etani delegated to a common whore," the man called out, and he dragged her to her feet, turning her around to face them.

Her lips looked swollen, her chin glistening with fluid none of them wanted to think about, even her breasts were shimmering slightly. She didn't look up at them, staring at the floor with tears streaking her cheeks and her hair a tangled mess in his grip.

"Mother ..." Jaia whimpered, his face distraught at the sight of her.

"Now ... get on top," Drizdan said in a gleefully loud voice as he pulled her back around to face him.

"Keep your fucking hands off her!" Kai screamed, finally breaking at what was coming next.

Etani flinched at the scream, but Drizdan ignored them as he led her back to the throne and sat down, then bundled up the hem of her dress and reached up under the fabric and then jerked down, her small frame swaying slightly as he moved her, and they found out what he had done a moment later.

He leant sideways around her body and, hooking one end of the fabric against his thumb, he pulled it back and flicked the delicate scrap of fabric across the room where it landed only a few feet away from them.

Her underwear, he had removed her underwear.

Kai vomited again into the bin, but Versalis could only watch in horrified fascination as the man grabbed her waist and pulled her closer to him, bundling up her dress and guiding her knee onto the throne beside his hip.

Dirdos pulled one leg free, his jaw set and eyes flaming as he was torn between getting to Etani and getting to Letari.

"Letari," Daemon hissed, and the woman looked around at them, fury in her eyes.

Versalis watched the woman he loved as the man arranged her over him, frustrated at the mass of her dress and finally simply ripping away a couple of the layers that were getting in the way and he spat onto his palm, reaching down between them and grinning up at her savagely.

Kneeling on the throne over his lap, the man slid down slightly to make himself more comfortable and pulled her down against him, his face intent as he guided himself to what he wanted while he traced his lips along her collarbone and down to her breast.

Her body flinched unconsciously at something, but when he pulled her down, Versalis saw the smear of blood on his cheek where he had bitten her breast.

Shifting his grip, he wrapped his arms around her waist and pulled her closer against him, his loud moan of pleasure announcing that he got what he wanted, and Kai was whimpering as he watched, the drow moving her against him as he fulfilled his promise, fucking her in front of all of them.

She had gone almost entirely motionless, responding only to his touch and demanding guidance and Versalis was certain she had detached from the situation, gone wherever it was she went when blocking out the world around her.

Drizdan reached up to grip her shoulder with one hand and the other remained on her hip as he pulled and pressed at her, forcing her to move against him, and Versalis could picture the man inside her, his pleasure as he used her body but after only a moment, he seemed to decide it wasn't enough for him.

Lifting her up off his lap with his grip on her thighs, he lowered her down onto the dais and Versalis closed his eyes as her dress fell down around her hips, exposing her bare skin and the ferocity with which he was fucking her.

Kai was talking to himself, his head bowed and mumbling, but Dirdos was at the cage, tall enough that he could reach up and touch the tip of Letari's foot and his fingers were glowing a solid red as she sat still, her eyes on her sister below being raped before them all.

He couldn't see it any more, couldn't watch her being abused like that, but he couldn't block out the sound, the groans of pleasure and the sound of skin on skin.

The lock on the cage melted and Letari climbed down with the help of the dragon and Versalis glanced at Etani, her head turning at the movement, though her face was blank, empty, and terrible.

Drizdan's cry was loud as he jerked against her, thrusting with a vicious force into her and going still while his head turned and his lips moved against her jaw, licking and teasing the pale skin.

Etani must have seen her twin free and her eyes slid shut, relieved, as Dirdos headed for Aurora and Letari crept closer, her short hair lifting up around her and then her foot scuffed the ground and Drizdan froze, panting hard and confused as his head turned. He growled as he saw Letari, her eyes flaming and the air seeming to sparkle around her.

Etani cried out in pain as Drizdan moved, sitting up and with one hand tugging up his pants. The other hand was smeared in blood as he held a very long, very elaborate knife in his grip, sunk to the handle in her side.

CHAPTER 39
REPAIRS

L etari screamed as she slammed into the man and he rolled with her, throwing the crazy woman off him while Etani struggled to slide the enormous knife free of herself, her legs closing and hips twisting to roll onto her side and hide herself from the view of the men around her.

Drizdan was on her in an instant, gripping the handle and ripping the blade free of her side only to kick her onto her back. "Little bitch ..." he snarled as he lifted the blade up above his head and her hands jerked up to grip his wrists, keeping him from being able to slam the blade into her a second time.

Letari flipped over onto her hands and feet, eyes furious as she found the man over her twin, trying to kill her. "Did you actually think I would submit to you, Drizdan?" She gasped, straining to keep him off her, though he had gravity on his side.

"No, but don't worry, little whore, I'll get what I want in the end."

"I'll burn in the underworld before I let you have what you want."

"You won't have a choice, my little pet; you'll come begging to love me," he snarled, her derisive laugh sounding pained and warped.

The instant Dirdos finished working on Aurora there was the sound of splintering ice and they froze for only a second, realising what was happening as Aurora was freed from the threat, and they all moved as one, sprinting forward.

Drizdan screamed a curse and yanked his arms free of her grip, springing for the door while Etani snatched for his leg, but before she could reach him, the man simply vanished into a streak of black and she froze, staring at the spot in disbelief.

Letari was on her sister, dragging her off the ground and into her arms while Versalis reached Aurora and dragged the terrified woman from the throne, hugging her tightly.

She clung to him while he pulled her along to Etani, but Kai was on her, his entire body shuddering with tears, and it was Etani trying to comfort him, her voice sounding small and hurt though she was working to calm him down.

"Are you all right?" Etani asked Aurora's left shoulder, unable to look any of them in the eye, or even at their faces.

"Yes," the pale, sweating woman said. It seemed that Dirdos heated them up to help burn off the toxin and her pale face was flushed red with the heat.

"Do you regret becoming my heir yet?"

"Almost," Aurora said in a half joke, her head turning to Versalis and her lower lip quivering.

Aurora turned back to Etani and, to their surprise, she reached for the small Queen and hugged her, a soft murmur causing Etani to nod slightly, though her expression didn't change.

Letari made a whining sound and moved forward, wedging her head up under Etani's arm, and squished between the women, forcing herself into the hug with a fierce determination.

Aurora laughed and kissed Letari's cheek though the exchange between the two of them was something that caught all of their attention, especially Etani's.

"Are you flirting with my sister?" Etani demanded and Aurora's face went pale, Letari only smirking.

"Mind your business," Letari said, nuzzling Aurora's jaw.

"You have Hunter."

"Hunter doesn't mind, so long as it's not another man," Letari quipped, and Etani let go of the both of them, indignant.

"You're absurd," Etani snapped, frustrated by the lot of them and in pain.

DIRDOS REACHED for her hesitantly and his fingers brushed her shoulder so as not to startle her, her head turning in his direction. He looked down at the blood covering her and frowned, curling his hand around the back of her head and pulling her face into his chest.

She didn't try and resist, going into his arms eagerly, and he wrapped them both around her, his face pained. None of them would be able to forget what had been done to her; none of them would be able to think of her the same way. She was stronger than any of them gave her credit for, able to withstand the abuses of those around her, but how much could she handle before she broke?

Something caught her attention, and she looked around at a strained voice calling for her, her tattered dress, wild hair and tear-streaked face giving her the look of a tragic spirit instead of a Queen, but his eyes were relieved when he found her.

Kneeling down at the man's side, she brushed his cheek with her fingers and his eyes slid shut.

He looked mostly human except for two long horns that grew out of his head and dark crimson eyes, though there was a very large dart in the left one.

He seemed to be almost steaming in the coldness of the room and she removed his helmet and studied the wound.

The closer she was to him the more he seemed to relax, and she must have noticed as she curled her fingers in his, holding them gently while she examined him.

"Dragon," Dirdos murmured from behind them, his eyes on the injured man. "I didn't know any of us joined the Court."

"Only a few," the injured man said, opening his eyes to look up at Dirdos. "We can't all be solitary old men like you."

Dirdos snorted his amusement at the casual, friendly insult.

"You're going to lose that eye," Etani whispered, her fingers tugging at the skin of his cheek, and he flushed as she bent over him, her face only an inch from his as she studied the injury. "Caught in the bone ... no brain damage," she was murmuring to herself, her brows drawn together into a frown.

"I know," he said, both in pain and captivated by her beauty. "What happened?" he asked, reaching up to brush back a wild strand of hair from the air between them.

"Don't worry," she muttered and moved away from him, looking up at them all. "We need to get him help."

"I'll go," Uzo said in a strained voice, and hurried away.

She moved around him until she was kneeling at his head and lifted it into her lap, her fingers gentle as she stroked his hair, the touch soothing him, and it seemed to be helping her in some ways, too. She avoided all of their gazes and dodged any attempts to touch her; they didn't blame her, but it was hard to deal with. They wanted to comfort her, but she wasn't keen to let them.

Uzo returned after ten minutes, and he was leading an odd woman who looked furious.

"I didn't know we were back at war, Uzo ..." she said as she approached.

"We're not," Uzo said.

"Oh ... it's you," the woman said, looking down at Etani. There was an enormous amount of contempt in those two words and Etani recoiled, her lovely face going paler.

The woman was small, only around five feet, with brownish-white skin and huge brown eyes. She didn't have hair in the normal sense, but instead a mass of yellow fur that trailed down her back and down her front, long enough that it stopped growing around her hips and the ends trailed down to her ankles.

Four sets of wings that looked oddly like leaves hung at her back, the tips of the wings reaching almost to the tips of her hair, and around her head was what first looked like a crown, but then he realised that it was more of a growth.

Four large grey-green leaves started between her eyebrows and spread up and out to around half a foot above her head in a series of little spikes, magenta flowers bloomed out of her skin at her right forehead and under each of her ears which were short but round at the base and then curled up into a point.

She had markings under her eyes like Uzo, though hers were longer and dark grey along with her lips and another marking that traced from her lower lip down under her chin in a wide band that ended in two points pointing outwards towards her jaw.

All around her head were little soft, flexible spines that swayed and moved with her movements. She had breasts, small and shapely though they were covered in fur, and wore a long loincloth.

The woman made a sharp jerking motion and Etani lifted the man's head off her lap, setting it gently down on the cool ice, but his eye snapped open and he looked around wildly for her.

"No!" he whimpered, reaching for her.

"Move," the tiny moth woman snapped, and Etani reluctantly obeyed, her eyes pained as she watched him being taken away.

"I'll come find you," she called, trying to see the man who had cried out for her in desperation, his gaze locked on her until he was taken from the room.

"Why does she hate me?" Etani asked quietly, her voice broken now that she had nothing to distract herself.

"She feels you are a dangerous, destructive force," Uzo replied gently.

"Well ... she's not wrong," Etani sighed, turning away from them.

"Will you be heading back to Ayathian?" Aurora asked.

"We should, there are things we need to take care of. The King is having a fight with another King or something like that."

"Men ..." Aurora sighed.

"I am glad you are unharmed," Etani said, still speaking to Aurora's shoulder.

"Thank you for coming to get us, he was getting impatient."

"Next time he needs to have a trumpet announcing his games. Last time I lost track of Letari it took me sixteen years to find her under a log pretending to be dead because I refused to let her eat Avadari."

Letari turned on her sister, indignant. "You said you'd never tell anyone!"

"I made no promise," Etani countered.

"You're a horrible sister!"

Etani's face paled once more and she swallowed, her lips parting, but she couldn't say anything in response.

"Let's go," Dirdos said, trying to break the silence that had spread between them as Letari frowned at Etani and Etani stared at the floor.

"Be safe!" Aurora called out as her eyes went around the room to figure out what to do with the destruction, and the world burst into flames around them.

THEY WERE DUMPED BACK out into her room in Ayathian, and she immediately moved away from them, correcting the disturbed items as the room had been repaired in their absence.

Dirdos moved away and Versalis' stomach twisted as he saw what the man had gone to collect: a jug of fluid that would ensure Etani couldn't carry a child.

"I don't need it," she whispered when he offered her the mug of liquid, and his face darkened.

"Etani ... he ..."

She stood frozen for a moment, unable to decide what she was going to tell them before she finally sighed and set down the little glass bell that had been placed on the wrong shelf.

"I made sure I wouldn't be able to have a child again when I reformed," she said simply, her back to them.

"You what?" Daemon snapped.

"I can't have children, Daemon. I won't go through that again," she told the wall, nudging the bell into the exact spot she wanted it to be in.

Something inside Versalis broke as he thought of what she could have done to make herself infertile, his image of her carrying his child shattering into a million pieces. No, he didn't blame her for wanting to ensure she couldn't have a third child stolen from her, but it was still devastating to find out.

"Fix it!" Daemon yelled, stalking forward while Dirdos grabbed him and pulled him backwards.

"No, Daemon."

"Fix it, Etani!" he screamed, and she turned on him, her pale face furious.

"No, Daemon! I will not have another child stolen from me! I—" She broke off and blinked in confusion as she looked down and all eyes dropped as they saw the sword that Daemon had ripped from Dirdos' sheath and driven through her chest.

"Daemon!" everyone cried, his face furious as he glared at her.

"I will kill you every day for the rest of eternity until you fix it," he snarled. "You are not allowed to choose this, Etani. You will be a mother one day. I will not allow you to lose that."

Ripping the sword free of her, she whimpered in pain and Versalis shoved a frozen Uzo out of the way, catching her as she collapsed.

"This isn't the way to convince her!" Dirdos cried and Etani looked up at Versalis, her face tense with pain.

"I'm sorry ... I couldn't let him hurt Letari," she breathed, and he closed his eyes as hers filled with tears.

Leaning down, he kissed her forehead hard. "I would have expected no less from you. Hurry back to me, I will be waiting for you," he breathed, his voice anguished as he felt her going still in his arms, her body limp and empty as she died.

"You can't just kill her to get your own way!" Uzo snarled.

"It only has to be a reform through her Celestrial side. She can't modify that," Daemon gasped, staring down at her limp form, her eyes shut and face relaxed. "Besides ... she won't have that bastard's scent on her."

They all froze, no one wanting to admit that the scent of her made them all want to be sick. It wasn't Etani they could smell, but his seed inside her, tainting her and turning what was once beautiful into something perverse and ugly.

"Now she can be clean and new. If we can't even keep her safe, then we should at least be able to wipe her body clean."

No one wanted to agree with or deny that thought, though Versalis had to admit it might be easier for her to cope with it if she didn't have to feel dirty.

"What do we do about him?" Jaia asked, sitting with Kai's head resting on his shoulder. "We are going to kill him, right?"

"I'm going to shove a lit torch up his—" Dirdos started.

"Etani is going to do it," Daemon snapped, speaking over Dirdos' imaginative torture.

"What?" Uzo snarled, livid. "She has been abused, raped, and tortured by that man; she is not going to be within ten feet of him ever again!"

"I know, Uzo, but what better way to give her some semblance of peace than to lop his fucking head off?" Daemon snapped back. "You saw her! She let him do that to her so we would be able to save her sister! She gave herself up to him to keep Letari safe!"

"I saw the exact same thing as you did! My niece being raped by that sadistic bastard! On the floor, in front of us all!"

They went silent, anguished and furious that she had been treated like that, that he had so completely humiliated and degraded her.

"You know she will believe what he called her," Jaia said. "She will think he was right in calling her a whore."

"Yeah ... she will. Why is it so hard for her to believe us when we compliment her, but she will immediately believe an insult?" Versalis asked, frowning as he stroked her pale cheek as her fingers began to melt away into black dust. How could anything that flawless think she was anything but perfect?

"She was raised by the Celestrials. They're all about racial purity," Uzo said, watching her corpse. "There is no breeding outside of the species. Belladonna did and as a result, Etani and Letari look very different to the others. Twenty years of mental development being told you are a hideous abomination and another nine hundred having someone scream that at you when they're trying to kill you ... It's entirely possible that she will never be able to see herself as anything but ugly."

Versalis jerked up and looked at Daemon, the demon frowning at him before he stalked from the room and into her bedroom, returning with a small pile of wooden figures. "This is how she sees herself," he snarled, lifting the hideous thing up, disfigured and terrible, with an anguished scream and misshapen body. "This is how she sees us," he said, holding the rest of the figures out on his palm.

"Gods ..." Hunter gasped as he saw them all.

"Where were they?" Uzo demanded.

"Under the mattress. We found them shortly after she died and decided not to tell anyone."

"We?" Uzo asked.

"I found them and showed them to Daemon," Versalis said, sighing as he collected her clothes, wedding ring, and earrings, folding them and setting them on the table as he moved to see the figures she had carved.

"I didn't know she could do that," Letari said, fascinated. "I'm not there."

"I don't think she's had time to herself in order to make any more. These look like they've been modified slightly, but we never leave her alone," Daemon said with a sheepish smile.

"You're all too nosy for your own good," Dirdos scolded, but he was just as fascinated as the rest of them.

Versalis twitched as she moved, and he tilted his head. "She's in the spirit world, I can feel her."

"I can feel her, too," Dirdos said in fascination.

"So, she did give you her magic?" Daemon said. "You could have told me."

"It was none of your business. She was struggling when she first came back. She couldn't get a hold on it and Hades suggested she give her magic to someone else until she could settle Winter down and then reintroduce the other two. She *was* born to hold that much magic, but the three are fighting for control and Winter is jealous of sharing her with any other magic. Daemon recommended it once and so she asked me to hold it."

"Lucky ..." Kai said.

"Sorry, little vampire, I don't think you would be able to hold her magic. Unless you're a Queen, you're simply not designed to have magic," Dirdos said in amusement while Kai pouted.

"And because I'm a King I can?" Versalis asked.

"Well, yes, the vampire Queens have magic, so you do too."

Versalis was taken aback by that. He knew he had taken the magic from the Queen, but did that mean he could actually use it?

"She's super pissed off at you," Dirdos said in amusement. "I'd suggest you invest in some body armour and a face guard."

"Let her be angry, at least she's whole."

"You didn't have any right to do that to her," Versalis growled.

"Please, can you honestly tell me that you aren't happy to know she can have children? Look me in the eye and tell me you weren't devastated when she said that she had made herself sterile."

He couldn't. It had been devastating to know she had done that to herself, but he had understood, and now that it would be repaired? He was incredibly glad for it.

"It doesn't matter how I feel about it, it's about what she wants," Versalis said, and Daemon's sneer was cruel.

"Well, if you feel that way about it why don't you pass her on to someone who does care? I'm sure any one of us would be glad for the chance."

Versalis growled, knowing the demon was goading him, but it was impossible not to rise, not after everything they had seen that day.

"Fuck off, Daemon, I want her just as badly as you do."

"Then how is it she isn't already pregnant?"

"That's none of your business!"

"Maybe you're not man enough for her?"

"Daemon, knock it off," Dirdos snapped, the lot of them incredibly tense.

"Have you even had sex with her yet?" Daemon taunted. "What's wrong, not able to get it up or is she not interested in spreading her legs for a vampire?"

Crunching glass sounded and Jaia was already gone, Kai slumping to the couch as the vampire fled across the room. Versalis knew it was how the demon worked out his anger and fear, but Mother ... It was so hard not to just jump the man and send him back where he belonged.

"Daemon!" Dirdos boomed, and they all jumped, looking around at the dragon. "Shut your fucking mouth! Now is not the time to be commenting on Etani's sex life after what just happened to her. Have some respect for the poor woman."

"Sorry ..." Daemon sighed, rubbing his eyes. "You're right, I'm sorry."

"Don't worry about it, we're all on edge," Versalis said, clapping the man on the shoulder even though he wanted to rip that stupid head off his shoulders.

"Yeah. But she'll be back soon, and we can hold him down while she rips out his spine through his chest."

"Sounds like a good plan to me," Dirdos growled and handed Uzo a handkerchief. Evidently the breaking sound had been his grip on the teacup which had shattered.

"None of you will ever ... Ever! Speak about her like that again. Do you understand me?" Uzo said in a deadly quiet voice. "She gave herself up to that man to keep those she loves safe. She has earnt your respect time and time again and all you do is make snide comments behind her back about whose conquest she will be. She is a fucking person! And if you can't respect her or treat her like the lady she is, then I will take her away from you all and you will never see her again."

That was a threat none of them could ignore and they all nodded, willing to agree to anything so long as the man didn't take her from them.

SHE HAD RETURNED by the next morning and Daemon was forced to run when she stepped into her room from Ceress. Her eyes swept the faces, finding him and lunging for a knife strapped to the bottom of the chair to her right, chasing after him, and they followed, watching as she dragged him to the floor and stabbed him six times in the back with a calm ferocity that reminded them all rather brutally that she was a fully trained murderess by trade.

It was easy to forget when faced with her beauty and seeing her as a Queen and all the other things. But she had chosen to become an assassin, and she was scarily good at it.

The demon couldn't outrun her, though, and so she had killed him quickly and easily. Then she had gotten off his transforming corpse and headed back into her room and into the bathroom to wash her hands and the knife.

"I keep forgetting ..." Dirdos said, staring out at the horrified guard who was inching back from the spreading pool of blood.

"That she's a trained murderer for hire? Me, too," Jaia said in a small voice.

Versalis eyed the rest of them and then headed for the bathroom, closing the door and meeting her eyes in the mirror.

He glared at her for a second and when her brows lifted, he crossed the room and grabbed her shoulders, spinning her around and pinning her against the wall.

Tilting his head, he kissed her hard and hungrily, her body tense for an instant and then melting into it as she kissed him back, her delicate fingers curling in his shirt to pull him closer as he deepened the kiss, his tongue tracing her lower lip. Her lips parted and her tongue traced his, eager and accepting while his fingers tangled in the long strands of feather soft hair and his body pressed her into the wall.

"If I'd have known that would get you riled up, I would do it more often," she purred against his lips and he growled, silencing her with another kiss that she met with just as much pressure.

His hand slid around her waist and then down to her backside, her breath hitching as he gripped her arse hard and pulled her hips against his.

He knew he was getting dangerously close to her shutting down, but he revelled in it while he had the chance. He knew she would be able to feel his arousal pressing against her. Breaking the kiss, she slid her arms up around his neck and he was surprised when she used his neck to jerk herself upwards, her legs wrapping tight around his middle and her grin was wicked as she met his confused and desperately hungry stare.

Her mouth came down on his and he pressed her into the wall once more, his fingers squeezing her backside enough to bruise, but he knew she liked it.

They kissed for several minutes, and he didn't mean to go too far for her, but his need was demanding. His fingers slid up under her dress and his fingers found her breast, soft and heavy in his hand. She liked that, and gasped softly, the peak hardening against his palm, and his head tilted, lips tracing the upper curve. His bite froze her in place, her breath stopping as the memory came into sharp focus, and before she could panic, he set her down and backed away. Her eyes were wide, and her hand rested on the basin for support as she gasped for air.

"I'm sorry, I wasn't thinking ..." he said, silently screaming profanity at himself as he saw her struggling to bring herself down.

"It's okay," she whimpered, and he watched in horror as she moved around the basin and sank down into the cramped space between the basin and wall. It was her safe place to hide when things got bad.

He moved closer to her and leant against the wall, sliding down until he was sitting close to her but didn't touch her again.

"He ... he bit me. In the throne room. Almost that exact spot," she whispered, and Versalis closed his eyes, realising where he had messed up.

"Sorry, love, I wasn't thinking at all," he said, and he was surprised when he felt her hand gentle in his.

"I'm sorry, I want to ... I just can't, not yet. I thought I could ... I did, and I really do want to ... but I can't ..."

She didn't need to explain to him. He understood perfectly and the mere fact that she wanted to brought relief flooding through him.

"Don't be sorry, it's not your fault. I shouldn't have pushed so far," he sighed, lifting her hand to his lips, and kissing it gently. It smelt faintly of blood and soap.

"I'm scared, Versalis," she whispered, her eyes on the wall as she stroked his thumb with hers.

"Scared about what?" he asked, revelling in the simple touch.

"I couldn't stop the broken part from fixing. Why couldn't he just let me have some semblance of peace?"

He looked up and saw that she was crying, her face anguished and tears trailing down her cheeks.

"I don't want it to happen again. I won't survive a third time."

His heart broke for her and he gripped her wrist, dragging her out of the corner and into his arms, wrapping her up in both arms and legs to keep her feeling safe and secure. "You won't, love. You won't lose another one," he breathed, rocking her while she cried into his shirt.

He didn't know if he was capable of fully understanding what it was like for her to lose a child, let alone two of them. He wasn't sure if any man could fully understand or appreciate the agony a woman felt when she lost something so precious, when it was taken from her so callously and without reason. Perhaps the father could, in a way, but she had been the one to carry it and feel it moving and she was the one who had lost it. How could Daemon take that relief away from her?

"Next time you die, you can stop it again, can't you?" he asked, hating himself for suggesting it. But he had spoken the truth; it was not what he felt that mattered, it was what she needed. "You can break it again and leave it broken until you're ready to fix it."

She shifted slightly, looking up at him, and his breath was stolen by the beauty of the woman. Even crying she was utterly, heart-breakingly exquisite.

"He would find out," she whimpered, her voice broken.

"It will be our little secret. If you need to, you can drink the potion Dirdos gives you and pretend it's working, Daemon will think you left it fixed and you only have to suffer for a few minutes pretending to be sick."

She stared at him, both hopeful and doubting him, but then her eyes narrowed, and her pain eased a little. "Are you presuming that there will be a lot of call for that?" she asked, her tone easing as her mood lifted. She had a plan; she could easily crush her pain if she had something to work towards.

"You can't deny my charm forever, Etani. Eventually it will weaken your resolve and then you'll come to me and beg me to make love to you because I'm clearly a stud," he said, giving her his best seductive stare.

Her pupils dilated and her lips parted, the colour darkening just slightly while her cheeks flushed. He hadn't expected her to have any form of reaction to his teasing.

He never expected any reaction at all from her, let alone one that suggested his attempt at a seductive stare might work on her. He smiled to help ease the tension and pressed a playful kiss to the tip of her nose, making her blink, seeming to come out of a deep thought. Her lips pulled up into an adoring smile and she strained up, but he leant back with a smug grin.

Growling, she reached up and grabbed his hair, dragging him down into another kiss.

THERE WAS a gentle knock on the door and they both looked around, snuggled up in the corner of the room, her still naked from her return to life.

"Come in!" Versalis called, and the door opened, Uzo peeking in. His face softened as he found them and understood instantly.

"Some of the Hunters are here to chat when you're ready," he said, and Etani nodded, reluctant to get up, but she was at least curious to know.

Kissing him once more, she got to her feet and pulled him up with her.

"I don't have any clothes left in here." She sighed, finding the little wardrobe empty.

"I'll get you some," Versalis said, stepping out of the bathroom to find Vincent, Dainin, Jason, and Cyle all sitting on the couch, Jason being the only one who looked relaxed. They were all masked, and it was a creepy sight when they all looked around at him in unison, jarring all sorts of eek metres in his head.

But he nodded to the four of them and headed into the bedroom and found a pretty dress set out on the bed. Shrugging, he picked it up and headed back to her in the bathroom and helped her into it.

It came to just above her ankles and flowed in a lovely, feminine, and almost innocent way around her body, curling up into a sweet-heart neckline with a series of ribbons criss-crossing her chest and curling up around her delicate throat. With her hair down it gave tantalising glimpses of her bare back with only a handful of ribbons holding the tight fabric to her body.

"New?" she asked, touching the delicate fabric.

"Not sure, it was on your bed." he said, his jaw nearly hitting the floor as she turned back to him.

She looked ravishing, and it was all he could do to keep from pinning her down and having his way with her. She smirked as she noticed the swelling at his groin.

"That good, is it?" she asked playfully.

He could only nod, reaching for her and dragging her closer. "Going to have to start leaving my mark on you if you're going to go out dressed like that."

"Well, there's always earrings," she said, and he froze as she slipped free and slunk from the room, leaving him to try to wrap his brain around the fact that she had just suggested the Fae marriage tradition. Had she just asked him to marry her?

It was another few seconds before he prowled after her, his eyes going to the others who stared at her with various degrees of appreciation.

"What are you all doing here?" she asked as she embraced Vincent, and then Dainin, both men squeezing her, and their lingering hands made Versalis glare at them both.

Jason and Cyle received embraces as well, though they were less warm. She didn't know them very well, and she wasn't much for touching strangers in any capacity. But they were both eager to get their arms around her.

"I wanted to discuss a prior arrangement that was made between myself and your demon, who appears to be missing," Jason said.

"Etani killed him a few hours ago," Uzo said, settling into the corner of the room with a heavy book and a cup of tea.

"How?" Cyle asked.

"How many times did you stab him, dear?"

"Six, I think. In the back," Etani said as she settled herself into the chair opposite the four Hunters.

"Did he try to grope you again?" Dainin asked.

"No, he killed me first," she said.

It was the oddest conversation, and Versalis found himself standing just behind her chair, his hands linked behind his back and watching the four men with cold glares any time they stared at her too long.

"Fair is fair," Vincent said with his one visible eye dancing.

"You should stick around and tell him that when he's back," Etani said with a smile, her eyes lingering on Vincent. "What prior agreement were you referring to, Jason? I'm afraid I haven't been informed as of yet, but a lot has been happening."

"Part of the agreement that I help in freeing you is that you and I would sit down to have a conversation for a few hours. The rest of it was Vincent wanted something, and the entire community would agree to a favour, but that's unlikely to ever happen. They squabble for several years over the simplest of things, let alone the favour of a Goddess."

Etani tilted her head towards Vincent, and then back to Jason. "Is that all you wanted?" she asked. "I expected more."

"I would like one if you're offering," Cyle said with a grin, Dainin nodding.

"Well, if you're offering. I'd take a proper courtship," Jason said.

Etani laughed, but Versalis growled. "I'm afraid I am already involved, Jason," she said, delighting in the man's flirting.

"Your shadow?" Jason asked and Etani turned, glancing back at Versalis as he loomed over her.

"Yes, my shadow," she agreed.

"A shame, I would have liked getting to know you better."

"As would I," Etani agreed.

"How many favours can I get?" he asked.

"You can barter," Etani said with a wicked tone that made Jason's head tilt slightly.

"You're a fascinating creature," he lifted the mask to rest atop his head, his odd blue eyes narrowed on her as he considered. "The conversation is non-negotiable. However, ten favours."

"One," Etani countered, her lips pulling up into a smile.

"Ten." Jason's lips turned down, but he was distracted as Etani shifted, crossing her right leg over the left at the knee.

"One," she said.

"Eight."

"Two." She traced her fingers over her thigh and Versalis saw her tactic. She was keeping him distracted, and it was working like a charm. His eyes were locked on her hands and then down to her calves as the fabric lifted.

"Six," he said and Versalis was curious to know that while he was going down in twos, Etani was only going up in singles. There would be no meeting in the middle for this, Jason was going to lose.

Vincent was laughing silently as Etani bent forward to scratch at her ankle and all eyes in the room went to her chest as she leant over.

"Two."

"Five ..." Jason said in a slightly breathless voice.

"Two."

"Four."

"Three," Etani said, straightening, and the motion jerked the fabric up to just above her knees and for one fleeting, soul stealing moment, the hypnotised man got a mere flash of her thigh up to her hip and possibly even a flash of the outer band of her underwear.

"Three..." he said, sounding as though his mouth had gone dry.

"Deal," Etani said, and Jason blinked hard, shaking his head and looking around in confusion as those closest to Etani burst out laughing.

"You're a sucker for a pretty girl," Uzo said.

"What just happened?" Jason asked, glaring at her wicked grin.

"You missed out on two deals because you were too busy ogling her," Vincent said.

"Oh, that's not fair," Jason pouted.

"You're dealing with the Fae, my dear fellow," Uzo said with amusement. "We love our deals, but we also love getting the best of them."

"You get three favours and a conversation for how many hours?" Etani asked, amused at how easy the Hunter was to trick.

"I want one full day," he said grumpily, and Etani shrugged.

"Very well, if you can find enough things to talk about. You can have twenty-four hours, either in one go or over as many days as you wish. What about you three?"

"Two favours," Vincent said, and Etani nodded. "And I want you to reinstate our old deal."

Etani looked at Vincent and his chin lifted in defiance as she considered him.

"Very well," she said. "When, and for how long?"

"Twenty-four hours, once a week."

"Twenty-four hours once a month."

"Weekly," Vincent growled.

"Monthly."

"Every ten days."

"Fortnightly ..."

"Deal," Vincent looked smug, but Etani was only amused, turning her eyes on Dainin who looked only somewhat frightened.

"Two favours is all I want," Dainin said.

"Are you certain?" Etani asked, watching the man.

"Yes."

"Very well, deal."

Cyle was last, and he was staring intently at Etani, frowning at her in consideration.

"What does your mask represent?" Etani asked, making the man's dark silver-grey eyes narrow.

"He hides that he is a demon. Cyle is much like Neah," Jason said, and Etani nodded.

"I do not have emotions; however, I am not a sociopath. I am not as stupid and reckless as Neah."

Etani watched the man for several seconds and the man stared right back at her.

"I want three favours, and to taste you," he said in a flat voice.

Etani's brows lifted and the room grew tense, even the Hunters looking around at him warily. "Taste me?"

"Your flesh, and your blood."

"Why?"

"I desire you, and am curious," he said shamelessly.

"You will not touch me in any other manner?"

"No. There will be nothing indecent."

"Very well. Where?"

Versalis growled, not liking this one bit.

"Your shoulder or neck."

Etani looked up at Versalis and he looked down at her, her eyes slightly anxious, but it was gone before she looked back towards Cyle.

"Very well. You have a deal," she said slowly, the only one that was making her nervous.

Cyle stood in one fluid, instant moment and approached her, his eyes intent on her.

Etani stood slowly, her chin lifting to look up at him.

Cyle wasn't that much taller than her at least, only a few inches, and it made them oddly even compared to many of the others.

"May I touch your arm and hair?" Cyle asked in a weirdly detached, impersonal way. "Your dress is in the way. You may want to undo the neck."

"You may do that," Etani said slowly, and Cyle nodded, reaching up behind her neck and pulling the ribbons free with quick movements, trailing them over her left shoulder to keep the fabric from falling down to her waist.

Versalis glanced at the other Hunters, all of them staring at Cyle as though he were out of his mind, but Cyle seemed indifferent to them, his fingers tracing across her skin to brush her hair back out of the way.

Cyle glanced up at Versalis, his lips pulling up into a smug smirk before his eyes dropped and his head bowed over her shoulder.

With one hand curled up around the back of her head, he tilted her head away from his and his free hand rested lightly against the small of her back to help support her, every touch polite and yet Versalis felt like he was molesting her.

Cyle's head shifted, and he inhaled the scent of her skin and hair, his eyes sliding shut as he revelled in the hypnotic perfume that was Etani.

His lips parted and his teeth cut through her skin like it was wet paper, her soft cry drawing Jaia and Kai to their feet, ready to defend her if the need arose.

He lingered for several seconds, the muscles of his throat showing his greedy drinking and his tongue lapping against the flesh. It was intensely intimate in a way only the three vampires would be able to understand, he was taking part of her, teasing the skin, and digging his teeth in deeper to make her whimper. It was an enormous turn on for the biter, to feel the victim trembling in their arms and hear their soft cries of pain.

He released her with a reluctance that had Versalis exchanging a glance with Jaia, both of them very wary of this man who took such great pleasure in the act.

Releasing her, he licked the large bite and drew back, her blood smeared across his lips and chin where a dribble had escaped. His cheeks were flushed with her blood while she looked paler, tired, and when she reached for him, Versalis moved immediately to her and wrapped her up in his arms.

Cyle used his finger to wipe her blood from his chin and then licked his finger clean, sitting back down with a thoughtful frown on his lips as he considered what he must have learnt from the bite.

"I'm tired ..." Etani whispered and Versalis nodded, leading her towards the bedroom. "Oh ... Just come back when you want that conversation," she said weakly to Jason, the man's attention on Cyle when Versalis glanced at the four of them sitting on the couch.

Guiding her down onto the bed, he smiled when she turned onto his side and dragged him down with her, nuzzling her face into his chest and dozing off with a vice-like grip on his shirt.

CHAPTER 40
LOVE

By the time she woke again it was late at night and she stirred, yawning and sitting up with a confused frown.

"What time is it?" she asked, finding them still alone in the room.

"I believe it will be midnight in an hour or two," Versalis said, looking down at his saliva-soaked shirt and giving her a dirty look as he took it off.

"Just means I was comfortable," she said, her brows lifting. It was true, she didn't drool very often.

"Mhm," he said in irritation, but her eyes were already on his chest, her cheeks flushing slightly as she studied the muscles. "It's rude to stare."

She looked up at his face and then grinned, leaning forward and licking up his chest to make him jerk back.

"What was that for?!" he demanded, indignant and yet incredibly aroused.

"Because I could," she said.

"Little beast," he growled, and she grinned

"Don't make me do it again," she threatened.

446

"Oh please, you couldn't even if you tried."

She took that as the challenge it was and he grunted when she tackled him, his hands on her shoulders and trying to pry her off him while she bowed her head with her tongue out, trying to reach his face.

"Eww get away from me!" he cried, his face turned and neck strained to avoid her tongue. "You're so gross!" He was laughing, and she was grinning, straining to get down to him.

"You love it," she said, the words muffled with her tongue out and she got him, the very tip of her tongue brushing the point of his jaw below his ear.

Taking advantage when she drew back in triumph, he flipped her off him and rolled on top of her, when she landed on her back on the bed, grinning as he gripped her wrists and leant down, licking from her jaw up to her temple.

She shrieked in disgust, turning her head to try to wipe her face on his arm and so he licked the other side as well.

"Now you're even," he said with a wicked grin.

"Jeez Versalis, you're so gross," she whined, throwing his words back at him.

"Please, you love me."

"I would sell you to Hades for a hug and half a grape ..."

He looked down at her indignantly. "I'm worth at least one full grape!"

"So you think ..." she said dryly, her smile smug.

He laughed and leant down, kissing that beautiful, brilliant woman that he loved so very much.

She kissed him back, her head lifting up off the bed to meet his lips, and he could feel her smiling, revelling in their banter that came so naturally.

"I love you, Versalis." She sighed, her face showing her contentment.

"I love you, too, Etani," he growled, something he had thought earlier popping up into his thoughts. "Before the Hunters came, you mentioned earrings."

Etani looked up, her eyes sweeping over his face as she considered him and her answer.

"It was only an option," she said defensively, her body tense.

"What did you mean, Etani?" His tone was serious, staring down at her. "Were you asking me...? Were you asking me to marry you?"

She swallowed hard, fear radiating out of her in almost visible waves. "Yes, I was," she said, her tone hesitant.

Versalis was frozen, staring down at the beautiful woman and, to his utter shock, she twisted her wrist until he let go and reached down, not under the mattress but into the side of the mattress wall, where none of them had ever thought to look.

Drawing out a small velvet box, she sat up while Versalis sat back on his heels, staring down at it.

She wasn't looking at him, her eyes locked on the wall just past his shoulder as she held out the box.

TAKING IT WITH SHAKING FINGERS, he opened it and found a twin set of ten earrings, one set somewhat larger than the other, one for him and one for her. They were delicate and elegant, engraved to look like the metal was twisted.

Inside the largest two loops he found miniscule words and, lifting them, he felt his throat close and eyes sting. 'My eternal heart is yours eternally.'

He didn't know what to say or do as he looked down at the earrings, never imagining that she would have wanted to give herself to him forever.

Setting the ring back into the squishy foam that held them in place, he closed the lid, and the force of his kiss was enough to tell her what his answer was.

Her arms snaked up around his neck and he clutched her to him, knowing he was probably hurting her with the fierce grip of his embrace, but he couldn't force himself to release her.

He was going to be with her forever, to be able to love her forever. He was going to be Etani's husband.

Her lips moved against his with a desperate need and he shuddered as she drew him closer, leaning into it, and as she drew him closer, she leant back until he was kneeling over her, and she lay flat on the bed.

He blushed as he swallowed and tried to focus on something else to contain the rush of blood to his groin, but it couldn't be helped. She was incredible and amazing, and he wanted her like he had never wanted anything in this life.

She met his need with her own, pressing up into the kiss when he wasn't using enough force, and he groaned against her lips, his fingers finding her jaw and then tracing down over the uneven scar that had been left by Cyle.

He ignored it, his fingers tracing down around the outer curve of her breast and down to grip her side. He could hear her racing heart and her uneven breaths, and he revelled in the sounds, hoping that it was desire that sped them up and not fear.

Breaking the kiss, he looked down at her and her eyes fluttered open, lips parted and glistening with his saliva. "Do you want me to stop?" he asked, his voice low and husky with need for her.

She looked up at him, silent and confused as she worked out what it was she wanted, and then smiled. "I don't want you to stop," she whispered, and his stomach clenched. Would she want him to stop at some point? He didn't know, but he would deal with that should it happen.

His mouth found hers again and his hand traced down over her side and then back up again, feeling the soft curves that so tantalised him.

Breaking the kiss, he shifted away just enough so that when he traced the hem of her dress up, he could bend down, and his lips found the skin of her stomach.

She was very well defined, yet her skin was so much softer than he ever imagined, silk and feathers, and it tasted like nothing he had ever imagined before.

Her breath sucked in as his tongue parted his lips and he trailed it up from the band of her underwear to the base of her ribcage. Looking up at her, he found her watching him warily, her eyes almost glowing with some hidden emotion he could only fathom.

Kissing his way back down, he stopped just at her underwear and her cheeks flushed with colour. It was the most beautiful thing he had ever seen, her slightly confused face and her flushed cheeks, her soft breaths that were nearly a pant as he slid the fabric down her hips. His fingers dragged down her skin and when she froze he stopped, her breath halted as she looked up at the ceiling.

She had disconnected from the situation, and he didn't know what to do, realising this was what Neah, Drizdan, and Zeus must have seen, a still body and unfocused eyes as she went elsewhere while they did whatever they wanted with her body.

Letting go of her underwear, he shifted himself up and laid down at her side, his hand cupping her cheek and turning her face to look at him.

She wasn't there and he sighed, knowing she couldn't help it. She had been abused so many times that she had become a master at going somewhere else.

Pressing his lips against her forehead, he stroked his thumb against her cheek and waited, murmuring softly to her as she travelled wherever it was she had gone to avoid what was being done to her. Reaching down, he tugged her dress down over her legs, hiding her from view once more.

It was almost ten minutes before she blinked, confused and uncertain as she came back to the gentle brush of his thumb on her skin and a soft humming tune he had picked up from Letari at some point.

"Where did you learn that?" she asked, turning away from him, and her beautiful face was ashamed.

"Letari, I think," he replied, not entirely sure but assuming.

"Our mother used to hum that when she was cleaning. I don't really know how she still remembers it. It was so long ago."

"Your sister remembers how many seeds were on a strawberry she ate three years ago. Do you really think she's going to forget your mother singing?" he asked, and she blinked, but then she smiled, a smile that could destroy any man and bring kingdoms to their knees.

"Yes, I suppose that's true," she said and shifted away from him and stood up from the bed.

SHE LOOKED DOWN at herself in surprise, then around at him before her eyes settled on the bed and there was an odd expression on her face.

"What?" Versalis asked, rolling into the cool spot she had vacated. Any chance to claim the cold left by her was a chance not worth ignoring and it was often a fight to see who could get to it.

"I'm dressed ..." she said, not able to understand.

"Yes, you're dressed," he said. "Did you think you wouldn't be?"

Her slow nod filled him with rage, and he sat up.

"What do you think I am?" he demanded, and she flinched, taking a step back from him.

"I said yes ..."

"But then you went away," he countered.

Looking up from the bed at his face, she was confused, her perfect face drawn in her lack of understanding. "But I said you could ..."

"Etani, I'm not going to touch you if you aren't here. I'm not going to take advantage of you."

She stared at him, her lips parted as she tried to take in what he was saying, and it slowly dawned in his angry brain what it must have seemed like to her.

The only time she had given herself to someone he had then turned around and abused her, everyone else had abused her, and ...

"Etani, your experience is not normal for a couple," he said, making her frown. "The man doesn't just take what he wants and then leave. The woman doesn't just endure his need. That's not a healthy, normal relationship, that's abuse. I won't touch you if you don't want me to touch you or are just going to let me do what I want to you."

"Why not?" she asked, and he paused, her genuine confusion throwing him for a loop.

"Because I'm not that kind of man. I can't just use you like that. I want to love you, and for you to want it, and enjoy it with me. I want you to be happy."

She was silent as she studied his face, trying to piece together what information she had on the subject, and then she frowned, coming to a conclusion she didn't like.

"I don't want to be hurt again. I don't want to remember it," she whispered, and his heart broke for her.

"I won't hurt you... or at least I'll try not to hurt you," he frowned as he thought that she had only just returned to life, and it might be difficult to keep her from experiencing any discomfort. "I would never intentionally hurt you like that. I want you to be satisfied."

She didn't understand, he could see that on her face, and her eyes trailed down his body, still dressed in his pants. How did one explain to a woman who had only known abuse that there could be pleasure in love? Neah had shown her only a taste of it before he turned rabid.

"I want to please you, not myself," he said, and her head tilted, considering his words. He expected her to reject him right then and there, but she was curious.

"How?" she asked, and he looked up at her, standing still and confused beside the bed.

"I would love you the way you deserve," he said.

"Show me," she said, and his breath caught in his throat.

"I ..." he paused, completely thrown before he held out his hand to her. "Come over here."

She looked at him doubtfully but accepted his hand and stepped closer to him. He stood with her and his head tilted, kissing her tenderly. She kissed him back, the kiss hesitant but eager to taste him again.

Reaching down, he gripped the hem of her dress, lifting it up over her head.

She moved willingly, curious and uncertain, but willing to let him work.

He wrapped his arms around her and she moved eagerly against him, his fingers tracing along her back and then finding the ties of her brassiere while his lips traced along the length of her ear to make her shiver.

He smiled at her reaction to the brush, and he caught the long-tapered ear in his lips, biting it gently with his lips protecting the delicate cartilage from his teeth.

She gasped, her arms contracting around him involuntarily, and he growled playfully, figuring out the pale beauty had a weak spot that he could exploit.

He managed to get the ties free, and he let go of her ear to move away, trailing the straps down over her shoulders and dropping the heavy, painful looking contraption to the floor.

His eyes drank her in, wanting to relish every inch of her, but his need demanded he keep going.

Turning her so that the backs of her legs rested against the bed, he looked down at her and he saw her doubt, her uncertainty as she stood almost naked before him.

"I will stop if you want me to. You only have to say it," he murmured, and she nodded once, a simple jerk of the head.

He had intended to pleasure her first, but he wasn't sure she would be comfortable with his mouth on her, and so he changed tactics, tracing his arms down over her sides and hooking his thumbs into the band of her underwear. She tensed, but when he looked up at her face, she nodded.

Eyeing her warily, just to be sure, he slid her underwear down and she stepped out of them, standing naked and glorious before him.

If only she knew how exquisite she was, or knew just how much his groin was aching with the need to be touched by her, but he blocked it out and instead guided her around to the side of the bed.

"Stay with me," he whispered as he pressed his lips against hers, scared that he was going to hurt her and damage her more. But she kissed him back just as eagerly and when he pulled back from her, she looked slightly less nervous.

"Lie down," he murmured, and she hesitated, their eyes meeting as she thought something he could only imagine, but she moved and the sight of her crawling onto the bed had his groin throbbing in agony. He clenched his jaw, needing to take things slow with her and not hold her down like he wanted. She was naked and on all fours, something he could barely resist, but then she laid down on her side, her movements feline and graceful.

Twisting on the bed, he knelt just beside her knees and with a playful grin, he gripped her calves and flipped her onto her back, tugging her feet to hold them on either side of his hips.

Something inside her flared to life and her eyes glowed a soft, liquid blue colour that he had never seen before, her lips parted and breaths coming ragged once more. She was no longer calling for him, she was screaming her demand at him, raging that he wasn't already inside her, but he did his best to ignore the scream.

Lowering himself onto the bed at her side, he placed two fingers against her jaw and turned her face to him, his lips finding hers as his hand left her cheek and slid down the length of her body, teasing, and stroking her until he coaxed a shiver out of her.

He would have another chance to do other things to her, but for now he traced his fingers gently against the velvet soft skin just below her navel.

"Are you sure?" he asked against her lips, and she nodded, her body tense, but she was still present with him.

He bit on her lower lip as his hand slid lower and his breath sucked in with hers as his fingers slid between her legs, cupping her sex and stroking her, slow, and careful. He explored her with a tentative touch, and when he heard her gasp, he knew he had found the right spot.

Pressing his fingers against her, he stroked her clitoris, teasing her and breaking the kiss to watch the expressions changing on her face.

She had been scared at first, but then her expression changed to wary curiosity and then wonder before turning to bliss, her eyes sliding shut and lips parting as she made a soft sound of pleasure. Resting his forehead against hers, he watched her face as his fingers worked with slow, deliberate care that was starting to speed up and it was when she shuddered that he realised something. Swallowing once, he realised exactly what position he was in, with the most desirable and dangerous woman likely to ever exist, and she was gasping as he teased her body, his wrist shifting, and he smiled as her body tensed, his finger sliding inside her.

The first time she moaned he shuddered, very nearly losing control of himself as his need to take her grew into an almost violent demand. It was driving him wild, just as he wanted to drive her wild.

Her fingers curled around his wrist, and he smirked as her other hand pressed down against the back of his hand, pressing his fingers harder against her and her back arched as he found that spot inside her. The sight of her like that was glorious and he moved his hand, sliding his finger into her, curling and he found the spot again.

She cried out, her breathing coming in short gasps as she did her best to remain quiet. He didn't care, he would stay there forever if he allowed her to.

Her voice was high as she cried his name and his eyes slid shut at the sound, a thrill of pleasure going through his body. It was a sound he had longed to hear since the first instant he had laid eyes on her and there she was, writhing in pleasure as his hand moved against her, his finger penetrated and worked her.

Her fingers clenched against his arm with enough pressure to draw blood and he ignored the pain, her ragged moans telling him exactly how close she was to release, and she cried out when she found it, her body shuddering beside him.

He didn't stop, working her until she was still and panting, her eyes clenched shut, and she twitched as he teased her clitoris, hyper-sensitive.

THE DOOR OPENED but she didn't seem to notice, or she didn't care and there was a soft snort of amusement before whoever it was closed the door again, confirming she was alright before leaving them to their fun. It must have been a sight to behold, though there wouldn't be any doubt of what he had been doing for her.

She made a soft mewling sound and reached for him, dragging him against her with an impatient growl when he was uncertain, but then he shifted obediently to her command and was surprised when her mouth met his in a deep hunger.

She clutched him to her and he kissed her back while her hand reached down between them, and her nails sliced the ties of his pants as though they were nothing.

He hesitated for an instant, but then he shoved them off and dropped down onto his hands over her, searching her face as she moved, sliding one of her long legs to the other side of his knees.

Searching her face, she met his hesitation with a faint hint of a smile, and he ran through a checklist of all the things he needed to avoid doing if he wanted to keep her with him, those things that would trigger a memory in her and send her into a panic attack. He knew them all, had drilled himself on them so as not to scare her again, but he hadn't expected to be in that situation, naked and kneeling over her, the scent of her pleasure tantalising and teasing him.

"I'm ready," she whispered, her hands tracing over his ribs and then around against his lower back, gently guiding him down.

He lowered himself down onto her, hoping that she was right. He didn't want to ruin what they had. "Are you sure?" he asked, knowing it would be agony to stop right then but he would do it for her.

"Yes," she bit her lip and then smiled, her chin lifting to meet his lips with hers.

He kissed her back deeply, passionately, and he shifted, positioning himself better as her legs parted and the feeling of her thighs against the outsides of his hips was electric.

"I don't want to hurt you," he murmured against her lips.

"Please..." she said in a kitten plea and he broke, unable to resist her.

He needed to focus on being gentle with her and yet it was so hard not to simply ravish her, to take what was his, but he moved slowly, the softness of her skin feeling delicious against his erection.

He kissed her deeply as he pushed against her, her returned kiss matching his need brush for brush. Her body resisted him, but her arousal and his persistence allowed him to push past the resistance and his world changed as his erection slid into her. It was odd, the cool temperature of her body, but she was so soft and wet that he couldn't resist either of their needs. He knew then that no other woman would ever be enough for him, though he couldn't put a name to why, and he could have found his release right then and there, finally inside her after years of fantasies, but he forced himself to think of something else to hold back his release.

She was tighter than he expected, but it was in no way uncomfortable, almost as though she had been made for him and the thought made him savagely gleeful. His hips found hers and he gasped, entirely within the confines of her body, and she was whimpering softly, her body clenching around him in a way that drove him mad. Resting his elbow against the bed beside her shoulder, he broke the kiss to look down into her eyes, stunned and amazed as she looked back up at him, need and impatience showing all over that perfect face.

Her body didn't seem to want to let him go as he drew back from her, and he watched her face as he clenched his stomach and pushed into her again. It was delicious to see her pleasure, and he kissed her again greedily, unable to help himself.

He moved slowly, not wanting to hurt her, but it was hard not to just fuck her like the ravenous animal he was. He wanted to dominate her and turn her into his keening mate, but he was working hard to keep himself slow and gentle.

She seemed glad for it, her head lifting to push up into the kiss and she sighed his name against his mouth, sending a shiver through him.

As her body relaxed around him, he was able to move more readily and she clutched him to her, her fingers leaving bruises on his skin as she tried to pull him even closer. He revelled in it, even when it hurt, and he moved against her with a new need, building up speed when his faster pace drew more moans from her.

He was addicted to the sound of her moans, and he was greedy for more of them, his movements almost demanding them of her, and she gave them to him.

"Versalis..." she moaned, her eyes opening, her skin glistening with sweat.

He groaned, his need growing to a fever pitch.

"Bite me..." she pleaded, and his mind went blank for just a second before his lips turned up into a vicious grin.

Nudging her jaw out of the way with his cheekbone, he dragged his tongue up the length of her throat to make her shudder, and then she cried out as his teeth sank into her flesh.

Her body seized around him, and he grunted as he was almost forced to stop, his eyes clenched shut as he fought back release once more, panting and trying to focus on something else even as her blood trickled into his mouth around his fangs. She was not like a normal woman, not even slightly. No woman had ever felt like that, as though she had muscles that were designed to grip him in the most pleasurable way. It was like nothing he had ever felt before, and he needed more.

Her blood, which tasted like magic and sex, tickled his senses, driving him mad with his need.

HIS MOVEMENTS GREW ALMOST vicious against her, and she gasped as he abused her hips and she moved, her legs wrapping around his middle, and he found a new depth inside her.

Lost to his need, he drove himself into her and she clung to him, his name on her lips every few groans and it too was driving him wild. Sucking hard on her throat, he swallowed her blood and gave into his feral nature. Dragging her up from the bed, he thrust her up against the wall and drove himself into her, demanding her body take him.

Her arms went around him and he snarled as her nails dragged down his back, his skin having the same chance as the sheets did.

Grabbing her wrists, he slammed them back against the wall and drew back from her, the light from his crimson eyes reflecting on her pale face.

She looked up at him, her lips parted and tilted up in a wicked smirk, and he growled.

Moving her slender arms up above her head, he gripped them both between one of his and reached down to grip her backside, using it to hold her in place as he thrust up into her, only joined by those points of contact, and he watched her body hungrily, taking her in from groin to face.

He couldn't help but watch his penis moving into her, almost hypnotic as he saw the smear of blood and his shaft glistening with her need. "Who do you belong to?" he growled and her eyes flared blue, a challenge in her eyes that had him driving harder into her, punishing her in a way that she liked.

"You," she groaned, and he growled, pride flooding through him.

"Me," he agreed, and his mouth came down on hers, possessive and hungry, but she met his mouth in a way that almost perfectly mimicked his.

"You are mine," she growled against his lips, and he smirked, fucking her with every ounce of force he could muster.

When he released her wrists, her arms went around his neck and she clung to him, her arms and legs allowing her to move with him as he gripped her arse and moved her against him, thrusting up whenever he could. He didn't care that he was standing in the middle of the room, fucking his mate even as those who would kill him to be in that position were in the other room listening. She was his, and he was hers.

How she had managed to untangle herself from him he would never know but he was reaching for her with a feral need, only to have her foot slamming into his ribs and his back hit the wall, then he fell forward onto the ground only to find her gripping his hair and dragging him up onto the bed.

He didn't have a chance to complain before she straddled him and he was inside her again, driving him into her and, reaching down, she gripped his hair and dragged him up into a sitting position, her body curled, and she kissed him hard, deep and passionate.

"Mine," she growled, her body moving against him in a way that made him gasp for air.

"Yours ..." he agreed, and he watched the glory of her body moving as she rode him, her body leaning back and the entire length of her rolling in a way only dancers could pull off.

Her hair tickled his legs, and his hands found her hips, moving her with him.

Blood was trickling down her chest and he licked and sucked on her breast, smearing blood against her skin and unable to help himself, he sank his teeth into her flesh.

She cried out, and he shuddered at her tightness, but she was merciless, refusing to stop pleasuring herself on his body even as her tightness almost hurt.

Gripping his wrists, she forced him down onto the bed, growling in anger as he lost contact with her skin but then she moved and he went still, lips parted as the new angle ground the underside of his shaft against her walls in a way that he knew would be his downfall.

She moved with a feral need, her eyes sliding shut, and she found her release, her body trembling and squeezing him hard, but he didn't want her to stop, he wanted more.

With her still, he thrust up into her and she cried out, her fingers squeezing his wrists until he was certain the bones were going to shatter.

He gave into the pleasure this time and thrust into her, demanding she take him, and he found his release not long after she did, driving himself as deep into her as he could get as his seed spilled into her.

He moaned her name, wanting to clutch her to him, but she had him trapped and slowly she relaxed, settling down onto his lap, and she looked down at him, the feral possessive need in her fading.

"Mine," he growled, and her brows lifted slightly.

"No, Versalis ..." she whispered and for one terrible, broken second, he thought she had changed her mind and terror filled him like he had never known before. "You are mine," she breathed.

CHAPTER 41

THE END

They fell asleep curled up in the relatively clean bed, his body wrapped around hers, and when he woke, he was still wrapped around her.

Standing, he kissed her cheek hard enough to make her growl in a threat of violence if he woke her, but he wasn't having any of it.

"Come on, we need a shower," he said and got up off the bed, throwing open the windows.

She flinched at the sudden bright light and moaned in an attempt to garner his sympathy. "Come back to bed ..." she complained and the sound of those words coming from her mouth sent a thrill of joy through him.

"No, love, get up."

"I don't want to ..." she muttered, pulling the sheets up over her head.

"Too bad."

"You go shower, I'll stay here," she complained.

Looking down at her, he frowned and crossed his arms. "You'd leave me all alone?"

"Ten more minutes…" she whined, and he rolled his eyes, pulling on his pants.

"If you're not in that shower in ten minutes I'm coming for you," he growled, and she lifted her middle finger, making him laugh.

Stepping from the room, he froze at the sight of so many of their friends asleep on the various surfaces and he realised that was likely one of the first times he had ever slept beside her without the rest of them ending up in there with them. Blushing at the thought of what they had likely heard, he turned to the bathroom, but Uzo was standing in the doorway, his eyes lowered to his cup as he swirled the tea.

"I don't like you, and I don't approve of you … but clearly she does," the Fae said as he approached. "But … I won't hesitate to sacrifice another teacup if I get even a whiff of you hurting her in any way. And I won't stop this time."

Versalis swallowed, his eyes drawn down to the cup. "I love her."

"We all love her, Versalis. That's what worries me. Etani's attitude towards Hunter is nothing to my attitude for you. I will destroy you if you do anything wrong, do you understand me?"

"Yes …" Versalis said.

He knew he was likely going to be a target now, someone who was hated for his getting to be with her. But it would be worth it in the end and they already disliked him for their relationship, now it was clear that she wasn't about to let him go, and he half expected that they would probably try to outright kill him again. It was only five minutes later when she came into the bathroom, dragging her feet and a blanket around her with a look of moody irritability that faded when she found him. Her eyes widened as he stood frozen in the shower, his arms up around his hair, just finished scrubbing the oil out of it.

Dropping the blanket, she was on him in a second and he thrust her up against the wall, burying himself inside her even as her lips found his.

He groaned her name as he thrust into her, her body eager and her mouth heavy on his, demanding more from him. He spilled himself inside her again and shuddered, gasping, and lost in the sensation of his … his fiancé. The thought of what she was made him tremble, and she looked around at him, panting and hungry, but his expression snapped off her need like a blown-out candle.

"Versalis?" she whispered, and she followed after him as he set her down.

He had fantasised about being with her for so long, imagined what it would be like to be inside her, and now he had been inside her twice and she wanted him to be hers forever, it was all just too much. He couldn't wrap his mind around it, and he realised with a shock that it was his turn to have a panic attack as it all hit him at once.

Sex with her had not been anything he could have ever imagined, it was so much more and better than he could have come up with in any of his wildest fantasies. He had never imagined she would almost demand him to be her husband. Never imagined she would be naked before him, his seed burning her insides and trying to comfort him as he struggled to suck in air. He could see her thighs glistening with it and it only drove his thoughts deeper.

He didn't deserve her, not in a million years. She left his side and he was alone; she must have read his thoughts and agreed with him. She would go to Dirdos or one of the others and choose them as her mate. She wouldn't want a man like him.

Why she had chosen him at all was beyond him.

A SMALL BOX appeared in front of his face, and he blinked at it, but he took it and realised what it was almost immediately. It was a small, ball-shaped wooden box, and he twisted it, trying to find the seam that would open it, but it eluded him.

"Haven't you seen the men after war?" she whispered as she

knelt at his side, a faint smile on her face. "They look exactly like that."

He remembered the scene, Kai sitting at her side as she crouched huddled against the wall, her heart slamming in her chest and her face terrified. She had been going through the first panic attack after Kai dragged her broken and bleeding from the dungeons, her child cut from her body, and her tortured for days by the man who had done it.

He had given her the box to help calm her down and there she was, giving it back to him.

"Etani ... how are you not insane by now?" he asked her, dragging his nail across the wood to try to open it. "How are you still yourself after everything you've been through?"

She tilted her head, watching his fingers working, and she frowned, trying to spot the seam as well. "I don't know. I learnt how to cope with the monstrosities of this world when I was younger."

"Even what the men have done to you?" he asked, lifting the box between them.

Her face went still and she looked up at him, those oblong pupils shrinking as she recalled the reason for that object.

"Men will do what men want. They will take whatever they want, and there isn't much you can do to stop it," she said, looking at the thing between them. "Men see me as an object for their needs and goals. I am not a woman, I'm a tool. I understand them, at least somewhat. Drizdan and Epharis ... they want a wife they can dominate and force into obedi-ence. But they want someone strong enough to bounce back and fight because a truly submissive wife would be boring. Drizdan wants that fight so he can feed his sadism and brutalise Epharis less so."

She spoke so calmly that he found it easier to focus on than the box, and he was fascinated. She had never been so open before and he didn't want her to stop.

"They are my husbands as well; I must perform my wifely duties. Daemon protected me when we were with the witches. He made sure I didn't suffer, and I am grateful to him for that. Zeus only saw me as a means to an end, it was simply a bonus that it felt good for him. For Neah I was a conquest. A toy for him to win over and then I was a tool to get a child, a thing he had once believed to be impossible. It's very likely that he would have hunted me down when he found out what I could do, even if he did not desire me."

Versalis watched her face, so perfect and pale. "And Jaia?"

Her face twisted and she looked away, pain written all over her. "Jaia ... I do not know with Jaia. He wants to own me for the sake of owning me. He believes I belong to him and should be with him. I would have forgiven him in time, likely would have loved him again, but now ... I don't know, Versalis. He broke my heart and my body."

Versalis pulled her closer and pressed his lips against her forehead, the truth of what had happened that night, what they learnt had happened to Jaia, making him burn with shame. He wanted to tell her and yet he was too greedy, too afraid that she would see Jaia again as something other than a man willing to hold her down and take what he wanted from her. She was such an unusual creature, like none other he had ever known. She was like a lioness in a pride of lions. They would hold her down and fuck her, but in the end, she was still watching for the one she would submit to willingly, and the others would no longer matter. Their actions were incidental.

She was not human, not even really a mythical creature. She was entirely other, and that made her wonderful.

He left the bathroom first, and came to a stop as he looked at the box that had been shoved in his face by a livid, recently returned to life, Daemon.

"What's this?" Daemon snarled, almost shoving the box down Versalis' throat.

"What is it?" Uzo asked, coming over to the two of them with Versalis still dripping, and the sound of water behind them.

"I can tolerate you two sleeping together, but not this," the demon fumed.

"You proposed?" Uzo asked, opening the box and staring down at the twin set of rings.

"No, she did," Versalis said.

"How did you know that?" Vincent asked, curious at the sight of the box.

"The Fae pierce their ears to show marriage," he said and the hostility in the room shot up as they all took in the news.

"She asked you to marry her?" Daemon snarled.

"Yes."

"Is that a good idea?" Uzo asked.

"No, it's not," Daemon snapped.

"Why not?" Versalis asked, his own anger flaring up.

"Because you two are a raging volcano of potential violence that is only going to take a pebble dropping onto your surface to set you off. You need to back off, Versalis," Daemon said.

"It's none of your business," Versalis snapped back.

"You know he's right ..." Jaia said, his eyes pained for his friend, but Versalis didn't want his pity; he wanted Etani.

"Fuck all of you. She chose me and I'm not leaving her."

"Grow up, Versalis, you know what will happen if you two erupt. Do you want the deaths of all those people on your conscience?"

"Nothing is going to happen."

"This is not happening. I forbid it," Daemon snarled.

"You have no choice in the matter," Versalis countered.

"If I kill you, she'll only be angry for a few hundred years," Daemon argued, looking at Uzo.

"Maybe not even that long," Uzo agreed.

"That's enough, we're all angry, but there's no need to get violent," Dirdos sighed, taking the sets of rings from Uzo and looking at them. "Etani made her choice, that's the end of it."

"And what happens when they erupt? What happens when they kill?"

"We will deal with that should it happen," Dirdos said and turned away, placing the box on the table between the couches.

"I'm going to train, who's coming?" the dragon asked, and the vampires stood, heading after the dragon. They both looked rather dejected.

"I'm going to kill you," Daemon whispered as Uzo moved away. "I don't give one damn if she is angry. You are not good enough for her and I will see to it that you won't get the chance to break her heart."

"I'm not going to break her heart," Versalis said in a whisper.

"You will, you're going to destroy possibly hundreds in your stupid delusion. You're just lucky it didn't happen. I saw what happened to the wall, that is only a flicker of what will happen when you two ignite. Enjoy her while you can, Versalis, I'll see that you don't survive a week."

The wall in question was the one he had hit, and he realised with a note of alarm that the stone itself had been damaged by the force of her kick and he hadn't even noticed. He had only cared that he get back inside her.

It was a sobering thought, but when she appeared and looked both tired and adorably grumpy, he forgot all about the damage and growled.

Her eyes met his in a challenge and the towel dropped, her hands finding his jaw and pulling him against her. "The others are gone," she purred. "Now we don't have to try and be quiet. We could have sex on the couch if we wanted."

She was a devious woman, and he growled as he gripped her backside and lifted her up off the ground, carrying her out into the living room where he dropped her down onto the couch and her toes pulled the towel free from around his waist, the fabric pooling on the ground behind him.

HE CAME BACK TO HIMSELF, looking down at her as she lay at his side, peaceful and calm in sleep, but there was something very odd about the situation. She was absolutely covered in blood and gore.

He vaguely recalled her on her hands and knees, stretched out before him like a cat as he fucked her with a particular viciousness, wanting to hear her pain and pleasure as he took what was his, his wife to be, but he couldn't fully recall. Even so, the vague memory was enough to get him aroused and more so when he remembered her bite that had driven him wild, lust and need driving their blood-lust to new heights.

He didn't know how many times he had taken her, but judging by how tender his penis was, it was a lot. Let no one say a vampire didn't have stamina.

Looking around, he had no idea where they were, and he began a slow exploration of the area. There was blood everywhere, including tree branches and the shattered remains of a village that had been obliterated by what seemed to be a hurricane.

Corpses lay all around him and he picked up a scrap of fabric from one of the walls. With a start, he realised it had been her dress. He didn't remember her putting it back on, didn't remember anything from the moment he woke up and fucked her in the shower and got threatened until waking up on the ground.

Mother ... they had exploded. Their volcano had erupted just as Daemon had predicted, just as they both knew it would, but they had ignored it.

The entire village had been decimated by them and then he found it ... the body of a child made his eyes slide shut in utter horror.

It showed all the marks of her kiss, and the signs of his teeth tearing at the throat. The boy had been about fifteen or so, young and innocent, but he had died at their hands, a taboo like no other.

There seemed to be only one child, but there were too many adults for his brain to wrap around and their corpses were every-where, both kissed and drained by the feral lovers in their blood rage.

"Versalis?" she called out, and he knew he had to hide that from her, he couldn't let her see.

Even as he turned away, he saw the rest of the corpses in a pile and his clothes were on top of them. They had been laid out like a bed and he shuddered as he realised he had likely fucked her on top of those corpses, like the people they had once been were nothing.

Hurrying back to her, he smiled as she studied herself. She was sitting in the grass, her hair a wild mess of knots and blood, her lips turned down into a frown as she considered what might have gone on.

"Wild night, hun?" he asked, putting on a smile for her.

"Did we go swimming in blood?" she asked, raking those glorious eyes down his body.

"No, but we did have dinner," he replied.

She looked confused, not recalling the events, but she forgot quickly when he kissed her, drawn into his affection like a starving woman.

He had to stop this. The others had been right, their love was impossible unless they could find a way to make it safer for them to be together, and he didn't know how that would be possible. They were destructive, violent, and soulless.

"Let's go home," he purred, but it felt meaningless in his heart. He didn't know what to do, he was madly in love with her and yet that love had destroyed their world.

Breaking the kiss, he watched as she bit into the tip of her finger and held out her hand, the drop of falling crimson causing the air to ripple just slightly and she pushed open the door for him, allowing him to walk through.

"What happened to you two?" Daemon asked, but Versalis only shook his head.

"Go ahead, I won't be long," he said to her and watched as she moved away from him, still curious about the blood.

"What?" Daemon snapped as the door closed. "What did you do?"

"We erupted," he said softly, feeling the man's anger like a fire at his side.

"How many?"

"At least twenty, probably more. Everyone, even children," he said, his voice broken.

Daemon turned green; his eyes wide as he struggled to take that in.

"You have to end it. Now. Before it gets worse. You will not tell a single fucking soul about what happened, do you hear me? You know what will happen if anyone finds out you killed a child. You will not tell her, you will not ever speak of this again," Daemon growled.

"I love her, Daemon ..." He was pleading with the demon, wanting an answer that would mean he got to stay with her.

"If you love her, you will end it. You know she would be destroyed if she ever found out."

Versalis closed his eyes, hating himself and the demon. He only wanted to be with her.

"Can we do anything else?"

"I can't make you into something else. You are what you are, and she is what she is. All you can do is try to be kind to her and make sure she doesn't think there's still a chance. "

"Tell Uzo so he doesn't kill me ..." Versalis sighed, looking at the door to the bathroom.

"I'll try, but no promises. Stay out of arm's reach if he has a teacup."

Versalis nodded, his head bowed as he approached the bathroom door and slipped inside, his heart breaking as he saw her there. She looked exquisite, blood washing off her and her head tilted back. Her long hair trailing down to past her backside.

"Etani, we need to talk," he said, and she froze, her eyes closed, but he knew she would be looking at him if they were open.

"Is that not the term they use when there is bad news?" she asked, her tone just as wary as his.

"Generally," he said.

"What is it?" She lifted her head and turned towards him though her eyes were still closed, pulling the mass of her hair over her shoulder to allow the water to wash off her back.

"You and I ... we can't do this anymore. I can't marry you."

Her eyes snapped open and she looked at him, her expression going neutral, but he had seen the flash of pain that coloured her features for only a second. His heart broke, knowing he was going to have to destroy her to keep her safe.

"What?" she asked, her tone flat.

"I do not want to marry you. It's been fun, but this has gone on long enough."

She was silent as she watched him, water running down her perfectly schooled face, her head tilting slightly to the side. "Is this a joke?"

"No, Etani," he sucked in a slow breath and put on a slight smile. He hated himself for what he was about to do, but it had to be done. He had to protect her. "I don't love you. I never loved you, I simply wanted to get between your legs. I couldn't love you, not really. You're just a plaything for me and now I'm bored. I got to fuck you, now I'm done." The words came out, and he felt himself dying inside, knowing that he had to tell her whatever it took for her to turn away from him. Even if it broke her heart, he had to do it.

"Get out, and take the rest of them with you," she said, her face going cold, and he shivered at the sudden temperature drop within the room as her magic drew to her anger.

He sighed and exhaled as he headed for the door, his heart broken and shattered into a million shards as he threw one last look back at her. She had turned away from him, her arms wrapped around herself, and he knew he had done something worse than any of them. Worse than Jaia. He had given her hope that she could have a normal, healthy relationship with a man and thrown it back in her face. He had broken every promise he had ever said to her, and he hated himself for it.

"She wants everyone to go," he said as he opened the door.

"Move," Uzo snarled, but he barred the way into the bathroom.

"Just leave her alone for now," Versalis said, his eyes lowered.

"I warned you ..."

"Please, Uzo, you can kill me if you want, just leave her be."

He didn't care if he died at that point. He would have welcomed it and thanked Uzo for doing it.

The long fingers curled in his shirt and he was yanked out of the doorway, glancing back to see her holding the wall, her arm tight around her middle, and he saw the way her body shook as she cried in silence, doing her best to remain quiet until they were all gone.

Uzo looked in at her, his face white as he pulled the door closed, and the last thing Versalis saw as Uzo turned on him was a fist coming for his face.

AFTERWORD

If you enjoyed The Vampire King, you can follow along on her adventures in book six "Queen of Nothing", available soon on Amazon.

Your opinions are valuable, please take a moment to leave a rating.

ABOUT THE AUTHOR

Born in Mackay, North Queensland in Australia, N. Malone's writing journey started at the age of nine. It wasn't until the age of twenty-nine that the career began.

The story of Etani had been building for nearly ten years, daydreams and forums until the character became a reality when book one had begun.
Now, with twelve books in the works, the story can continue.

"If you like writing, then write."

https://www.nmalone.net

facebook.com/Author.N.Malone

twitter.com/NMalone8

instagram.com/authornmalone

goodreads.com/NMalone

amazon.com/dp/B08BWJMKSH